THE GRIM

REQUIEM FOR THE MORTAL ELVES

K H NELSON

This is a work of fiction. Names, characters, places, and incidents either are the product of the author's imagination or are used fictitiously. Any resemblance to actual persons, living or dead, events, or locales is entirely coincidental.

Copyright © 2022 by K H Nelson

All rights reserved.

No part of this book may be reproduced in any form or by any electronic or mechanical means, including information storage and retrieval systems, without written permission from the author, except for the use of brief quotations in a book review.

ISBN 9781736271612 Ebook

ISBN 9781736271605 Paperback

ISBN 9781736271629 Hardcover

Cover art © 2021 by Lily Dormishev lilydormishev.com

*For the poor souls who have listened to me talk about this nonstop for the past five years: thank you.
I know it hasn't been easy.*

DISCLAIMER

This tale contains material that may be disturbing to some readers. Such material includes, but is not limited to:

- Graphic Violence
- Sexual Encounters
- Mentions of Child Abuse
- Depictions of Mental Illness
- Sexual Assault
- Foul Language

Reader Discretion is advised.

KARTHI SEA

KARTHÉN

BAFOREIS

CIUDELACO

ÁFGAL

PRASTÖMI

TAELONAEL

OASIS CITY

OROVÍN

TIA

NETHU

DRAGON'S HORN

BANSUNGEI

DRAGON SEA

ISLI O
KAMOTIYEN

ISLE OF THE
CHAINBREAKERS

THE EASTERN
LANDS

SOUTHERN SEA

IRSEN

GARMATHIAN
GULF

GARMATH

EASTERN OCEAN

BLACK SEA

N
W　　E
S

CAST OF CHARACTERS
AND THEIR PRONUNCIATIONS

Áfgal [AHF-gall]

- Sólan de Ciudelago * [SO-lan de KYOO-de-LOG-oh]
- Prince Irragrin de Ciudelago [EER-ah-GRIN de KYOO-de-LOG-oh]
- Monrél de Maseño [mon-TRELL de mah-SAY-nyo]

Garmath [GAR-math]

- Kil-Alira-Non, AKA "Chainless" [KEEL ah-LEER-ah nohn]
- Kil-Rasheed-Nol [KEEL ra-SHEED noll]

Karthénos [kart-HEN-ose]

- Duke Jannon O'Corin * [JAN-on]
- Senator Moira O'Jannon [MOY-rah]
- Senator Siobhan O'Jannon [shah-VONN]
- Dame Saoirse (family name unknown) [SEER-shah]
- Sir Cadman (family name unknown) [KAD-men]
- Senator Kiera (family name unknown) [KEER-ah]

Nethuania [NET-wane-yah]

- Tirsen Bonlak [TEER-sen]
- Elena Bonlak
- Tala Bonlak
- Bayani Lin * [BYE-ah-NEE]
- Kadek "The Vile"
- Kalasin of Tianag [KAH-la-SEN of TEE-ah-nag]
- Dakil Papuan * [DAH-keel]
- Roman Ho'su

Orovín [or-oh-VEEN]

- Oleg Kinev [OH-leg KEE-iv]

Prastömin [PRASS-tou-men]

- King Diarmuid O'Cian [DEER-mid]
- Queen Ethna O'Burnell [ETT-nah]
- Prince Alsantör O'Diarmuid * [al-sen-TOUR]
- Maid Rhona O'Frasier * [RO-nah]
- Sir Faerin O'Aiden * [FAIR-in]

Taelonael [TAY-lone-ALE]

- King Jabali Nir [jah-BALL-ee NEER]
- Prince Kabir Nir [kah-BEER NEER]

Vaoirsen [veer-SHEN]

- Sir Naoise McManstair [NEE-shah]
- Sir Giaven McManstair [GEE-ah-vin]

1. * Characters with POV sequences
2. List of main and major secondary characters. This does not encompass the entire cast and extras.

"For where [thy] treasure is, there will [thy] heart be also. The light of the body is the eye: if therefore thine eye be single, thy whole body shall be full of light. But if thine eye be evil, thy whole body shall be full of darkness. If therefore the light that is in thee be darkness, how great is that darkness!"

— MATTHEW 6:21-23 KJV

PROLOGUE

*S*team. It engulfed the massive cavern in its haze. The burn of sulphur tingled Duke Jannon's throat as he finished his prayers at the edge of the hot pool he knelt before: the Sacred Pool of the Wizards and Gnomes. Hundreds of years had passed since Jannon last visited this holy place; before his father seceded the tundra from the forest. Before, even, the late King Eamon was killed in the victory of the Great War.

The pool's white-clad monk, Brayson, Speaker of the Wizards, concluded the ceremony with a tender kiss atop Jannon's head of straight taupe hair. Jannon's pale face winced in response to the rotting stench of the monk's breath, inadvertently baring his elfish fangs.

"Be cleansed, child of the tundra," said Brayson. "Go and sin no more." His twisted back crinkled and popped as he straightened his posture to slink away into the shadows of the cave.

For a fellow elf of silver blood, ye truly age like a mortal of crimson, lamented Jannon. *Gnomes be merciful, friend. What has Diarmuid done to ye?* He sighed, covering his head with his blue cloak's hood. Its fur dripped with condensation, but Jannon paid it no mind. He wasn't here on holiday. He was here for business.

"The red bloods are breeding with our people, Jannon."

And so our business begins, without so much as a greeting fer lost time. Does our friendship mean naught to ye? thought Jannon as the much broader silhouette of the forest elf's king glided through the cave as though 'twas his private quarters, rather than the hallowed ground of their deities. Jannon rose to his feet, his damp cloak sticking to his much slimmer, yet taller, frame.

"The royal colours of Prastömin look better on ye every time I see ye, dear friend," said Jannon. He cocked his head as he inspected the beautiful green cloak that hung off one of King Diarmuid's shoulders. His thoughts soured at the glimpse of his own dirty covering.

"As do the noble colours of Karthénos," said Diarmuid. "Apologies, I forget my manners in these troubled times."

"Ha!" As Jannon threw back his head in a laugh, his hood fell once again to reveal his pale face. A face that, unlike his forest kin, was free from the freckles that decorated Diarmuid. "When are times untroubled with ye? What is the disturbance this time? Mortal men 'breeding' with elves? Ye know better than I that they have been crossing fer—"

"But it has gotten far out of hand, Jannon. They must be stopped. Even the Wizards believe these beasts are a scourge upon these lands, as they are unbound by both mortality and the Oath of Light."

Jannon sighed, rubbing his glacial eyes with one hand. "And how, pray tell, do ye expect to stop them? Outlaw their conception? Their birth? Gnomes be merciful, Diarmuid, ye're not the emperor of the whole of the Eastern Lands. Have ye thought not of yer allies to the West? To the North?"

"Of course, I have thought of them. Which is why I intend to wipe out these mortal elves. Not by law or diplomacy—but by blood."

Ye warmongering prick, thought Jannon, eye twitching with a sudden rage. "I cannot condone this massacre. I refuse to allow the Karthi to be responsible fer the bloodshed of innocent beings again."

"Yet your western villages are still raided at will by these mongrels. They must—"

"Wizards be good, Diarmuid! We are not your people!" Jannon

grabbed fistfuls of his own hair, each syllable spitting from his mouth like shards of ice. "Ye're not the gnomes-damned King of Prastömin and Karthénos!"

"I may as well be as you wear no crown."

Jannon held his breath, stifling the insults he longed to hurl. "I could never be king, Yer Grace," he said through clenched teeth. "I've toyed with that idea, but 'tis merely a dream. The Republic of Karthénos shall remain independent—me senate already held a emergency vote over the matter. Besides, I have no son. Only a young daughter."

"You are a terrible liar, My Laird. I heard about that Áfgalese boy."

"What Áfgalese boy?" Outwardly, Jannon merely frowned. However, his heart raced up into his throat, and it took every ounce of concentration he could muster to keep his hands from shaking. He knew precisely of whom he spoke. Deep brown hair and olive-toned skin haunted his memory's eyes. *Who told ye about him?*

Diarmuid's mouth curled into a smile as though the duke's thoughts manifested before him. "My son, Alsantör, tells me of a child he helped rescue at Prastömin's western border. A red-blooded boy of twelve who claims to be your bastard son. I believe he is called 'Sólan de Ciudelago'? I am told he has an uncanny resemblance to you, despite the darker colours in his skin, hair, and eyes."

"Oh, that boy!" Though feigning ignorance, Jannon's cracked voice betrayed him. "That boy is dead." *And as such, is the evidence of me drunken jealousy of yer ability to father sons.* "Me finest knights watched him tumble from our highest waterfall, never to emerge at—"

"He's alive and you know it!" Diarmuid grasped Jannon's cloak with a tight fist and stared evergreen daggers into him. "Tell me it's not true, friend. Tell me he's merely poisoned my son against you! What Alsantör tells me is distressing enough, but he has seen merely thirteen years and is cursed with the same sympathy as his mother for those halfblooded beasts. If your senate discovers that you sired a son by means of rape—of crimson blood—your life will be forfeit, and your corpse forever cursed to Eclipse Aeturnum."

Jannon wriggled in the king's grasp, but Diarmuid's grip was strong as iron. "It's true, Diarmuid, alright? It's true! Just let me go!" The wind howled across the rocks and trees at the cavern's entrance, as though the Wizards themselves wept.

The king released, and Jannon pushed himself away. Stifling his tears with a clenched jaw, Jannon fumbled with his brooch and straightened his cloak. "I cannot lie to ye, friend. Every word of it is true." His eye twitched in hesitation as the sting of shame flashed through his veins. After all, that boy was still his son. His firstborne, even. "How long do ye expect this massacre to last?"

"Massacre?" Diarmuid placed a hand over his chest and winced. "My dear Jannon, do you believe I mean to murder even those who would be willing to swear the Oath of Light? Nai, friend, this is no mere massacre. This is the 'Crusade of Light'."

"Hmph. And be it blessed by the Wizards *and* the Gnomes? This 'Crusade of Light?'"

"Funded by the very servants of the pool before which we stand."

Jannon licked his lips. Why was he pondering this? Why was he giving into this warmonger's bloodlust? *Ye just swore never to do this, Jannon! What are ye doing?*

"Well?"

Jannon sighed, lowering his head in defeat. *Me bruised pride is going to destroy millions of innocent lives, and all fer what? The death of a single boy? The murder of me son?* "Fine," he whispered. His face burned with the rush of disgrace at the sound of his own voice. "But Karthénos removes itself the moment of that halfbreed's demise—with proof! I will need more than mere word of it."

A wicked grin crept across Diarmuid's mouth, his elfish fangs glistening in the murky light. "That can be arranged, dear friend."

Gnomes be merciful, what have I done?

PART I

THE WAR OF RED AND SILVER

THREE HUNDRED YEARS LATER

1

FISHING FOR DEAD MEN

"Yusa God, smile on us today!" the fisherman shouted as he and his two companions pulled the taut, heavy rope over the bow. A large school of mackerel struggled against the netting as it surfaced.

As the sun beat on the ruddy skin of their burned necks, the fishermen sorted through their catch, tossing the younglings back into the clear turquoise water. All three had the same coarse black hair, dripping with sweat and salt. The youngest—a man of twenty-five, by his looks—grasped what he thought was a slick starfish. But when he looked down, he yelped. In his hand was a stiff foot attached to a fresh corpse.

The crew cleared the fish from the net, revealing the tattered body of a man who had obviously been in his prime at the time of his death. An unkempt long beard of deep brown obscured his sharp face, matching the matted waves of his tangled hair.

"Where he from?" the young fisherman asked.

Scars littered the dead man's chest and abdomen, likely due to a multitude of attempts on his life prior to drowning.

"Is no obvious?" the third man said, as if in challenge. "He escape from dungeon. I smell his stench when we pull up net. He look like escape murderer from Bansungei, or worse... a monster of Taelonael."

The other two gasped.

"Áfgail," the dinghy's owner said, wiping the sweat from his sunburnt brow. "Can you not see t'e point of his ears? The hair on his chest?"

"How, Tirsen?" the third man asked. "How can northern man drown in t'e Southern Sea?"

"What we do with him?" said the younger one, ignoring his comrade's question. "We cannot let his death ruin our good fish."

"Tie something heavy on him, Bayani," Tirsen said. "Gesang"—he turned his attention to the second fisherman—"what if he alive?"

Gesang flared his nostrils. "If he dead, we cannot let t'is evil omen of Misó ruin other's good fish, either." He reached over and placed a hand on the corpse's belly. "But, he still warm. I t'ink he alive."

"Bayani, wait!" Tirsen barked.

"Tirsen. What if he murderer? Slaver? Or worse? Do you truly t'ink—"

Without warning, the man they thought to be dead lurched forward, spewing seawater from his lungs. His speckled amber eyes opened as he gasped for breath.

"Pantot!" Bayani fell backward, flailing wildly.

Gesang snatched his fishing knife and prepared to strike.

Tirsen, however, merely rolled his eyes. He removed his shirt, revealing sharp tan lines along his arms and neck, and wrapped it about the sputtering man's shoulders to soothe him. "Hush, now," he said. "You dry and free."

"Th-th-thank you," said the man, his teeth chattering as he shivered. He wiped his face with Tirsen's sleeve, wincing as the rough cloth touched his skin. "I," he tried, only to break into a dry cough. "Water," he finally managed. "I need water."

Tirsen snapped his fingers and pointed with his lips. "Bayani. T'e water skin." Returning his attention to the man, he said, "My name Tirsen Bonlak. T'is is my brother, Gesang Bonlak, and my found-nephew, Bayani Lin. We are humble fishermen of Bansungei and servants of God of the Sun, Yusa. Who you are?"

Clearing his throat, the man again tried to speak. "Lu—" He coughed. "Lucero de Grimana." His wheeze grew louder with each breath.

Bayani handed the leather flask to Tirsen, who uncorked it for Lucero. "Here. Drink."

The man obliged, guzzling faster than he could swallow. Water sputtered out of his mouth between gulps. "Thank you for this," he said, continuing to gasp. "I cannot swim."

"You no should be alive, Lucero de Grimana," Bayani said with a growl, his accent butchering the name. "And you smell of dead man."

To his left, Gesang tightened his grip on his knife.

Lucero glared at him. "What do you imply?" Though his voice was little more than a wheeze, his tone still stung like hot metal.

The young fisherman snarled and said, "I felt you hand! It was cold and wet like a corpse. You no should be alive!"

"You are aswang," snarled Gesang.

Tirsen jumped in front of his fellow fishermen. "Stop it, Bayani! Gesang! He is only a man."

"We should have tossed him over when he was dead," Gesang said. "T'en he would stay dead."

Lucero stiffened. He locked a frantic gaze with Tirsen before—

WHEN LUCERO STIRRED, HE FOUND HIMSELF LYING UPON A THIN PILE OF sour-smelling hay. The ground beneath was one of compacted dirt, and as he inched himself up to seated position, he winced at the caustic throb inside his head.

"Medría," he cursed, gagging on the telltale stench of the city's slums. As he surveyed his surroundings, his vision somewhat lopsided, he belched; the acrid taste of bile coated his tongue. He was off the fishermen's boat and inside what appeared to be an abandoned stable.

Lucero's lungs burned as he inhaled deeply, though a sensation of constriction prevented him from filling his lungs. Looking down, he frowned at the sight of a bloodied bandage wrapped tightly about his chest. He lifted its edge to reveal a fresh cut that split the skin. It appeared to have been cleaned and stitched to perfection. Someone had stabbed him, no doubt, but had they also dressed his wound? 'Twas of no matter, however, as the scar would get lost among the ones he already bore.

Grimacing as he pushed himself to his hands and knees, Lucero cursed once more. *Was I also trampled by a fucking horse?* His head swam as he shifted to a kneeling position, the tender spots on his ribs and skull announcing themselves with sudden pangs. He prodded each contusion and rubbed his face in frustration. Wait. Someone had shaved him and detangled his hair, too? And where were his clothes?

"Hundi!" a child's voice shrieked nearby, followed by the loud thump of a wooden bowl as it dropped to the ground. Lucero flinched in pain, the fresh curse on his tongue overwhelmed by a projection of vomit.

"¿Qir medría lo posa, aeh?" *What the fuck is wrong with you, aeh?* A searing pain flashed in his eyes as he looked up to see a trembling girl standing before him. She remained perfectly still as Lucero blinked up at her, a dribble of bile still dripping from his chin.

Shit. "I... I am sorry, sañeratota. I did not mean to curse such insults at you." He leaned back with an apologetic shrug. Looking down to his nakedness, he cupped his manhood with a blush.

The child didn't move.

He tried again. "Do... uh... do you speak Garmathian?"

This time, the girl nodded.

"What is your name?"

"Elena," she squeaked.

Lucero smiled warmly, wiping his chin with the back of his hand before asking, "How old are you, Elena?"

"Ten." Elena knelt and lifted the bowl she had dropped. "Why you eyes glow?"

"Glow? What do you mean?"

"You eyes glowed green when you angry. Why? Is true you aswang?"

Lucero clenched his jaw, grumbling, though unsure if this was an insult. "What the hell is an 'aswang'?"

"It monster. From haunted islands far to t'e south." The girl's face suddenly lit up. "I never meet aswang before! You no scary like—"

"Elena!" a man's voice rumbled toward them from the stable's entrance. "Negasan po bo suya?"

The hair on Lucero's neck stood on end. *What kind of language is this?*

"Ta!" Elena called back. She returned her attention to Lucero and whispered, "I come back, aswang. I want to hear you stories." Clutching her bowl to her chest, the little girl skipped her way to the door.

The newcomer approached with a chuckle, carrying a bundle of linen in his arms. "I sorry, tual Lucero, for my daughter. She like to make wild fantasy."

Lucero's shoulders slumped in relief. *Oh, thank the Gods. 'Tis you, Fisherman.*

Tirsen smiled and offered him a hand. "I was afraid my friends closer to kill you than t'e sea," he continued, hoisting Lucero to his feet, "but it seem you no easy to kill."

Lucero stretched. "Heh, it appears as though I owe you two of my lives, sañero Tirsen." He laughed nervously. "How will I ever repay you?"

The old fisherman's eyes darkened. "Tell me who really are you."

"I"—Lucero gulped—"I have already—"

"Grimana no real village. I know the trade maps well."

A cold breeze sent stray bits of hay scuttling across the floor as Lucero's demeanour changed to one that matched the shift in atmosphere. "Do you call me a liar? I do not enjoy being accused of such."

"T'en why you angry if you no lie?"

Clenching his fists, Lucero puffed out his chest and ignored the pull of the stitches on his breast. "Whether lying or not, why do you insult a man you supposedly saved?" Lucero took an ominous step forward and bared his teeth. They were jagged like fangs, hinting at a lineage his countenance did not otherwise betray. "And why call him a 'monster,' as your daughter so graciously informed me?"

"I know why you hide, tual," Tirsen deflected. "I know you blood run red just like any other man." He raised his eyes in knowing as he continued, "But be aware: if anyone find you blood also silver, God help you."

The warmth drained from Lucero's face, and he clasped his hands together in a failed attempt to stop the from shaking. "Tirsen, who have you told?"

"I never like Crusade of Light." Tirsen shook his head as though he had not heard the question and scratched his beard thoughtfully. "It only murder, no save. Why kill mortal elfs? Why would false gods of those—"

"I will not ask you again. Who. Have. You. Told?" The pain in Lucero's eyes burned hotter with each word he spoke.

Glaring, Tirsen flared his nostrils and answered, "Not a soul. You no like to be called 'liar'? Well, I no like being accused of betraying man I saved."

Lucero opened his mouth to challenge him but stopped. The searing pain in his eyes faded as he relaxed his posture. Running shaky fingers through his hair, he said, "I apologise, sañero. There are few beings willing to preserve the life of a mortal elf. Especially those who will not swear the Oath of Light." He rubbed his right palm sadly, as though nearly regretting missing the telltale silver scar of that dreaded oath.

A moment of pause, and Tirsen finally handed Lucero the bundle of cloth he'd been carrying. "Here, take t'is. It fit short on you arms and legs but will keep you covered. My brother, Gesang, told me to give you it. It his way to ask you to forgive him for what happen on boat."

"Tell him 'thank you' for failing to kill me."

"*That* no was him."

Lucero hissed a curse in his own tongue as he awkwardly slipped into the shirt and trousers. The heavy tread of a soldier's heavy boots stopped Lucero's words, and the towering silhouette of an elf warrior suddenly filled the entire doorframe. Tirsen shuffled toward him as Lucero skittered into the barn's shadowy corner.

Clearing his throat, the intruder said, "There be a rumour, fisherman, of a man residing here who should not be alive." The smoothness of his baritone voice was unmistakable: he was Prasti. A warrior of the forest elves' kingdom..

Jidir, thought Lucero, heart now racing. *I suppose you will betray me now.* His stomach twisted, and he felt as though he might vomit again.

"An Áfgalese man, to be precise," the elf continued. "A mortal *elf*, perhaps?"

Tirsen puffed out his chest. "I have man here t'at I save from the sea."

Lucero hung his head in defeat. *I should have known you were a coward.*

"But he never dead. A man from Áfgal, yes, but of red blood alone."

¿Mondé? You still protect me, even after I threaten you?

"I'd like to see him," the warrior demanded. "Does he have a name?"

Medría. I am a dead man.

"He, um…" Tirsen fumbled and looked at his feet. "Loo… Lucero dee, uh… Greem-ahnah."

"Grimana?" The elf scoffed. "We were just in Áfgal not three fortnights ago, and we'd never heard of 'Grimana.'" Grasping the handle of his short sword, he snapped his attention to the dark corner. "Step aside, fisherman."

Lucero held his breath as Tirsen slid to his left. There was no escaping the stable without being seen. He was trapped. A cold sweat glazed his forehead as he stepped forward. "Make it quick, silver-blood, for I will not swear." He knelt, exposing his neck to the warrior.

But the elf merely rested the tip of the blade under Lucero's chin. "Get up," he said. "You're being ridiculous."

Lucero snapped his head up and locked his gaze on a familiar and freckled face: Prince Alsantör of Prastömin.

Chuckling, the prince said, "Sólan de Ciudelago. Of all the mortal elf *bastards* in the Eastern Lands." He frowned. "Why're you always on your knees when I find you?"

Sólan, as he was rightly called, flashed a grin, and his words came out before he could stop them. "Perhaps I am curious about the size of your cock."

"Ha! That's not surprising, given your bedding appetite."

"I will admit, I am disappointed in what I see, amógo."

Alsantör's smile disappeared. "Get up, Sólan. I won't ask you again."

Tirsen tentatively stepped forward. "Sólan?" he asked. "The Grim?"

The two glanced at the sputtering fisherman.

"If I knew who was he—"

"You'd have died trying to do what you think you'd have done," said Alsantör.

Sólan snickered. "You know me too well."

"Wizards be good," the prince muttered, sheathing his sword. "What the hell happened to you? Last I'd heard, you'd gotten yourself killed in Garmath five years ago."

"Heh. I had planned for it to be the last anyone had heard of me." Sólan rubbed the back of his neck. Still, his hands shook with the waning adrenaline.

"Shite, ciradh. You shoulda stayed hidden. I was days away from getting the Speaker of the Wizards to declare this crusade over. You fucked up with that damned water-steel hatchet."

"First of all, that was the best weapon I have ever owned. I forged it myself," said Sólan, crossing his arms in defiance. "Secondly, I could not—"

"You murdered a gnomes-damned *child* during that raid!" Alsantör snapped, all humour gone from his face. "You couldn't wait one more season? Three moons and the end of the crusade would be declared throughout the Eastern Lands. You could've gone back to scouting without the rumours of your return. Those rumours're all that Jannon needs to keep his hatred of you alive."

Tirsen gasped. "A child! Oh Yusa, protect my Elena from him."

Sólan paid the man no mind. "I am aware, sañero," he growled at the prince. "But forget not that mad king of your Prasti forest. Diarmuid is as warm and welcoming as the fell beasts that haunt the grasslands and the canyon ruins of Garmath. Was it not his hand that wrote the declaration of this massacre?"

Alsantör curled his lip, revealing one of his sharp fangs. "I'd be careful with your tone, Sólan de Ciudelago. Not every being in the Eastern Lands thinks the way you do."

Though ignored once again, Tirsen grunted in agreement.

"Perhaps not." Sólan shrugged. "However, I know there are many of us Áfgaliards who share a distaste for your fa—"

"Ah, there we are," the prince cut in. "Yet, you're only *half* Áfgalese. Do you forget it was your father who started all this? Mine never would've signed that scroll without his backing. The Speaker of the Wizards would have never endorsed it had it not been for Jannon."

Sólan bristled at the mention of the Karthi duke's name. Jannon may have been his father, but 'twas by title alone. He wasn't his "átha"—the male figure every child looks up to and hopes to be. No one had the luxury of that name to him, and no one ever would. "Of course," he croaked, a single tear escaping the corner of one eye. "That fucking duke of the tundra would rather watch millions of innocent lives be destroyed than to give his legacy to a halfbreed bastard son sired by rape."

As though to remind the comrades of his continued existence, Tirsen cut in, "Why is he still alive, then? He should burn for what he did to you mama. But, she never should carried you. It why you now cursed to be 'The Grim.' She should have died with him."

Sólan's face contorted into a snarl. "I will kill him, Tör." He lunged forward, but Alsantör blocked his path. "Get out of my way, " he hissed and tried to push past his friend.

"Sólan, stop."

"Niníl." Sólan dropped his voice to a rumbling growl so low, that only Alsantör's keen elf ears could hear. "Do not make me use The Dark." His eyes burned as he allowed his powers to bubble in his chest, their colour likely pulsing in an unnatural green glow. "Move."

Alsantör gripped the man's shoulders in warning. "If you kill him, I'll have no choice but to execute you."

Sólan shot daggers at Tirsen as he stepped back. "¡Vo ta qemir et lu enfríno, pundijo!" *Go to hell, asshole!* He spat at the old man before switching his attention to the prince. "You heard him. He insulted my athóta."

"I know, Sólan. It was out of line," the elf said, releasing his hold, his eyes piercing Sólan with the sharpness of sorrow. "But you can't just curse him to hell in his own home. I hate that Jannon despises you so."

At this, Sólan's eyes prickled. He wiped away another tear before it could fall and said, "I am a threat to his *pride*, amógo."

Tirsen opened his mouth, but another glare from Sólan stayed his voice.

"This crusade will not end until I am truly dead. You know it as well as I, Tör."

"It doesn't have to be that way, Sólan. Just swear the bloody oath," the prince begged. "You can go home if you swear."

Sólan turned away, kicking at a stray clump of straw. "I am not swearing, Tör, so stop trying to force it. I need those powers to survive."

"Have you even used them since your disappearance? I doubt you'll miss them."

"Until I get another knife to my chest." Sólan gestured toward the cut from the fisherman, which was nothing more than a pink scar. "I will not die a mortal's death and give victory to that asshole in the tundra."

Tirsen gasped. "That was from today! How it heal like t'at?"

"My 'curse,'" said Sólan through a harsh laugh.

"I—I sorry. I no mean to insult you." Tirsen bowed his head, placing a hand over his own heart. "And I no intend to insult you mama. I sorry for that, too." His voice sounded sincere, but Sólan didn't know if he could trust it.

Alsantör prodded his comrade with his eyes, waiting for a response.

Sólan sighed. "Fine. I forgive you, I suppose." When the prince kicked his foot, he begrudgingly added, "You have saved my life more than once, today, Tirsen. I am in your debt. There is no need to apologise." He shifted his gaze back to Alsantör. "So, what now? You will not kill me, and I will not swear your 'precious' Oath of Light. It appears we are at a crossroad, amógo. Perhaps—"

"A h-uale ded creat, mi phriannso?" Sólan was cut off by the appearance of a second elf in the doorway. Though knowing the prince's native tongue, this phrase was unfamiliar to him.

"Shite," Alsantör muttered under his breath. He turned his head slightly to speak over his shoulder. "Eil. The a h-uale ded creat, Anlon."

Sólan opened his mouth to speak, but again was cut off by the second elf. "Ilb maoirsetach, o dhiune maoirsetach?" *Mortal elf, or mortal man?*

This time, Sólan whispered before the prince could reply. "I look Áfgalese," he said, his voice quavering as he locked panicked eyes with Alsantör. "I am mortal. I am a man. I can get out without revealing myself."

"You *also* look Karthi." The prince shook his head sadly. "I'm sorry, Sólan. I can't lie to my men." The clink of his sword as it was drawn a second time reverberated ominously in the small barn. Lowering his voice so only Sólan could hear, he said, "Follow my lead," and then he thrust his blade into Sólan's tender abdomen. As his friend gasped in shock, he cried out triumphantly, "Nao ilb maoirsetach! We got another one!"

Tirsen yelped as he stumbled backward. "No! I hate t'is crusade!"

"He's a mortal elf who's refused to swear the Oath of Light!" Alsantör spat. He locked his eyes on the friend still skewered on his sword. "Sólan de Ciudelago, it be under my authority to sentence you to die for your crimes and your refusal to cleanse your blood from The Dark through the Oath of Light. Any last words, half-breed?" Alsantör yanked his blade out of Sólan, who immediately collapsed in a pool of crimson blood.

The wound was deep, and Sólan clutched his stomach in desperation as his innards threatened to spill. Hot, sticky blood gushed through his hands and stained the dusty ground below. *Fuck you, Tör. That one hurt.*

Sólan spat a glob of frothy blood at the prince's feet and garbled, "Vita i le medría, asshole." *Fuck you, asshole.*

Alsantör laughed. "Anlon," he called. The second elf dutifully stepped forward. "Send a raven to my father. Tell him Sólan the Grim is dead."

"Eil, Commander." Anlon spun and marched out of the stable as the prince raised his bloodied sword again.

Playing along, Sólan exposed his neck, but the sword thwacked as Alsantör dropped it into the dirt. Leaning closely to the Áfgaliard's ear, he hissed, "Stay hidden. Don't leave the city." He then stood and tossed a small leather pouch of coins at Tirsen's feet. "Be sure to burn his body," he said with a wink. "You don't want his ghost haunting you."

The fisherman trembled as he said, "He will burn tonight."

"Good." Alsantör grabbed his shirt and pulled him close, their faces only mere centimetres apart. "Don't let 'him leave the city. And keep 'him alive." He shoved the old man back before strutting out of the stable without another word.

Tirsen bent to pick up the pouch at his feet. When he turned to face Sólan, he was met with nothing but a sticky puddle of blood. "Oh Yusa," he groaned. The ground gave no clues of where the wounded Áfgaliard had gone. "Where in t'is city will I find him?"

2

TYPHOON

Sólan perched himself on a roof by Bansungei's northern gate and took in his surroundings as he had done every day since leaving Tirsen's home two moons ago. Before him, the trade road meandered its way northward alongside the Runedein River's eastern bank, where it forked and crossed over the water into Orovín.

The memory of that western kingdom's small dungeons made Sólan shudder. He recalled how small were the Orovite oddlings, no taller than a young Áfgalese child, and built like a pig from the waist down. Standing beside Sólan, even the tallest of them would reach little higher than his hip at their own floppy ears. Their dungeons had been built for their own kind, which left little room to accommodate any larger beings. As the eastern sun lowered in the sky, its vibrant colours made the western horizon deceptively beautiful.

Sólan twisted to peer over his shoulder. Behind him, beyond a vast estuary half-hidden by rocks, the Runedein opened wide to meet the Southern Sea. He let his eyes follow the golden coastline as it curved two leagues to the south, thus completing the semi-circular bay.

A clang echoing from somewhere below him directed his attention to the bustling baker's shop upon which he sat. He took a deep breath, savouring the perfume of ocean salt and fresh herb bread and purposely oblivious to the dark reminders of the man who raised him.

Up here, he could find peace. Since the day Alsantör had left him in a pool of his own blood, he struggled to find a moment of rest. Every day had been spent hiding, scrounging for food, and looking for means to escape the city. Though the Prasti prince had told him to stay here in Bansungei, Sólan wasn't one to follow orders. He hated feeling trapped, and this city? 'Twas the greatest cage he'd found himself in since his tenure in the fighting pits of Taelonael.

A tear trickled down his cheek as memories of the family he'd outlived flooded him. They were the good memories: his mother's soft smile as she sang him to sleep and his brother's braying laugh as they played in the open streets of Ciudelago. Sólan yearned for the lush prairies and vineyards of his native kingdom. In Áfgal, the summers were warm and the winters mild, with only the occasional dusting of snow. He leaned against the building's sunbaked chimney and sniffled.

Suddenly, a cool breeze bit through his thin clothing. Shivering, he again peered over his shoulder to the south to see a wall of dark clouds approaching, forewarning a late summer typhoon. "Medría. This one is coming *here*." He clambered his way down the roof, barefoot, and dropped onto the main road.

"Áp-galiard!" a voice called from behind. "Lucero! T'ank God I find you!"

Sólan spun to find Bayani, Tirsen's young comrade, jogging toward him. He clenched his fists and jaw at the fisherman. "Have you come back to finish killing me?" Sólan snapped. "Perhaps you should have let me drown."

Bayani startled. He opened his mouth to respond, but bit his lips instead at the Áfgaliard's scowl.

Sólan continued, "What, are you going to deny your attempt on my life?"

The fisherman muttered, "Perhaps I should have let you drown." He then shook his head and added, "I needed to find you. I—"

"Whatever it is you offer, I want no part of it. I do not enjoy being stabbed."

"And how you know it no was—"

"I know a liar when he speaks, cabróde." Sólan turned his back and stomped away.

Bayani followed, much to Sólan's dismay. "But... but t'is storm! It t'e first to hit Bansungei in many years, and you have no shelter! It will kill you."

"I have survived far worse than this coming storm."

"And t'e thunder! I seen many die of such things!"

Sólan stopped to glare at Bayani. "Why do you continue to follow me, aeh? Is my show of disgust toward you not clear enough?"

The fisherman merely flared his nostrils at the insult.

"You tried to fucking kill me. You should be thanking your 'god' that I did not respond in kind."

"I trying to be kind to you," Bayani said through clenched teeth. "Gesang gave you clothes. Let me shelter you. I made mistake on boat."

You are correct in that regard, cabróde.

"But I hope to try and show you I not a bad man."

You have made a poor impression so far, pundijo.

"Please, Lucero," the fisherman begged. "Tirsen. He tell me—"

"Tirsen?" Sólan stiffened. "What did he say to you?"

"That you lost in the city and need shelter." Bayani trembled. "My home on high ground. It no will flood. Tirsen there with Tala and Elena."

Tala? "And Tirsen's brother? Will Gesang be joining this family gathering?"

"He with his wife's fam—" A bright flash and deafening boom interrupted Bayani's words.

"Fine." Sólan growled through his fangs. "I will go with you... but only for Tirsen and Elena. Not you."

The rain from the blackened sky pounded against the city of Bansungei. Bayani and Sólan struggled to trek through the storm as wind toppled palm trees and whipped debris about them. Sólan slipped and stumbled as his feet lost traction on the muddy ground.

"We almost there!" Bayani's voice nigh drowned under the wind's howls. "Just up t'e hill!"

Sólan squinted through the darkness. A flash of lightning illuminated the wealthier portion of the city that was much further away than he expected. *Jidir*, he cursed. *I should never have left that godsdamned stable.* He crossed his arms and shivered as the gusty wind chilled him to his core.

The duo trudged up the hill against the flood of wreckage. The slick mud gave way to sharp gravel, and his tender feet bled and throbbed with each step until it cleared to cobblestone. He prayed thanks to Áfgal's gods as he and Bayani finally reached the top.

"You need shoes." Bayani motioned to the ground as he spoke.

Do I, truly? I cannot believe I never thought of such a thing! You are such an intelligent man, Bayani Lin. Perhaps you can be my personal advisor some day. Sólan gritted his teeth and gave the fisherman a strained smile to keep from verbalising his disdain.

Bayani knocked on the heavy bronze door of his home. It creaked open with a familiar young face behind it.

"Binyego! Aki-yo bahi!" Elena jumped into Bayani's arms despite his soaked clothing. He chuckled as he squeezed her and kissed her forehead.

The girl broke her embrace and leaped into Sólan's arms next, giggling. "Thank Yusa you here, aswang!"

"Elena," Tirsen scolded. "Atogil mei yin."

Elena stepped away and hung her head.

Her father wiped the scowl from his face as he averted his attention to Sólan. "I was afraid you left the city, tual, after the elf told you to stay."

Sólan shrugged as he followed him inside. "He always tells me to stay wherever I am. I never listen to him. To be honest, sañero, the thought of leaving weighed heavily on my mind. Especially after what—"

"Well, thanks be to God you did not," the fisherman deflected.

Elena skipped to the back of the house, oblivious to the growing tension.

Bayani shifted his gaze between the men, pondering them with a frown. "Lucero, have you never seen t'e storms here? They not like the ones in Áfgal."

A young woman entered from the kitchen just as Sólan opened his mouth to retort. Her thick black hair, which perfectly framed her oval face, coiled its way down to her waist. "I was worried that you'd died, tual," she said. "I saw the blood in the stable."

As Sólan looked her over, the sudden twitch of lust fluttered in his chest. *Gods, Tirsen. You make beautiful daughters.* He cleared his throat and smiled. "Apologies, sañeratota. Have we met?"

The woman nodded. "Yes, but I'm no surprised you forgot. How is your chest? I hoped it wouldn't fester after you disappeared."

As Sólan took a breath to reply, Tirsen cut him off. "I forget! Sólan dee Coo-dee-log-oh, t'is is my wife, Tala."

Sólan clamped his mouth shut and held out his hand. "A pleasure, sañerota."

Tala placed her fingers in his palm with a stiff smile. He clasped her hand and brushed his lips against the back of her knuckles.

Bayani tensed before tightening his fists with a snarl. "Wait, I t'ought you name was Lucero. And now you kiss other man's wife? I knew you no trustworthy."

"'Tis a simple gesture of respect," said Sólan. He turned to Tirsen. "Apologies. I meant no offence to you nor your bride. We Áfgalese are—"

Bayani stepped between them. "Who you are, hah?" he asked, shoving Sólan. "What you are?"

Sólan's eyes pulsed with an unnatural searing pain as he bared his fangs, and Bayani growled at the likely colour change. "You more t'an Áfgaliard, I see now. You eyes glow like a demon. You teeth sharp like a lion—no—like a snake."

The pain in Sólan's eyes flared alongside his temper. "I am a man who should not be alive. A man who has been cursed by the gods to bear this burden of The Dark within me. A man who has looked death in the face a thousand times and conquered it. I am Sólan de Ciudelago. The Grim." As though they feared him themselves, the thunder rumbled and the wind howled.

The colour drained from Bayani's frightened face, and he took a tentative step back. *Yes, coward. You know to fear me and my true name. Choose your enemies with care, pundijo.*

Elena, who had reappeared at her father's side, crossed her arms and pouted. "So... you no aswang?"

Sólan peered at the child with a raised eyebrow. "No, sañeratota. I am no aswang. I apologise for disappointing you so."

"What you are, then?"

"A kapiret-liho," Bayani muttered.

Tala backhanded the young fisherman's ear. "He's you *guest*, Bayani Lin! Have respect, hah!"

Sólan rolled his eyes at the slur and returned his gaze to Elena. "Have you heard of 'mortal elves,' or the Crusade of Light?"

"We don't speak of that to her," said Tala. "She's only ten."

"Right. Apologies, Tala." Sólan pursed his lips in shame.

"Elena, time for bed," Tirsen commanded.

"But... but I no tired—"

"Listen to you papa. We no want t'e babuwaya to steal you."

Elena gasped and clamped her hands over her mouth at her mother's words. Sólan lowered his head to hide his laughter. Tala winked at the Áfgaliard as Tirsen followed close behind his daughter. "T'e crocodile woman."

"Why he care, Tala?" said Bayani with flailing arms. "He foreigner and he no have children."

Sólan scowled at the fisherman. "I do not suppose, Tala, that you would check my wound? I no longer have need for the stitching."

The woman nodded with a curious frown and led Sólan to the kitchen. At her direction, he removed his tattered shirt, as her delicate fingers untied the bandage's knot with ease. Removing the linen, she paused to reveal his powerful physique. The rough hair on his torso covered just enough to outline his muscles and the myriad of scars from previous attempts at his life. Tala's eyes followed the thin strip of hair that meandered down the centre of his lower abdomen until it disappeared beneath his low-waisted trousers. She stared at the top of a circular tattoo peeking its way over the hem. Her hand reached toward the black design and—

"Are you alright, Tala?"

The woman snapped her eyes back to Sólan's, gulping with a nod. "Ta." She then went to work with an edged pin and cut through the sutures. Once they were removed, she traced her fingertips over the pink scar left behind.

Sólan grimaced at her touch and took a deep breath, the scent of lust overpowering his senses. Gods, he needed to get away from her.

"This shouldn't hurt," she whispered. "It's fully healed."

"'Tis not my chest that pains me."

Tala inspected his torso again. She gasped at the sight of the ugly scar left behind by Alsantör's sword. "That one's new!" She reached out and placed her palm over his abdomen. "What happened?"

Sólan blinked as he realised she'd studied him closely the last time she had seen him. Then, the memory of his nakedness came rushing back. *Shit. You saw—*

"I refused to die," was all he said.

"It still pains you."

"Of course it does. The pain reminds me that I am still alive."

Tala crossed her arms, frowning. "There's no need to be rude. I'm trying to help you."

Sólan's jaw dropped at her words. "I"— he clacked his mouth shut at her reproachful scowl—"apologies, I just... you... aeh..."

Tala scoffed. "You're not a child, tual." She reached over and brushed her knuckles against his wrist. "You have the power to heal. Why do you carry your scars?"

"I try not to use that power. The Dark is greedy. I wish not to lose control of it." He inched himself closer with his head cocked and eyes smouldering.

Tala's breath quickened and her pupils dilated as he rubbed her thumb with his own. When he bowed his head toward hers, her lips parted in anticipation.

"You are a claimed woman, sañerota. Yet, I can see you want more than a mere story from me."

A mischievous smirk curled her mouth as she stepped away. "We have little eyes watching."

Sólan glanced over his shoulder and stiffened at the sight of Elena. "Thank you for your help," he said. "This wound would have festered had you not sewed it." He slipped into his shirt before excusing himself from the kitchen.

"You should be in bed, pitru," he heard Tala say. He peeked around the corner to watch the interaction, his heart aching in memory of him and his own family.

Elena shuffled to her mother with a lowered head. "I know. But binyego Bayani—"

"Told you to watch him, I know." Tala kneeled to embrace her daughter and kiss her head. "You don't have to obey him, yet. You're still mine to hold."

Elena stared at her mother with curiosity. "What T'e Dark is, mama?"

"What?" Tala scoffed. "Why you're asking about The Dark, silly girl?"

"It what tual Sólan say is a curse. What kind of curse it is?"

Her mother flared her nostrils, her smile disappearing. "Evil, pitru. It's nothing but a curse of Misó." She glanced to the doorway. "You need to go back to bed. Don't worry about Sólan. He's not evil like Bayani says."

Sólan closed his eyes with a grimace and silently slipped away. *Oh, how I wish your words were true, sañerota.*

3

THE ÁFGALIARDS

The boy ran, breath fogging in the crisp morning air. His eyes and nose dripping with tears of irritation and fear, the thunder of horses chased after him with fervour.

"Dispár lu!" a commanding voice shouted.

The boy dug his foot into the ground and cut to the side, an arrow missing him by mere centimetres.

"Móta lu!"

Again, the boy changed direction. This time, however, the arrow hit its target, burrowing into the back of his knee. He tumbled down an embankment and splashed into the narrow river at its bottom. More arrows whistled past his ears as he lurched across the cold water to the other side. There, the kingdom of Áfgal ended, and Prastömin's domain began.

Jidir, the boy sobbed. He ripped the arrow from his leg and closed the flesh with his newfound powers. To his dismay, the pain remained.

He scrambled to his feet and hobbled to the edge of the Prasti forest. The splash of horses in the river reached his pointed ears, their approach growing louder with each passing second. The boy shivered in his wet clothes, his teeth chattering as despair hit his stomach—he was trapped.

A hand gloved in leather snatched his shirt collar and dragged him into a clearing. The boy shrieked. "Please! Please, sañero! I beg mercy! Mercy!"

"Silence, mastázo! You know the punishment for murder and flight."

Hot tears streamed down the boy's face as he argued, "You believe *lies* about me! Montrél tried to save me! It was the baker! The baker killed him!"

"Keep your venomous tongue behind those fangs of yours, half-breed!" The commander punched the boy, the impact sending him to the ground. "I pray to the Gods I never see you in Terría Vareno. You deserve the deepest pits of enfríno. You and all the rest of your kind."

The boy was racked with sobs at his captor's words, choking and sputtering. "Please, sañero Lorenzo. Please believe me."

Lorenzo wiped his nose with the back of his hand and announced "I, Cabillero Primero Lorenzo, sentence you to die for the murder of a man of Ciudelago." Turning to his men, he nodded to the one closest. "Javiér, móta lu." *Javiér, kill him.*

The mounted archer smiled maliciously as he pulled an arrow from his quiver. But before Javiér could nock it, his wrist was pierced between the bones by another arrow. His steed reared in surprise, throwing him to the ground with a thud.

The boy cursed himself for failing to hear the approach of a new swarm of attackers amidst the chaos. He trembled as his speckled amber eyes flitted around him— he was in the midst of a standoff. A score of elf warriors surrounded him and the men who hunted him.

"And what brings a group of armed Cabilleros across our borders unannounced?" the commanding elf asked in his deep Prasti voice. "Take care with your words—you don't want to start a war."

Lorenzo cleared his throat. "We chase a murderer, sañero. We apologise for the intrusion into your kingdom, as we were unaware of our proximity to the border."

A young elf no older than thirteen approached the boy. Kneeling with concern, he asked, "Are you hurt?"

The Áfgalese boy trembled as he nodded.

The elf reached out and placed a gentle hand on his injured knee. "You're safe now."

"I do not feel safe," the boy said. "And I know not if I can trust you."

The elf boy winced, sucking at the back of his teeth. "My name's Alsantör. I'm the crowned Prince of Prastömin. You can trust me."

The Áfgaliard's lip quivered as fresh tears dripped down his cheeks. "S-S-Sólan de Ciudelago."

SÓLAN'S EYES FLUTTERED OPEN AT THE HOWL OF THE WIND. HE RUBBED his face and groaned. *I still trust you, amógo.* He sat up on the hard ground of Bayani's home, shook his head, and stretched, his back and shoulders popping. The only light in the room came from the occasional flash of lightning and the soft glow of an approaching candle.

"You awake, tual. You are afraid of thunder, too?" a small voice whispered.

Sólan smiled warmly at Elena, raising a curious eyebrow. "I am afraid of many things, sañeratota, but the thunder is not one of them. Why do you come to me? Should you not go to your mother and father?"

"Uh... I no want to wake t'em." Elena fidgeted with her candle as she stammered. "And... uh... and I want... uh..."

"Let me see that candle, before you burn yourself." Chuckling, Sólan reached out his hand toward the girl, who obliged his request. "You have a very curious mind. If not careful, you can get hurt."

Elena crossed her arms with a frown. "Why you are cursed?" she finally asked. "What T'e Dark is?"

It was Sólan's turn to stammer. "Aeh... you... aeh... you need not worry about The Dark. 'Tis not a curse that can... aeh... be spread from." He paused, a new thought occurring to him. "Tell me something, Elena. Is Bayani always so angry?"

Elena blinked at the sudden change of conversation. "Why?"

"He seems like a very angry man, and I am surprised by your father's deep friendship with him. Is he always so unhappy, or…?"

"Ta." The girl dropped her head in shame. "He angry a lot. Papa says it because he young but… he old to me." She flitted her eyes around the room, as though she was afraid someone would hear. She leaned in close and whispered, "He already twenty-four."

"Ha!" Sólan shook his head through his laughter. "He is young, Elena. Very young, especially to me. Do you want to know how old I am?"

Elena nodded eagerly, and a playful grin curled across Sólan's face.

"Three hundred twenty-two."

The girl gasped and clamped her hands over her mouth. "How you no dead yet? You so much older than Papa!"

"My father is an elf," said Sólan, snickering. "My mother was a 'regular' woman. So, that makes me half of both. It is why my eyes 'glow,' as you say."

"Is t'at why Bayani call you a… uh…" Elena trailed off, seemingly losing focus. She pinched her lips together and flared her nostrils. She paused for a while, thinking. "Papa say wisdom come with older age. Maybe you can talk to him. I no want to marry binyego Bayani, but Papa say—"

"Marry?" Sólan cringed at her words. "Why would you… what?"

"I almost flower, so I need husband soon. Papa say he young and bless by Yusa with wealth."

A wave of nausea engulfed Sólan, and he belched; last night's meal threatened to escape as sour bile reached the back of his tongue. "You are promised to a man more than two times your age. Gods, do all girls marry so young?"

Elena gave a sad nod. "God no smile on whores, tual. To know my husband first and only is what is pure. It my duty to—"

Tala's voice echoed from the back. "Elena. Kimbelo ko timpet tudo."

"But Mama," the girl whined, "I no—"

"I don't care. Bed. Now."

Sólan chuckled as Elena crossed her arms in a huff. "You should listen to her," he whispered with a nudge. "The wrath of a mother is one thing I am afraid of."

Elena gulped. "Sorry, Mama," she said with a squeak, then sprinted to the bedroom and shut the door.

Tala shook her head. "I'm sorry, tual, for her," she said. "She know of boundaries, but she can be stubborn."

Sólan shrugged. "She is a child. At her age, she is still learning."

"Do you have children?"

"Aeh…" Sólan scrunched his nose as though the idea appalled him. "I would be a terrible father. How old were you when your family forced you to marry Tirsen?"

"Twelve." Tala lowered herself to her knees with a forlorn expression. A tear slid down her cheek as she said, "Thirteen when Elena was born."

Sólan gasped. "Gods! You are younger than Bayani!"

Tala rolled her eyes at the mention of the young fisherman. "Only by number," she said. "It's better for girls to marry older men. They know Yusa better. Know his ways and his laws"— she grimaced— "'better.'"

"That sounds like something a tyrant would teach you. This god of yours… Do you truly believe that?"

Tala tried not to frown as she declared, "It's my duty to believe it." Her fiery eyes burned chasms into Sólan's own. "But… it's not easy."

His breath quickened as she leaned in close. "Tirsen is a lucky man," he said, and then reached to brush a wisp of hair out of her face. Pinning it behind her ear, he inhaled deeply, savouring the scent of ocean salt and coconut. "You are a beautiful woman."

"I'm the lucky one, Sólan, for I have a husband. My beauty is a curse, like The Dark is to you."

Sólan winced. "Beauty—within and without—is never a curse, Tala. Only those who do not possess it are doomed to hate it." He gently ran a hand along her hip as though aching to pull her closer. "And you have been blessed with both."

"Stop saying that," Tala whispered, and Sólan removed his hand. "That beauty makes me exposed to the evil Misó. Exposed to the ways of a whore. So"— she grasped his hand and brought it back to her hip— "a 'whore' I will become." She brushed her lips against his as she inched her body closer.

Sólan, however, stiffened at the sudden change in her demeanour. "Wait. We cannot be doing this. You are a claimed woman. If I were to give you a child to carry—"

"You can't." Tala's voice caught as she spoke, though her eyes burned with lust. "I lost my womb when Elena was born. I didn't give Tirsen a son, so I'm nothing to him now. I have been untouched since before Elena was born… and bound to t'e Temple of Yusa. T'ere, I am sworn to live the rest of my life untouched by a man, never to see my child again." She grasped the front of Sólan's shirt and pulled him in, their mouths meeting in a passionate kiss. "Take me," she whispered. "Make me a woman again."

Sólan groaned, a wave of desire tearing through him, and he buried his face into her bosom. She clambered onto his lap and allowed him to slip the sleeves of her dress off of her shoulders, exposing the soft skin beneath. He kissed and nibbled each breast. "I cannot promise my heart," he whispered, tracing her neck, collarbones, and chest with his nose and lips.

"I don't want your heart," Tala said, shivering. "Just your touch." She reached into his trousers and grasped his erection with a tight fist.

Sólan's head snapped back as he growled with passion. He fumbled with the hem of her heavy linen dress and help her onto his manhood. In one swift motion, he swept her onto her back and thrust, accidentally knocking over the candle over and extinguishing its flame. Tala kissed him to stifle his groans. She explored with her tongue the sharpness of his fangs and the taste of his mouth.

Sólan broke the kiss to nuzzle her neck as he pushed himself deeper, stronger, faster. A well of pressure built inside him as Tala writhed beneath his body. The heavy rain and thunder masked their noises as they climaxed together in the darkness.

The flicker of a new candle brightened the room as Sólan pretended to sleep. "Áfgaliard," Bayani's voice whispered, "what you have done?"

"¿Perdón?" *Pardon?* Sólan pushed himself upright, his mouth gaping in a false show of fatigue. "I am unsure if I understand what it is you imply," he finally said with a glare. "I—"

"Don't lie to me, Lucero," Bayani snarled. "Or it is Sólan? You have so many names, I get mix up."

"Hmph. I am hardly intimidated by you and your temper, cabróde. What does my name matter to you? I will be gone once this typhoon—"

"And leave Tala to be stoned?" Bayani stooped to pick up a loose hairpin. Tala's. "Because of you and your seduction, she is now a whore. You rapist of Misó."

"¡Jideta, putathóta!" Sólan jumped to his feet and gripped Bayani by the throat. "The deepest pits of enfríno are too kind to a man who takes an unwilling lover. She came to me. She wished to speak to me on what ails her. Do you truly believe I would—"

Bayani slammed a knee into Sólan's groin, forcing him back to the ground.

"Fuck... you..." Sólan croaked as tears flooded his eyes. He curled his body into a ball and took deep, rhythmic breaths, but the pain refused to stop.

"I welcome you in my home, give you food and shelter," Bayani snarled. "And, you t'ank me by violating the mother of my bride? What kind of man would—"

"Binyego! What you are doing?"

Bayani spun to face Tala. "You no speak to me, whore. This no concern you."

"Fuck you!" Sólan staggered to his feet and yanked the fisherman's hair. He threw him to the ground and said menacingly, "Call her a whore again." He kicked Bayani's hip with enough force to make him yelp. "Go on! I will suck the life out of you with a twitch of my eye, and I shall enjoy every moment of it."

"He's right, Sólan." Tala placed a desperate hand on the Áfgaliard's shoulder. "Please stop." She spun him around and stared deep into his eyes as she spoke. "I would rather be stoned and have my daughter live a fruitful life with Bayani than to live in exile while another woman take my place at Tirsen's side, teaching my daughter the ways of Yusa in her marriage while I wonder in misery."

Sólan swallowed as his stomach twisted. He stepped away from the woman and nodded reluctantly. *This is wrong.* "Tell me, in what world is it accepted, no, encouraged for a man his age to marry a child? He is twice Elena's age!"

Bayani scrambled to his feet and stepped between them. "Tala," he whispered. "I promise to be good to her. Forgive me, I speak in anger. T'at is not Yusa's way. And I promise t'is kapiret-liho will no violate you again."

"Indionta lo piezo de medría," Sólan said as he rolled his eyes. *You stupid piece of shit.*

Hushed voices then reached them from outside. Sólan's ears twitched and his heart fell at the familiar language: they were soon to be joined by slavers from Áfgal. "Shit," he said, turning to Tala. "You need to hide."

Bayani scoffed. "What now? You going to threaten me ag—"

"Shh!" Sólan held up a hand and motioned to the door. "Slavers," he whispered.

"Pantot," Bayani cursed. He scrambled to the back of the house in search of weapons.

A flash of lightning illuminated the room just enough for Sólan to locate a dull hatchet on a corner table. Bayani returned with a heavy cargo hook and several knives, Tirsen in tow.

"What happening?" the older fisherman asked as he prepared for the fight.

Before Sólan could answer, the thick bronze door burst open. Five hooded men swarmed inside, touching their torches onto the window drapes and wooden floors. A young girl's scream pierced through the roar of flames, gathering the men's attention. "¡Vipar lus chócas!" *Get the girls!*

Sólan attacked the speaker, leaving Tirsen and Bayani to fend for themselves against the four remaining intruders. A swift punch to the nose knocked Tirsen to the ground, unconscious. Bayani disarmed two opponents, killing one with ease. He nigh finished the second before he, too, was tackled. The dismembered head of Sólan's victim gaped at him in a pool of crimson blood.

"Papa!" Elena screamed as she rushed to her father's side. Before she could reach him, a slaver scooped her up and threw her over his shoulder.

"Elena! No!" Tala removed a large pin from her hair and lunged after her daughter. She embedded her makeshift weapon into the slaver's eye and grasped Elena's arm. "Run!" She again brandished her weapon, ready to strike once more. But before she could, Tala's feet were swept out from under her. She swung and managed to lodge her pin into her attacker's arm, only to lose her grip as she hit the ground.

The man ripped the pin from his flesh and rushed toward Elena. The little girl screamed and kicked as he threw her again over his shoulder.

Tala scrambled to her feet, this time arming herself with a fishing knife left unattended. She lunged for Elena's captor, who only kicked her back to the ground. He stepped on her wrist, snapping her arm with a twist. As she writhed and screamed with pain, the slaver spun toward the door. He almost made it before a dull hatchet collided with his throat. The sudden collapse of his airway made him drop Elena and fall to his knees. Sólan finished his kill by snapping the man's neck.

Tala and Tirsen's attackers charged Sólan from behind, but he twirled around and slayed them effortlessly. His eyes pulsed green as he channelled his powers, drawing every flame in the room to his hatchet. A swirling mass, the fire danced about his arm. He swung at the last remaining slaver, but the flames snuffed out before they reached their target.

There was another mortal elf in the room. Sólan launched himself onto his opponent's shoulders. The impact brought them both crashing to the ground and they grappled over the hatchet, their hands and faces slick with blood and sweat. Without warning, a cargo hook embedded itself into his collarbone, followed by a swift kick to his face, and his world turned black.

Sólan awakened with a start. He groaned as he shifted, the hook in his shoulder digging deeper into his muscle. He clenched his teeth nigh to cracking as he extracted the grapnel from his flesh and closed the wound. There would be another inevitable scar.

Tirsen and Bayani stirred as Sólan noted how calm the weather had become. The typhoon had passed.

"My God," Bayani croaked.

His words were cut off by an anguished cry from Tirsen. "Look what you kin have done!" he snarled at Sólan. He buried his face in his hands and wept. His body trembled with melancholic sobs as he rocked back and forth on his knees. "They took my wife! My daughter!"

Bayani placed a gentle hand on his shoulder in a failed attempt to comfort him.

"They are not my kin," Sólan growled. He scanned the corpses at his feet while monitoring Bayani in his periphery. *Thank the Gods.* He quickly went to work stripping the clothing off of the largest body. "These putathótas do not hail from Ciudelago. They are likely from the southern districts of Yubina or Piulenoro." He slipped out of his bloodied shirt and trousers as he continued, "These districts are poor in resources, thanks to their proximity to the Taela desert and the dunes of the 'Trial by Fire.'"

"Oh, Yusa. Please bring t'em back," Tirsen begged to the sky as though he were alone in the room. "Iso minhon pidoma." The thump of a corpse's leg as Sólan discarded it interrupted him. "You steal clothes from dead man?" he said, gaping in disgust as the foreigner placed a foot into a fine leather boot. "Is no good of you. Yusa frown upon—"

"My Gods care nothing about what happens to these fuckers, nor their possessions," said Sólan. "They are condemned to the eternal fires of enfríno, never to enter Terría Vareno." He sighed in relief at the boots' perfect fit—the oiled leather hugged his ankles and shins, and the padded soles of cork supported his weight with a pleasant bounce.

"You false gods allow theft and impure acts," said Bayani.

"And your 'god' demands that young women to be sold to his temple and isolated from their families, simply for bearing daughters instead of sons." Sólan's eyes flashed as his anger flared. "And the marriage and fornication of old men to children? Tell me how that is pure!"

"You will never understand, tual," Tirsen argued. "Not until you baptised in the temple and washed clean by Yusa's love."

Sólan's nose twitched, and he clenched his fists in forced restraint. "These men," he spat, "have murdered, raped, abducted, and sold men, women, and children that belong not to the slave masters of Taelonael. Their possessions belong to those in greater need. Not wasted by being buried or burned with them." He knelt and rummaged through each corpse's pockets for anything valuable —gold, weapons, or food, his eyes widening at the discovery of a small papyrus scroll. While he could not read its words, the numbers scribbled on it confirmed his fears. *That mortal elf was a Taela slave. These are no slavers—they are breeders!* He jumped to his feet in a panic. "I need a horse. Now."

Tirsen hiccoughed as he said, "I thought—I promised t'e elf to—not let you leave this—"

"Do you want your wife and daughter back or not?" Sólan's glare pierced Tirsen like a pair of arrows. "I know where to find them, where they are going, and how to get them back."

"You need to tell us why they were taken!" Bayani demanded. "You seem to enjoy killing you kin, Sólan t'e Grim. I know you pretend to be hero, pretending now to be slave scout. If you slave scout, why I never hear of you, except as murderer?"

Sólan sighed heavily and muttered, "Kírpa, Diosota de Mersi-corda, savienlí de luste indionta." *Kírpa, Goddess of Mercy, save me from this idiot.* Crossing his arms with a scowl, he said pointedly, "Because I do not barter with slavers who work outside of their laws. I kill them. Will you tell me where to find a fucking horse?"

Tirsen fidgeted as he tried to stifle his hiccoughs, so Bayani rose to his feet and proclaimed, "I go with him, binyego. I no let him run away."

In unveiled contempt, Sólan wrinkled his nose as the older fisherman nodded his approval. "Bring t'em back, tual," said Tirsen to Sólan. "Especially Elena. My life be without purpose if you fail. But I have no gold to pay you. Only t'e silver from that el—"

And what of Tala? You piece of shit, thought Sólan. "You have done enough for me, sañero. Take this as my debt repaid." He then turned to Bayani with annoyance. "Horse?"

"I have gelding, stallion, and mare. I give you gelding. I know to handle stallion when t'e mare in heat."

"You must have great wealth if you can afford to breed your own horses." The Áfgaliard eyed Bayani sideways with suspicion. "Yet, a fisherman's life is not—"

"We must go. T'e longer we stay and argue, t'e farther away they get."

4

SCOUTING

Sólan and Bayani rode into the gusty wind and through the wreckage left behind by the storm. Broken palm fronds, bits of houses, and even dead bodies littered the road that were streaked with the muddy evidence of the devastating storm surge.

They reached the northern gate and were met with several armed guards blocking their exit. Poised archers were arranged atop the white brick wall as a guard asked the duo, "Sa'on ku pipinta?"

Sólan gulped as flashes of memories flooded his mind at the unfamiliar tongue. *Hunted by his own people as he escaped Ciudelago at the mere age of twelve, tossed from the top of a thousand-metre waterfall by his father's knights, beaten and raped by the Taela guards in the Oasis City's fighting pits.* On and on, the images flashed by in an escalating whirlwind of panic.

"Numo suya Bayani Lin," the young fisherman replied.

The familiar word mercifully snapped Sólan back to the present.

"Dun oni Lucero dee Greem-anah. Kumo birboro sokilimpo baduk Áfgaliard."

As Sólan fidgeted with his reins, Bayani reached out to calm him. A second guard approached from behind, one hand on his double-edged sickle. "Áfgaliard iso pong poner-daya?" His voice trembled as he spoke.

What the hell is he saying?

"Hundi," said Bayani. "Áfgaliard hundi oka kapiret-liho."

Did he just call me a halfbreed to them? Sólan stiffened at the slur. "Did you just give away—"

"No. He ask if you mortal elf, and I tell him you no halfbreed."

Jidir, I need to learn this tongue. Sólan's eye twitched as he repressed a scowl. "Do any of you speak the common tongue of Garmathian? I cannot speak yours."

"I speak, yes," the first guard said. "Why you come?"

Oh, thank the Gods. "We hope to rescue a woman and child taken from their home during the storm. Have they—"

"I know why you here. But why *you*, Áfgaliard? You a foreigner here. We saw it was your kin who took them."

"I hire him," Bayani said before Sólan could react. "He slave scout I pay. They took my promised bride and her mother. I only here to see that my gold no wasted."

Sólan clenched his teeth, nodding stiffly. "Tíal. He is very concerned for the safety of the *child* set to marry him."

The guard nodded, despite the Áfgaliard's obvious disgust, and motioned to his archers to relax their weapons. "Yusa be with you."

Despite his disdain for the man beside him, Sólan savoured the warmth of the setting sun at his back. He and Bayani stopped at the river crossing to give their steeds one more deep drink and light meal before they moved on toward the western edge of the desert.

Sólan washed his hands and face, removing the remnants of dried blood from the previous night's fight. "Do you think, sañero, they stopped us because of the blood on us?"

Mere metres upstream, Bayani filled their waterskins and chuckled. "Hundi. Blood on faces is common sight in Bansungei. 'Specially close to Yusa's solstice. Men get brave on rum and try to fight cavalry guards."

Water snorted out of the Áfgaliard's nose at his sudden laughter in response.

"But," Bayani continued, "they no like men or women leaving the city. Not without papers endorsed by t'e temple, anyway. It only way they can keep control of the people."

"Hmph." Sólan continued to scrub his skin, washing even beyond his hairline. His heart rate jumped with each passing second as he felt Bayani's stare. "What?"

"You confuse me," Bayani finally blurted. He handed Sólan his waterskin. "I meet other Áfgaliards before. You nothing like them."

Sólan raised an eyebrow. "Being a 'kapiret-liho,' as you say, should not be very confusing to you. I am only half Áfgalese, remember?" *'Tis what everyone prides in reminding me of, at the least.*

"Are t'e stories true?"

"Why are you so concerned with the truth of my life, aeh? It hardly matters to me, so it should be no concern of yours."

Bayani rolled his eyes. "For Yusa's grace, why you always so angry?"

"*What?*" Sólan dropped his jaw in disbelief. "I should ask you the same, *Bayani Lin*. You have been nasty with me since the moment you plucked me from the sea. Why? Are you afraid I am going to steal your bride? I assure you, I am not. I do not have an attraction to children."

"No. But you steal Tirsen's," the fisherman grumbled.

"I stole no one. To claim such makes it no different from calling her a slave."

Bayani shrugged. "She may be better off as one."

"¿Mondé?" Sólan sputtered. "Have you seen what the Taelas do to their slaves?"

"No. Have *you* seen what the temple cavalry guards do to barren women, or women who only bear daughters?"

"I am unsure if I want to."

"You don't." The fisherman rubbed his nose with the back of his hand. "It will be merciful for Tala to be stoned." Before Sólan could respond, he added, "I know. I hate it, too. The way those temple men desecrate Book of the Sun for their own selfish power…" He let his words trail off, not needing to explain further.

"I made a promise to Tirsen," Sólan whispered. "At least Elena will… aeh… well…"

"She safer with me than her papa, I promise you. But if I had chance to escape? I take both Tala and Elena with me."

Sólan scratched his chin thoughtfully. "Now would be your most opportune time, what with—"

"I be hunted down and killed for that."

"There are many sanctuary camps inside the walls of the Oasis City," Sólan argued. "While I hate nearly everything about those fucking putathótas—particularly their most lucrative trade in slavery—they, at least, will protect you from the cavalry guard."

"It's not Cavalry Guard who'd hunt—" Bayani snapped his mouth shut. "We should move on." The young fisherman mounted his stallion without another word and headed toward the bridge. "If we hurry, we might catch them by dawn."

THE PAIR RODE THROUGH THE NIGHT, ONLY STOPPING ONCE TO FEED AND groom their horses with the measly supplies they had mustered in their haste. Their surroundings transitioned from tufts of grass and chaparral to coarse sand as they reached the western cusp of the desert.

As morning broke, Sólan halted and held up a hand. "Just over that dune," he whispered. The glare from the rising sun threatened to blind them and expose their approach. Sólan descended from the gelding and handed the reins to his companion. "Wait here."

Bayani flared his nostrils. "These are my family. You no command—"

"I *will* command you, cabróde," said Sólan through a hiss. He stepped forward and reached up to snatch the front of the fisherman's shirt. "I have scouted for more than ten of your lives. If you wish to see your beloved Elena again, you need to fucking listen to me. If you refuse, I will kill you before you can blink. Understand?"

Bayani nodded with fervour.

"Good. Wait here."

Sólan released his grip and scrambled up the dune. *Five men*, he spied, *eight horses, two mules, and four girls*. He gasped at the sight of two familiar faces, though they belonged not to Elena or Tala. *Those double-crossing fuckers.*

"What you see?" Bayani asked as Sólan slid back down the dune toward him.

Sólan snatched the gelding's reins and murmured, "They outnumber us more than two to one."

Bayani inhaled sharply, the sour stench of fear assaulting Sólan's nostrils. "We only kill three in Bansungei," the fisherman whispered.

"I know. They also have a mortal elf slave."

"What! You no tell me of—"

"Are you too afraid to face one?" Sólan snapped at the fisherman. "You seem so damned confident around me. I never expected you to be a coward."

Bayani bared his teeth and snarled. "I no afraid, kapiret-liho. 'Specially of you."

A mischievous grin stretched across Sólan's face. "I thought not." He mounted his steed and faced the western horizon with a grim look. "We must be delicate in our approach. I have discovered a… aeh… complication."

"What you mean?"

"Two of these monsters used to work for me."

Bayani gaped wordlessly as the Áfgaliard bowed his head and whispered, "The saviours become the slavers, and the deepest pits and hottest fires of enfríno are too kind to these traitors." Sólan lifted the hood of his cloak over his face. In the shadow of his covering, his eyes once more pulsed in that burning pain. "I bring to them the wrath of Javiénto. May the God of Death do his worst."

5

BETRAYED

*I*t took little time for the two scouts to reach the slavers' camp. A short Áfgalese man stood, gaping at them in what appeared to be disbelief. "Akeem? I thought you were dead when you did not return with the others."

"I am not Akeem," Sólan growled, "nor am I a Taela mongrel. Your companion is dead, whoever he was." He cocked his head to the side and added, "Raúl de Yubina."

The man tensed. "Who are you? How do you know my name?"

"Perhaps you should have ensured my death by sending my head to the Karthi Duke." Sólan removed his hood and stared him down with the pulsing green glow in his eyes. "My *father*."

Raúl gasped. He reached out as though to touch his old comrade's arm. "Sólan? Thank the gods," he whispered, lifting his arm to embrace him when—

"Fuck you, pundijo! You left me for dead in Orovín!" Sólan's shout gathered the others' attention.

Bayani slapped his own forehead, but Sólan ignored them all in his anger. "And now you work for the gods-damned Taelas? There were other scout gangs to join. I might have forgiven you for your betrayal if—"

"We did not choose to become slavers, Sólan," a second man cut in. "They forced us. Besides, the business all but died when we failed to save that Maseño girl. And very few Taelas really are—"

"The 'business,'" Sólan scoffed. "I thought 'twas more than a mere business to you, Frásco. I trusted you. Áfgal trusted you." He bared his fangs, snarling, "The *Gods* trusted you."

"We had no choice," Raúl stammered. "They brought us before King Jabali himself!"

Sólan ignored Raúl's excuse. "And you stole my hatchet! You know better than to take a man's prized weapon. How much gold did you gain for it?"

"Listen to yourself, amógo. We are not thieves."

"Stealing women and children from t'eir homes is no theft?" Bayani butted in. "You people twisted."

"Stay out of this, Nethuanian," Frásco snapped. "You steal entire lives and freedoms in the name of your false god."

"Sólan," said Raúl, "do you think we wanted to be tortured and killed at the hands of the men we spent years slaughtering? It was work for the Taelas or die."

"Then die," Sólan barked. "I told you from the beginning that was the risk of joining my gang. What about Armando? Felipe? Lucero? Did they betray me as well?"

"Wait," Bayani frowned at the familiar name. "Is Grimana a real—"

"Well, no"—Raúl fidgeted as he spoke—"but they made us watch as they—"

"You fucking cowards. If you valued your lives above those we served, you should have joined Humberto de Casaca or Matteo de Pueblanrío."

Frásco gasped. "You think so little of us, amógo?"

"I am not your friend, apparently."

"You would have us tortured and killed by our sworn enemies?"

"¡Tí Dioses lío! This Nethuanian's *bride* has bigger balls than you! And she is merely ten years of age!" Sólan jeered. "Have you apologised to your daughters, Raúl? Your sisters, Frásco?"

Both Áfgalese men silently glared at him in response.

"You swore oaths on their graves, putathótas. I thought you were men of your word."

"Vita i le medría, Sólan," Raúl cursed. "What oaths have you sworn, aeh? You survived Orovín's gallows, after all. How else, without the Oath of Light? You are worthless without your powers. A mere mortal now."

"Sólan," Bayani cut in, his voice urgent. "We have problem."

Sólan brushed him aside. "I have survived just like I always have," he said to Raúl. "By killing."

Without warning, Raúl collapsed to the ground, his skin instantly becoming shrivelled and ashen like a well-seasoned corpse.

"¡Qir medría, Sólan!" Frásco cursed. "He was like a brother to you!"

"Sólan." Bayani tried. Once again, he failed to gather the man's attention.

"And I like a brother to *you*!"

"Sólan!" the fisherman finally shouted. "They getting away!"

Sólan turned to see the remaining members of the party sprinting toward the sunrise, the women dragged by chains into a black covered wagon. The heat from the sun was nothing compared to the hot flash of fury that engulfed him.

"Shit!" Sólan clumsily ducked to dodge Frásco's sudden attack. "Stop them, Bayani!" he yelled as he lunged at Frásco, stabbing him in the ribs with his dagger. They swung, sprung, and twirled in a deadly dance of Áfgaliard mist-combat, Sólan with his dagger and Frásco with his—*Wait*.

A sudden bubble of rage boiled within Sólan at the sight of his opponent's weapon. He attacked again with greater fury, the dance continuing until Sólan slit Frásco's throat in a torrent of crimson blood. The life faded from his eyes as Sólan watched with glee.

He stooped to pick up his lost weapon, a rare Casacan water-steel hatchet with a polished ash handle. *Piezo de medría*, he thought as he spat on Frásco's fresh corpse. He mounted his steed and galloped to join Bayani.

The fisherman had raced his stallion to the front of the slavers' carriage, causing the mules to rear in fright. The cage-like wagon nigh toppled over at the sudden stop. Two of the mounted slavers flanked Bayani, but he held his ground.

You are no mere fisherman, sañero, thought Sólan as he dismounted. His eyes flashed as he commanded his steed, "Stay!" The horse sat like a trained hound at his direction. "Good boy," the Áfgaliard said before approaching the carriage, hatchet in hand. He pulled open the door, sighing in relief at the sight of Elena and Tala.

"Nisu-muzalin," said a voice thick with the Taela accent. The far corner of the cabin was in shadow, save for two eyes glowing green.

Sólan blinked as he entered, his eyes slowly adjusting to the darkness. "Fellow mortal elf," he said with a smirk. "What a pleasure to meet such a worthy opponent." He cocked his head and added, "You surprise me, sañero, for you have not betrayed your masters. Has the thought of freedom never—"

"I will kill them all, nisu-muzalin!" the mortal elf snapped. "Drop your hatchet."

Of course. Your free will has been washed clean with Taela alchemy. Sólan bared his fangs as he threatened in the slaver's own tongue, "Ita kuma no biso-una, n'digo, isu nivuk-eh. wa'ochi endi ka." *You would be wise, brother, not to cross me. Let them go.*

"Kopinakshi!" the Taela cursed. "They matter not to me! Drop your hatchet!"

"Don't listen to him, tual!" Tala begged. "He'll kill you too!" The Taela snatched her by the hair and placed a knife at her throat.

Elena's scream pierced the carriage. "Mama! No, Mama! Please!" She fought against her chains, her wrists already raw, and choked on her sobs. "Let her go! Please! Mama!"

Tala's lip trembled as a tear trickled down her cheek. "Hush, pitru," she whispered. Her captor pushed his blade into her soft skin, its edge threatening to draw blood as she grimaced.

Jidir. "Okay, okay, sañero." Sólan acquiesced and placed his hatchet on the floor. He slid it to his opponent with his foot. "See? No need to spill any more blood. Now, let the woman go. She—" His words were cut short at the sudden constriction of his airway.

The Taela grinned wickedly as Sólan struggled with his shirt and cloak, to no avail.

You fucking Taela bastard. I gave you a chance. With a flick of his wrist, Sólan flung his dagger at the slaver, but the blade missed him by mere millimetres.

The slaver flinched, the movement loosening his grip on Tala. She gritted her teeth and smashed her head into her captor's nose.

Chaos ensued in a flurry of blades and blood. Sólan retrieved his weapon and embedded its pick into the slaver's throat. Before the Taela could heal himself, Sólan grasped his hair and swung the hatchet's edge into his neck. With that single blow, the Taela's body detached and tumbled to the floor. The Áfgaliard slammed the severed head against the bench and turned to face the captured women, his face and hair dripping with crimson blood. He counted two girls just shy of womanhood, plus Elena and...*Where is Tala?* "Are any of you hurt?" he asked.

All three girls merely trembled at his words. He surveyed the carriage and broke open each lock with the pick of his hatchet.

"Elena! Tala!" Bayani cried as he slid to a stop outside the door.

"Binyego!" Elena fell into his arms and wept, her body racking with sobs. "Calomot i Yusa."

The other two girls embraced with joyous tears. Sólan, however, continued to scan the carriage in search of Tala, his heart sinking when he found her lifeless body. *Fuck.* He scrambled to her and lifted her torso to his own with a delicate touch. Droplets of blood slid from her mouth and nose as her gaze fixed itself on the ceiling. Her hands were already cold, but her torso was still warm.

He placed an ear on her chest, begging the Gods for a small breath, a heartbeat… anything that he could heal. But there was nothing. Solemnly, Sólan closed her eyes with his fingers and kissed them forever shut. He removed the slaver's knife from her chest with a wince and dropped it to the floor.

The metallic thud gathered Elena's attention. "Mama?"

Sólan scooped Tala's body into his arms and carried her out of the carriage.

"Mama! No! No, no, no!"

Bayani held the distraught girl tightly against his body. "Hush,

Elena. You safe now. You mama safe now." His voice cracked as he stifled his own grief.

"Mama!" Elena wailed. "Glisong ni! Wake up!"

Sólan placed the woman on the sand and cleared the hair from her face. He reached into a hidden pocket of his cloak to reveal her hairpin, still stained with blood from the previous fight. "You were a fierce woman," he whispered, "and a delicate soul. Tirsen was lucky to truly know you." He placed the pin on her chest and folded her hands around it. Then he dropped to his knees and bowed low toward the sun, softly placing his lips on her forehead. "Javiénto," he prayed, "Iliva i luste mujóta te Terría Vareno. Lí, lo servente hambode, lo pador mondé lu ceptiantes. Qormondé lu dio falsto lu a abaniñota." *Javiénto, lead this woman to Terría Vareno. I, your humble servant, ask you to accept her. For her false god has abandoned her.*

Once he finished his prayer, Sólan reluctantly rose to his feet and trudged back to the fight's survivors. His eyes pulsed hot as behind him, a spark ignited from Tala's chest, and flames engulfed her body.

Elena screamed. "You burn Mama! You damn her to Yirno, kapiret-liho!"

"There is nothing more pure than fire," said Sólan. "The worms cannot rot her, evil men cannot violate her any longer, and her ashes shall feed the ground to bring forth new life for generations to come."

Bayani cleared his throat to speak, but Elena cut him off. "She was pure!" She moaned. "You send her to Yirno as a whore! She knew only Papa. She no was violated like me!"

"*What!*" Bayani and Sólan bellowed in unison.

"Pantot!" Bayani cursed as he pulled the girl into a tight embrace. "Hush, Elena. Hush, hush. T'ey dead now. You hear? Those monsters dead now."

"I sorry…" Elena's words morphed into wails as she hiccoughed and sputtered through her tears. "I no wait. I no pure for you, binyego."

Sólan trembled as his vision turned red. He turned to the others and asked, "Did they rape you, too?" They stared at him in terrified silence. *They do not speak Garmathian, indionta.* He turned back to see

Bayani rocking Elena in comfort. He chewed his lip as he struggled to find his words—his tame words, at least—words of comfort, not curses.

"I promise, Elena, you papa won't know," Bayani soothed. "Right, Sólan?"

Sólan's mouth twitched into a forced smile. "Of course. He will not hear such foul news from me."

"See? You papa will never know."

Tíal. Your átha will never know.

6

LAIRD OF THE TUNDRA

*D*uke Jannon's cloak was soaked and dripping as he halted his steed. He could hear the rain as it clinked upon the golden armour of the approaching Prasti knights: his escort. The taste of the muggy air churned his stomach. *Curse this gnomes-damned kingdom,* he thought. He hated the forest. 'Twas naught but a dirty atmosphere laden with moss, pollen, dust, and mud. *O, the wretched mud.* The mere thought of stepping off his horse made him feel the urgent need to bathe.

"I was expecting me escort much farther back on the road, Sir Naoise," he said. "Was I not promised six knights to meet me in Baforeis at the Karthi-Prasti border?"

The knight's commander removed his green crested helmet and rested it on one of his four saddle horns. "Apologies, m'laird. Upon their journey, we discovered a risk at the Áfgalese border. I thought it best f'r ya to avoid an ambush, so I sent y'r escort to investigate."

Jannon's eye twitched as he clenched his jaw. *Save me yer theatrics, ye two-faced Veer.* "I suppose I should thank ye, then." He darted his glacier-blue gaze around, counting six additional golden helmets. "However, I fail to see the risk that Áfgal could bring, aside from rogues of their northern district attacking my western villages at random. Are they not yer allies?"

"Eil. That they are, 'cording to their bylaws. However, the longer this Crusade of Light continues, the higher the strain on even the strongest alliances. After all, allies can turn like the weather in winter."

Jannon stiffened. *Ye mock me with yer late father's words?* "A peculiar saying. One I haven't heard since the conquest of Vaoirsen." He watched Naoise's mossy brown eyes narrow. *Ah, I've struck his nerve.*

"An unfortunate truth," the knight said through an emotionless smile. "'Specially since 'twas they who turned on us, the—"

"Tell me, Sir Naoise." Jannon tapped his lips in a false show of deep thought. "How did the two sons of the treasonous Veerish Earl Manstair gain such covetable Prasti roles such as yers and yer brother's?"

Naoise's mouth twitched as he appeared to stifle a smile. "Transparency, m'laird. A willingness to repent 'afore the Wizards and distance ourselves from our father's crimes. Surely, *you'd* understand the necessity of honesty, and the gravity of honour it brings."

Jannon fought a scowl as the knight's words stabbed at his core. "I don't expect a meeting with the prince, no? Just the king?"

"We don't see how Commander Alsantör could meet with ya—"

'Commander.' Psht.

"—as His Grace is hundreds of leagues to the south with his covetable comrades."

Jannon's teeth threatened to crack at the force of his clenched jaw. This Veer was just like his father, indeed, with aggression so passive, any onlooker might think they were friends.

"However, he is quite aware of y'r arrival," Naoise continued. "He is chief commander of Prastömin's army and charged with the protection of guests within all our borders. He cannot protect you in his father's kingdom if he doesn't know of y'r travels through his lands."

"How can he possibly protect me whilst hundreds of leagues to the south?"

"Shall I request he delegate such responsibilities to his first knight?"

You prick. "So, we'll go to the king now? Or de me bones hafta soak as well?"

Naoise's mouth remained stoic, but the gleam in his eyes threatened a smile. "M'laird." He donned his helmet and turned his horse toward the southeast. With a quick whistle, he commanded the escort to surround Jannon as they led him toward the main keep.

Ye've won this battle, son of Manstair. But I will win the war.

It took the remainder of the day to reach the hidden palace. There was nothing particularly glamorous about the dull granite fortress, save for the sheer number of gold- and leather-clad soldiers that patrolled its grounds. *'Tis quite unnecessary to maintain such large patrols for a single kingdom.*

The outer walls of the keep were encompassed by a climbing ivy that bloomed a sickening pink for little more than a fortnight every spring. *Gnomes be merciful,* Jannon thought with a sigh, *as if ye weren't already overrun with such green rubbish.*

As the cedar portcullis creaked open, the smell of livestock and wet hay hit the Karthi duke like an arrow to his sinuses. The nauseating scent permeated the back of his throat and forced his eyes to water. Jannon clasped his burlap sack of dried mint and rosemary under his nose to stave off the stench. He dismounted, his feet squishing in the shit-filled mud, and gave a young elf boy his mare's reins. The sloppy bubbles at his soles released a pungent odour that made Jannon's stomach retch.

He both sweat and shivered at the same time in the hot, muggy rainstorm. *Curse this forest,* he thought again. *Our next meeting'll be in me Tundra. Mark me words, Diarmuid, I shan't return.* He immediately scoffed, for he'd thought the same words every previous visit to the forest, no matter how many hundreds of years in between.

Jannon followed his escort through the courtyard to the heavy cedar door. *Cedar, cedar, and more cedar. Naught but granite and cedar.*

The keep's boxy architecture rose far beyond what the duke could see, the towers extending skyward as though attempting to reach the heavens for a beggar's handout. In their shadows, the keep's mundane entrance was foreboding.

The heavy door boomed shut. Jannon slumped his shoulders as the wafting smell of burning incense filled his nostrils—a stark and welcome contrast to the ambience of the stables outside.

"You may all take y'r leave now," said Naoise.

The six other knights removed themselves from the sparsely decorated foyer as Jannon wrung the excess moisture out of his straight, taupe hair. His eyes wandered around the room as Naoise slipped off his helmet and shook the water from his own copper curls.

Fragrant sage burned beside scores of flickering candles. The warm light bounced off the gold-embellished tapestry that covered less than half of the walls. *Hmph. No son, no queen, no history beyond yer rule. Yer self-indulgence has never lacked, has it?* Diarmuid was as close a friend as any. However, like any friendship, they were not in agreement on all things. Such a relationship was welcome, but still, Jannon found it exhausting at times.

Naoise's flat tone snuffed his thoughts. "Follow me, m'laird."

The duke glared at the first knight's back, the tension between them thickening with each step. They reached the base of a wide staircase of which each granite step was trimmed with gold and emeralds. At the top, Naoise handed his helmet to a servant woman who blushed as she scurried away. *Wizards be good, he's not that pretty.*

Jannon let out a loud sigh and whispered, "Finally." He pursed his lips with a frown at the knight's lack of reaction.

A short walk down a broad corridor of stone and gold led to the intricately carved cedar entrance to the crowded great hall. The duke and first knight approached the stately throne and knelt at the king's feet. "Y'r Grace," said Naoise, "may I present to ya Jannon, son of the late Corin, Duke of Karthénos and Laird of the Tundra."

A chorus of gasps and whispers echoed through the room at this announcement. It was in that moment that Jannon realised just how dishevelled and underdressed he appeared. *I should have waited until the morrow. Damn ye, McManstair! Ye and yer conniving banter.*

King Diarmuid stood and descended from his chair, a warm smile stretching across his freckled face. His heavy green robes were draped across his broad shoulders, and as he approached, they dragged on the floor behind him. "Jannon! Dear friend! Get up and embrace me. You've no need to kneel."

Jannon looked up to see the Prasti king greeting him with open arms. He stood and welcomed the warmth of Diarmuid's embrace.

"It's been far too long since you came down from the Tundra. Please, join me for a cup of wine!"

A nervous smile crept across Jannon's face. "I'd have no greater pleasure, yer grace."

Diarmuid chuckled. He clapped the Karthi's shoulder and said, "Sir Naoise! Please escort my other guests to the ballroom. The bards have been begging for an early performance!"

At his words, the first knight emptied the great hall. Many of the king's guests grumbled and whispered in protest. Some commented on Jannon's tattered appearance, while others lamented their own lack of wine. Duke and king, meanwhile, set themselves at a table—Diarmuid at its head and Jannon at his immediate right hand.

A young woman entered with a golden tray of two delicate emerald chalices and a crystal decanter of wine. She filled each cup nigh to the brim, placing what remained between the duke and king. Diarmuid whispered something to her, and she smiled, skittering off as though he'd promised her queendom.

Latest concubine, I presume. A sniff and quiet cough reminded Jannon of Naoise's continued presence. He glared at the Veer, who posted himself at the closed door of the hall. "Does *he* hafta stay here and watch us?" he whispered.

"He doesn't," said Diarmuid, frowning. He cleared his throat to address his first knight. "You may take leave, now, Sir Naoise. I will call for you when you are needed next."

Naoise bowed at his waist and answered flatly, "Y'r grace."

Jannon waited until the heavy door thumped closed before he

relaxed his posture. "Apologies, friend. I wish for as few ears to hear as possible, particularly the ears of Manstair's eldest son."

Diarmuid snorted. He swallowed a sip of wine before he said, "His father's blood has been beat and trained out of both him and his brother, Giaven. I received great pushback from several of my advisors when I knighted them."

"Understandable."

"However, they've both proven far more loyal than those advisors."

"I see. I wondered why complaints of those lords have been absent of late. I also wondered why I smelt satire in yer words." Jannon smirked at the king's shrewd expression.

"Tell me, Laird Jannon, how close do you keep your friends?" Diarmuid asked, cocking his head with a curious evergreen gaze.

"Quite close. Why?"

"And your *enemies*?"

Jannon frowned before slipping into a quiet chuckle. "I forget, old friend, how much of a cunning prick you can be."

The king burst into hearty laughter nearly loud enough to shake the granite walls. Jannon snickered along before he finally took his first sip of wine, quietly sighing at its tart spice. He rarely drank such a fine vintage and found that the dry finish soothed him. "Áfgalese wine?"

"Eil. Áfgalese wine," said Diarmuid. "A wondrous red blend from Áfgal's District of Arriya Taca. This particular vineyard is well known for their use of pepper."

"And their expense, I gather." The duke took another sip, savouring it. "A wondrous blend, indeed."

"Only the best for my last friend in these gnomes-forsaken lands."

Jannon snorted at an inopportune moment. While the burn of the wine felt pleasant on his tongue and in his throat, 'twas much less pleasant when it flooded his nose. "Ye're too kind, yer grace."

Diarmuid refilled his chalice with another smile. "So, what news from the tundra?"

"Well, I have finally considered yer offer."

"Oh?" The king leaned in at his words. "Are your senators aware?"

"Only of me absence. However, they believe I'm here on simple holiday." Jannon shook his head with a chuckle. "Me daughter, Senator Siobhan, can be quite the giggling dunce."

"Must take after her mother."

Jannon's eye twitched. "Senator Kiera is a quick-witted woman, a powerful ally, and the best partner an elf could ask for. Gnomes be merciful, I don't deserve her, nor the fact she has defied nature in surviving beyond our daughter's birth, unlike Moira's mother."

"And yet, you've failed to tell her of your... parlay."

"Parlay?" The duke stiffened with a touch of panic in his throat. "Are we at *war*, Diarmuid? I dare say, friend, I am most hurt by—"

"Worry not of a war beween us. Yet, said" Diarmuid, and before the Karthi could argue, he added, "Sólan de Ciudelago is dead."

Jannon stiffened. "I"— he hummed and fidgeted with his half-empty chalice—"I will believe such things when I receive his head."

"That wasn't part of the arrangement. You were to pull out of this crusade, and I to end it with the Speaker when you received word your son was dead. You have received such word."

Jannon snarled, baring his fangs. "That halfbreed cunt wished he were me son. I shan't grace that bastard of crimson blood with such a title." He took a gulp of wine to stay his anger. "How many times have we received word of the Grim's demise, ey? How many times has he slithered away from certain death? I told ye three hundred bloody years ago: I need *proof*."

"My son dealt the final bow. That should be proof enough."

"Begging yer pardon, friend, but I'm afraid that—perhaps—Alsantör may have... ulterior motives? Was it not *he* who presented that red-blood to—"

"Are you calling my son a traitor, Laird Jannon?" Diarmuid revealed his own fangs as he spoke. "With your evidence being a *mistake* he made at thirteen years of age?"

Shit. The blood drained from Jannon's face. "I, ehm, was," he stammered. "Was it yer order to kill that Áfgaliard-Karthi mongrel? No, 'twas mine, and merely implied, at that. After all, was that not the purpose of me involvement in this crusade?" His voice cracked with his words.

"Then, if you don't call him a traitor, you call him a liar."

The duke winced through clenched teeth. *Ye bloody fool, Jannon! Ye know his swinging moods!* He'd insulted Prince Alsantör. Worse, he'd insulted the king. His heart pounded in his throaty as his thoughts raced. "I suppose I misspeak," he whispered.

"I suppose you do."

"Forgive me, friend. 'Twas uncalled for."

Diarmuid leaned forward with a snarl and whispered, "I like you, Jannon. You're a good friend—a much-needed friend—but, don't ever insult my son again. Are we clear?" Jannon's frantic nod allowed the Prasti king to relax and chuckle. "Now then. To business."

Naoise paced the hall and grumbled. *Fookin' ice-goblin. You can go to Eclipse Aeternum f'r all I care. "Son of a traitor." Fook ya! That bloody Veer wished I'd called him "daela."*

"Naoise," a soft voice whispered. "Come 'ere."

The knight spun on his heel to see a freckled woman. The pale moonlight shining into the cold stone corridor danced off her emerald eyes and golden ringlets as she approached.

"Queen Ethna." He bowed. "To what do I owe the pleasure?"

"Why the hell is Jannon here? He hasn't left the bloody tundra in three hundred years," she said. Rarely did the queen waste time for niceties with the first knight. That moment was no exception.

Naoise scoffed. "Couldn't tell ya. You know how he—"

"And the prince? Any word from *him*?"

The knight bit the inside of his lip. *Facts, Neesh. She doesn't want y'r complaints. She's not y'r friend.* "Eil," he said through clenched teeth. "A raven came just after dusk."

Ethna raised an eyebrow. "And?"

"And he executed Sólan de Ciudelago, per the letter. He 'nd his fellow hunters'll be home 'afore the winter solstice."

The edge of the queen's mouth twitched. Whether in relief, joy, or annoyance, Naoise couldn't gather. "Alsantör's always had a weakness for that halfbreed bastard of Jannon's," she finally said. "Sólan the Grim is not truly dead."

"Likely not. But I doubt he'd lie so brazenly. Besides, if Jannon were to discover—"

"Do you take me for a fool, Naoise?" Ethna snapped. "I've been Queen since long before my husband usurped my brother's crown, and I intend to keep it that way until the timing is fresh for Alsantör to take his father's throne."

Naoise bit his lip again, barely refraining from rolling his eyes. "Beggin' y'r pardon, y'r grace. What does that hafta do with Alsantör and his acquaintance with Jannon's bastard?"

"Jannon and Diarmuid are far more alike than meets the eye. They both have sons who have been killed, or shall be killed. If we could end their alliance..."

"You imply treason," Naoise whispered as the queen's words trailed off. "I woen't play that little game, 'nd I doen't wanna present you to y'r husband f'r such a crime."

"You're the first knight of Prastömin." Ethna pressed her body against his armour and stroked his jaw with her delicate hand.

Wizards be good, Naoise thought. *As if ya think I can be seduced by* —. He grasped her shoulders and pushed her away with a snarl. "Ya walk a dangerous path, my queen," he said. "I'm not my father."

Ethna snorted. "And yet, you still won't go to the king."

"Y're gon' get us both killed if y're not careful with y'r hollow attempts at seduction."

"Save me your lectures on honour, Veer," said the queen. "I know the risks of our conversation." A wicked smile contorted her freckled face until she appeared more demon than elf.

Shite, thought Naoise. It was a smile of knowing—of extortion. *What does she know?*

"A risk not unlike that which you took with Ina."

The blood drained from Naoise's face at the name.

"Surely you haven't forgotten my last handmaiden, have you?

'Tis a shame she was so determined to carry that child. She might've survived if she'd taken the piaraberry I'd offered."

Naoise's voice wavered with panic as he said, "Not a soul knows who the father was o' that child. Cadman and I both questioned her. She took that secret to her grave."

"Did she?" The queen cocked her head with a smirk, tapping her chin in a show of deep thought. "I seem to remember a young knight of Prastömin who was quite interested in her infant girl." She narrowed her eyes, staring daggers into the knight.

Do you threaten me?

"Find Jannon's purpose for his travels, or else, you will wish you'd died with Ina and that bastard daughter of hers."

THE TRAIL TO THE WIZARDS' SACRED CAVE WAS NARROW, FLANKED BY massive boulders of grey granite that held shimmering veins of quartz and gold. It pinched inward just wide enough for a single elf to squeeze through before opening back up to reveal the cave's gaping mouth. On each side stood a statue of an ancient elf hero. To the right was King Nielann of Garmath: the Great Unifier of elves. 'Twas said he was the Champion of Freedom, he who led the elf slaves of Garmath into liberation. He was the founder of Ūendevail and the empire of elves, before his unfortunate death during the Great Plague.

On the other side, King Burnell, also known as the "Bear of Ūendevail," kept guard. He was renowned as the only elf gifted by the Wizards the power to slay the ancient bear faeries that haunted the forest, the likes of which had all but disappeared before the Great War. Ethna's father.

A green-cloaked woman of alabaster skin and ebony hair entered the cave after placing one silver coin at each of the statues' feet. Once inside, the sulfuric fumes of a steaming pool burned her throat as she approached. There, she lowered herself to her knees and folded her hands upon her lap.

The Speaker of the Wizards soon joined her. His thin white robes were draped over his hunched figure as he hobbled over to the woman. The top half of his dusky face was covered by a deep hood, hiding the mangled flaps of skin that covered what used to be eyes. "What brings you to the sacred pool today, handmaiden of the queen?"

The woman averted her gaze to the ground and pressed her lips together in a thin line. "The same as every day, Speaker. The same questions I ask and the same answers I seek."

The blind elf placed his arthritic hands on each side of the handmaiden's head. "You are bound by an oath, Maid Rhona. Bound by the laws of the crown. You already know that which I will say."

Rhona's lips trembled as her eyes filled with tears.

"Ah"—the Speaker inhaled, as though savouring the smell of a fragrant flower—"I sense a disturbance in you, daughter of Karthénos. One that haunts you… and soon, your master."

Rhona grimaced. "The queen—"

"I know Ethna's words." The woman clamped her mouth shut as Brayson continued, "The wind whispers to me her thoughts. The pool shows me her dreams, even now."

"She's charged a friend with an impossible task."

"The failure of which shall mean his life."

"Yes." Rhona took a shaky breath. *I shan't let ye die like yer father did, dear friend.* "Do ye know the purpose of Jannon's travels?"

"I do."

"Tell me."

The speaker snatched his hands back with a hiss. "You *dare* command the Wizards, Handmaiden?"

"No!" Rhona pressed her face to the ground. "I don't! Fergive me, please!"

"You must learn, daughter of the tundra, to take great care with your words. For what the Wizards have in store for you shall be your greatest trial."

7

THE CRUSADE OF LIGHT

*T*wo moons of travel came and went as Alsantör and his crusade hunting party followed the trade road to the north. Every three days, they would reach a small village of mortal nomads to replenish their supply of dried meat, water, and aged cheese. Sometimes, the river disappeared far below the ground and reemerged in the occasional small oasis or hand-dug well. The group settled and made camp outside one of those small villages at the sun's eastern descent.

"Sólan the fuckin' *Grim*!" said Anlon. "That orange-eyed devil of Áfgal's been slitherin' out our grasps f'r three hundred gnomes-damned years!" He took a sloppy gulp of Taela port wine from his hard, leather flask.

"Yeh, but out of your grasp f'r a mere ten years, ya radge," a comrade said through a snort. "And you already f'rgot he's half Karthi, too?"

Anlon hiccoughed. "Like any Karthi'd take credit f'r siring that mongrel, Carsen." He handed his flask to Alsantör, who obliged without hesitation.

"Ha! Anlon, y're full of it!" a fourth elf cut in. "He was the fookin' bastar' of Laird Jannon."

"Save us from y'r Veerish morality, Giaven," Carsen groaned. He placed his hand across his forehead as he faked a swoon.

"Ya think I care that monster's 'dearest daela' is Jannon?" snickered Giaven. "I thought we were friends, Carse. I'm hurt."

"Yeh, Carsen," said Anlon. "Just 'cause this fucker looks like Naoise, don't mean they're the same."

Giaven flashed a fanged grin. "He's so broody, isn't 'e?"

Alsantör shrugged as he passed the wine over to Carsen. "You could say I'm quite broody, too. Since we both have to deal with all your shite." He tossed a hunk of dried goat at Giaven. It bounced off his golden breastplate and landed in the sand between his legs.

"Oi! That's perfectly good grub ya've ruined there!" The knight picked up his food and attempted to shake off the sand, but to no avail. The group roared in laughter.

Anlon snickered. "Maybe the sand'll chafe enough to make you a man!"

"Careful, there, *Annie*." Alsantör chuckled. Carsen and Giaven snickered at the name. "You're the youngest here by fifty years."

A mischievous grin crept across Giaven's face. "Yeh, maybe you should eat the sand. Give ya the 'trial by fire' out y'r ass in the mornin'!" He threw the piece of meat at his comrade.

"Even a half-bred beast would die at the stench!"

As Carsen howled, Giaven added, "Ya coulda kill'd ol' Sólan the Grim with just y'r wind!" They both fell over in the sand at the weight of their laughter.

Alsantör rolled his eyes and stood. "I need to piss," he grumbled.

"Dinnae pish y'r boots, Commander!" Anlon called. "Can't have those rustin' when ya see y'r father next!"

The prince flashed a scowl behind his shoulder.

Carsen stiffened. "Shite, Anlon," he whispered. "I think ya—"

"Bloody hell lads! Just shut up and eat your sand, will you?" Alsantör snapped. "I've got first watch."

His three companions swallowed nervously at his sudden anger. "Eil, Commander."

The prince never bothered to investigate who'd spoken.

ALSANTÖR'S MIND WANDERED AS THE SUN DISAPPEARED BELOW THE eastern horizon. *Dammit, Sólan. I hope you're really hiding this time.* He loosened his golden bracer and pulled out a small kerchief that had been tucked around his forearm. It was made from the finest green silk, with an eagle's head embroidered upon it in golden thread. 'Twas the symbol of the woman he loved, and to carry it was forbidden. Their love was punishable by death.

"*Simple friendship. No more nor less,*" they'd promised to one another. Yet, deep in his heart, Alsantör knew they had both lied. Was it the temptation of rebelling against his mother's law that drove his infatuation? Or was it, perhaps, the secret—of knowing and loving outside of his father's grasp? He knew not, except that she was untouchable by all, except his mother.

"Tör?"

Startled, the prince quickly stuffed the kerchief back into his gilded bracer before addressing the voice behind him. "Yeh?" he said.

His comrade snorted. "No need to hide that thing. I'm still the only one who knows about you two."

Alsantör slumped his shoulders and sighed. "Fuck, Giaven. Don't sneak up on me like that."

The knight plopped himself onto the soft sand beside the prince, chuckling, and said nothing more. Silently, they watched the stars emerge as the sky darkened, twinkling gems against a deep blue canvas. Giaven cleared his throat to finally break the silence, "So, tell me, Tör. Did ya really kill 'im?"

"Why would I lie about that?" Alsantör asked. "You think I'd help him fake his death and send a false raven to my fa—"

"Yes." Giaven's mossy-brown eyes burned into the prince's own. He nudged him with his elbow. "Y're a good liar, friend. I know ya too well. Y're like a brother to me. Naoise too."

A tear escaped Alsantör's eye as he fought a smile. "And you both are like the brothers I never had." He wiped his nose and sniffled. "And Sólan—"

"Wasn't the monster ev'ryone said 'e was. Ah ken." Giaven revealed a clay bottle from his cloak and uncorked it. He took a gulp and coughed before offering it to Alsantör, his eyes watering from the burn in his throat. "That Nethuanian 'god' might treat his followers like shite, but he's sure got an excellent taste in liquor."

"Dammit, Giaven. Did you steal from their temple again?" The prince dropped his head in disbelief.

"Hey, now. We are at war, in all technicality," Giaven argued. "Alvara would condone—nai, encourage—the collection of spoils."

Alsantör scrunched his nose. "We're not at war with Nethuania. The Wizard and Wizardess of War wouldn't encourage theft from a sovereign theocracy."

"I wouldn't call 'em, 'sovereign.' Tyrannical, maybe."

"Wizards be good," the prince grumbled, rubbing his forehead at his comrade's impish grin. "You've got to stop stealing from their temple, alright? It's a war crime."

"Ha! And slaughter isn't? We should be endin' slavery, not murderin' a people based on the colour of their blood."

"That's the Veer in you talking."

"Ya ken y'r mother feels the same way."

"Give me that fucking rum." Alsantör finally surrendered, chugging the coconut-flavoured liquor. He emptied half of the bottle in one breath. "Shite," he said. "You weren't kidding. That is good rum."

Giaven beamed in triumph as he shoved the cork back into the bottle. Wiping the smile from his face, he asked, "You think this crusade'll end soon?"

"I know it will," said Alsantör. "Victornia herself promised me so in a dream last moon."

"What? You can speak with the Wizards and Gnomes?"

"Just the Wizards," the prince confessed, running a nervous hand through his mahogany hair. "I'd have to wield The Light to speak with the Gnomes."

"Heh. Fat chance o' that. Ya doesn't have a single drop of orc blood in ya."

"Eil. I know." Alsantör looked up to the sky as the stars continued to flicker awake one by one.

"Does y'r father know? About y'r gift?"

"You think I'd still have my head if he did?" the prince asked. "Look what he did to Shira and Brayson—Shira's dead, and Brayson's doomed to forever live as a blind old madman. The Wizards deserve a better speaker, and the Gnomes? Fuck. We haven't heard from the Gnomes since—" He snapped his mouth shut. "Never mind."

"Since what?"

"Well, since your father, eh—"

"No need to bring *that* traitor into this." Giaven growled in disgust. "I may be a Veer by blood, but I'm Prasti by heart, through 'nd through."

"I'd have to give up my title, my crown, and my bloody future to be Speaker of the Wizards. No one else needs to know of my 'gift,' alright?"

Giaven's nose twitched in a poorly stifled guffaw. "Nice parry. So, what now?"

"You go get some rest. You've got third watch after Anlon."

"Fine." The knight pushed himself to his feet and stretched. "Y'r secrets're safe with me, Tör. All of them."

"Go to *sleep*," the prince demanded. "The moon's starting to rise."

"As you command, y'r grace."

Alsantör sighed, watching Giaven trudge back toward the others. His thoughts raced as the moon continued its ascent, thoughts of Sólan and his brash words. *The mad King Diarmuid.* He clenched his fists and scoffed. *Save me your lectures, Sólan. As if your father isn't mad himself.* He scowled, knowing the truth of his friend's words.

His father was paranoid and prone to all manners of torture he deemed appropriate for perceived and unfounded accusations of treason. 'Twas said he could hear the dead, even those taken by The Dark. Alsantör had learned at an early age: when the king's eyes fogged over, his voices had returned.

He prayed day and night for his father's mind. He prayed to

Kendra, Gnomess of Mercy, to heal him of the affliction and to Ethar, Gnome of Protection, for himself and his mother. He even prayed to Anza, Wizard of Strength, and Dana, Gnomess of Kindness.

But still, his father's mind darkened. In fact, the king's fragility had forced nearly all his subjects into poverty, as there were no more lords and ladies to govern the houses. Diarmuid's demons had seen to that. What remained were only his knights—young boys plucked from their families at the age of five, trained to do the impulsive biddings of their king. *Dammit, Sólan. You're right about him.*

Alsantör lowered his head into his hands and sniffled. *This is all my fault,* he lamented. *Not Jannon's, not my father's. Mine. Mine alone.*

"Commander?" A voice yanked him back to the present. "It's my turn f'r the watch."

The prince looked up at the half-risen full moon and sighed. "Right." He stood and stretched the stiffness out of his joints. "Nothing to report, Anlon."

"Eil, Commander. Get y'r rest."

Alsantör acquiesced with a yawn. *Mûntak, Gnome of Justice,* he prayed as he laid his head next to those of his sleeping comrades. *Forgive me of my deceit.*

Alsantör awakened at Carsen's screaming and the unsettling sensation of sinking.

"Get up! Get the fuck up!" the knight bellowed.

The prince leapt to his feet and scrambled to safety from what was rapidly becoming a sinkhole. Anlon and Giaven were close behind with their swords in hand.

Carsen rushed to pull them further away. "You alright?"

"Fine," said Giaven. "Thank the Wizards you were last watch."

Anlon's voice shook as he added, "I don't remember the ground ever doing that here."

"It doesn't," said Alsantör, peering to the west to see the rising sun and—*Káil.* "Ilb maoirsetach," he whispered, his heart missing a beat. *Mortal elf.*

His three companions shot their gazes to the horizon and tensed. The silhouette of a massive figure blocked most of the sun's light in a sudden appearance.

"That's not a mortal elf, Tör," said Carsen. " Look at those damned tusks from its mouth. That's a bloody giant."

Anlon trembled. "I thought the giants of the west died out after the war."

"They did."

"And, weren't they docile be—"

"Look at its eyes. That thing's got elf blood in it," Alsantör cut in. *Shite. The Taelas're breeding elves with giants?*

"Is that why the ground opened up like that?"

Behind the elf-giant stood a group of five mounted men boasting the unmistakable armour and weapons of Taelonael. Their helmets were of iron atop their heads, and their faces were completely hidden by chain mail, save for two small holes for their eyes. Their heavy linen tunics were also covered by an even heavier coat of mail that draped to their thighs, followed by lightweight trousers and hard leather boots that rose to their knees. Finally, their armament was comprised of a short bow with a hip quiver, a bronze dagger, and a broad-headed spear that glistened orange in the bright sunrise.

The elf prince slid his sword back into its sheath and pulled a white linen cloth from beneath his breastplate. The common signal of parlay. "We can't afford a fight with them," he said in a low voice.

"Tör, what the hell're you doing?" Giaven asked.

Without answering, Alsantör waived the kerchief above his head and motioned for his companions to put away their weapons.

In the distance, a Taela warrior shoved his spear into the sand before trotting his way toward the elves.

"Do you even speak Taela?" Carsen asked, trembling.

"Enough," the prince replied.

The rider came to a stop before them and growled, "Untak-ika nino?" *What do you want?*

The prince held back a snarl as he answered with his own question, "Unzungimz'ek Garmathian?" *Do you speak Garmathian?*

The Taela exhaled sharply and said, "Yes."

Oh, thank the Wizards. "I see you have a ... eh ... fierce companion," Alsantör said, nodding toward the giant. "Have you come on behalf of King Jabali?"

"No." The Taela made no effort to hide the disdain in his eyes.

"I see." Alsantör sucked the back of his teeth and peered around the rider. Further behind the giant, a black carriage led by two mules creaked to a stop. *Shite. Slavers.* He cleared his throat and looked up at the Taela. "'Tis a shame, since I have news from your eastern kin in Nethuania."

The horse fidgeted under the rider's shifting weight. "What news?"

"Sólan the Grim is dead."

"Is that so?" The man's eyes curled, suggesting a smile. "You killed him?"

"Eil. I did. And it would be best to let us on our way." The prince glanced at the man's thigh, noting how his grasp tightened around his dagger. *Dammit. He wants my head.* Before returning eye contact, he clocked the missing link in his mail between his breastplates. "I'd like to end this bloody crusade, and—"

"Tör!"

In one fluid motion, Alsantör ducked beneath the man's swing before he unsheathed and impaled his sword into the Taela's chest. He yanked the man from his steed and twisted his weapon until he saw the spray of crimson blood spurting from a severed heart. "They're slavers! Positions!"

His three comrades grabbed their swords and scrambled into a defensive box with their backs pressed together. An ominous wind howled and swirled a black cloud of dust and sand about them.

A second Taela charged the group and struck Carsen dead with his sidearm.

"Káil!" Giaven cursed and swung his gladius at the rider, cleaving off the horse's back leg.

Alsantör lunged and made quick work of the Taela, severing his head. At the thundering approach of a third horse, he spun and caught its rider through his abdomen. The man was dead before he hit the ground.

An arrow pierced the prince in his back. The searing pain radiated to his flank and forced him to his knees. Gritting his teeth, Alsantör snapped the arrow's shaft where it entered his flesh.

"Phriannso!" Anlon cried. He jumped to the prince's side and helped him back onto his feet.

"I'm fine!" said Alsantör, pushing his comrade away. "Just find that halfbreed fucker and kill him!"

The three remaining elves gripped their swords and peered through the haze. A massive, burly shadow separated itself from the darkness. The elf-giant approached, his eyes alight with a green glow that pierced through the dust like demonic fire.

Giaven screamed, "Doen't look 'im in the eyes!"

But he was too late. Anlon gaped as he stared up at the giant's snarling face. It didn't matter whether he'd looked or not. He was the target, and his death would come swiftly.

The creature's voice rumbled, "Kó suna inik afi." *And now you die.*

Without warning, Anlon's breath was stolen. His face turned to sunken leather, his flesh disintegrated into ash, and the weight of his armour pressed him to the ground, his bones shattering as the metal crushed him.

"Anlon!"

The elf-giant spun to face Alsantör and Giaven.

"M'kū, Alsantör," the mongrel growled. His tusk-like fangs glistened as though tainted with venom. His voice lifted in mockery as he said, "'The Hunter of the Forest.'" Throwing his hand into the air, he transformed the particles of sand into a sharp blade, which he aimed and thrust at the elves' chests.

Alsantör ducked to avoid the blow. Giaven, however, launched himself off his comrade's back to jump. Despite the giant's incredible height at nearly five metres, Giaven flew over the enemy's head— such was the ferocity of the Veers. Each second felt like an eternity as the knight sailed through the air. He flipped and spun, sword in hand, slicing his blade through the creature's neck as he landed. The wind and swirling dust halted at the creature's death, his head still teetering on his shoulders. Giaven rolled away as it collapsed to the ground, thrusting his sword through another attacker's throat.

Two remaining slavers charged the elves with jagged spears. The prince jumped to his feet and cut through them with ease. After a quick survey to ensure no further attack, he grinned in triumph.

"Gnomes, I can't wait to see your brother's face when"—he turned to face his comrade and gasped—"Káil! Giaven!"

His companion was slumped over the broad head of a Taela spear that had pierced through his armour and into his chest. Alsantör raced over to him and broke off the shaft with his bloodied sword. He grimaced as he supported the his friend's torso with his arms. "Shite, Giaven. You—"

"Fookin' 'ell," the knight gargled. He spat up a lob of frothy silver blood and took a ragged breath before speaking again. "Naoise's gon'"—he winced—"throttle ya when ya tell 'im of that kill."

Tears flowed down the prince's face as he attempted to laugh through his sobs. "You mean 'we,' Giaven. When we tell him."

"Doen't be stupid, Tör," the knight said weakly. With shaking hands, Giaven removed the silver ring from his second finger upon which a crowned eagle clutched the hilts of crossed gladiī. Two emeralds sat on each side of the ring, contrasting with the shiny metal and black tarnish between the engravings.

"No, no, no. Don't you dare take that off," said Alsantör. "You're not dying on me. Not you too."

Despite his pleas, Giaven's face grew pallid as his breathing shallowed. "Take it," he gasped, "you crowned fucker. Tell Naoise"—he choked and coughed—"I love 'im." The life faded from Giaven's brown eyes as a final tear slipped down his ashen cheek.

"Dammit, Giaven. Wake up. This isn't funny." Alsantör lowered the knight to the ground and gently closed his eyelids. He pressed his face into Giaven's limp body and wept; his body was racked with sobs and hiccoughs. "Wake up. I promised Naoise I'd keep you safe. Wake up!"

Alsantör lifted his head to take in the surrounding carnage. Five dead Taela slavers, the headless elf-giant, and ... *All three of you.* A wave of nausea hit the prince like a horse's kick to the gut. He was alone. Alone, injured, and afraid.

Shite. I have to get home. His thoughts jumped to the forest, to his knights, his mother—to her. *I have to warn them.*

The prince scrambled to his feet and checked his supplies. He counted his gold—there was enough left to buy food for the remaining travel. A small scroll fell from his pocket, the green wax seal already broken.

Naoise's writing sprawled across the sheepskin parchment as a reminder of the tundra duke's travels. *Jannon!* A sudden rage coursed through his veins at the thought of Sólan's murderous father. *That blue-eyed goblin of Karthénos is going to start another fucking war!*

8

THE VILE

The bronze gate to northern Bansungei creaked as it opened for Sólan, Bayani, and the three rescued girls. Elena trembled as they reentered the city's limits while the two older girls wept, embracing each other.

"Calomot i tual. Calomot," said one through her sobs.

Bayani leaned over to his companion. "She say 'thank you.'"

"Ah." Sólan nodded and stored the new phrase. "How do I respond?"

"Tell her, 'Colomot ki Yusa, su piganabay nuya suya kin.'"

"¿Mondé? Slower, please."

Bayani exhaled with a groan but still obliged. Sólan stumbled over the words as he repeated them in the unfamiliar tongue. Forcing a smile through gritted teeth, he whispered, "What the hell did I just say, sañero?"

"'Thanks to Yusa for guiding me.'" The fisherman snickered as he added, "You accent need work."

Sólan hissed. "As does *your* Garmathian."

A cavalry guardsman approached from their side. "You now follower of Yusa, foreigner?"

"Just nod, Sólan," Bayani whispered. "T'ey kill pagans here."

"The *Taelas* are pagans, worshiping false gods of death and destruction. I am a servant of—"

"For Yusa's grace, tulalo. Just lie."

Sólan's eye twitched as he turned toward the guard. "Tíal, sañero," he said. "I am a follower of the god of"—he glanced nervously at Bayani.

The fisherman coughed and motioned toward the eastern horizon with his lips. Sólan frowned, confused. *The sky? The stars?* Bayani coughed again. *The sun!* "Apologies, we breathed a lot of sand." Clearing his throat, he stammered, "I am a new follower of Yusa, god of the sssunnn?"

Bayani smacked his own forehead as the guard smiled a toothy grin. "Welcome, child of Yusa. We rejoice you accept t'e one true God and turn away from you false idols."

Fuck you, pundijo. I am a servant of the Gods of summer and life! Not your abomination and rapist of children.

"If it please t'e prophet of Yusa," Bayani cut in before Sólan could react, "we seek rest and prayer."

"It no please me, but Yusa, yes. T'e poor's kitchen behind the corner temple should offer you such." The guard handed Bayani a leather pouch of coins. "Take this as reward for saving Yusa's daughters."

"Calomot ki tual." Bayani clasped his hands together and bowed his head in thanks.

"Hundi. Calomot ki tual." Without another word, the guard gathered the three girls and led them away.

Sólan's stomach churned as he watched the children follow him, Elena peering over her shoulder unhappily at the duo. "Where is he taking them?" he asked.

"To t'e High Prophet," said Bayani. "T'ey must be cleansed and baptised again, to remove t'e stains of Misó."

"I really hate your 'god.'"

"So do I, sometimes."

Sólan scrunched his nose, and his nausea morphed into hunger as the sun threatened to set in the east. "Does he allow drink? Ale? Wine? Brandy?"

"Rum." The Áfgaliard's ears perked up at Bayani's words. "But it watered down so you no get drunk."

Dammit.

"T'e kitchen he speak of two blocks to the west. Their pork adobo with rice is the best in Bansungei."

"Adobo?" Sólan's mouth watered despite being unfamiliar with the dish. "I have never heard of this 'pork adobo,' but it sounds divine."

Bayani chuckled. "You will be true follower of Yusa after just you first bite of—"

"So, where is this kitchen?"

THE *PEOPLE'S KITCHEN OF THE SUN*, AS IT WAS TRANSLATED INTO THE common tongue of Garmathian, was exactly where Bayani promised it would be. 'Twas hardly more than a massive bamboo shack with a steep thatched roof made of palm fronds. The foundation was set on hard stone that was carved with stairs and ramps leading to a myriad of curtain-covered doors and windows. Floor tables and straw cushions littered the kitchen's dining hall, upon which its patrons would sit cross-legged to enjoy their meals.

The steep ceiling allowed a surprising airflow to circulate the room. Inside, the muggy temperature dropped just enough to be bearable.

The smell that engulfed his nose was one for which he was unprepared. He had expected the same stench of Bansungei's slums, yet he was hit with the aroma of simmering pork, sugar, and ... *what is that scent of heavenly goodness?* Something warm yet sour filled his nostrils. Yeasty, but not in the way of fermenting ale. Nay, like rising bread dough, with a hint of vinegar, garlic, and ... salt?

His mouth watered as he watched a young woman slip by with a steaming bowl of rice and shredded pork drowning in a thin, dark sauce. He nudged Bayani with his elbow. "What is *that*?"

His companion snickered. "Adobo, tulalo." Handing the Áfgaliard several silver coins from the cavalry guard's pouch, he said, "Eat. Drink. Rest in t'e hospitality of Yusa. It rare for foreigner to be welcome like this."

Sólan paused, frowning. "You are a confusing man, sañero."

"Not here. Not now, Sólan. Please?" Bayani whispered. "We have image to keep."

"¿Mondé? Of what sort of image do speak?"

The fisherman darted to the back of the shack without another word. Sólan clenched his jaw as he watched his companion approach a corner separated from the rest of the patrons by a heavy orange curtain. Bayani was using a private dining area meant for the higher privileged, the pretentious bastard.

Another, slightly taller, man appeared from behind the curtain. His black waist-length hair draped over his shoulders, and he grasped the hilt of a decorated rapier while addressing Bayani. He scanned the room as though searching for enemies, and when he momentarily locked eyes with Sólan, his nose twitched.

The Áfgaliard's stomach flipped into his chest. Blushing, he broke his gaze with the man, though he turned his ear toward the corner. Sólan stiffened as his keen hearing caught Bayani's whisper: "Siso no dens-i kami." He snapped his gaze back to the curtain as both Nethuanian men slipped behind it.

Not pretentious. Just a worm in the Taela drug trade.

SÓLAN SLURPED DOWN THREE BOWLS OF ADOBO AND A PINT OF WATERY rum. The amount of liquor was little more than a thimble's worth—just enough to tame the grit and bitterness of the murky water. 'Twas a problem he could have easily mitigated with his power, but for what use? The more he used The Dark for such menial tasks, the quicker he would lose control and become like the Sprites of old. The food, however, tasted even better than he expected, which—based on the smell alone—had been perfection.

Bayani finally reappeared as Sólan finished scraping the last grains of rice from his final bowl. The fisherman snorted at the pile of dishes on the table. "You eat more t'an my mare when she pregnant," he said. He lowered himself to the ground across from his companion and chuckled.

Sólan licked the oil from his lips. "I have never tasted anything so …" he trailed off, unable to find a word that could do the food justice.

"I told you. T'e best in Bansungei."

"At least I know I can trust your palate, if nothing else. Particularly your career …"

"Pardon?" Bayani's posture stiffened. "After everything, you still no—"

"I am fluent in Taela." Sólan's eyes narrowed as he growled and leaned forward, that pulsing pain burning in his eyes. "The *Silent Dancer*? Really?"

The colour drained from Bayani's face. "Wh-what about it?"

"Captained by the most feared pirate in the Southern and Dragon Seas?"

"Smuggler," Bayani corrected. "Pirates only steal and rape. We earn, and we never take unwilling lovers."

"Smugglers do not murder—"

"We cannot talk here."

"You work for Kadek the Vile and expect me to believe that Elena will be safe with you?" Sólan bared his fangs as he clenched his fists to stay the angry tremors. "I may be 'The Grim,' but I am not known to drown *infants* for sport."

"You ask who hunt me if I escape Bansungei, remember?" said Bayani. "I am bound to Kadek until my twenty-fifth summer solstice. Only t'en can I marry Elena and leave t'is godforsaken place."

Sólan scoffed. "Please. As though I can trust any word you vomit at me."

"Why you come back to Bansungei after rescuing Elena? You hate it here—our God, His people. You had chance to go back to where you come. I'm tired of seeing you face."

The Áfgaliard stared daggers into the fisherman. "We are talking about *you*, putathóta. But, I am as trapped as you until this fucking crusade is over. So, get used to 'seeing my face.'"

"You are hero in Áfgal. So, go back to Áfgal."

"Tíal, I am a hero there. Heroes are well-praised in that kingdom, making it a dangerous place for a man who should not be alive." Sólan leaned back and crossed his arms, as though his words were challenging Bayani.

The fisherman took the bait. "You stand out. You no safe here, either."

"I am the most hated man in both the desert and the tundra. The prince of Prastömin just helped me fake my own death a mere two moons ago, *and* I am being hunted down by the oddlings for a crime I did not commit in Orovín. I think I will take my chances here." Sólan raised an eyebrow and cocked his head with a smirk. "Your turn."

"Why do I bother to help you?" Bayani grumbled as a young man placed a bowl of food in front of him. He snatched the wooden spoon and began shoving bites of rice and pork into his mouth.

"I could ask you the same thing." Sólan looked over to the long-haired swordsman and shifted the conversation. "Who is that over there? A cavalry guard? A former cavalry guard?"

Bayani wiped his mouth with the back of his hand. "He was never a cavalry guard. He Kadek's bodyguard for ... fifteen years? He been on *Silent Dancer* since he fourteen."

Sólan made a sound of disapproval. "His bodyguard? Or his lover?"

"Dakil no lover of men, tulalo," Bayani snarled. "And he will kill any—man or woman—who breathe such disgusting lies."

"Ah, yes. For such love is forbidden by Yusa, of course." Sólan shook his head as he spoke.

"It unnatural. Disgusting. A vile abomination—"

"Careful, cabróde," Sólan said in warning. "You are speaking to an Áfgaliard. An Áfgaliard with a ... an eclectic appetite in a variety of lovers."

"You ... you are ..."

"Yes?" A wicked grin stretched across Sólan's face as his eyes flared with wicked flames. The fisherman clamped his mouth shut and returned his attention to his food. Sólan sneered at his obvious discomfort. "Be careful with your words, putathóta. They are likely to get you killed someday."

"Binyego!" Elena's small voice echoed through the shack from the kitchen's entrance. Both men snapped their heads toward her as she sprinted through the crowd and leapt into Bayani's arms, tears flowing down her cheeks.

"Calomot i Yusa, Elena." Bayani kissed the top of her head as she buried her face into his chest.

Sólan's gaze wandered toward the back corner just as the thick orange curtain twitched opened, revealing a well-dressed and ornately decorated man. He whispered to Dakil—his "bodyguard," apparently—with a deep scowl cut across his face. Even from where he sat, Sólan could feel the tension between the two men. When they parted, Dakil's eyes again met Sólan's, and in that moment, the malice that blazed within them was unmistakable. *Bayani is wrong. That man is no mere bodyguard, but a lover scorned.*

Bayani led Sólan and Elena back to his damaged home, where Tirsen had prayed and fasted for days. They entered through the broken door. Elena bolted into the main room. "Papa!"

"Elena!" Tirsen scooped his daughter into his arms and collapsed to his knees. He wept and rocked as he held her close to his chest. "Calomot i Yusa!" 'Twas all he could say, over and over again until he was breathless.

Bayani leaned over to Sólan and hissed. "Not a word about Kadek."

"Do you take me for a fool?"

"Where's Tala?" Tirsen still clutched his daughter as his question interrupted the bickering between Bayani and Sólan.

Both men lowered their heads and shuffled their feet, fidgeting.

"Well ..." said one.

"We ... aeh ..." added the other.

"She fought hard," Bayani finally managed.

Sólan nodded with a nervous twitch. "Tíal. She was a fierce woman when—"

"You fail her." Tirsen's tone stung like nettle. "Now how can I receive new bride from temple?"

"¿Mondé?" Sólan trembled, clenching his jaw as another surge of rage tore through him.

Bayani stepped between him and the old fisherman. "I help you, binyego. I marry Elena in ten days, instead of summer."

"What the fuck!" Sólan shoved Bayani aside and grasped Tirsen's shirt; he yanked the fisherman to his feet, leaving Elena to crumple on the floor with a scream. "Even in death, she is no more than—"

"She was my everything!" Tirsen's voice cracked at the seething man's outburst. "Don't pretend to know our way, Áfgaliard … you *pagan*."

"He admit to cavalry guard," Bayani declared. "He now follower of Yusa."

Sólan's eye twitched as he met Tirsen's gaze with a glare.

"He will learn. Just as I learn t'anks to you and Gesang." The young fisherman's words softened the older man's expression, but Sólan refused to relax his grip.

"I failed no one," growled Sólan . "Tala fought for her child. She *died* for her child." He released Tirsen and ran both hands through his own hair. He grimaced and shook his head in order to keep his darkening thoughts from turning into spoken words. "I see I have overstayed my welcome in this 'holy' city."

"Wait." Tirsen's eyes widened. "You not leaving, tual. Are you?"

"Of *course* I am. I have been faced with nothing but hatred and mistrust since you and your family 'saved' me from the sea. Hatred and mistrust that has been masked by your god's directive of kindness."

"I promise t'e elf—"

"That you would keep me in the city and keep me alive. However, you misplaced me for two fucking moons. You have already broken your promise to him."

"Wait," Bayani cut in. "You tell me—"

"I have told you many things, pundijo"—Sólan snapped at the

young fisherman—"and yet, you still continue to take my words as undeniable truth."

Tirsen grunted. "You tell me you no like to be called a liar, yet you call you-self one now."

"I really do hate that word," muttered Sólan. His lip lifting into a sneer, he spat, "I say whatever I need to say to survive. Given my reputation, this should not surprise you."

"Can you at least wait until t'e end of the elf's crusade?" Tirsen begged. "Bayani need help to fix his burned home. Elena needs a safe place to live after she married."

"*I* need a safe place to stay until I can return to Áfgal. To be quite honest, sañero, I am unsure if I can find that here. Why do you demand my presence when you clearly despise it?" *Have the Gods sent you to punish me for my repeated failures? I swore an oath to them ... time and again, I have failed them.*

"Papa?" Elena finally broke her silence with a quivering voice. "I no want him here anymore."

A river of guilt and shame threatened to drown Sólan as Elena recounted nearly everything. As he remembered both his impassioned night with Tala and the flames that engulfed her body merely two days later. *Indiónta. You have brought this upon yourself with your incompetence and pride. This truly is a punishment for my failures. O Javiento, will you ever forgive me? Elék, will I ever again be worthy of your mercy and protection?*

"He *what!*" Tirsen's outburst snapped the Áfgaliard's attention back to the half-burned home.

Sólan opened his mouth to defend himself, but Bayani got there first. "I tell him to burn Tala, binyego." The silence that followed the young fisherman's words was deafening.

Tirsen's teeth chattered as his expression contorted into a mixture of anger, sorrow, and confusion.

"She was murder by evil men and no bear son for you in her life. It was Yusa's will for her to be purify in His fire." Bayani stepped forward and placed a gentle hand on Tirsen's shoulder. "You will see her again in Linget. I promise you."

Tirsen burst into tears and fell to his knees. "Yusa bless me with you," he said between sobs.

Bayani turned to Sólan and whispered, "I have place in my stables for you. Please stay ... help me protect Elena."

Sólan squinted and made no reply. *Gods, Bayani. You are a confusing man, indeed.*

9

KNIGHT DOWN

"Faerin." A gruff voice startled the lower knight awake. Faerin's sleepy eyes darted around the darkness and landed on the broad silhouette of his commander—an upper knight, Sir Marlen. He rubbed the sleep from his eyes and sat up. "B-beggin' y'r pardon, sir, but … I thought you ordered me the-the-the watch at dawn."

Marlen sighed and Faerin could practically hear the roll of his eyes. "Dawn'll arrive by the time ya start movin', at your rate. You're supposed to be there at dawn. Hurry up."

Faerin yawned and inched himself to his feet. His donned his thick leather armour, which was so constricting that he was awakened further by the discomfort. He then descended the steps of his barrack into the armoury and kitchen, where he snatched a cold chunk of salt-cured pork and stale sour-cake from the previous morning. It wasn't much, but it halted the growls of his empty stomach.

"Morrow, Sir Faerin." A young academy knight grinned as he handed him a gladius, a bow, and a quiver of arrows. "Nice cool breeze out today. Should wake ya oup in no time."

Faerin gave a tired smile as he tied the sword and quiver each to a hip. "Thanks." He trudged out of the building and met a chilling gust of wind. A shiver ran down his spine as he pulled his tunic's hidden scarf over his face and plopped his wool-lined helmet over his head with a grumble.

It took him hours to reach his post—hours that he could have spent sleeping. The crescent moon'd hardly begun its descent as the sky brightened from black to a deep indigo. *Marlen was right. Dammit.*

Faerin approached the lower knight he was to relieve—a lower knight who, unlike himself, was not in contention for a promotion to upper anytime soon. The lower commanders hardly tolerated the minimum standard, and they saved early promotions for the most honourable and hardworking lower knights. The vast majority, however, were elevated in title simply because they had served their maximum fifty years at such rank.

At a mere age of twenty-five, Faerin was—by nearly ten years—the youngest lower knight up for such honour. The youngest, at least, since the brothers from Vaoirsen—Naoise and Giaven.

"About bloody time, Faerin." His fellow knight's whines and yawns pierced his eardrums like red-hot needles.

Peevish prick. I bet ya slept through y'r watch. "Stars're still out, Conor. I'm on time."

Conor merely grumbled and rubbed his eyes until they were puffy. "Fook me. That had to be the dullest night I've had in a hundred years."

Definitely slept through y'r watch.

"Not even an owl or mouse!"

"You sure about that?" Faerin crossed his arms with a frown. "Not a single squeak?"

"Ask any o' the other lads. The whole damned forest was silent. Even the crickets slept."

"Shite," Faerin whispered. "That's a poor start to-to the morrow. You have the h-h-horn?"

Conor nodded and slipped a leather strap off of his shoulder. "Pray hard, Faerin. There's somethin' not right out there." He pressed one finger to his lips and pointed two others at Faerin.

"Thank you, C-c-c-conor." The young knight repeated the salute and strapped the twisting, gold-trimmed horn across his back. "See you this-this ev'ning."

"Hm? Oh ... yeh. Our spar." Conor dragged his feet as he trudged back to the barracks.

When Faerin was sure he was out of earshot, he sighed. *Fuckin' bastard.* He inspected the mouthpiece of the horn with a scowl—it was both slimy and gritty. That was a difficult combination to achieve, but it seemed to be Conor's specialty. Only the Wizards knew what he did with that horn. Faerin shuddered at the thought.

A small sound of movement beneath the brush snapped his attention to the west. A brown-spotted elk squirrel carried three hornless babies on her back as she sniffed the air, detecting the intruder. She scurried away once Faerin moved.

"A bit late in-in the year t-to be raisin' babies, yeh?" He chuckled and started his patrol. The sky continued its transition from indigo to maroon to crimson as he walked. *Shite. Red.* A red sky at dawn meant one of two things: ally blood spilled, or the infiltration of an enemy. Nerves heightened, he couldn't help but flinch with every sound, whether it be a winged gecko taking flight, or the incessant knocking of the featherless woodpeckers high in the trees. Considering the lack of a blowing horn last night, Faerin prayed he wouldn't be find an intruder.

He wasn't so lucky. Heavy boot prints meandered their way toward the barracks through a hole in the outer wall. Fresh. Likely made mere hours before his arrival. Faerin's heart thumped in his fingertips as he drew and nocked an arrow. *One man.*

After following the makeshift trail for nearly a kilometre, the prints disappeared onto a granite shelf, upon which were smears of dirt, water, and silver ... *blood?*

Faerin gasped. He put his arrow away and clambered to the opposite side of the rock where a steep embankment dropped several metres below its edge. Whoever had broken through the wall had then fallen and tumbled—at least, that's what the clumsy trail of slides and impacts in the needle-covered ground told him.

He slid down to the bottom where a seasonal brook bubbled its way to the southwest, and a painful groan filtered through the noise of the running water. *What the—*Faerin rushed to his left. He leapt across the brook and landed by what appeared to be a dead animal. Yet, at closer inspection, he saw that it was no animal.

Gnomes be merciful! Panic set in as he fumbled for the patrol horn and pressed its dirty mouthpiece to his lips. He didn't care; he *couldn't* care. Three blows. Pause. Three blows.

Knight down.

Rhona entered the southern garden, her pockets empty after her prayers with the Speaker of the Wizards. Her ears perked at the sudden clamour of shouts and horns echoing from the western courtyard. She scurried across the keep's grounds—such racket was rare and such panic unseen since the start of the crusade.

A crowd of commoners and knights alike formed behind the centre fountain. She pushed her way through them and froze at what she saw—a gold-armoured knight slumped across a rider's lap, corpse-like, the rider shouting for help.

The handmaiden sprinted to his side and helped him ease the motionless body to the ground. "Who is he?" she asked. Matted hair and dried blood obscured the dead man's face.

"Ah dunno," the rider answered. "'Nd I'm n-n-not sure if he—"

Suddenly, the body rattled with a sharp gasp. Rhona wiped the blood and hair from his face and called out, "Get the dotaires!"

Several onlookers ran from the scene, shouting for the prestigious healers.

Rhona snapped her attention to the rider. "Who found him?"

"I ... I did," the rider said.

"Yer name?"

"F-F-Faerin. Sir Faerin."

Rhona was too distracted with her assessment of the injured knight to acknowledge she heard him. "Help me remove his armour."

Faerin trembled as he helped her untie and loosen the wounded's breastplate.

Eyes of evergreen shot open at the release of pressure from his chest. "Giants!" His breaths were short and fast. "The Taelas. Giants!"

"What ha-ha-happened, sir?" Faerin's question went unheard.

"Move!" The commanding voice of a high-ranking healer boomed as he pushed his way through the crowd.

"Over here, dotaire!" Rhona called.

Faerin looked into the wild eyes of his fallen comrade. "What's you-you-your name, sir? What happened? Are-are you a c-crusade hun—"

"Káil!" The dotaire dropped to his knees and shoved Rhona to the side. "Your grace! Wizards be good, not the prince!"

"Tör," Rhona whispered, "stay with us. Ye're in Brennan's care now. What happened?"

Alsantör's disconnected gaze fluttered in panic as though surrounded by enemies. "Giants!" was all he could say.

"Shite," said Brennan, jumping to his feet with alarm. "A fever of the mind. Get me the other dotaires! We need to move him!"

Six knights stepped forward as volunteers. With three on each side, they hoisted the prince up and followed Brennan, who ordered, "North wing, lads. He needs the north wing's care."

Rhona gracefully rose to her feet and helped Faerin to his. "Tell me again. What's yer name, sir? Ye deserve great honour fer what ye've done."

"F-Faerin, m'lady."

"I'm not a lady," said Rhona. "I'm the queen's handmaiden."

Faerin stiffened. He looked to the ground as he stuttered, "A-apologies, M-maid Rhona. I didn't intend—"

"No offence taken, Sir Faerin." She pressed her lips together and frowned. "What's yer title?"

"Lower knight, m-maid-maiden."

"I see."

Faerin fumbled in his pocket. "The upper knight of my b-barrack has ch-charged me with finding First Knight Naoise 'nd giving him-giving 'im this." He placed a tarnished silver ring into Rhona's outstretched hand. "Do-do you-do-you know where I could find 'im?"

The handmaiden rolled the ring around her palm with a sad sigh as she recognised the crowned eagle. "The fencing arena." Without hesitation, she removed a gold-chained necklace from around her neck. She plopped its pendant into her pocket before slipping the chain through the ring. "Here." She handed the jewellery back to the knight. "It was Sir Giaven's … his brother."

Faerin's face fell at Rhona's words. "Káil," he whispered. "The L-lord Knight? He"—the young knight sniffled—"he taught m-me ev'rything I know." His teeth chattered, tears welling in his eyes. "Thank you, Maid Rhona. I'll go d-deliver this now."

"Nai, Sir Faerin. Thank *you* for yer courage. Had ye not broken that silly protocol, the heir to the throne would be dead."

"DOEN'T CROSS Y'R FEET." NAOISE WIPED THE SWEAT FROM HIS COPPER hairline as the high noon's sun filtered its way through the forest's muggy atmosphere. The fencing arena was small, hardly larger than the horse trainer's bullpen. Beneath his thick leather armour, his body was drowning in sweat— drips of it even fell from his elbows as he lifted his wooden gladius to his face. *Wizards*, was this heat stifling. Ignoring the discomfort, he said, "Again."

His opponent nodded despite the utter exhaustion painted across his face. Still, the man hardly looked warm—not a hint of sweat. Such was the resilience to heat the Prasti contained in their blood. "Eil, sir."

Naoise lowered to a slight crouch and shuffled to the side, his steps effortless across the loose soil that scraped along his ankles. The other knight stumbled, and his posture twisted as his legs crossed at the knees. Naoise lunged. The tip of his dull blade poked his ribs between the halve of his breastplate.

"I told ya, Rowan. Doen't cross y'r feet." Naoise placed his free hand over his own underarm and added, "Ya just exposed the weakest part of y'r armour, 'nd now y'r heart's been severed. Dead 'afore ya even hit the ground."

Rowan dropped his head. "I'm sorry, sir. I—"

"Doen't apologise, neither. Y'r a bloody knight of Prastömin. Not a child being scolded by his maela." Naoise shut his eyes to keep the salty sting of his sweat from blinding him. He shook his head before opening them once more. "Again."

Rowan took a sharp breath. "Eil, sir," he said through clenched teeth.

The two squared off as before. They shuffled, crouched, stepped. Round and round they danced, their twitches and threatening lunges keeping the other in constant focus.

A third knight entered the arena. "Ehm … Sir Naoise?"

Naoise flashed a glance at his name, and Rowan took the moment to attack. Despite the break in his concentration, Naoise parried with ease before he shoved his open hand against his opponent's throat. The impact sent Rowan to the ground with a guttural heave. A tap with the waster's blade across the back of his neck finalised his defeat. "Dead," said Naoise.

"Yep," croaked Rowan. "No argument there."

Naoise chuckled as he stooped to take the young knight's weapon. He then helped Rowan to his feet and clapped him on the shoulder, a warm smile stretching across his face. "Doen't be hard on y'rself. That was excellent timing, even if the movement's a bit slow. Now, go get some water … and a bath. Ya stink worse than my horse's shite after a bout o' colic."

"Eil, sir," Rowan said through a snort. He crossed to the arena's entrance and passed the newcomer. "Good luck," he whispered. "'E loves his swordplay."

The newcomer's mouth contorted into a forced smile. "I n-noticed." He gulped nervously as he approached Naoise with tentative steps. "Ap-ap-pologies f'r the, ehm, the intrusion, sir, but—"

"Name 'nd title?"

The knight's tone made the new opponent stutter. "S-Sir Faerin. Ehm, lower knight of-of the, ehm, southwestern patrol."

Naoise frowned as he looked Faerin over. "I doen't recall an appointment with ya."

"Eil. I know, sir. I d-don't have one with—"

"Wait." Naoise's mouth curled at the corners. "You're Dotaire Aiden's boy. That young lad up f'r promotion next moon, yeh?"

Faerin blushed and shuffled his feet in the soil. "Eil, sir."

"Well, this is a surprise. Finally get to put a face to the name. I was lookin' forward to meeting ya."

Faerin snapped his head up to meet Naoise's welcoming gaze. "Sir?"

"To what do I owe the pleasure?"

The sudden discomfort in Faerin's expression was unmistakable. "Ehm ... well ..."

Shite. What happened?

"I'm, ehm, I'm not sure if ... if you're gonna find m-much pleasure in this, sir." Faerin fumbled through his pockets. He held his fist out to Naoise, who opened his own hand. The gold chain and silver ring plopped into his palm.

Naoise froze. *No, no, no, no. No!* He bit the inside of cheek to quell the flood of tears that threatened to burst from his eyes. So hard, in fact, that the metallic taste of silver blood filled his mouth. It was to no avail—the tears flowed anyway. "Where'd you get this?" His voice quivered through the growing lump in his throat, his gaze never lifting from the ring.

"It was on-on-on his grace's person when I found 'im early this morrow."

"What d'ya mean, by 'found him?' What happened to the prince?"

"He ... ehm ..." Faerin trembled.

I'm not the king. I doen't murder messengers. "Spit it out, lad. Where's the chief commander?" Naoise, too, was shaking. He held his breath in attempt to ease his racing heart. Again, he failed.

"The infirm'ry. Ehm ... n-north wing with Do-dotaire Brennan."

Káil! That arsehole's gonna kill him! Naoise dropped his wasters and sprinted out of the arena, his brother's ring clutched inside a tight fist.

10

OF POISONED BLOOD

*R*hona sprinted through the keep's stone halls. The beams of sunlight that pierced through the walls flickered as she passed by, casting odd shadows. Just three more doors, a sharp turn to the right, and a climb up a winding staircase—never had the route felt more endless.

She paused at the top. Her lungs burned and her feet ached as fatigue washed over her. *Shit. I need to stop trying to run up these.* Rhona shook her head and laughed at her own thoughts.

"What's so funny?"

Rhona froze at the deep, gritty voice behind her. She spun around and promptly averted her gaze to the ground. "Nothing, yer grace. Just the silly thoughts of a silly girl."

Diarmuid clicked his tongue. "And your haste?"

"I have news to deliver. If it please ye, yer grace, I'd like to deliver such news to ye. It's regarding yer son and his health."

"His health?" Diarmuid stepped back with a frown. "Has he returned from Nethuania?"

Rhona nodded. "Eil, yer grace." *Please, Wizards, don't let him rage.* "He's in the north wing of the infirmary, fighting for his life. The dotaires believe his blood's been poisoned by an arrow wound." She winced at the king's sharp intake of breath.

"Fuck." Diarmuid's hand trembled as he clasped it over his mouth. He took slow, rhythmic breaths through his nose before he spoke again. "Apologies, Handmaiden. I meant not to curse in front of you."

Rhona blinked to hide her surprise at his kind tone. "No apologies necessary, yer grace."

"Who's in charge of his care? Brennan?"

Rhona nodded.

"Thank the Wizards." The king paused. His eyes began to lose focus, but he shook off whatever demon threatened to subvert his thoughts. "How did he return—was he alone? Under his own power?"

"Alone, eil. However, he was found down at the southwestern wall by a lower knight of this season's patrol. Dotaire Brennan assumed his care shortly thereafter."

Diarmuid squeezed his eyes shut. "Lower knight? Did he break their casualty protocols? He could have *killed* him by doing so." A fog threatened to form around the edges of his pupils, but he blinked it away. "Carry on, Handmaiden. His mother should become aware promptly."

"As ye command, yer grace." Rhona said as she bowed her head and curtsied. Without another word, the king descended the winding stairs. Rhona sighed. *Thank ye, Creator—Gnome Ethar, for yer protection,* she prayed before turning to continue on her own way.

The handmaiden's adrenaline surged as she regained momentum and peaked as she reached the corridor to the royal chambers. It contained six doors—three on one side, two on the other, and one against the back wall.

Each cedar door was gilded and emblazoned with an eagle clasping a gladius in one talon and a javelin in the other. Though, one was remarkably plain, and that demarked the prince's abode. He had despised the gaudy monstrosity that previously decorated his entrance, so he'd requested a simpler one. One made of unglued cedar.

First Knight Naoise, King Diarmuid, and Queen Ethna with Rhona all had chambers along the halls. Without a duke of the forest, however, one chamber sat abandoned.

The last door of the corridor was the most decorated, featuring two carved eagles instead of one, their talons clasped together. Behind the entryway was a heavily decorated bed, two plain stools, and … nothing else. 'Twas only used once per hundred years, when Diarmuid and Ethna renewed their marriage vows by a witnessed consummation. Namely, the first knight of Prastömin and the queen's handmaiden. Rhona shuddered at the thought. *Gnomes be merciful, only fifteen years left until that passionless ritual repeats.* She paused outside the queen's door and gulped. *Ethar. Would it be too much to ask again for yer protection? Would it be too soon?*

She pushed against the door, first lightly and then with increasing force, but it didn't budge. Grumbling, she rapped her knuckles on the golden eagle's chest.

Rhona's nerves flared as the adrenaline pumped throughout her body in the short, yet agonising, moment it took for the queen's door to open.

"Back so soon, my dear?" Ethna's voice almost sang as she spoke through the opening.

"Eil, yer grace," said Rhona. "I have urgent news regarding—"

"Have you told the king?"

Rhona shut her mouth and nodded. "I passed him on the way here."

"Then there's no further news to deliver." Ethna opened the door just wide enough for her handmaiden to slip inside. "Don't mind the mess. I've been weaving."

A welcomed warmth spread through Rhona's cheeks as she looked over to the queen's loom, upon which a half-finished tapestry revealed itself in splendour. The threads were of a deep emerald green, woven together with vibrant shades of red, gold, and copper. "It's beautiful, yer grace. How—"

"Oh, come now. I'm Ethna when we're alone." The queen sat back down on her stool and continued to weave, adding one painstaking layer of thread at a time.

Rhona blushed. "Right." She shook her head and crossed to the open window, leaning against the wall to admire the view spread beneath the afternoon sun. The rose garden's scent wafted up to her nostrils like a sweet Prasti perfume. Thousands of flowers blossomed below, creating a mosaic of colour that rivalled even the brightest lights of rainbow cast by freshly cut diamonds. The trees of the orchards surrounding the courtyard bowed under the weight of their plump fruit: pears, peaches, plums ... Rhona's mouth watered at the thought of sinking her fangs into the crunch of a honeycrown apple, the delicacy of a self-pollinating hybrid tree of pear and apple. It had been discovered by Ethna on pure chance and had become a royal luxury enjoyed only by the three elves of the crown. At least, that's what was publicly known—Naoise, Giaven, and Rhona were well-trained in the art of palming the fruit for their own summer solstice picnics.

A tear slid down Rhona's cheek as she pictured Giaven's ring in Faerin's hand. He and his brother were the last of Vaoirsen and the closest friends a woman of her stature could afford. Unlike his brother, however, Giaven was the only being in all the eastern lands who knew the secret she shared with ... *the prince!* Her sense of duty came crashing back to her like an avalanche in the Blue Eye Mountains to the east.

Rhona spun around just as Ethna said, "I hear they found a knight dead at the western gate this morning." The queen raised an eyebrow and glanced sideways at her handmaiden, noting the mud and silver blood on her hands. "And it appears you've ruined your gloves."

Rhona removed her hand coverings and mumbled, "Replaceable pieces of fabric. I still have their pattern on parchment." She pressed her lips together into a fine line before plopping into the padded chair beside a heavy cedar table. Reaching across its face, she uncorked a glass decanter of red wine and poured a significant amount into two golden chalices.

Ethna frowned. "What in Eclipse Aeternum do you think you are doing? it's not even tea-time yet!"

"Trust me, Ethna. Ye'll need something much stronger than tea."

The queen clamped her mouth shut and sucked the back of her fangs. "What happened?" she asked, moving from her stool to an identical padded chair.

Rhona swallowed a mouthful of wine and grimaced. "That 'knight' is a crusade hunter—the only survivor in his crew."

"Is?" Ethna swirled her burgundy drink around in its glass thoughtfully before taking a sip. "Who is he, then?"

The handmaiden again pressed her lips together as the queen took another drink of wine. "Well?"

Rhona said quietly, "A-Alsantör."

Ethna froze, though her grip on the chalice's stem tightened. The gold bent beneath the pressure, its jewels clinking out onto the table.

"He *is* alive, Ethna ... and was even awake when—"

Ethna released her hand, casting wine about the room as she screamed. The queen slipped from her chair and onto her knees. Sharp jewels cut through the linen of her dress and into the soft skin of her shins. She hugged herself tight, rocking herself as she sobbed.

Káil! Rhona leapt to her feet, nearly slipping on the wet ground, and wrapped her arms around the devastated mother.

"Gnomes be merciful, not him!" the queen wailed. "*Please* not him!"

"Hush, Ethna," Rhona murmured. "He's in excellent hands, I promise ye." But her words fell on deaf ears. *He's not dead. There's still hope.*

Ethna clutched her handmaiden's arm and buried her face into the crook of her elbow. Her body was racked with sobs, and her attempts to calm herself were rewarded with hiccoughs. Finally, she sat upright and wiped away her tears with the back of her hand. "Shite. I'm sorry, Rhona. I didn't—" A ragged breath interrupted her words.

In response, Rhona only tightened her embrace, bringing Ethna's face to her own. With their cheeks pressed together, the handmaiden said reassuringly, "He's in Dotaire Brennan's care, Ethna. The best healer in the forest."

"Yet—" Ethna hiccoughed—"'tis still not enough."

Rhona stiffened. "What are ye saying? He woke up and was brought to the western courtyard shortly after. Brennan is—"

"A Prasti." Ethna broke her embrace to stare into her handmaiden's confused gaze, her emerald eyes as cold as the green stones they matched.

Shit. I know that commanding look.

"You, however, are the daughter of the greatest dotaire of Ūendevail. Frasier knew medicine nearly as well as the Wizards know creation, and the Gnomes compassion."

Rhona slowly rose to her feet. "He also died of the very plague he sought to cure. What is yer point?"

"My point," Ethna said as she also stood, "is that he taught you and your late siblings—"

Rhona winced.

"—everything he knew. Brennan would die for half as much knowledge as you have."

Dammit. Rhona hung her head. "Ye want me to oversee the prince's care."

"Precisely."

"Begging yer pardon, yer grace … I'm not a dotaire, and Brennan knows this. He wouldn't dare take advice from a woman of Karthi and Ta—"

"Bollocks. That was an order, Rhona. You are to report to me at sundown."

Rhona gritted her teeth and said, "As ye command, yer grace." *Even if yer commands are dangerously reckless.*

"How is he?" demanded Naoise as he stormed into the private infirmary room. He struggled to hide his panic as he watched the dotaire wrap Alsantör in wet, tepid cloths. Heavy wafts of mint and cedar attacked his sinuses, making him wipe his runny nose with the back of his hand.

"Not well," said Brennan, not bothering to look up from his work as he addressed the first knight. "I cut a pestilence from his back.

Likely an arrow of some sort. It's deep, and it's festered into his blood."

Káil. Naoise bit the inside of his lip to staunch the well of tears prickling his eyes. "Will he"—the knight cleared his throat and silently cursed his voice for betraying his apathetic façade—"will he live?"

Brennan grunted in a mixture of annoyance and fatigue. "That remains to be seen, Sir"—he looked over to Naoise and studied him—"Sir Giaven."

"It's Naoise, actually."

"Oh! Apologies. I … well. You Veers look so much alike."

"Hardly," said Naoise. "Besides, Sir Giaven's dead."

Brennan's lack of reaction proved his inattention—or his inability to care. He finished his work by placing a final cloth over Alsantör's forehead. "Look, I don't know how poisoned his blood is, and I won't until the morrow, if he even survives 'til then."

Naoise stiffened at Brennan's grim words. "What the hell do ya mean by 'if'?"

Sighing irritably, the dotaire grabbed the bowl of lukewarm water and shuffled out of the room, without a word.

Naoise glared after him as the heavy door slammed shut. "Arsehole." He sighed as he turned to take in his surroundings.

A single stool sat at the foot of the plain wooden cot. Beside it was a table just large enough for a small servant's tray. Splashes of water had soaked the wood, save for a bowl-shaped patch of dryness. The plain stone walls were covered with little more than white linen sheets. Half of the eastern wall was appropriated by a large window overlooking the distant entrance to the sacred pool. Thick drapes on either side had been opened to allow the afternoon sunlight to illuminate the room. Just beyond the stool and table at the bed's foot was a cold hearth carved into the granite. In the mugginess of the summer season, there was no need of a fire's warmth.

A tear escaped Naoise's eye as he gazed upon the unmoving figure in the bed. "Fook." He dragged the stool to the prince's side. Stifling a sob, he sat and placed a calloused, dirty hand on Alsantör's chest. He gasped at the heat searing through the wet cloth. "Gnomes, Tör. You'll melt away if ya get any warmer." His shivered as his emotions cracked through the walls of his heart. He clocked the sweat on the prince's skin. *By the looks of it, y've already started.*

The prince groaned, grimacing as he attempted to shift himself on the cot. Naoise leapt to his feet and slipped one arm beneath Alsantör's shoulders and the other, his hips. Even through the thick leather bracers that armoured Naoise's forearms, the fever burned.

"Dammit, Tör." Naoise laid the prince down in a more comfortable position and then dropped to his knees, resting his forehead against the edge of the cot's feather mattress. "I can't lose you, too. Both my brothers in one day? Wizards be good …" He curled a tight fist around the prince's wrist while he held his brother's ring with a vice grip in his other hand. "Wake up."

Sudden sobs tore through his body as his heart's defences finally crumbled. He coughed and sputtered as his tears flooded his nose. "The forest be lost without ya. Y're the only one here who cares about the men ya lead. The only one who cared about Giaven—reckless prick that he was." A new onslaught of emotion swept through him, and he looked to the ceiling with increasing despair. "Gnomes, Giaven was a good lad, wasn't he? I bet he was teasin' ya through his last breath. Laughin' at us now from across the gilded veil."

Naoise couldn't let go of either Alsantör's hand nor Giaven's ring. Not even to wipe the tears that now slithered down each side of his jaw and neck. "Please," he whispered through his sobs. "I can't lose you both in one day. Doen't leave me alone with your bloody parents. Y'r father'll go mad if ya do."

Alsantör shivered and groaned beneath the wet cloths. Naoise straightened and watched in earnest, but the deep grimace across the prince's clammy face snuffed out whatever glimmer of hope he had. *Ya burn too hot, Tör. Where's Brennan?*

Naoise sighed and hung his head once more, letting the tears drip off his nose. "Ya can't die, Tör. That's a fookin' command, ya ken. You will survive this. Silver blood will flow like the damned Runedein if ya doen't." A sudden passion ignited the first knight as he added, "Your father will kill all the dotaires and their pupils, and

I'll be the fookin' man swinging the sword. Just like with Ina … and … and her."

Two and a half hundred years had passed since Naoise was forced to swallow his grief of losing her. As the previous handmaiden, Ina was forbidden to touch any man—let alone carry his child. Alsantör had planned to help Naoise smuggle her to Karthénos as she carried their daughter.

The child, however, had arrived too early. She was small, underdeveloped, and likely to die a painful death of cold and starvation. It would've taken days, even if Ina hadn't been executed for treason immediately after giving birth.

Ethna took pity on the infant girl and ordered for her to be smothered in her sleep. "Her suffering would've been inevitable," she'd said to Alsantör, and yet, Naoise refused to believe 'twas mere pity that inspired the queen to act.

Twisted waves of rage, grief, and loneliness poured out of Naoise's mouth as he screamed into the feather mattress. He screamed for Gaiven, for Ina, and for the nameless daughter upon who he'd never laid eyes—and never would.

He cried for Alsantör, begging him to survive, however unlikely.

He wept for Vaoirsen, the home destroyed because of his father's treason, and for his mother, the woman who'd carried him and Giaven—only to die fighting to protect them both.

The sorrow continued to crash over him until he was mercifully drowned, succumbing to sleep at the prince's side, his late brother's ring still clutched in his fist.

A SOFT HAND ON NAOISE'S SHOULDER STARTLED HIM AWAKE. HE LEAPT to his feet, hand on his gladius's hilt, and spun to face the intruder behind him. "You should be with the queen," he said, slumping his shoulders as he met Rhona's gaze.

The handmaiden simply raised an eyebrow. "You should be with the king. Yet here we are."

Naoise scrunched his nose. "Here we are, indeed. What's the time?"

"Quarter day 'til sundown." Rhona shifted her pale green gaze to Alsantör. "Her grace sent me to ... em ... *oversee* Tör's care. She wants to be sure Brennan does his job."

"Hmph." Naoise rubbed his freckled chin in thought. "I haven't seen him since I arrived at high noon." He paused. "You shouldn't be alone in here. The dotaires and their pupils are curious men—they don't know the meaning of the word 'no.' Gnomes know what the hell they'd do to ya if—"

"Ye don't hafta worry about me." Rhona crossed her arms, her lips pressed together in her signature smirk. "I welcome the change. Ethna—" she stopped and pawed at her loose ebony braid as her nerves flared.

Naoise gave a knowing nod. To speak ill of the queen was treason, and committing such a slip of the tongue in possible earshot of the dotaires was suicide. "Ah ken, Rhona. She's a powerful woman, and 'twould be best f'r neither of us to cross 'er." He plopped himself back onto the stool and lowered his head into his hands.

"Ye've been weeping, friend," said Rhona. She knelt at his side and placed a comforting hand on his knee. "Is it about yer brother?"

Naoise flinched. "It's summer. All the pollen 'nd heat—"

"Bullshit." Rhona squeezed his kneecap. "I know the difference between yer tears and yer sensitivities. Ye can't lie to me, *Sir Naoise*."

The first knight's bottom lip trembled. *Ya know me too well, friend.* "I miss him." He hiccoughed. "Giaven was as kind as he was stupid ... and the best brother an elf could hope to have."

Rhona dropped her head and sniffled. "I miss him, too. He was a wonderful friend ... and a carefree cunt."

"Ha!" Naoise wiped his dripping eyes with the heel of his hand. "Yeh. Nothin' like Manstair ... nothin' like me."

"Oh, come now, Naoise. Ye're not always so uptight."

"I suppose not." Naoise bit his lip. "That must've been a damned deadly halfbreed to—"

Rhona grimaced.

"Shite. I'm sorry. I keep forgetting 'bout y'r blood."

"I know," Rhona whispered. "I hide it well." She grasped Naoise's hand and looked up to his mossy brown eyes. "But ye're right, Neesh. That mortal elf must've been quite strong to kill him, Carsen, and Anlon."

As if on cue, Alsantör moaned. They snapped their attention back to him.

"Káil," Rhona said under her breath.

Naoise gulped. "What's wrong?"

"His heart is racing. Can't ye see the pulse in his neck?" Rhona jumped to her feet to scan the room.

"He's far too hot, ah ken. But isn't that what y'r heart does with a fever?" asked Naoise, voice shaking in panic. *What's she searchin' for?* "Brennan says he may not last the night."

"He won't with only damp, tepid linens," said Rhona. "He's got the sweat. If he doesn't get coriander oil under his tongue soon, he'll convulse from the fever." She placed the back of her hand on the prince's forehead. "Get Brennan."

Alsantör's hand suddenly clenched as his arms extended. His wrists spasmed outward, his jaw tightened, and his breath became shallow. Naoise watched in horror at his contortions. "What the—"

"Get Brennan!" Rhona bellowed, her voice echoing throughout the room.

Naoise spun toward the door just as Brennan marched in with a deep scowl cut across his face. "What in Sprite's Hell is going on in here?"

Alsantör's thrashing intensified. His eyes fluttered and rolled, and he even lost control of his bowels and bladder.

"Brennan! Help me!" cried Rhona.

The dotaire darted to the bed and shoved Naoise aside. "Get off, get off!" He grabbed Rhona by the hair and yanked her off his patient. Her head snapped back before she stumbled over the stool. Naoise caught her fall and helped her remain on her feet.

As his convulsing slowed to a stop, Alsantör vomited. "Shite. Shite, shite, shite—" Brennan snatched the cloth off the prince's forehead and wiped his lips, only to then shove his fingers inside the prince's mouth in an attempt to scoop the vomit from his throat.

Alsantör gagged and heaved, reaching weakly toward the dotaire's arm to no avail. Rhona growled and slammed her body into the Prasti's, knocking him against the granite wall. "Ye're choking him." She reached across the prince and grabbed his far shoulder and leg. She pulled and rolled him onto his side, his mouth draining a frothy mixture of mucous and bile.

Grasping his shoulder as though injured, Brennan growled, "Naoise, arrest this woman."

The knight merely scoffed. "F'r what?"

Rhona slumped to her knees as she held Alsantör on his side. His breath was deep, wet, and forced. Tears fell from her eyes as Brennan continued his rant.

"Look at her! She touched me. She touched my patient. She's no dotaire, yet she—"

"Rolled him." Naoise frowned. "She rolled him to drain his throat. I'm a fookin' knight and I know to do that. Ya doen't hafta be a dotaire to protect a man from his own vomit ... Have ya never drunk too much mead?"

Rhona smirked. Naoise flashed her a wink as Brennan snarled, "She's the queen's handmaiden, ya thick-headed Veer. She's forbidden to touch any, save f'r—"

"I've heard differently." Naoise clenched his fists. "Take care of y'r insults, dotaire. This thick-headed Veer's the first knight—and the executioner—of Prastömin. Now then." He cleared his throat and rolled his shoulders back in a show of authority. "I know the laws of this forest. It be my job to know them. 'The handmaiden of the queen shall mother no sons nor daughters. No act of sexuality, fornication, or otherwise shall be permitted outside of the queen's needs. Such an act is treason and punishable by beheading. Any man or woman besides her grace who touches her for the act of fornication or procreation shall be convicted of rape and hanged without trial.' I'm sure that excludes helping protect y'r patient—the bloody *prince*—from suffocating after convulsion. A convulsion you shoulda been here to prevent by bringin' his fever down."

Brennan's eye twitched. "The king'll hear of this."

"Oh, eil. Of course, he will."

"As will the queen," said Rhona. "Ye'd best hope she's in a forgiving mood when she does."

"*Fuck* you, handmaiden. I didn't authorise you to speak." Brennan spat at her feet. "Naoise, I demand again that you arrest her!"

Naoise crossed his arms with a glare. "I refuse to arrest an innocent party. But while ya speak with the king, do be a kind lad 'nd tell him why you were absent when his son had a fit."

The blood drained from Brennan's face. He opened his mouth to respond, but Naoise held up a hand and said, "I'm not done. You have several messages f'r Diarmuid, Wizards bless his Crown. You will also tell him why you touched his queen's handmaiden by pulling her hair. 'Tis quite an *intimate* thing to do to a woman, nai?"

"That's preposterous! I had no intention of—"

"I doen't give a fook what be y'r intentions, Brennan!" Naoise brandished a pair of iron shackles as he spoke. "Ya threaten the first knight and executioner of the crown, ya insult the integrity of her grace's highly honoured personal servant, and ya abandon y'r patient nigh to his *death*! The king'll hear of this, and you'd best hope his demons are quiet today." With that, Naoise snatched the dotaire's wrist and locked it in a shackle.

Brennan spat once more, the glob of saliva splattering upon Naoise's cheek. "You fucking royal puppets. Both of you! I'll be *damned* if I let you humiliate my prestigious guild of healers! Madness, this is! Utter madness!" He swung his free fist at Rhona but missed by millimetres.

Naoise swept Brennan to the ground and pressed his face into the stone floor, shoving his knee between the dotaire's shoulder blades. "You've earned y'rself a new home, arsehole. It's the haunted dungeons f'r you."

11

BOOK OF THE SUN

"**K**in gunyan ey pananakin no suya, if they love him so!" Elena shouted as she sprinted into Bayani's stable. She hid herself in the shadows of the far corner.

Her arrival stirred the horses and startled Sólan out of a shallow sleep. He yawned and rubbed the fatigue from his eyes and sat upright. Stretching, the bones of his bare back, neck, and shoulders popped. "What's wrong?"

"Is no you concern, kapiret-liho!"

"Alright." Sólan shrugged and scrambled to his feet. The waves of his dark brown hair stuck out in multiple directions, adorned by bits of entangled hay. He rubbed the debris from his hair and trousers before shaking the wrinkles from his wadded shirt.

"Elena!" Bayani's voice echoed from beyond the stable's entrance. He jogged inside just as Sólan finished slipping into his boots. "T'ere you are, manag ng su. Come here."

"Hundi! You lie to me! You and Sólan!"

Sólan stiffened. "¿Mondé?" His gaze flitted between Bayani and Elena. "What do you mean *we* 'lied to you'?"

"We no lied, Elena. It no was us who—"

"I hate you!" Fresh tears streamed down the girl's cheeks as she shouted at them. "You burn mama! She no 'violated' by evil man. She was pure. I hate you both!"

Sólan hung his head in defeat. "I imagine you are wishing you had escaped with her now," he whispered to Bayani.

"With every breath," said the young fisherman. He glanced at the door and cursed. "I … um … I need to feed t'e horses."

Sólan groaned as, without another word, Bayani shuffled away from the confrontation. *You fucking coward.*

Tirsen soon entered the stable, the indignation on his face matching that of his daughter.

"What happened?" said Sólan.

The older man sniffled, streaks of moisture glistening upon his cheeks. "T'e temple cavalry cancel her marriage to Bayani. My daughter's maidenhood was taken by Áfgal man. She no longer virgin."

Sólan's eyes narrowed. "Bayani and I were there. We know not—"

"You both also proved to lie. How can I trust those who steal from dead men like you? Who work for Taela servants of Misó and burn the bodies of pure women, like Bayani? Unless there something you hiding from me? You both seem so concern wit' Tala even after she die."

Sólan bared his fangs. "I was *told* to burn her."

"That not what Elena tell me."

"¡Tí dioses lío, Tirsen! Are you so incapable of understanding genuine kindness?" Sólan pulled at his hair with both hands, his knuckles white from the force of his grip. He took several deep breaths and paced the length of the stable to calm the rage bubbling inside his chest. "I need to leave," he finally said.

"You can't. You will be hunted by cavalry," said Tirsen. The old fisherman puffed up his chest and awkwardly raised two fists. "I won't let you leave my daughter to—"

"I can—and I will—leave. I have nothing to fear from your false god's servants, as I have already—"

"Elena will be stoned if you do."

Sólan's breath caught. He could feel the blood draining from his face. *No. No, no, no, no. You are right, Tirsen. I cannot leave.* He gulped. "What must I do?"

"You must marry her. To atone for the sins of you kin."

Sólan's eyes widened. He crumpled to his knees and rocked back and forth, his vision tunnelling as his stomach retched. *Be this my punishment for laying with a claimed woman? Forced to marry a child in exchange for her mother's life?*

"It must be today, before sundown. If you refuse, t'en she will be stoned, and her body will be placed at you feet while you burn alive."

"But ... but Elena is no whore," whispered Sólan. He heaved again. "She ... she ..."

"You think I no know this? A man rape her, Sólan! She not a whore. She can't be whore. But I also can't let you leave. I'm doing what I must to protect the family I have left."

Sólan snapped his gaze up to Tirsen. "There is another way." He crawled toward the fisherman and grabbed the knee of his trousers. "Taelonael. The Oasis City. I can lead you there, with no debt to me. Run, Tirsen. You and Elena must run. I will protect you on the way. Please, do not make me do this."

Tirsen trembled as fresh tears flowed down his cheeks. "The guards already waiting outside. I no can let you kill them or run away. It not Yusa's way."

Sólan stared at the ground in defeat as Tirsen continued to beg, "Please, tual. Yusa already punish me for my unkindness. Don't let Him punish Elena, too. She still pure in my eyes."

Jidir. Sólan's fingertips tingled from his heavy breathing. Swallowing with a look of disgrace, he whispered, "I will do it, if that is what is needed to protect her. I ... I will marry her."

This time, it was Tirsen who fell to his knees and pawed at Sólan's clothing. "Calomot ki, Sólan. Calomot ki."

Sólan placed a hand on the fisherman's shoulder. "Nimíl. Thanks to ... aeh ... to Yusa for guiding me." *Oh, Elek. Protect me from these zealots.*

Sólan was soon shackled and led through the rough streets of Bansungei as two cavalry guards "escorted" him toward the high temple. Their iron and leather-scaled armour flared at the shoulders and the helm, granting them the illusion of a broad frame. Lining the route were people of all social statuses, jeering and throwing rotten fruit and horse dung at him. Some even splashed cups of their own urine and faecesfeces at him as he passed. In their eyes, he was naught but a foreign adulterer. A rapist of Áfgal, although he never touched Elena.

After what must have been two kilometres or more, they finally reached the temple. The heavy bronze doors were held open by two massive chains and flanked by several intricate columns of marble. The building itself was built mostly of marble, though it had a sturdy brick foundation.

Sólan tripped as he climbed up the hundred steps to the entrance, his hands still shackled tightly behind his back. His captors beat and kicked him as they forced him back onto his feet, his eyes pulsing with hot fire with every blow. *Ansalá,* he prayed, *give me your courage, God of Strength. Elék, protect me from The Dark as these men abuse your humble servant.*

When they finally reached the top, Sólan's feet were swiped out from under him—he landed on his knees with a loud thud. A sharp pain burst inside his leg as one of his kneecaps shattered. He yelped instinctively at the sensation, only to be promptly silenced with a punch to the back of his head. The surging crowd below roared in approval. *Fuck you all.* The Áfgaliard's vision swirled as he channelled his powers to heal the bone that crunched beneath him.

Two boys clad in orange appeared from behind the ornate pillars. They could be no older than Elena, yet appeared as devout as her father. *Gods, they start young.* They approached Sólan with careful steps. Their orange silk robes were wrapped around one shoulder and draped down to their knees, where they then split and twisted around their shins to the ankles. The boys were barefoot, save for what looked like a white rubbery resin that had hardened on the soles of their feet.

In silence, they tore off Sólan's shirt and tossed it down the steps.

They then scrubbed him from his face down to his abdomen with what he assumed to be—based on its fragrance and the way it melted from the heat of his skin—ground coconut shell mixed with a solid oil. Sólan clenched his jaw to keep from rolling his eyes at them as they spoke to him in their tongue. *I am a foreigner, indióntas. I cannot understand you.*

He flinched as Tirsen suddenly appeared at his side. "They said, 'A sinner you were. This is you atonement: t'e walk of Misó, and the cleansing by Yusa's love.'"

"I am not a criminal, putathóta," said Sólan through a hiss. "I am only doing this for Elena, not—"

"Just stay quiet and do what they say." Tirsen's eyes stared into his, pleading. "I no care if you die from you atonement after the ceremony. Just save my daughter."

Sólan's eyes flared as he snarled. "*I* care if I die." Before he could argue further, he was dragged to his feet once again. *Gods, Bayani. Why did you make us return?*

The cavalry guards, indifferent to his limp, led him down the temple's centre in naught but his dung-stained trousers and boots. After climbing another dozen marble steps, he was forced to his knees a second time. He groaned as his kneecap cracked again. *Dammit.*

Sólan fell forward onto his hands when the guards removed his shackles and shoved him, hard. His eyes pulsed as he glared at them from underneath his arm. Despite the near-overpowering desire to kill them, he redirected his dark powers to his broken and rebroken knee. *You are not making this easy, Ansalá. Is this your intent?* His captors backed away far enough to let Sólan crawl about the room, but close enough to restrain him if necessary.

Tirsen remained at his side as a wrinkled man approached. "That is t'e High Prophet," he explained. "He will baptise you before t'e wedding ceremony."

Sólan grumbled, "Fantastic," and with Tirsen's aid, rose to a semi-upright position on his knees. One still ached, despite its repaired bone. *Medría. The pieces were unaligned.*

The prophet slowly shuffled toward them. His gown and robes

were of a heavy wool that had been dyed red and were embellished with buttons of silver and ivory. His bony frame hunched under their weight.

'Twas the ivory that forced Sólan to take a double glance. *Odd. I thought the tusked buffalo of Garmath were wiped out thousands of years ago.* His gaze travelled up the prophet's figure, where an oversized yellow turban was tied to an engraved bronze plate by a thin red cord. A white beard twisted to the old man's waist, ending in a sharp point.

With both his hands, the prophet carried a massive pewter chalice. Filled to the brim with water, it splashed and sloshed with every step. Two more temple boys hummed and chanted as they waved large palm fronds around the old man. When the prophet stopped, the boys dropped their fans to help his weak arms lift the chalice high. "Gui suya ina suya paniran si tumbag ng Yusa," he said in a voice even more frail than his appearance.

Sólan turned an ear toward Tirsen. "What did he just say?"

"He say, 'Now you will be baptised in t'e Holy Water of Yusa.'"

"And what, exactly, is this 'holy water,' sañero?" Before the old fisherman could explain, the Áfgaliard received his answer as the chalice's contents were poured over his head in a slow and steady stream. It burned his eyes and nose—like salt. Of course. Seawater. Sólan shivered as it soaked him from head to knees, the trickle proceeding to flow past him and down the steps of the altar.

When the chalice was finally empty, the temple boys placed a heavy orange robe upon Sólan's shoulders. He slipped his arms through the sleeves and shrugged the wool into place. The prophet then bid him to stand, which he obliged with a glare. At his full height, Sólan stood more than a head taller than the old man. His pointed ears twitched at the sound of the armoured guards as they fidgeted behind him. He stifled a victorious smile as the scent of their fear reached his nostrils. *They are no fools, I see. They know to fear me.* He turned his gaze over his shoulders to watch a score of cavalry guards entering the temple in pairs. Wrapping up the rear was a bronze-armoured guard whose arm was linked with that of a small being. A light wooden mask carved and painted red into the demonic likeness of a fanged lizard with a long moustache hid his features. The heavy doors boomed shut behind him and the child he escorted.

Sólan's heart sank. He would know those sad, round eyes anywhere—they belonged to Elena Bonlak. The girl wore a formless gown of bright orange silk. Red and yellow embroidery twisted and swirled down its sleeves in no specific pattern. Her hair and the bottom half of her face were covered by a thick red veil draping down her shoulders and elbows.

A wave of nausea hit Sólan as the masked guard escorted the child up the steps. He then muttered something in her ear, and she burst into tears as he stepped away. Sólan shivered. *You have survived thus far, Sólan. Let her not fall prey like you did.* His eyes watered, so he tore them away to let them wander about the front of the temple. Against the wall stood a small wooden table with a silver chalice and an ivory bowl. A ten-pointed sun made of pounded iron and bronze was erected two metres above. The light from the setting sun shone through the myriad of high, glassless windows, illuminating the altar and bouncing bright orange hues off the monument.

The high prophet took Sólan's hand and placed within it Elena's small one. Sólan swallowed back the bile rising in his throat as he wrapped his fingers around hers, and a quiet sob escaped from behind the child's veil. The prophet ignored this and sandwiched their hands between his own, and then spoke.

Tirsen leaned over to translate into Sólan's ear. "T'e Sun," he said, "symbolise the commitment of our fleshly lives to t'e one Living God, Yusa. It symbolise the commitment you bring to each other on this day of marriage. Man and woman of sin—"

Man and child, you mean.

"—you were, husband and wife you will become."

Sólan gagged quietly.

"Each ray of t'e sun symbolise a single virtue of our body, mind, and spirit."

"How many of these virtues are there?" asked Sólan.

"Ten."

"Will he recite them all?"

"Ta."

Sólan groaned.

"The first ray is faith. It what separate us from animals and what make us more pure than any other. Without it, we can't enter Linget, the place of eternal bliss."

Pure. Hmph.

"The second is peace. It no mean lack of war, but peace among people. All relationships between people must have peace—brothers and sisters, parents and children, husbands and wives."

Tyrants and their subjects? Slavers and their masters, too? Not all relations thrive in peace.

"The third is patience. It—"

"Ha!" Sólan's outburst echoed through the temple. The sharp ring of brandished weapons filled his ears as he chuckled. "What patience have you and your people shown to me, sañero? 'Tis a dim ray of Yusa's sunlight, indeed."

"Sólan, please," said Tirsen. He grasped Sólan's robe and yanked him down to his level. "I swear to Yusa, if my daughter die because of you, I will find great joy in lighting the fire that kills you."

"And you think your flames of 'Linget' will harm me?" Sólan's glare pulsed hot enough for only Tirsen to see. He squeezed Elena's hand and asked, "What is the fourth ray of your precious idol?"

"Kindness."

Sólan's eye twitched. *Another façade of your kind.* He nodded and shrugged himself out of Tirsen's grip. His scowl melted and the prophet continued his speech with an ignorant smile. A collective sigh accompanied his words as the surrounding guards sheathed their weapons.

Tirsen cleared his throat. "Kindness it t'e act of putting others' needs before you wants. Five is purity. Yusa live in all of us that accept Him. It important to control our flesh and wait to know one another until you vows sealed in t'e oil of God. Six is joy. In all things we do for one another, it mean nothing if no joy in our hearts."

So, your apologies meant nothing. Only your threats.

"Seven is control of self. Our flesh born of evil. But if we master our flesh, we destroy the power of Yusa's enemy, Misó. Only then are we saved from Yirno. Only then can we become Yusa's children."

Some father he is. Nearly better than mine.

"Eight is goodness. Keep goodness in you heart, and the first seven rays will shine ever brighter."

Yet you murder innocent and unmarried girls who were raped. Gods, what do you do to the boys? To men who love other men, or women who love other women? Sólan shuddered at his own thoughts. Distant memories threatened darken his eyes, but he stamped them down with another prayer.

Tirsen paid him no mind as he continued his translations. "The ninth ray is gentleness. All actions we perform must come from a gentle place in our heart. When we speak, it must be soft. When we act, it must be to show t'e good of Yusa. Or else, we no better than unbelievers."

Sólan snorted. Another tense pause rang throughout the temple. "Please, continue. No need to stop on my account. I assure you that I am not leaving until after our vows."

Tirsen lowered his face and rubbed his forehead with a thumb and finger. "Yusa, bogyin ma oka ng lekes."

"Ten, Tirsen," said Sólan. "What is number ten?"

Tirsen's nostrils flared. "Love," he said through gritted teeth. He motioned to the prophet to continue speaking. The old man gave a toothy grin and obliged. "And the tenth, above all, is love. Love of Yusa. Love of our brothers and sisters. Love of our children. Without love, none of the other nine virtues can shine. If we allow t'e sun to stop shining its light, we will fall into the darkness of evil."

Sólan scratched the scruff on his chin. "Yet, 'should the light always shine, we would never grow wise in the shadow of despair.'" His gaze was intense as he looked over to Tirsen. "That saying has kept me alive since my brother's death, sañero. A small proverb from ancient Ūendevail, of all places."

Tirsen startled. "You have a family?"

"Had." Sólan raised his eyebrow. "What next? I doubt that was the end of—"

"Now, tual Sólan, you will look upon you bride and vow by t'e ten rays of Yusa's Sun. This will bind you to her, and her vows will bind her to you."

Sólan sighed with resignation. "Tell me what to say."

The prophet instructed Sólan to loosen Elena's veil just enough to reveal her face. His fingers shook as he saw her tears fall from eyes burning with unmistakable hatred. The old man, however, paid her no mind. He gripped Sólan's elbow with surprising force and said, "Suya nyokita dima di wa motahori ..."

Tirsen leaned close to translate by whisper. Sólan repeated his words with a quivering voice. "By the power of the sun, I declare that my faith in Yusa shall always be present. I will keep peace in my heart, in our union, and in our home." The words grated his ears. "I will be patient in all actions I perform and all words I speak. I vow to be kind to you and your kin, from this day until the end of my days."

He stopped. What Tirsen said next punched him too hard to repeat. *Shit. How much longer can I keep up this act?* "I ..." He cleared his throat. *You are lying to them, Sólan. Remember, you believe not in these vows.* He shook his head and grimaced. "C-could you repeat that? I missed a few words."

Tirsen obliged with a groan. "It you vow of purity, Sólan. This t'e reason we in this mess."

"I know, I know. I just ... I could not hear." A sudden longing for the caress of a woman's bosom, the feel of a man's kiss, or the warm embrace of either filled him. He needed someone to save him from the empty loneliness of his nightmares. Sólan took a deep breath and rolled his shoulders. "Right. I will remain ... pure, g-giving my body to you and you alone." The sour taste of bile filled his dry, sticky mouth. *Gods, this is wrong.*

Elena's small body shook with sobs.

Sólan stumbled over his words in his effort to end both of their discomfort. "I will bring joy in our midst. Even in anger and sadness, I will control my tongue and my flesh. I vow to always be good, helping the less fortunate." *In that, I am honest.* "I pray to Yusa" —*Damari*—"that his goodness shall overflow out of our union. With gentleness, I take you as mine for the rest of our days"—*in this wretched city*—"and I vow to love you. To love Yusa. To love the family we shall begin after today." *Never. There will be no family between us after today.*

Sólan released his upright posture with a loud exhale. He held his breath as steady waves of nausea forced his muscles to contract, breathing only when the burn in his lungs overpowered the churning of his stomach. Elena tearfully repeated the vows in her native tongue, sniffling and hiccoughing all the way to the end.

Finally, the high prophet nodded in approval. Bowing low, one of his temple boys then handed the old man an ivory bowl. He dipped his wrinkled fingertips into its oily contents and then reached for Sólan's face.

"Fuck no!" Sólan grabbed the prophet's wrist with a snarl. "Do not touch me again, putathóta." The surrounding guards brandished their weapons once again.

"It's almost over, tual. I promise," said Tirsen. The panic in his voice was palpable. "You vows still need to be sealed with Yusa's oil."

Sólan bared his fangs as he glared at the prophet. He savoured the fear in the old man's eyes—it was, for a moment, more invigorating than his desire to save Elena or even his hatred of Tirsen.

Elena coughed through her sobs. *Medría. What am I doing?* Sólan released the prophet's arm but maintained his scowl. Again, the old man reached up to draw a ten-pointed star on the groom's forehead. The temple boys removed the bowl from his hand as he repeated the drawing on the bride.

"Now, is the sacrament."

"¿Mondé?"

Tirsen drew a sharp breath. "You each will sip from t'e Holy Cup of Yusa. If He bless you marriage, you will be fruitful. If not, you both burn alive, sending you souls to Yirno—the realm of eternal suffering."

Sólan's eyes widened as he slowly turned his head toward Tirsen. "What the fuck kind of sacrament is this? Blood?"

A tap on his forearm snapped his attention back to the old man, who was holding a silver chalice full of a dark liquid. Reluctantly,

Sólan lowered his face to sip. The strong, vanilla-like taste of cane rum filled his mouth. He savoured the tingle on his lips and the burn in his throat. *Gods, that is good.*

Elena, however, cared not for the strong liquor. Her body heaved as the sacrament hit her tongue. Tirsen and Sólan both stiffened as she struggled and held her breath. After a long moment, she finally swallowed. Her face contorted and twitched at the stinging aftertaste, but she managed to keep it down.

The prophet set the chalice down and lifted his arms. He bared his yellowed teeth in a joyous smile and bellowed, "Calomot i Yusa!"

Tirsen and the surrounded guards all shouted back in chorus, "Calomot i Yusa!" *Thanks to Yusa!*

Sólan leaned down to Elena's level and wiped a tear from her cheek. "I am so sorry for this, Elena. I promise I will never harm you."

Elena's face hardened into a mask of malice. "You already have, kapiret-liho."

12

THE FACE OF DEATH

*T*he boy dropped to his knees, desperate to free his wrist from the sweaty grip of an oversized man. "Átha! Please, Father. Please!"

A second man leaned against the brick oven's wall and wiped his flour-covered hands on his white apron. "I am not your átha, mastázo." He stuffed a carved bone pipe with dried apyin flower bud and lit it with a kindled reed. He took a long drag and coughed as the pungent smoke filled his lungs. "Medría, Hidalgo," he said to the boy's captor. "Where did you get this shit? The butcher's ass?"

"That's not mine, baker, remember?" The man replied, shoving a fat hand over the boy's mouth to muffle his screams. "It's Orovite, not Taela."

"Ah. I see." The baker lit his reed again and took another effortful drag from his pipe. "Still better than none, I suppose."

The boy bit Hidalgo, drawing crimson blood with his fangs. He kicked, pulled, and sobbed. "No! I will not—"

"Silence, mastázo!" Hidalgo punched the boy with his bleeding fist. "They will hear you."

The baker waved his hand lazily. "Aeh. They care not, so long as you pay them well enough."

A bright red welt expanded under the boy's eye. He shook his head to gather himself before struggling to free himself once more. "You promised, Hidalgo. You promised."

Hidalgo growled and tightened his grip. With his other hand, he wiped his thin black hair from his sooty brow before shoving a dirty rag into the boy's mouth, chuckling. "Shit. You were telling me the truth. This one is a fighter."

The baker grinned and tapped the spent apyin from his pipe. "You will wish you had started him earlier. He surrenders much more easily now."

Hidalgo raised an eyebrow. "Does he? That is a shame. I enjoy it when they squirm." He grabbed a chunk of the boy's dark brown hair and yanked it back to see his face. "You hear that, mastázo? That is your job." The boy's eyes flooded with hot tears. "Gods, do his eyes sparkle. He's prettier than that girl I sold back in Casaca."

"Ha!" The baker reached over the wood countertop and kneaded a ball of leavened dough. "I don't intend to sell him just yet. He turns nine at the end of the season. Hardly worth half his weight in copper until his voice drops."

Hidalgo snorted. "By then, he will be a fine blacksmith as well. So long as I can keep my hands off him, that is." He licked his lips and caressed the boy's head. "You hear that, you little halfbreed? I will make you the finest blacksmith of Ciudelago"—his smile melted into a scowl—"but only if you please me. You are an expensive apprentice, Sólan de Ciudelago. Very expensive."

He stroked the boy's cheek with his knuckle before plopping a musty linen bag over his head. Young Sólan coughed and wheezed as he inhaled a puff of stale flour.

"The storage," said the muffled voice of the baker. "No one will hear you in there."

The boy felt himself being slung over Hidalgo's shoulder and carried off to the back of the bakery. He kicked and sobbed, fighting with what little strength his eight-year-old body had.

"Now then," said Hidalgo. He dropped the boy onto a large sack of grain and removed the bag from his head. "Let's see if you really *are* worth all that gold I spent on you."

SÓLAN AWOKE WITH A GASP. HIS FOREHEAD DRIPPED WITH COLD SWEAT as his heart pounded in his throat. He held his breath to stifle a sob as the images faded from behind his eyes. Three hundred years had passed since he last suffered such nightmares—memories, rather—yet this one just as vivid, haunting, and true as they'd always been. *Damn you, Tirsen. You should have run, not forced me onto your daughter.*

He looked over to the empty pile of blankets beside him. Sitting upright, he took a ragged breath and rubbed his eyes with the heels of his hands. When Tirsen had given him and Elena a private room for their "consummation," Sólan had begged Elena to run away from Bansungei. He had begged her to nullify the marriage. She had refused to run, of course, and Sólan had refused to touch her. As a victim himself, he had sworn long ago to never touch a child in like manner. He had held onto that promise. He'd argued with his bride … but what good was arguing with an indoctrinated child? After all, the younger the child, the stronger their faith in anything.

The sound of a blade being unsheathed rang in his ears. He straightened his posture and slid his hand beneath his pillow. His ears twitched and his eyes narrowed as he scanned the room for his impending assailant, his fingers wrapped around the handle of his own weapon.

A low grunt and the flash of thin metal came from his side. Sólan blocked the blow and jumped to his feet. Adrenaline pulsed through his tensed muscles as he turned and shuffled, searching the darkness. *Gods-damned elves.*

Suddenly, a sharp pain tore into his back and through his chest. He sandwiched the rapier-like blade between the heels of his hands, his hatchet falling to the ground with a thud.

He glanced down and stomped, feeling the gratifying crunch of his attacker's toes as they shattered beneath his foot. He threw an elbow, expecting a jab into the ribs, and was rewarded with a satisfying grunt from behind. *Not an elf. An oddling, perhaps?* No more time to think—the shadow had kneeled to pick up the dropped hatchet.

Sólan kicked, hard. His assailant's head snapped sideways and hit the doorframe with a sickening crunch. The rapier's blade still pierced his ribs as he reached behind his back for the hilt. *Jidir.* Warm blood oozed down his torso in identical rivers from each break in his skin. The taste of metal and salt filled his mouth, and he fell to his knees with a thump. He was dying, and he couldn't reach the weapon that was slowly killing him.

The door banged into the wall as it swung open. "What happen—no! How could you?"

Sólan directed his wavering gaze onto the newcomer. "¿Mondé?" He coughed, blood frothing out of his mouth.

The intruder dropped to the ground and wailed. "Kapiret-liho! You monster of Misó!"

Sólan's vision focused just long enough for him to see … *No!* "Tirsen … please … forgive me," he said through gargles. "I knew not … knew not."

Tirsen brought the small body to his chest and wept. "My daughter! Elenaaa!" He rocked her and sobbed, nearly drowning from his watery eyes and nose.

"Don't, Tirsen …" Sólan's teeth chattered. The pools of blood around him continued to grow, his shirt and trousers more red than white. He shivered as death loomed close, even as his chest ached and throbbed from The Dark within. Pain radiated down his arm, up his neck and around his jaw. "Make it quick. Please …"

Tirsen glared at Sólan. "You will suffer. I swear on t'e Sun of Yusa, your soul be damned!" The old fisherman rose to his feet awkwardly, still clutching his daughter's body to his chest. But as he took a halting step forward, his throat was suddenly split open. It spewed across the room, covering the little part of Sólan yet unstained in Tirsen's blood.

Medría. "Are … are you here to … kill me, too?"

"No. I hear to save you, tulalo."

Sólan moaned at the familiar voice. "Please kill me, Bayani. I refuse to—"

"Dammit, Sólan! We need to run." Bayani shuffled through the sticky puddles and grasped the rapier's hilt. "Pantot. She almost pierce you heart."

"I know that!" Sólan's outburst sent him into another coughing spell, causing more blood and froth to ooze from him. "Just get this fucking sword out of me."

"I'm trying!" Bayani struggled to hold his hands steady as he inched the blade out of Sólan's flesh.

Centimetre by agonising centimetre, Bayani pulled while Sólan screamed. His powers flared as he stitched his arteries and lungs back together, but the pain, exhaustion, and loss of blood all united against him. "Bayani," he whispered. "I think"— his eyes rolled back, and he fell with a thud.

13

DANCING WITH TYRANNY

*T*he door to Prastömin's Great Hall swung open with an echoing bang. The rattle of chains and the thumps of boots bounced off the polished and marbled granite floor as Naoise led a disheveled Brennan toward the throne.

Diarmuid paid them no mind as a potato farmer from the eastern province pleaded his case against the lord over his lands. "Please, y'r grace. 'E's taken so mooch, we'll starve coomb wintar."

The king held up a hand and nodded. "I understand your predicament, good farmer. I shall see to it that a master knight and two score of lowers go back with you to investigate. Thank you for bringing this to my attention. Next!"

Naoise tightened his grip on Brennan's chains. *He's in a forgiving mood today.*

"Oh, thank tha Wizards, y'r grace! Thank ya!" The farmer clasped his hands together and bowed low before shuffling toward the exit.

Another farmer—a wheat grower from the southern province—stepped forward. Naoise, however, cleared his throat before the elf could speak.

Diarmuid snapped his attention to the knight and dotaire, stiffening at the sight of Brennan's chains.

Naoise gulped as a flash of horror danced across the king's evergreen eyes. *Shite.* Taking a breath, he pushed all emotion to the back of his mind and flattened his expression. "Apologies f'r the intrusion, y'r grace. This requires your prompt attention."

The king's lip quivered as he looked to his most recent messenger girl—concubine, really—and shouted his orders. "Girl! Go fetch the queen!" The woman nodded in silence and sprinted out of the hall. Diarmuid turned his gaze back to Brennan, his face pale and stiff. "Is ... Alsantör ... is he dead?"

A smattering of nobles and servants loitering in the hall gasped.

"Likely," said Brennan.

Naoise jabbed his ringed thumb into Brennan's flank and said, "Nai, y'r grace. The prince still lives."

Diarmuid slumped his shoulders with a heavy exhale. "Thank the Wizards." He rubbed his temples with his hands. "Why are you here, Brennan?"

"Ask your first knight, since he's the one who put me in these Gnomes-damned chains," Brennan snarled, baring his fangs.

"I did not ask *who* shackled you. I asked *why*." Diarmuid's eyes narrowed. "Why did my first knight bring you before me, as a criminal?"

"This bloody *Veer* seems to think that festered blood and fever can be healed over mere hours!"

"May I remind you, this 'bloody Veer' is the man whose word stands between you and the axe block?"

Brennan snapped his mouth shut and gulped.

Diarmuid stood, his heavy green robes trailing behind him as he descended the half-dozen marble steps. He loomed over the cowering Brennan and snarled. "Tell me, why are you here?" Each word stabbed like a thorn from a thistle.

"The ... ehm ... His Grace—"

"Sir Naoise!" Diarmuid snapped his attention to Brennan's captor. "What happened?"

Gnomes be merciful, he's impatient. "His Grace suffered a convulsion from his fever," said Naoise. "Brennan, however, was absent from the room when—"

"Lies!" Brennan's cheeks grew bright red, his eyes wild and his mouth twisted. "Fuck you and your brother!"

Diarmuid backhanded Brennan with a force that sent him to the ground. "Another outburst like that, and I'll relieve you of your head. Lord Knight Giaven, Gnomes rest his soul, was a *hero* to this forest!"

The sharp clack of women's shoes echoed throughout the room, emanating from its western entrance. All eyes averted to Ethna as she rushed into the hall with Rhona trailing close behind. The queen's eyes were red and puffy, the sure sign of duress.

Brennan grumbled. Naoise, however, bowed at his waist. He gave Rhona a subtle glance before standing upright and addressing the queen. "Y'r grace. Apologies for the intrusion on y'r—"

"Where is Alsantör?" Ethna's voice pierced the air like a Nethuanian rapier.

"Still in the north wing infirm'ry," said Naoise. "Dotaire Aiden has taken over his care." In his periphery, he watched Rhona close her eyes and soften her posture. "His fever broke shortly after sunrise."

King and queen visibly relaxed. Ethna raced to Diarmuid and embraced him. Poorly stifled gasps bounced off the granite walls at this rare display of affection, and Naoise exchanged a curious glance with Rhona.

The queen stepped away from her husband to wipe away a tear with her finger. She turned to the shackled elf and said, "It's a shame, Dotaire Brennan, that you couldn't do the same for my son before he convulsed." Her tone burned like molten steel. "If I hadn't sent my handmaiden to spy, perhaps we would be planning his *funeral*."

A dark scowl etched across Brennan's face. "Your handmaiden is a harlot. She shoved me as I was treating him. Pushed me against the wall and—"

"Silence!" Diarmuid's voice was guttural. The force of his outburst shook even the gold-embellished oil lamps that dotted the hall's columns and walls. He turned his attention to Naoise, who stiffened. "Are you certain, Sir Naoise, that you have the correct elf in chains? Maid Rhona is not a dotaire, is she?"

Naoise took a breath to respond, but the sharp icicles of a Karthi lord's voice cut in.

"If I may intervene, yer grace." The startled crowd turned its attention to a dark corner as Duke Jannon stepped into the light. He wore a simple white tunic under a blue jerkin, embroidered with white thread and studded with silver buttons. His dark grey breeches were formfitting and tucked into his matching leather boots.

"The Lady Rhona is a well-known pupil of her late father, Dotaire Frasier of central Karthénos."

Rhona blushed and looked to her feet, pressing her lips together.

Diarmuid rubbed his forehead and sighed. "Jannon, she's not a lady. She's the handmaiden of the queen."

Jannon cocked his head with a single raised eyebrow.

"And you're not of the royal council," the king continued.

The Karthi snorted. "Perhaps not." He took slow, methodical steps toward the centre aisle made of green marble. His gaze never broke from Rhona during his approach. "However, am I not yer closest ally? Yer friend?" His icy voice cracked beneath the weight of that last word. "Rhona is of Karthi blood. I am within me rights as the laird of the tundra to defend those who were born north of our shared border." He finally moved his eyes to Diarmuid. "Perhaps 'tis time for her to speak?"

Diarmuid's nose twitched in threat of a snarl as a fog began to form at the edges of his pupils.

Shite! His demons're wakin' up. "I was witness, y'r grace." Naoise's voice was weak, but his word stopped the fog from covering the whole of the king's gaze. "After Alsantör's convulsion, Brennan shoved a dirty, wet cloth into his throat. After, of course, he pulled the handmaiden into himself by her hair." Naoise continued.

Ethna's face contorted as her features grew pale. "He what!" She burst forward and slapped the prisoner. The force nearly sent him back to his knees, but he recovered.

"Calm, Ethna," said Diarmuid. "Let the dotaire defend himself."

"It's true, yer grace," said Rhona.

A pale green malice burned in her eyes as she took a step closer. Or was that a faint glow? Naoise blinked, but it disappeared before he could confirm anything.

"And, he attempted to strike me and Sir Naoise during his arrest," the handmaiden continued.

More gasps ricocheted throughout the hall. Diarmuid studied the trembling dotaire before him as Naoise simply nodded in agreement. "I need no further evidence," whispered Diarmuid. He turned to Jannon and nodded. "I accept your defence on behalf of Maid Rhona, friend."

Jannon gave a shallow bow and stepped back toward the shadowed wall. "I thank ye, friend."

"As for you, Brennan, son of Bowen, I hereby strip you of your title as dotaire, and I sentence you to seventy-five lashes at sundown."

Brennan squealed in protest, but Naoise yanked on his chains and kicked his knee. The force sent him to the ground.

The king continued, "You will spend your nights in the eastern corridor of the dungeons until Alsantör makes a full recovery from your ignorance and pride. Should he die, however, your head will be mine."

Rhona sat impatiently, watching Ethna shake as she pruned her summer roses. Most days, the queen could garden them with little more than a single prick or superficial scratch from their thorns. Today, however, her hands and forearms bled.

"Káil." Ethna hissed and sucked the pad of her thumb.

Rhona sighed and rose to her feet, placing her basket on the flagstone pathway. "Here. Let me see."

"No, no. I don't need your *skills*. It's just a small puncture."

"That's not what I'm reaching for, Ethna." Rhona snatched the pruning shears from the queen's hand. "Talk to me."

A tear trickled down Ethna's cheek. "You're too kind to me."

"Please." Rhona went to work trimming the dead stems and rose hips off the chest-high bushes. She tossed the hips into her basket. "Ye're the queen, and I'm yer servant. Our friendship is just a happy coincidence."

Ethna snorted. "You do much more than what's required for your role. I don't force my appreciation."

Rhona smirked over her shoulder. "I didn't say our friendship was forced. Just lucky."

"Still." Ethna looked to her feet and rubbed her toe against the pathway's pink stone. After a moment, a small rose hip bounced off her forehead and into the basket.

Rhona grinned at the queen's failed attempt at a glare.

"You *dare* strike your queen with such weapon?" Ethna said through giggles.

"Eil, yer grace. I have committed such a terrible crime, haven't I?"

"That you have, dear. That you have." Stooping, Ethna picked up another of the round red bulbs and rolled it in her palm. "And you shall be punished accordingly." She threw the tiny projectile at Rhona. It hit the handmaiden's chest and tumbled down the front of her dress.

The women burst into laughter as Rhona squirmed and bounced, Ethna stepping forward seductively.

Rhona braced for her kiss as an icy voice cleared its throat behind them. They ceased their laughter to face the newcomer.

"You're still here," said Ethna, her smile disappearing into a scowl. "I thought you'd be halfway to that frozen wasteland you call home by now."

Jannon gave a shallow bow. "To leave for that 'frozen wasteland' without bidding farewell would be quite impolite. Nearly a crime against Victornia the Hospitable, Queen of the Wizards."

Words of honey from the voice of lemon peel, thought Rhona.

"Farewell, Jannon." Ethna's curt voice stung, and her eyes glistened with emerald hatred. Eyes that had shone with lust mere moments before.

"Not one fer niceties, I see. Never have been." Jannon gave a flat smile and turned to her companion. "Maid Rhona. I also bid ye farewell. If not for yer training in Karthénos, Alsantör would likely be dead."

Rhona's mouth twitched. *Ye pandering son of a sprite.* "I cannot thank ye enough, me laird, for yer help in Brennan's ... 'trial'." She clenched her teeth and stepped behind the queen.

"I suppose I should pray to the Gnomes to protect you on the journey home," said Ethna. "Safe travels, Jannon."

A coy smile danced across Jannon's thin lips. "I suppose I could ask no more than that. Perhaps I should pray to both the Wizards *and* the Gnomes for yer son's recovery ... or swift justice on Brennan." He bowed again, turning on his heel to plod toward the stables.

The women scowled after the Karthi duke. "That fucking bastard," sighed Ethna.

Eil, thought Rhona. *And far more "Grim" than his own.*

R<small>HONA SNEAKED THROUGH THE HEDGE LABYRINTH AS SHE DID NEARLY</small> every night in the summer—at least, every night when she *didn't* sneak to the stables for a moonlit ride through the forest. Her silk slippers made no sound as she tiptoed onto the smooth flagstones she knew so well. She reached the middle of the labyrinth, stepping into the clearing under the waning half-moon, and stiffened. On one of the stone benches sat an elf, his back turned toward her.

Even in the dull light of night, she knew Naoise's slightly crooked frame. Prasti dotaires blamed it on a curse from his father's treason. Rhona, however, assumed 'twas simply his archery. He was, after all, the best marksman in all of Prastömin, thanks to his Veerish blood. She cleared her throat to announce her presence. In acknowledgement, Naoise merely glanced over his shoulder. A shallow smile curled Rhona's mouth as she approached. "Ye should be in the keep, resting. The new academy recruits start on the morrow."

Naoise snorted. "And you should be keepin' the queen warm, bein' her handmaiden and all. Yet, here we are."

Rhona's grin crept up to her eyes. "Here we are, indeed." She shivered and pulled her dusky blue cloak around herself. "This seat taken?"

"Nai. Always reserved for you 'r Tör."

Rhona sat on the bench and placed her head on Naoise's shoulder. "Ye've been weeping again, friend."

"Eil. I have." Naoise wrapped an arm around her back and rubbed her shoulder. "Didn't want the king to hear, since Tör's snoring's not echoing through the hall."

"Ha!" Rhona clamped her hand over her mouth to stifle the rest of her laughter. "Gnomes, I can't sleep without it."

"At least you're across the damned corridor. I share a wall with the fooker."

Rhona's snickers continued, but Naoise's face grew solemn. A sniffle and a shaky breath brought her amusement to a halt. "Talk to me, Neesh. Ye've seen too much damned loss these days."

Naoise shook his head. "I'll be fine, Rhona. I *am* fine. Just needed some air to keep from cr—"

"Dammit, Naoise, it's okay to cry. Ye're no less of a man fer it!"

"I feel like it, though." Naoise squeezed his eyes shut. "Losin' more and more of myself every day. More of my family ... my hope." He hiccoughed. "Shite. I'm the last of Vaiorsen. The last of my kin ... last of the mountain elves." A barn owl screeched in the distance as though in weeping. The knight's mossy brown eyes glistened in the moonlight. "Ah dinnae ken what I'd do if I lost Tör, too."

Shit! "Naoise, ye're not thinking of ..."

"No, no. Not yet. I'm just a bit hopeless." Naoise rubbed his face and sniffled. "I'm safe from myself, I promise."

Rhona pursed her lips. "Have ye considered taking the—"

"No," said Naoise. A sharp scowl cut across his forehead. "Ya ken I woen't too."

"Why not? What are ye afraid of?"

"I've already lost too much, as you've said. I can't lose myself, too."

"But—"

"But nothing, Rhona," Naoise snarled. "I refuse to medicate f'r this. I can handle losing what I have. Just …" He sniffed, grabbing his hair with both hands.

Just what? Let ye drink and fuck yer way into a grave? "I worry, that's all," said Rhona.

Naoise's lip trembled, and tears fell down his face in a steady stream. "Ah ken," he whispered. "Y've every right to."

Embracing each other, the knight buried his face into the handmaiden's shoulder and shook with his sobs.

There you are. Let it out yer bottle. "I won't let him die, Neesh. I promise."

14

FORBIDDEN

The morning sunlight filtered through the trees and illuminated the small room in the infirmary, the window's thin white drapes to glowing a soft yellow. Rhona's pale green eyes glistened as she smiled at the dotaire sleeping by his patient's bedside. She held a basket of bread, cheese, and salt-cured pork in the crook of her elbow. "Good morrow, Aiden."

The dotaire startled and sat up with a jump. His thick but straight hair stuck out in nigh every direction but down. "G-good morrow," he said, wiping the drool from his mouth.

Rhona winked. "It's fine. I won't tell anyone." She placed the basket on the bedside table. "How is he?"

"Better. Much better." Aiden yawned and rubbed the sleep from his eyes. "The coriander oil's kept his-his fever at bay, and the boiled honey seems to've m-m-melted away the last of the pestilence. If we can prevent it from-from festering again, the wound shouldn't take any longer than half a season to heal."

"That deep, eh?" Rhona scrunched her nose. "Won't be easy to keep clean, will it?"

"'Fraid not, M-maid Rhona." Aiden yawned again and dragged

himself to his feet. "Would it be alright f'r me to-to start the morning rounds? Since Brennan's gone, and … well."

Rhona snickered. "Ye don't need to ask me permission. I'm not even a dotaire." She motioned to the basket with a warm smile. "Take this. A gift from her grace."

"Gnomes, thank her for us. That bread smells divine." Aiden stooped to snatch the basked before he turned toward the door.

"One more question—has he awakened yet?" Rhona's heart thumped in her throat.

"No, I'm afraid not." Aiden looked over his shoulder with a frown. "I'm unsure of the delay. I hope it's not residual from the convulsion."

Rhona winced. "Wizards, that would be cruel." She glanced at Alsantör. His eyelids twitched as though they'd just opened. *You stupid fucker.* "Go, Aiden. Ye've other elves to tend."

"Thank you, Maid Rhona." Aiden shuffled out of the room, allowing the heavy door to close with a thud. His clunky footsteps soon faded into silence.

"Dammit, Tör," said Rhona. She turned to the cot and crossed her arms.

The prince opened one eye and held a finger to his lips. "Shh. I'm sleeping."

Rhona rolled her eyes. "Then ye'd be snoring."

Alsantör rolled onto his side and propped his head on his knuckles. "I don't snore, do I?"

"Wizards be good. Ye're a conniving prick at times. Did ye know that?"

"Ha!" Alsantör's laughter sent him into a coughing spell and painful groaning. "Káil. Why do I hurt to breathe?"

"Ye haven't moved in days, and've had an arrow in yer back since … Gnomes know when."

"Hmph." Alsantör struggled to sit upright, only to fall back into a fit of coughing. He panted with the effort.

Rhona grasped his hand and helped him straighten.

"Bloody hell."

"Well, ye're awake. I suppose I should go fetch the queen."

"Fuck that." Alsantör tightened his grip on her hand. "If she didn't come to see me at my worst, she can wait a few moments more."

A coy smile danced across Rhona's mouth. "Well, ye've commanded me, yer grace."

Alsantör sucked the back of his teeth with a look of distaste. "I hate it when ya call me that. I'm not—"

"Not a graceful being, and I've got no one to perform for in here." Rhona curtsied in play as the prince snickered. She sat next to him on the bed. "This seat taken?"

"Never." Alsantör reached up to brush aside a wisp of black hair from her face. "You're blushing," he said, his hand nestling in the crook of her neck.

Rhona closed her eyes and nuzzled his hand. "Ye always make me blush."

Without warning, Alsantör's mouth pressed against hers.

She instantly pushed him away. "What the hell, Tör? Ye know we can't do this. And did ye forget? Yer royal blood doesn't preclude ye from consent." She crossed her arms with a huff.

Alsantör looked to his lap with pursed lips and a bright red face. "I'm sorry. Ah ken." He reached over and cupped her elbow. "I won't do it again. I swear."

"I swore an oath," said Rhona. "An oath to yer mother. Besides, she was in dire need of me *services* last night. Do ye understand the strangeness of be a queen's concubine, then falling in love with her son?" *Káil, does it ache to deny ye so.*

"I know, Rhona." Alsantör's hand now rubbed up her arm and shoulder. "It's just … of all the women in the Eastern Lands, it has to be you."

Rhona quivered, a dull burn pulsing through her eyes. "Of all the men …" She relaxed her arms and leaned into his touch, closing her eyelids as the burn behind them flashed intensely. "Oh, fuck it all." She pulled his face toward hers and whispered, "Kiss me again."

Alsantör obliged passionately. With one hand, he tangled his fingers into the base of her braid. He wrapped his other around her and pulled her close to him, her chest pressed against his, all the while exploring her mouth with his tongue.

The handmaiden adjusted herself onto his lap and felt his erection as it pressed against her with desire. They kissed more deeply. Her womanhood tingled as it swelled and moistened. Slowly, she lost control of her hips as they rocked back and forth, grinding on Alsantör.

The prince's lips and nose traced down Rhona's delicate jawline to her neck and collarbone. The featherlike sensation of his breath on her skin made her shiver. Reaching behind, she guided his hand to the hem of her dress. *Gnomes, Tör.* His calloused hand trailed up her thigh and rested on the cusp of her entrance. "Ye tease me," she whispered.

Alsantör removed his face from her chest and smiled. "As do you." He inserted one, then two, fingers inside her.

She gasped, squirming as he massaged her and pressed his thumb against her bud. Reaching under the sheet, she clasped his erection with a tight grip. He grunted, his hips moving with hers as she stroked and fondled.

"*Wizards*, Rhona."

"Shh." Their mouths met again, the hunger between them tenfold. Finally, Rhona whimpered, and her writhing peaked as she climaxed against Alsantör's hand.

He removed his hand to steady himself. "More?" his evergreen eyes pulsed with unmistakable lust.

"Eil, more." Rhona's movements continued, even as Alsantör teased her opening with the tip of his manhood. "Damn you, Tör." She growled, settling herself on top of him.

He filled her completely with a thrust, her pressure filling once again. She clenched her teeth and stiffened. Her hips, however, betrayed her.

Alsantör's breathing accelerated as his movements grew more forceful. 'Twas nigh as though he'd forgotten his wounds when—

"I see y're feeling much better, y'r grace."

Rhona gasped and Alsantör yelped. They separated at once, their faces pale as they looked to the newcomer.

Oh, thank the Wizards.

Naoise leaned against the doorway with his arms crossed, barely able to control his snickering. "Shite, you two. At least be subtle." He closed the door behind him and plopped onto the bedside stool. "You should thank both the Wizards and the Gnomes the queen didn't catch ya. She's on her way."

"She's *what*!" said Alsantör.

Rhona trembled. "Shit. She's gonna—"

"Eil, Rhona," said Naoise. "She'd be all up to high doh if she found out." He cocked his head and winked. "So, fix y'r hair. You look like ya just fooked a prince."

Rhona pressed her lips together and unravelled her braid. "Where is she now?"

"Not too close. If ya catch her at the door, you can tell her Tör's awake. It might look as though 'twas recent."

Alsantör scrunched his nose. "I need to talk to my father, not Maela."

"Fookin' hell. Ya doen't need to talk to *either* of them in y'r state."

Rhona rolled her eyes at them both. "Yer mother's been worried sick."

"And you still need to rest," said Naoise to the prince. "You're in no condition to rush back into your duties."

"He'll be fine." Rhona tied the end of her new braid and straightened her posture. "I told ye, Neesh that I wouldn't let him die."

Alsantör hung his head with a sigh as Naoise snorted. "Dammit, Rhona," said the knight. "It's dangerous to do that. 'Specially during this damned crusade."

"No more dangerous than what the Taelas are preparing," said Alsantör. "They're breeding western giants with elves."

His companions froze, Rhona's heartbeat again in her throat. *There's only one purpose for that kind of power.* "I'll fetch the queen."

Naoise nodded. "'Nd I the king."

15

SMUGGLER'S BANE

*B*ayani dragged Sólan's body through a labyrinth of tunnels that ran parallel to the sewers, the stench of which seeped its way through his sinuses and throat. *Pantot!* the fisherman thought. *You weigh more than barrel of rum.* He tripped, dropping the Áfgaliard on his back with a thud.

Sólan grunted awake. "What the f—"

"Shh!" Bayani clamped a hand over Sólan's mouth. "We right below the temple."

Sólan shoved Bayani off him. "Where the hell are we?" he whispered.

Oh, Yusa, save me. "I just tell you. Below t'e temple. Where the High Prophet live."

"And where are you taking me?"

Stupid fucking Áfgaliard. Bayani dared not to verbalise his thoughts—'twould be suicide.

"Well?"

Bayani flared his nostrils and rubbed his forehead. "Where you t'ink, tulalo?"

"Medría." Sólan got to his feet with a grimace. "Have you

already forgotten how I feel about that gods-damned pirate?" He spat the last word out like a bitter poison on his tongue.

"He no monster like you say he is, Sólan. Like you, stories of him are stories, not truth. So, will you come with me or not?"

"How about I kill you and find my own way out?"

"Really?" Bayani stared hard into Sólan's amber gaze with mild amusement. "*More* threats? You no have killed me yet, and I no think you will now."

Sólan's eyes narrowed. "Fine."

"Fine. Follow me." Bayani knocked his shoulder into Sólan's chest as he walked by. To his dismay, however, the halfbreed stopped him once again.

"Before I do, however, I need you to tell me something."

Oh, Yusa's grace. What now?

"You have made quite clear these last moons your distaste for me and my kind. Why help me? Why now?"

Bayani clamped his mouth shut. "I don't know, kapiret-liho," he said through clenched teeth. *Perhaps you just like my dead brother? Perhaps I see t'e good in you? Respect you as slave scout and for trying to help Elena and Tala?* "Maybe I just want you out of Bansungei?"

Sólan furrowed his brow and looked Bayani over. "I see."

"Can we go to *Silent Dancer*, now? I tired of talking."

A dirty look cut across Sólan's face faster than Bayani could blink. "I have no desire to smuggle that stinking flower bud, nor that sticky oil of The Dark."

A chill breeze bit through Bayani's clothes. *You control t'e air, too?* "Neither do I," he croaked. "But here we are." He puffed up his chest to stifle the shiver ricocheting throughout his body. "You mouth will get you killed."

"My mouth has saved my life many times, pundijo," said Sólan. "What has yours done for you?"

"It done enough for me." Without another word, Bayani spun on his heel and led Sólan through the sparsely lit tunnel. Echoes of dripping water and the humming from commotion above them filled Bayani's ears. The occasional thud of loaded crates being dropped above made him flinch.

"So how do you do it?" said Sólan.

Bayani stiffened. "Do what?"

"Smuggle such fragrant herb into the city. Surely even this 'Cavalry of Yusa' would know 'tis no dead skunk every time you walk by."

"Where you t'ink we are, Sólan? Look around. *Smell* around."

The colour drained from Sólan's face. He wheezed, heaving, and held his breath.

To stifle the bubbling laughter in his chest, Bayani also held his breath. He failed. "You should see you face, kapiret-liho! Oh, Yusa. It never get old. I bet I look t'e same the first time Kala—"

"You giggle like a fucking apyin whore," said Sólan, growling.

"And you angry like kabotay beggar!"

"I have no need for either." Sólan grasped the front of Bayani's shirt and pulled him close. "I am already tormented enough by the spirits of The Dark. Lead the way or leave. I care not."

MOMENTS OF DARKNESS AND SILENCE SLITHERED BY AS THE MEN TIPTOED through the tunnels. The further they walked, the narrower the corridor became. Even the dull light of the oil lanterns failed to reach this portion of the passage.

Sweat dripped down Sólan's face at the increased effort of crouching and crawling. *Gods, I should have gone back home.* "How much further?" he whispered.

"Not far."

Sólan sighed. *Not far. Common words for 'further than desired.'* "If I am going to be stuck with you for the foreseeable future, perhaps we should get to know one another?"

Bayani stopped and glared over his shoulder.

"How long have you been indebted to Kadek?"

"You no stuck to me much longer. And is no you business how I meet Kadek." He mumbled something in his own tongue as he started moving again.

"Dosilpas de pruganteni, pundijo," Sólan muttered. *Apologies for asking, asshole.*

Bayani stopped again and slumped his shoulders. "Nine years. When Elena was baby."

"Fifteen is young, even for mortal men," said Sólan. "Why did you do it? Why did you swear ten years to Kadek?"

A faint sniffle came from Bayani's nose as he plopped into a seated position on the ground. "It no was Kadek. It was Dakil who help me. Kadek only know me by promise, not by reason."

"That does not answer my question, sañero."

The still air grew stale, the rustling from Bayani's bouncing knee the only thing keeping the silence at bay. "Love. Being brave. Whatever you like to say." His breath quivered.

Sólan swallowed the lump that threatened to swell in his throat. "Love," he whispered. "Or stupidity." He shook out the unsettling memories that tried to creep into his head. "A thing I have been blessed to avoid since my family's death three hundred years ago."

Bayani shrugged. "Blessed? Or cursed? I would rather love Tala and try to help her, t'an not know her."

"Hmph." Sólan shifted his weight and fidgeted before he placed a tentative hand on Bayani's shoulder. "Well … aeh … I apologise for being so harsh. But we need to get moving. I do poorly in such close quarters."

"For what point? I do all t'is for nothing. For promise I fail to keep."

"You have kept your promise to them. You promised to free them from the tyranny of Yusa—to end their suffering. I would like to think death is that freedom. They suffer no longer."

Another sniffle. "You no helping."

Of course not. "Look, I—"

"But we should move. Kadek expecting me."

Sólan scrunched his nose at the name. "Right. Lead the way, I suppose."

Another kilometre passed, and the oddling-sized tunnel opened onto a corridor that reeked of sewage and mildew. Sólan gagged as the stench seeped into his gullet. To his left, more oil lanterns lined the tunnel's path, illuminating the packed dirt trail and rough-hewn wall they followed. He shuddered at the sight of what lay to his right — a deep creek of piss, excrement, and dirty bathwater slopping and flowing from the slums above them. He swallowed the sour tasted of bile and belched.

The passageway suddenly widened into a massive chamber in which multiple streams of waste converged, leaving Sólan no choice but to collapse to his knees and vomit.

Bayani rolled his eyes. "You over-drama. I thought you fearsome killer."

"Blood and violence, I can do. Even torture," said Sólan between heaves. "But this? Please tell me we are close."

"Ta." Bayani pointed with his lips. "Up t'e stairs."

Stairs? Sólan's eyes flitted around each corridor's entrance, stopping at the far side of the chamber. *Oh, thank the Gods!* He and Bayani rushed up the steps towards a small door, bursting through it with relief.

The sun assaulted Sólan's eyes and made him sneeze. Bayani fared little better. After three—no, four—involuntary expulsions of air from that indionta's mouth, Sólan's nerves were sufficiently frayed. "Where are we?" he said curtly.

Bayani remained silent.

"Pundijo"—he smacked the young smuggler on the back of his head—"where the hell are we?"

"Shh!" Bayani motioned south with his eyebrows.

Sólan took in a sharp breath as recognised the hidden estuary he'd seen from the rooftops of Bansungei. A deep and narrow channel cut through it in a dark turquoise that contrasted with the dull brown crags and bright blue shallows flanking it on either side. Metres downstream sat the *Silent Dancer*. Her red, battened sails folded in accordions to the tops of five masts. Salt-proofed teak encompassed the hull, its blemishes caulked with ground lime and dry oil.

The loud scratch of a boat being landed snapped the Áfgaliard's attention to his right. Bayani was helping a fellow smuggler—one much broader and more weathered than he—secure a small rowboat.

A white cataract blemished the brown iris of his left eye. His other was forebodingly dark, nearly matching the black of his hair.

"Kalasin," said Bayani, "calomot i Yusa nondika su pa'ng."

The newcomer snorted. "Nipantot ki, bingal," he said with a voice as rough as the surrounding rocks. "Binket ne danila oka kapiret-liho? Pong Áfgaliard? Pantot, Bayani! Kadek—"

"If you are going to piss from your mouth, do so in Garmathian," snapped Sólan, eye twitching. "I wish to be here as much as you want me here. Tell me, am I to meet Kadek or not?"

Kalasin snarled. "Who you are?"

A mischievous thought flashed through Sólan's mind, and Bayani's stiffened posture indicated its gleam had reached his eyes. "That is for me to disclose to your captain. His minions are not worth my time."

Bayani hung his head and muttered in his own tongue. Neither Kalasin nor Sólan paid him any mind.

"We 'minions,' as you say, decide if you worth Kadek's time," said Kalasin. "I no ask again, kapiret-liho. Who you are?"

Gods, Bayani. You are more pleasant a man to speak to than this pundijo. "The Grim. You?"

Kalasin opened his mouth to respond, but Sólan held up a hand. "Wait. I already know. Kalasin, correct?"

The smuggler's eyes narrowed. "If you really the Grim, why would I—"

"I know your words, pundijo." Sólan's Taela accent was flawless as he said, "'Siso no dens-i kami.' Ita kuma no biso-una isu nivuk-eh." *"We are the Silent Dancers." You would be wise not to cross me.*

Kalasin bared his teeth. "Fine. I take you to Kadek. You life be in his hands."

Sólan grinned, winking at Bayani, the young smuggler smacking his own forehead.

As Bayani helped Sólan on board, a silky tenor voice spoke. "I see you brought a newcomer."

Sólan's turned to see a familiar sight—the swordsman from Bansungei's "People's Kitchen." This time, Dakil's raven-coloured hair was now pulled back into a tight braid, its tie embellished with a single-edged blade about the size of his thumb. The edges around his short beard were sharp from a fresh shave.

Sólan's chest fluttered at the fine smoky lines that streaked out from his pupils through his russet irises. *Medría, Kadek is a fool for letting you go.* Clearing his throat, he said, "Are newcomers unwelcome here, sañero?"

"I wasn't speaking to you, Áfgaliard." Dakil's tone tore through Sólan even deeper than Elena's blade.

Bayani stomped forward. "Dakil, t'is man requesting passage to … um … his camp in Taelonael. He slave scout who—"

"I know what he is, Bayani." Dakil's eyebrows furrowed over his upturned eyes. "But we neither smuggle men nor serve adobo."

Sólan blinked. *What the hell does that mean?*

Chuckling, Dakil gazed at Sólan with a mischievous smirk that made the smokiness in his eyes smoulder. Again, Sólan's heart raced. *Halaña, Goddess of Love, stop toying with me.*

"You bring him"— Dakil finally broke his suddenly intense gaze with Sólan to address Bayani—"but not the child. Why?"

"I still have one more summer with—"

"After what happened last moon, Bayani, it's time. Bansungei is too dangerous for her. Look what they did to her mother." Dakil placed a hard hand on Bayani's shoulder. "She's alone? This time, you left her to die."

"But Kadek—"

"Nipantot Kadek na suya." Dakil spat at his feet and snarled. "No amount of prayer to *Yusa* will change a man like that. I promised to help you. If we can at least get her to the Island of"—he stopped and clenched his mouth shut. Stepping back, he turned to study Sólan. He cocked his head and moved toward him with accusation in his eyes. "She's dead, isn't she? The girl? … How?"

Sólan couldn't speak under Dakil's burning gaze. Perhaps it was the perfectly trimmed facial hair, the flawless musculature on his toned forearms and nimble fingers, or the sharp edges of the geometrical tattoo that peaked from beneath the collar of his loose shirt. "It … it was an accident," he whispered.

Impossibly, Dakil's stare intensified.

He can read me like a fucking papyrus.

"Bayani," said Dakil, never taking his eyes off Sólan, "it's your turn to swab the lower decks."

The fisherman grumbled before obliging.

"How did you get him on such a tight rope?" said Sólan as soon as Bayani was out of earshot.

Dakil ignored his question. "You want to speak with Kadek, yes? Or should his 'minions' deliver your message?"

I see where Bayani learned his insolence. "Lead the way, cabróde."

"I would be more careful with your words around Kadek … pundijo."

I suppose Kadek was no fool, after all. Ansalá, give me strength with this fucker.

Dakil led Sólan to the heavy door of the cabin and knocked. He wiped all emotion from his face as soon as a gruff voice answered, "Ta."

"Ng suya poner-daya," said Dakil. "A slave scout from Áfgal."

The door creaked open just enough to reveal half of Kadek's plump face. "Hundi nagana kapiret-liho," he hissed.

Dakil's mouth curled at the corners. "Ng na 'Singut.'"

Kadek stiffened, stepping aside to open the door further. Dakil nudged Sólan with his shoulder to guide him past the protruding belly that blocked the entrance. Sólan squeezed by with Dakil close behind to shut and latch the door.

"So," said Kadek. He waddled his way to a plush, velvet chair behind an elaborate mahogany table, upon which sat vials of oils, perfumes, drinks, and—Sólan assumed—poisons. The melted candlesticks embedded in silver and gold candelabras gave the cabin an even more ominous feel.

Kadek motioned for Sólan to sit on a similarly luxurious chair across from him. "Please sit, tual. Let us talk."

Tentatively, Sólan obliged. The fat smuggler leaned back, tapping each of his fingertips together. Neither man moved, thickening the room's tension. Dakil shifted on his feet, resting his hand on the hilt of his rapier. Sólan glanced at him in his periphery. *Kill me, already. Or speak. Either one, get me out of this stinking chair.* The odd bouquet of heavy perfume and sweat irritated his sensitive nose until his eyes watered.

"Tell me, what your name is?" said Kadek.

Sólan could practically hear Dakil's eyes rolling in his skull, and a smirk creeped across the Áfgaliard's face. "That depends entirely on you. Which of my names do you wish me to utter? The one my mother gave me or the one feared by the Taelas?" His smile disintegrated into a deep scowl. "As far as I have gathered, putathóta, you know *exactly* who I am."

Dakil shifted his weight again, and Sólan's keen ears picked up the sound of a fist being tightened over leather. Kadek, however, burst into hearty laughter. "Kalasin was right about you, kapiretliho! You tongue sharper than edge of you hatchet!"

The dull slide and click of a sword re-sheathed made Sólan startle. *When was that sword drawn?* He peered over his shoulder to meet Dakil's intense russet gaze. *Well played, swordsman.*

Kadek wiped the smile from his face and said with a snarl, "He also tell me you rape and murder child. T'en you burn her body."

Sólan returned his attention to Kadek and spat a glob of sticky saliva onto the captain's robust cheeks jumping to his feet. "You *dare* accuse me of such filth?" The Dark bubbled eagerly inside Sólan's chest, a searing pain in his eyes pulsing. "You, of all monsters? 'The Vile'?"

Dakil again drew his sword. This time, however, Sólan was ready for it. "Touch me with that blade, sañero, and I will kill you both with a mere twitch of my eye."

"Not if I pierce your heart first," said Dakil.

Sólan bared his fangs as he slowly lowered himself into his seat. "I do not rape, and I will not hesitate to behead those who do."

Kadek merely chuckled. "I see. Kalasin always one to add … alternate facts to his reports." He reached over the table and grasped two crystal chalices in one meaty hand. With his other, he held up a matching decanter filled with sour-smelling wine. "Port? It Orovite."

"No, thank you," said Sólan, the smell of vinegar and brandy offending his nose. "I am Áfgalese, remember? We take great pride in our wine, unlike some."

"Dakil?"

"Hundi, Captain. I'm on duty." The salt in Dakil's tone was enough to cure a full loin of pork.

A wicked grin stretched across Kadek's face. "How could I forget?" He poured himself a glass and sipped. He smacked his lips before returning to Sólan. "So, you no rape the child. But you burn her?"

"I burned her not. Only her mother after her death," said Sólan. "And the girl tried to kill me first."

Dakil stiffened at the confession.

Kadek, however, merely snorted. "Prove it."

Sólan stood to remove his tattered shirt. He motioned to the fresh scar on his chest, just below his heart. He slowly spun to face Dakil. The swordsman's eyes flashed as he looked over Sólan's bare torso. *Is that—*

Kadek clapped slowly, chuckling. "She was a fighter."

Sólan rolled his eyes to face the captain. "Are you finished? I would like to move on in this conversation, and the death of a child is the least of my priorities."

"Nánco lu ternimando. I le dilar il lis ufos qir doéla lu mótua," whispered Dakil. *He's never done. And the sorrow in your eyes tells me that her death grieves you.*

Sólan's breath caught as the flutter returned to his chest. Gods, was his Áfgalese flawless.

"So," said Kadek, "how you—"

"Silver blood, indionta. You call me a halfbreed and already forget my bloodline? My powers?"

"T'at not what I ask. You do well to listen, *halfbreed*." Kadek leaned forward threateningly. "How you intend to leave this ship alive?"

Sólan clenched his jaw. *You conniving putathóta.* He rolled his shoulders back and popped his neck. "I am unsure if I intend to leave this ship at all." His back burned under Dakil's hot stare. The subtle sound of the swordsman's hand gripping his leather hilt again tickled Sólan's ears.

Kadek, however, merely chuckled. "You have large bounty on you head, Sólan the Grim. What will stop me to take it off your shoulders and deliver it to Taela king?"

It was Sólan's turn to chuckle. "Nothing," he said, exposing his fangs.

Kadek swallowed. A spark of fear flashed and disappeared from his eyes faster than a blink.

The unmistakable scent of lust that suddenly filled Sólan's nostrils ... coming from the man behind him. He forced himself to focus. "However," said Sólan, "there is also nothing stopping me from doing the same to you—with my bare hands, no less." Sólan kept his intense stare on Kadek, waiting for the moment to strike. Tensing, he stopped himself at a new scent in the room. His heart pounded as he watched Kadek's pupils dilate in a way that could only mean one thing.

Kadek took a shaky breath. "Dakil. I must speak to this ... kapiret-liho alone."

There it is.

Dakil grumbled in his native tongue and slipped out of the cabin. As the door shut with a heavy thunk, Kadek and Sólan both relaxed their postures.

"When you first arrive, I thought you came for my ship," said Kadek. He watched Sólan over the edge of his chalice as he sipped.

Sólan snickered. He reached across the table and snatched a different bottle, one made of clay and already half-empty. Popping the cork, he took a sniff and then a swig. "You and your bodyguard would be dead, and the *Silent Dancer* would be mine by now." *Gods, your brandy is rough.* "Ninîl, sañero. I came for the very reason your crewman said: I need passage. Preferably with my neck intact."

"I see." Kadek licked his lips. "Passage to where?"

He took another swig and was rewarded with a burning cough. Sólan shrugged lazily. He wiped his mouth before answering, "Anywhere that is outside of Taelonael, Orovín, or Nethuania."

"Huh." Kadek threw his head back to down the last of his port.

"That no leave much coast for me to drop you." He frowned. "Why not with oddlings?"

"An island would suffice." Sólan dodged the question with ease. "There is one in particular I have been searching for in the last ten years, or so. One on which I wish to gather information—from you."

"What kind of information?" Kadek's face was close enough for Sólan to smell the wine on his breath.

Ti dioses lío, sañero. Your breath alone makes you "Vile." Sólan swallowed his disgust and relaxed. "Rumours, mostly. However, I have been hearing them more and more as of late." Taking another several gulps of brandy, he shuddered at its foul burn. He replaced the cork and set the bottle down. "'Tis said that the 'Chainbreakers' have come out of hiding."

Kadek frowned. "'Chainbreakers?' T'e slave scout ring? Why?"

"You do know what I am, do you not?" Sólan sneered at Kadek's confused expression. "How do you think I became 'The Grim,' aeh? Certainly not by my cheerful nature." He flashed a fanged grin at Kadek. "However, if I wish to maintain this career of mine, I need help. I can no longer trust my fellow Áfgaliards to follow my methods, as I have recently discovered."

"And you think the twins will help you?" Kadek snorted. "There's reason they went to hiding."

"Are you going to take me there, or not? I am running quite short on patience."

Kadek's mouth danced in a coy smile. "I know where are they." He fidgeted with his hands and licked his lips.

Sólan took a breath to savour the change in scent of the room. *Ah, there it is.*

"But I must ask you first—"

"Are you trying to seduce me?" Sólan's eyes smouldered. He bit the lower corner of his lip and slid to his feet, the brandy rushing to his head in a pleasant buzz. Kadek followed suit, seemingly entranced by the flames of Sólan's gaze.

"You … um …" Kadek's eyes meandered down to Sólan's low trousers, where the black tattoo was showing just enough to pique curiosity. "What is that?"

Sólan glanced down with a smile. He lowered the waistband just enough to reveal the palm-sized circle embellished with thirteen symbols around and inside it. Each one twisted and swirled in simple patterns, representing one of the thirteen gods of Áfgal.

"A reminder of whom I serve," said Sólan.

Kadek licked his lips once more and stepped forward. "I serve Yusa. T'e one true God. And He forbids—"

"Fuck Yusa." Sólan closed the gap between them and wrapped his arm about the man's hips. Nose-to-nose, he hovered his lips over Kadek's. "He cannot deny what we are ... who we love."

Their mouths met. Kadek let out a groan as Sólan rubbed his hand inside of the captain's trousers.

Almost have you. Sólan reached with his other hand toward the table. Grasping a glass vial of oil, he pressed himself into Kadek until they thudded against the wall.

Kadek growled and tangled a hand in Sólan's hair. So impassioned were they, their teeth clacked together as their tongues fought. The men spun to the ground with Kadek on top. "Take off your pants," he whispered.

Sólan chuckled. "You take them off." He swept Kadek onto his back and ripped off his clothes, his circumcised erection only just visible beneath his well-fed stomach. Sólan licked his lips and slowly slid his mouth over the tip of Kadek's manhood.

Kadek gasped and moaned, squirming and writhing as Sólan oiled his hand to insert one—then two—fingers inside of him. "Oh God," said Kadek. "Don't stop."

Despite his pleas, Sólan stopped. He crawled over the top of Kadek and nibbled his earlobe. "Dakil was a fool to lose you," he whispered.

"Such a fool," Kadek breathed.

Gently, Sólan pushed his own oiled erection into Kadek. He thrust, slow and shallow at first, then faster and deeper. Heavy breaths turned to groans as Sólan's pressure built. He slowed. *I almost have you.* Kadek's moans turned into begs for more.

Their mouths met again. Sólan's thrusts waxed and waned as he toyed with his own pressure as well as Kadek's. "You were a fine lover, sañero," he sighed. "'Tis a shame I shan't feel you again."

Kadek cooed. "Oh, but Sólan. T'e Island of Chainbreakers is far. You will feel me again."

"You misunderstand." Sólan stopped. His eyes pulsed in pain as he grinned villainously. The air between them chilled, and as Kadek trembled beneath him, the Áfgaliard leaned in and whispered, "I am going to relieve your shoulders of your head."

Kadek squirmed as Sólan wrapped his hands around his throat, thrusting even as he squeezed and collapsed his airway. Sólan's movements grew rapid and violent. His pressure continued to build, climaxing just as Kadek stopped writhing. The release sent shivers down his spine. *The Silent Dancer is mine.*

He stood, his hands shaking in either victory or orgasm—it all felt the same to him. The pulsing burn from green flames in his eyes diminished as The Dark retreated from his chest. Looking down at his handiwork, a new shudder filled his shoulders. *Fuck. What have I done?*

16

THE SILENT DANCER

*B*ayani's head popped up on the top deck and looked around cautiously. Dakil rolled his eyes at the sight. *Damn tulalo thinks he's hidden.* "You should be swabbing the deck," the long-haired smuggler barked.

"I heard something," whispered Bayani. "I think they trying—"

"I know exactly what they're doing in that room, and we both know only one will leave alive." Dakil crossed his arms with his head cocked and challenged, "Which one do you prefer?" *At least he's not making me watch this time.*

The colour drained from Bayani's face, pleasantly ignorant of the meaning behind Dakil's words. "If Kadek die …"

"Then the *Silent Dancer* will be mine. And if the Grim dies, Kadek is mine. Once we get to the island, I will take it. That part of the plan has not changed. This is Kadek's last voyage, if he even makes it to open water."

"Right. I know already, but … what if Sólan claim the ship?"

"Then I'll kill Sólan the Grim in a duel, as is custom." *He's already struggling to kill that boy who thinks he's captain. That kapiret-liho will be easy to kill in return.* "You think he can do that unchallenged? How do you think Kadek got this ship? *He* didn't build her."

Bayani hemmed and hawed. "Then ... um ..."

Dakil rolled his head back and sighed. "I told you, Bayani. You bring Tala and Elena here, and I take you to Chainless. I kill Kadek, take the ship, and we go on with our lives." *And if your new "friend" gets in the way ...*

Bayani looked to his feet and flared his nostrils. "Fine. But is there any way to—maybe—keep Sólan alive?"

Dakil snorted. "Why? Have you fallen in love with him since Tala died?"

"No! I loved Tala and Tala only! Dammit, Dakil. Why you always—"

His words were cut short by the slam of the cabin's door as it opened. A freshly severed head covered in blood bounced and rolled to Dakil's feet—Kadek's.

"What you have done, Áfgaliard!" cried Bayani.

Dakil spun and unsheathed his rapier in one fluid motion. The blade's tip threatened to puncture the scruffy flesh beneath Sólan's chin. "You're still alive, kapiret-liho."

Sólan growled and clenched his fists, which were sticky with blood and bits of flesh. Every bit of the unstained linen left on his shirt and trousers was now soaked in crimson. "I believe you must now call me 'Captain.'" *Unless you wish to join your former lover.*

A small crowd began to form around the two men, some gasping at the sight of Kadek's severed head; others readied themselves with weapons.

Dakil tightened his grip on his sword as his body shook with cold laughter. "It seems Sólan the Grim thinks he can take the *Silent Dancer* unchallenged!"

The entire crew joined Dakil and jeered.

The swordsman wiped the smile from his face. "You don't know anything about the sea. You're a mere scout of the desert. A man who buys slaves just to sell them back to their families."

"I will not be threatened and shamed by a fucking pirate." Sólan bared his fangs. "Particularly the *concubine* of that fat imposter."

Dakil increased the pressure of the blade against Sólan's skin. "I told you to be careful with your words."

Gods, you are an irritating—yet beautiful—man. "Perhaps you should be careful with yours, 'bodyguard.'"

One side of Dakil's nose twitched. "Bayani," he said without breaking his stare down with Sólan, "give this man a weapon."

The crew backed away to create an egg-shaped stage, leaving Bayani standing alone. "W-why me? I—"

"*Now*, tulalo!"

Bayani flinched and clambered below deck.

Sólan raised an eyebrow at Dakil. "You are making a mistake."

"Perhaps. But perhaps it's *you* who made a mistake already," said Dakil. "Oligo e lúas enomógos cil carño," he half-whispered in Áfgalese. *Choose your enemies with care.*

Sólan opened his mouth to respond but was cut off by Bayani's quick return. "I t'ink this belong to you, Sólan."

The forge marks of Sólan's hatchet glimmered in the afternoon sun like water. *You fucking thief.* "You stole it."

"I save it. You drop it when Elena—" Bayani stopped as though choked up with sudden emotion.

Sólan snatched his weapon from Bayani's grasp, though his expression softened. Flashing a conflicted look to the swordsman, he whispered, "We will grieve on her later. But I must first silence that man's mouth with blood." *Though I would rather silence him with passion.*

A coy smile curled Dakil's lips. "Two heads in one day? Most gods don't give such blessings."

"I do not serve 'most gods.'"

Flashes of lust, sorrow, and anger crossed Dakil's eyes. *What have I done? Halaña, you wretched temptress.*

"On any other day, we might've been friends, Sólan the Grim."

Stop it! You need to kill him, Sólan. The Áfgaliard coughed to steady the flutter in his chest. Twirling his weapon, he rolled his shoulders back and took his stance. His eyes pulsed once more with The Dark.

"No magic. Only skill," said Dakil. "The winner takes the *Silent Dancer*."

Sólan growled. "Of course." he said, stuffing his greedy powers down. "I prefer to kill in a fair fight."

Their fatal dance began. Sólan flinched in an attempt to keep his opponent on edge. Dakil, however, never dropped his posture. They stepped, glided, and stepped again—round and round they went. The men surrounding them grew restless at the boiling tension.

Suddenly, Dakil lunged. Though Sólan dodged the deadliness of the blow, the rapier sliced through his cheek as though 'twere nothing but water. He grunted at the sting, stumbling backward at the swordsman's second swift attack. *Shit, is he quick!*

Sólan landed on his arse and kicked upwards, the hard sole of his boot's heel cracking against Dakil's knee.

"Pantot!" Dakil jumped to the side as he cursed. He limped back into position.

Sólan used the force of his next kick to return to his feet and swing. His hatchet's blade missed Dakil's throat by millimetres. "Jidir!"

The enemies reset, and the dance began again. "Anyosa, Diosóta de Gierra, eyudalí," Sólan muttered under his breath. *Anyosa, Goddess of War, help me.*

Dakil whipped his head with such speed that the blade in his hair sliced a deep cut above Sólan's eyebrow.

Sólan hissed. Snatching Dakil's braid, he yanked his opponent to the ground.

Dakil yelped before landing with a thud, his rapier clattering out of his reach.

Sólan swung.

The smuggler dodged and kicked.

"Fuck!" Sólan's elbow cracked against the deck as he fell. The burning pain shot up his forearm into his fingers. His grip went limp, the hatchet sliding away.

The fighters grappled. Despite the pain in his elbow, Sólan maintained the upper hand, though Dakil somehow slithered out of each submission.

Dakil jabbed, kicked, and punched his way to the mount, only for Sólan to sweep and overpower him. The swordsman jabbed his flat hand into Sólan's throat—and he was free.

Sólan garbled, wheezed, and grunted, but it took little time for him to recover. He looked up and glared. *Dirty move.* Scrambling to his feet, he eyed his hatchet behind Dakil's foot. *Dammit!*

Dakil flashed a victorious smile before striking again. The tip of his narrow blade embedded into Sólan's chest. The crew cheered.

A searing pain in Sólan's eyes flared as The Dark bubbled through him unprovoked. "You missed my heart, putathóta." He lurched forward, forcing the rapier to impale him to its hilt.

Dakil gasped. He stumbled backward, pulling on his sword to no avail.

A wild grin blanketed Sólan's face. He laughed as he finished his bull charge and slammed his opponent's back against the wall. With a headbutt to the nose, Dakil crumpled to the ground.

Tears, snot, and blood dripped down Dakil's face, soaking his facial hair and the shirt about his chest. He shook his head and sniffed, his new bruises already threatening to swell.

Sólan removed the sword from his own chest. He twirled it with one hand and stopped to grab his hatchet. "The Silent Dancer is mine," he said. The wounds over his face and chest healed, and the blood stopped flowing, leaving behind raw, pink scars. He towered over Dakil in victory, raising his weapon to deal the final blow when—

"I'm not dead, yet, kapiret-liho." Dakil kicked to his feet, a previously unseen dagger in hand.

What the—Sólan yelped as the dagger's blade sliced beneath his wrist. He dropped Dakil's rapier at the pain. "Fuck you!" He booted the sword across the deck and blocked Dakil's next blow with his forearm. A knee to the groin and a quick grasp-and-twist was all Sólan needed to subdue his opponent.

Dakil struggled against Sólan's tightening grip to no avail. He stopped as the Áfgaliard rested his hatchet's blade against his throat.

"Yield," whispered Sólan.

"What?" Dakil struggled again to break free.

"You heard me. Yield."

Dakil snarled. "Never."

Sólan sighed. "Dammit, sañero, I cannot waste a talent like yours. *Yield.*"

"That is not our way."

"It is mine." Sólan lowered his hatchet. His grip, however, never loosened.

Dakil's head slumped. "Fine." He cleared his throat to announce, "The *Silent Dancer* is yours, Captain Grim."

The crew gasped as Sólan released his opponent. He slumped to the side as simultaneous waves of relief and dread overtook him. *What the hell have you done, Sólan? You have made an enemy and let him go, you fool.*

SÓLAN PERCHED HIMSELF ATOP THE SHIP'S CENTRE MAST AND STARED OUT at the sea. Shortly after winning his duel, he'd gone to work removing Kadek—and all his blood—from the cabin. He'd scrubbed, tossed, and swept every corner of the room to claim it as his own. He scoured the man's belongings—his clothes, jewels, hats, and scarves —to claim what might be of use. Each piece was heavily perfumed and made Sólan's eyes water. To his delight, he'd found a simple Áfgalese cotton shirt, unstained trousers, and a thick wool cloak not unlike the one he'd stolen from the slavers.

Stars littered the inky sky, their shimmer mirroring the silver and blue specks that he knew danced across his own amber irises. *Varín, oh wise one, help me. I am losing control.* A tear trickled down his cheek as he lifted his desperate prayers, his mind replaying his meeting with Kadek. *I swear to you, Varín, I shall find a bull in offering the moment I reach the island.* Over and over again, he saw the images of the captain's pleasure, of the fear in his eyes, of his struggle for life as Sólan strangled and fucked him in synchrony. The brutality made him shudder. *Halaña. Forgive me. I have disobeyed your great law and used seduction for murder.* He cursed and then slapped himself in the face, but there was nothing he could do to himself to dull the pain of his shame.

No doubt, Kadek had deserved to die. He was well known to murder children, rape men and women for sport—he was Sólan's opposite in nearly every way. Hell, the man even dabbled in the slave trade for a time. However, there were cleaner, more honest ways to kill a man. Even with weapons, Kadek was weak. His death was inevitable the moment Dakil had left the room. So why such deception? Sólan knew not, except that the Goddess of Love forbade it.

The breeze gusted and changed direction. Sólan's eyes refocused on the southern horizon. Far in the distance, a black wall of clouds loomed and snuffed out the light of the stars. *Shit. Another storm.* The half-moon soon disappeared as well. He climbed down and dropped to the main deck with the gracefulness granted by his elf blood.

"Do you never sleep?"

Sólan spun, hatchet suddenly in hand. He prepared to strike as Dakil approached with a soft chuckle.

"Worry not, Captain. You've proven your strength. I don't question it."

Sólan's eye twitched. "Mere hours ago, you tried to kill me." His grip tightened around his weapon. "Would you not try again?"

Dakil snorted. "Ta. I tried to kill you ... and failed." He walked over to the starboard rail and leaned his hip against it. With crossed arms and cocked head, the swordsman studied Sólan carefully. "I challenged you for the helm and lost. I know my place. No need to keep threatening me."

But how far can I trust you? Sólan swallowed his rebuttal and lowered his weapon. "Caution has kept me alive for nearly three and a half hundred years. I would be a fool to lower it."

"Caution," scoffed Dakil. "Caution is for the child who steals copper coins from the Temple of Yusa."

He pushed himself off the railing and moved toward Sólan. He stopped at a half-arm's length and looked hard into Sólan's curious gaze, his smoky eyes flickering with an unfamiliar emotion. "There's more than simple caution behind the mask you wear, Sólan the

Grim. You fight a darkness that haunts both your dreams and your waking moments."

Sólan stepped back, his brow furrowed over his eyes. "You speak as though you are wise beyond your years." He slowly walked around Dakil, taking in every detail—the slicked back hair once more in a tight braid, the streak of grey hairs through the middle of his short beard, the perfectly upturned shape of his monolid eyes with shallow creases at the corners. His ears, Sólan noted, were no sharper than were any other man's of pure crimson blood. "Given your lack of elvish features, you must be of noble birth rather than silver blood."

The burn from Dakil's glare confirmed his suspicion. "Why'd you do it?" the swordsman asked.

You dodge as smoothly as you strike. "Do what—kill Kadek?" Sólan shook his head with a chuckle. "The same reason you tried to kill me. I wanted the ship."

"I know why you *killed* him, tulalo. The man needed to die." Dakil rubbed his face with a sigh. "No, no. Why did you fuck him first? Is it not forbidden?"

Sólan tried not to roll his eyes. "Not in Áfgal."

"No?" The mischievous smirk returned to Dakil's lips. This time, it reached one of his eyes. "What about using seduction as a weapon?"

Is that not what you are doing now?

"He was famous for that tactic, you know," said Dakil. "Rarely did his victim survive after."

"Hmph." Sólan rubbed his scruffy chin, a curious frown creasing his forehead as he met Dakil's gaze. "Neither did he, when he was the receiver. But you survived him. You are one such rarity, no?"

Dakil's nose flared. "Bold words."

"And you *thought* he was in love with you?" Sólan shrugged. "Perhaps he was."

A deep scowl cut across Dakil's face. "I would be a liar if I denied our … romance. But it faded once he 'found God.'"

"Ha! And then he grew fat and used you for your actual sword."

Dakil's face softened. "Only for show. His mind grew soft like his belly. It was 'Yusa's way' to stop killing. To stop smuggling. To stop loving me."

Oh Halaña. You punish me with Kadek's attempt at redemption. Sólan shook guilty pangs from his head. "This *Yusa* seems to be excellent at making his followers hate each other."

"And themselves." Dakil looked Sólan over with curious eyes. "You don't follow him. Yet, I can see your self-hatred as well."

Sólan scowled. *Perhaps I should have killed you, after all.* "I would be a liar if—"

"No need to dwell on our lies, Sólan de Ciudelago." A shiver ran down Sólan's spine at Dakil's perfect pronunciation of his name. "I know a broken man when I see one."

"¿Mondé? I am no broken man, Dakil … aeh …"

"Papuan." Dakil smiled, his eyes glistening in the darkness. "It's Dakil Papuan." A soft chuckle escaped his lips. "And yes, you are broken. You just don't know it yet." He gave Sólan one last look before turning away. "Get some sleep, Captain. That storm is getting stronger."

Sólan gulped as he watched Dakil disappear below deck. There was something different about the swordsman, something about the way he struck Sólan's thoughts. Arousal? Perhaps, though Sólan had bedded enough men and women to know that this feeling tugged far deeper than his cock.

The captain shook the lustful thoughts from his mind and turned toward the cabin. Wrapping himself in his cloak, Sólan curled up in a far corner of the room—one that didn't still stink of Kadek as much. He squirmed and fidgeted as images of Dakil's smile and nimble build threatened his sleep. *Medría, Halaña! You conniving …* He dared not finish his thought. The Gods didn't take kindly to insults, particularly those that came in silence. *Fine!*

Grumbling, he shifted his weight and grasped his throbbing manhood. Halaña, forgive me, he thought. He yanked with increasing speed until, finally, he was relieved. *Two of your laws in one day, Great Goddess,* he lamented. *I shall never again be worthy of your blessings.* Tears trickled down his cheeks as he cursed himself over and over until he finally fell into a restless sleep.

17

BLOOD FOR BLOOD

*K*nock knock knock! Sólan bolted awake in naught but his trousers, his neck twanging in painful protest. Inhaling through clenched teeth, he clamped a hand over the stiff muscle. *Where the fuck am I?* He frowned as he looked at his surroundings. His cloak was wadded at his feet, and his shirt had fallen behind his back as though he'd used it as a pillow, though he held no recollection of removing any clothing before he'd fallen asleep. *Wait. Is it dawn already?* The surrounding darkness proved that the sun still slept, and the escalating knocking pounded the fog out of his consciousness.

"Captain!" Dakil's voice was frantic enough to get Sólan moving —albeit, slowly. Slipping into his shirt, he staggered toward the door and swung it open. Before he could snap in his irritation, Dakil said, "We're under attack!"

Sólan's stomach dropped. "Gods-*dammit*!" He pushed Dakil aside and hustled to the bow, confirming the swordsman's words. Three large ships blocked them in the estuary—one in front and the others close behind. He spun to ask the nearest crewman, "Who are they? Pirates?"

"Hundi," said the weathered, one-eyed man.

"Cavalry guard," said another.

"Pantot," whispered Dakil. "We're trapped."

Fantastic. "Unfurl the sails." Sólan spun to face the swordsman. "Dakil, come with me. I need you to speak to them." He hurried below deck to shout orders.

Dakil followed, translating for those who spoke no Garmathian. The crew reacted quickly and scurried on deck, leaving the two men alone for just a moment. Sólan's breath hitched as their eyes met.

"What are you thinking, Captain? Their hulls will shatter ours."

Sólan blinked. *Not the conversation I hoped for.* He bared his fangs and loosened his hatchet in its holster. "That storm out there—we need to use it. 'Tis our way of escape."

"What! You're going to get all of us killed!"

"I swear to the Gods, Dakil, perhaps I should have taken your head."

Dakil's shoulder knocked Sólan into the stairwell's wall as he pushed past him. "A shame I missed your fucking heart," he grumbled before sprinting up the steps.

Sólan's eyes flashed as The Dark awakened within him once again. *This man is going to be the death of me, whether by his sword or my own hand.* He punched the wall before rushing up the stairs, taking two at a time.

Bayani stood at the bow, staring out at the ships ahead. Sólan knew not whether he stood in fear, triumph, or anger.

"Bayani," the captain said, "why are you simply standing there?"

The smuggler turned, flaring his nostrils. "This no make sense. We never trapped like this until you come." A dull flash lit the sky, followed by the roll of distant thunder.

Sólan's teeth were clenched as he challenged, "Are you accusing me of something, sañero? Perhaps I should ask you if—"

"Niong gonawiga no?" Dakil's voice beside him was sharper than his rapier. "Bimulak ko suya tobaho."

Gods, not you again. What the hell are you saying?

Bayani snarled. "Hundi! Hundi ng na tobaho ey poner-daya!"

Sólan's eyes narrowed. *What did you say?* "Hundi" ... no ... some-

THE GRIM

thing, something ... "mortal elf." We have no time for this. "Garmathian, Bayani," he hissed. "I cannot speak your tongue."

Dakil wasted no time in unsheathing his rapier. Sólan grasped his hatchet in preparation for a fight, but the rapier's blade pointed at Bayani's chest. The swordsman's voice roughened to a grit as he said, "Weigh anchor, pantot ng."

Sólan stiffened, the flutter returning to his chest. *Halaña, you bless me. Though, your timing is terrible.* A tingling prickled his scalp, and his hair—even the curls on his chest—stood on end. He looked up to the sky, smelling an odd scent of electricity. *Medría!* "Move!"

He shoved Bayani and Dakil away and thrust his hand upward just as a violent bolt of lightning glanced off its heel and out to sea. His eyes flashed with pain, and he screamed in sudden agony. Falling to the ground, Sólan grasped his wrist—the flesh on his hand sizzled and cracked until a waxy scar formed over the bottom half of his palm.

His burning eyes pulsed with The Dark, and his fangs dripped as he snarled, "Get this fucking ship *moving*!"

Dakil's eyes widened. "My God, what *can't* you do?"

Sólan never answered. Instead, he scrambled to his feet and peered straight up into the black sky above them. More thunder boomed. Electricity and wind filled the air as the storm grew around the ship. He paid the panicked crew no mind as he wrapped his thoughts around the weather's power. "Javiento, Diota de Mardano, niníl li llives todivota," he whispered. *Javiento, God of Death, do not call me yet.*

The Dark tugged at his heart. His chest throbbed as pain radiated down his arm and up his jaw, and yet he simply gritted his teeth and concentrated deeper. Sweat covered his pallid face as the air electrified again. Sólan pulled the forming bolts of lightning from the sky and then threw them at each of the three cavalry ships blocking the estuary's opening.

The ships ignited. The stench of burning wood and tar filled the air, nigh choking those aboard the *Silent Dancer*. Echoes of screams drifted through the smoke, and the sounds of crackling flesh tickled Sólan's ears like music. He suddenly laughed at the chorus of flames, the thunder, and the cries of drowning men. The Dark had a strange way of festering his mind. His chest throbbed again, sharper this time. Tighter. He heard a deep whisper in his mind, yet he refused to listen. Refused to hear the words they spoke.

The *Silent Dancer* moved through the channel with ease, and Sólan tightened his grip on the weather. The wind pushed the ship into the open sea but spun it in no real direction, whipping and tearing the sails. Fragments of the cavalry's ships were lifted from the surface of the churning water, becoming projectiles that impaled anything—or anyone—in their path.

Waves engulfed the bow, stern, and sides, tossing the buoyant hull every which way. Black, frothy swells flooded the deck. Two—no, *three* men were washed overboard, their screams cut short as they drowned beneath the water.

The clouds above began to spin. A funnel descended—slowly, at first, and then faster and faster. The wind whipped and twisted even more. Water on both sides of the ship rose toward the sky. The air and clouds lifted and swirled the ship. The draft of wind seemed to suck the air out of Sólan's lungs, even as The Dark battered his chest. Shouts and prayers from his own crew were drowned out by the crushing roar of the wind—a stampede of wild Áfgalese horses would be but a whisper compared to this deadly howl.

Medría! Sólan released his grip on the lightning and pushed the heels of his hands at the twisting spout. It inched away just enough for them to dodge its destructive path. Finally, the ship descended.

The vessel lurched forward, knocking Sólan to his knees. More men were bounced and flung overboard. Sólan slid toward the bow and the splintering rails below him. *Shit!* Hatchet in hand, he embedded its pick into the deck's floorboards to break his fall. The ship levelled, but not before another body slipped and tumbled toward him.

"Watch out!"

Sólan looked to the direction of the shout, just before he was body slammed by Dakil.

Sólan's eyes burst open, and he sat upright with a gasp. Despite the suddenly motionless ship, his vision swam. His eyes finally focused to see a teasing grin close to his face.

"You're either more powerful than you think or more stupid than you're willing to see," said Dakil.

The fluttering in Sólan's chest returned, gnawing at him even as his temper threatened to flare. The swordsman was close enough for him to see a gold-capped tooth behind his incisor.

"Did you always insult Kadek in such a way?"

Dakil chuckled as he helped Sólan to his feet. "Only when he needed reminding of his mortality."

My mortality is far less fragile than his was. "And now you have insulted me."

Dakil shrugged. "I think my knee's more damaged than your head. Your mortality isn't in danger."

The swordsman's mischievous grin fanned the embers of Sólan's lust while also provoking a nigh overwhelming desire to snap his neck.

Dakil continued. "I hope your pride is less fragile than his was. Here." He held out the water-steel hatchet for the Áfgaliard to take.

Sólan grumbled and snatched his weapon, this time knocking his shoulder into Dakil as he walked away to the splintered rail. The Dark threatened to bubble up again as the swordsman's quiet laughter bounced off his eardrums. Rolling his shoulders back, his joints popped and stretched. The overcast sky drizzled with mist, hiding every star—even the sun. "Where are we?"

"I'm not sure," said Dakil. "The sun hasn't risen yet, and that storm you controlled pushed us in many different directions."

Could you be any more unhelpful? Sólan clenched his jaw and squinted into the heavy fog, tucking his weapon neatly into the holster behind the small of his back. "Well, I suppose the lack of wind has played to our advantage. Wait." He spun to face Dakil, frowning. "How did the cavalry know where we were?"

Dakil frowned. "I don't know, and too many men were washed overboard for us to suspect anyone in the crew."

Says the man who has already tried to kill me. Yet, how many chances have you had since then? And ... us? What do you mean by "us?"

"But it happened far too soon after Kadek's death. I don't think they were after you."

"Regardless ..." Sólan's wandering gaze drifted over the deck, coming to a rest upon the back of Bayani's head. He glared daggers at the man, clenching his fists at his side. "Tell me, sañero Papuan, has Bayani always—"

"Never." Dakil's voice was sharp, like a needle hidden within the usual silk of his timbre. "I'm unsure why he hates you so."

Sólan rhythmically clenched and released his jaw in thought. "Force of habit? Though, I doubt 'tis hate, considering all he has done for me these past days." *Likely a mere mistrust, like everyone else who meets me ... and I to them.* He raised an eyebrow and shifted his gaze back to the swordsman. "After all, I did fail to save the family he had. Perhaps even stole his 'true love.'"

"You did," said Dakil.

"¿Mondé?" Sólan stiffened. "He was actually in love with that child?"

"Hundi, not her. He did what he could to stay close to her mother."

She wanted you, Sólan. Not him. There is no shame in that. "I see. No wonder he hates me." Sólan scoffed and looked askance at Bayani, who was assisting his crew-mates with repairs. "And to think it was because he was jealous of my cock, not my marriage."

"Ha! So am I." Dakil clamped a hand over his own mouth at his own outburst. "I mean, I've seen Tala. She truly was a star of Yusa." Dakil gulped and flicked his smoky gaze to Bayani. "I'm surprised you haven't killed him yet."

Sólan snapped his attention back onto the swordsman. *Good parry.* "A waste of entertainment, I suppose. Besides—" Sólan shrugged "—he has saved my life on more than one occasion, though he had no reason to." A smirk curled the side of his mouth. "Perhaps he can tell me more about the 'aswang' within me."

Dakil snorted. "Ah, yes—the famous monster of the southern islands. A true terror for children."

Bayani spun to face them. "Have you never seen dead man rise, Papuan? I swear to Yusa—"

"I hope to your god that you threaten not your former master's swordsman," said Sólan, reaching behind his back. *His ears must be better than I thought.* "I was just starting to like you." He once more loosened his weapon from its holster, praying he wouldn't have need of it. *I have already shed too much innocent blood of late.*

"But you promise to kill Dakil, yesterday," said another crewman, stepping forward. A gaffing hook rested in his hands. "He lost to you, yet you keep him alive. Why?"

A wicked grin stretched across Sólan's face, though he lamented at the challenge. "Are you questioning my authority, sañero?" The pulsing burn of The Dark returned to his eyes as laughter bubbled in his chest. "Do you call me a liar? A breaker of promises?"

The man's scowl merely deepened. "It is not our way. Why we trust you when you say you take his head?"

"I made no such promise—merely to silence him with blood." Sólan cocked his head and chuckled. "But perhaps you would prefer your life as payment for his?"

Before the man could answer, his throat was split open. Crimson blood spewed over Sólan, Dakil, and Bayani, the latter falling to his ass with a yelp.

"Does anyone else here have doubts?" Sólan demanded. He lifted his arms in a show of power, blood dripping to the ground. "Any more challenges to my authority?" His pulsing glare met each of the smugglers' frightened gazes. "No?" *Gods, what is this curse making me?*

Some of the men shook at the knees, and others squirmed under the Áfgaliard's fiery stare. A voice shouted from the back. "Sólan ng na Singut! Capti na ki!"

"Capti na ki!" the crew repeated, throwing their fists into the air with a cheer.

"They call you their captain," whispered Dakil, his warm breath on Sólan's ear sending a shiver down the Áfgaliard's spine.

Gods, do I want to kill you or fuck you? When Sólan turned to face the swordsman, Dakil was assisting Bayani to his feet. He could hear them speaking curtly in their native tongue. The scent of lust reached the captain's nostrils and sent a tingle down to his groin. *Halaña, I swear to you, I shall not disobey you again.* His mind was set—Dakil would live, regardless of his insolent mouth. *His perfectly groomed and beautiful mouth.*

18

DEMONS OF PRASTÖMIN

*A*lsantör marched down the marble corridor of the castle's northern keep, his heavy boots echoing with each step. The parchment holding Jannon's letter crunched in his tight fist. The gaping windows lit the hall with filtered sunlight, though the summer birds were silent. Beads of sweat threatened to form upon his brow from the muggy air.

Naoise had tried to fetch the king but was unsuccessful. Per Diarmuid's concubine, the king was "unavailable", though she had not been as scantily clad as her norm, which meant the king was occupied by something other than her.

Finally, Alsantör reached his destination—his father's private solar. Only once in his life had he entered the massive, library-esque room, and that time, he had nigh lost his thirteen-year-old head. *What the fuck are you doing, Tör? You know better than to go in there.* The heavy gold-plated door stood ajar, giving way to the sounds of a quill scratching on paper. The prince took a deep breath and straightened his posture before knocking and entering.

Diarmuid jumped to his feet. The imported oak chair tipped and thudded to the ground, and the candles flickered in the sudden movement. Brandishing a dagger, he accidentally spilling his inkwell on the parchment. Black fluid spread across the matching oak desk and dripped to the green marble ground. "Káil ti pash—"

"Daela!" Alsantör jumped back with his palms out in surrender, the crumpled scroll fluttering awkwardly to the ground. "It's me, your son." The prince took a slow step forward, his evergreen gaze matching the king's. "It's just me, Father."

Diarmuid lowered his weapon. The gloss over his eyes faded as he looked the prince over. "I see Jacobo has been kind to you. Rarely is the Wizard of Disease so generous with his healing." He rolled his shoulders and re-sheathed his dagger. "What brings you here, Alsantör? You know you're not allowed here. No one is allowed here."

"I understand, Daela, but—"

"Don't call me that."

"Apologies, your grace," said Alsantör with a stiff bow. *Is that all you can say to me? After everything?*

"You haven't answered my question, Commander. Why are you here?"

The prince grimaced at his father's tone. "It's an urgent matter, your grace. One that I could not entrust with a messenger." *He's going to think I'm a bloody fool.* "It's about the Taelas."

Diarmuid sniffed in annoyance. "Have they declared war?"

"N-no. Not yet. But, they—"

"Then what is so urgent that you had to come to me now?" A fog threatened to cloud the king's eyes once again.

Shite. They're coming back. "At what time would you like to discuss these matters, then, your grace?" Alsantör knelt, slowly retrieving the Karthi scroll by his feet. "Because I'm afraid that—"

"If you let fear control your decisions, you'll be no better a king than your damned uncle was." Diarmuid now scowled. "Get out. I'll have no scaremongering in my presence."

The prince sucked the back of his teeth. *He's calmer than usual.* "As you command, your grace." He turned to leave but stopped at the doorway.

"Gnomes, if my son were here," said Diarmuid mournfully. "He would've been such a king."

Alsantör winced. *I'm right here, Daela. Remember?*

"I said leave!"

Tears filled the prince's eyes as he faced his father again, silently cursing at the thick fog that now covered Diarmuid's pupils and dulled the colour of his irises. "I merely wish to extend my condolences, my king." His lip trembled, but he forced his voice to stay strong. "My apologies. I allowed my pride to cloud my judgement."

Diarmuid bared his fangs and spat at the prince's feet. "See that it doesn't happen again, son of ... of ..."

Alsantör clenched his teeth. *Don't say it. Please don't say it.*

"S-son of ... Wizards, remind me of who you are? I don't leave the solar much, especially after the death of my son."

You said it. The prince swallowed the lump in his throat. "Prince Alsantör, Chief Commander of the legions of Prastömin, son of King Diarmuid, Gnomes bless his crown." A tear escaped the corner of his eye, trickling down his cheek in outward defiance. *Not now. Don't show your weakness to him now.*

"You lie!" Diarmuid lunged forward and backhanded his son with a tight fist.

Alsantör braced, but the impact still sent him to the ground. Anger pulsed through him, and it took every ounce of strength he had to keep from retaliating.

Diarmuid stood over him, trembling. His eyes wild, he removed his dagger from its sheath once again. "I swear to the Wizards, Eamon, if you ever challenge me again—"

"Father, *please*!" Alsantör shielded his eyes with his forearm and waited. Last time, it was a quill. A superficial wound that permanently embedded a black ink stain in the bottom of his wrist. This time, however, the prince was certain an attack would likely lead to his death. He waited for the blow for what seemed like a fortnight. Peeking under his own arm, he watched the king's expression twist and twitch.

"Wizards, look at you," said Diarmuid to himself. "You can't even remember your own son."

Oh, thank the Wizards, and bless the Gnomes. Alsantör lowered his arm but remained on the ground. It wouldn't be long until Diarmuid would join him there. 'Twas his norm: the demons would whisper in the king's ears, turning him against those closest to him, and then an epiphany would strike, and he would crumple to the floor to weep.

As predicted, Diarmuid did just that. He hiccoughed and sputtered, rocking back and forth on his knees. "What have I become?"

The prince took a shaky breath. "Father?" He reached out to place a hand on the king's shoulder but stopped. *He just tried to kill you, Tör.*

"I'm back, son. It's quite alright," whispered Diarmuid.

Alsantör swallowed. "You never left." Flicking his pinkie, he pushed himself to his feet. "I should take my leave. I'll send for you later. Midday, perhaps?"

"Wait." Diarmuid scrambled up and leaned on his oak desk. "We need to talk."

"I know, Father. There are many things we need to discuss, but you're not in the right mind to speak on the Taelas. I'll send for you at high noon."

"I'm not speaking of those gnomes-damned savages."

Alsantör looked to the vaulted marble ceiling and groaned. "Sólan the Grim is dead—not that he mattered much to us. He was just a halfbreed slave scout of Áfgal who likely killed more of his own kind than anyone else during this damned massacre."

Diarmuid straightened. "Then we must redouble our efforts. We must remove the Taelas from the map like the Garmathians nearly did to us!"

"They're crossbreeding their mortal elves with giants"—Alsantör stomped to emphasise the last word—"and they're allies with Nethuania and Orovín! You'd risk open war with the entire southern half of the eastern lands? Just us versus all of them? We've *got* to sue for peace, or else Prastömin will be the one wiped off the map!"

"Karthénos would come to our aide, as would Áfgal." Diarmuid placed a hard hand on Alsantör's shoulder. "Shall we send a pigeon to them?"

"We don't have a written alliance with Áfgal—'tis only by word —and I just executed their most beloved hero a mere *season* ago. They'll turn on us quicker than our hounds when they starve. And

Jannon?" Alsantör shook his head. "He's already pulling out of the crusade. He won't risk more of his knights' blood for *our* squabbles!"

"Ah, yes. Speaking of Jannon ..."

The prince clenched his fists. "Have you heard naught of what I just said? Is this damned crusade all you care about?" He trembled, but his voice grew stronger. "My men are dying out there. Our people are losing hope. I nearly lost my life because of this campaign. Yet, all you care about is staging another attack? You want even *more* warfare and bloodshed? When was the last time you even left the damned halls of this keep?"

The king's silence was deafening. He opened his mouth to respond but then snapped his mouth shut in a rare show of restraint.

"Look, Father," said Alsantör gently. "I'm not questioning your abilities as king. I just ... I see too much. I hear too much. I'm not even inside these borders as often as I should be."

Diarmuid sighed. "I don't expect you to understand, Alsantör. You won't until you are king."

Alsantör closed his eyes. *Fat chance of that.* "There's only one way I'll ever sit atop that throne, Father. Wizards willing, that will never happen."

"There is another way." Diarmuid raised an eyebrow and looked hard into his son's eyes. "A way for the throne to be given to you. But you must promise me, my son—"

Not this again.

"Promise me you will be merciful and—"

"Stop it. Please." Alsantör shook his father by his shoulders. "I can't do it. I won't."

"Oh, Alsantör," whispered Diarmuid. "If only you could see ..."

I see, Daela. I see more than you know. Taking a shaky breath, Alsantör cleared his throat and picked the crumpled scroll off the ground. "I received a letter in Nethuania regarding Jannon's travels. What did he want?"

ALSANTÖR SLOWLY ENTERED THE CAVE OF THE SPEAKERS AFTER placing his two silver coins at the feet of its guardian statues. He shivered despite the summer heat surrounding him. The clouds above wept, sending rain throughout the forest and cleansing the air of pollen. As he stepped further inside, a different warmth enveloped him. The pungent scent of the sacred pool's mineral steam tickled his nose until his eyes watered. His muddy boots crunched over the gravel and calcified silt that composed the cave's floor.

His heart jumped as he caught sight of the hunch-backed elf draped in white: Brayson, Speaker of the Wizards. *It's alright, Tör. He doesn't know yet.*

"What brings you to the sacred pool, Prince of Prastömin?"

Alsantör grimaced at Brayson's thready voice—it sounded like rusted metal being dragged across a stone floor. "I come on behalf of all affected by the Crusade of Light."

Brayson's head tilted. "An unusual call, coming from the son of a king."

Alsantör squinted. "I could send my father, instead."

"That would be unnecessary," said Brayson, suddenly stiff. The distant roll of thunder rumbled, sending tiny ripples through the pool's still water.

The prince's mouth twitched in a victorious smirk. "I also come for another reason, Sacred One. I wish to see the face of Üendevail."

Brayson bared his yellowing fangs. "Even I can grant you no such gift. The mirror of the Wizards shows only what it wishes."

Alsantör frowned. He opened his mouth to respond, but—

"Take off your clothes, Prince of Prastömin."

Hesitantly, Alsantör obliged. He slipped his shirt over his head, dropping it to the ground between them. *What the hell are you doing, Tör? What kind of madness are you letting him do to you?* His thoughts raced as he untied the golden rope that held up his trousers. He shimmied them down to his knees, letting them fall to his ankles.

"And your undergarments."

Brayson's demand struck the prince as excessive. He looked around the sparsely lit cave. Odd shadows from the forest's ferns and moss danced in the flickering light of the torches, and a shiver slithered down his spine. "But—"

"You cannot bathe in the sacred pool with anything clinging to your fleshly self," Brayson hissed as he motioned to the water. "Remove your clothes, or face death upon your entrance into the place of the mirror."

The prince gulped and slipped off the rest of his clothing, stepping out of his boots last. He crossed his wrists at his groin, cupping his manhood as though the blind elf beside him could see. *This is ridiculous. I've swum in this pool plenty a time without stripping down to naught but my skin.*

"You may enter, son of the king."

Finally. Alsantör stepped into the pool. The warmth of its water tingled his toes, his ankles, his knees. He stopped when he was submerged to his waist, as he'd always done.

Brayson then removed his own cloak, revealing his mutilated skin and missing manhood. Alsantör winced at the sight. He imagined Brayson had once been a handsome man, perhaps had even been a soldier during the Great War before the Wizards called him to serve the Sacred Pool. But he had become hunched, wrinkled, and scarred. He shuffled around like an elderly mortal, blind to all except what the Wizards gave him. He, too, entered the pool. Placing an arthritic hand on Alsantör's shoulder to steady himself, Brayson pressed the heel of his other hand to the fresh scar on the prince's back. Alsantör grimaced as the icy burn of pain radiated up to his shoulder and down to his tailbone.

The speaker hissed again. "You come before the Wizards, having been touched by The Dark? 'Tis sacrilege to do such a thing."

Alsantör frowned. His gaze shifted back and forth as he shuffled through his recent memories since returning from Nethuania. *The giant? No, he never touched me like that. Rhona! Was it—* A flare of intense pain exploded in his body. "What are you *doing*?"

Brayson was digging his knuckles even deeper into his back, kneading with a surprising strength. "You must be cleansed, child of the forest. Washed of The Dark ere the Wizards bring their wrath upon you once you enter the place of the mirror."

Gnomes, I need to learn more of this. What good is a gift if I know not how to use it? "Apologies, Speaker. I should never have brought my pride into this sacred pool."

"What you ask of the Wizards, Prince of Prastömin, is not for the weak of spirit." Brayson moved his hand from Alsantör's scar and onto the top of his head. "Sink. Let the blood of the Wizards wash you clean so that you may enter the divine space of the mirror."

Alsantör's heart raced, and a cold sweat frosted his forehead. *Wizards, give me strength.* Trembling, he knelt. His instincts screamed and clamoured. The cries of his fallen comrades echoed in his ears, and he could see the fear in those speckled amber eyes that watched him from afar. Hot mineral water covered his head as flashes of memories haunted him. Flashes of futures coming. A minute passed. Panic threatened to open his lungs for a breath—for a scream that would mean his doom. Never before had the Wizards required such torment. Never before had they required the drowning of their followers.

A second minute, and the prince's lungs burned. The edges of his vision narrowed. Bright white light shattered the blackness in pulses, images of golden hair, emerald eyes, and winged shadows flashing with it.

Wizards be *damned*. Heart pounding in his ears, Alsantör flailed, sweeping the speaker's hand off his head and screaming even before his face even broke the surface. The bitter, hot water scalded his tongue as it hadn't done to his outer skin. The guttural cry that reverberated throughout the cave was of a man who'd seen death's face clearer than any summer's sunset. Than any full moon on a cloudless night.

The prince clasped his hand about Brayson's throat, hissing at the shrivelled man. A dull pain flashed throughout his chest, thumping down his arm just enough to startle him. Releasing the Speaker, he scrambled out of the pool, trembling, and staring at his steaming palms. *What am I doing?*

PART II

THE TREATY OF TAELONAEL

19

THE REPUBLIC OF KARTHÉNOS

*O*il lamps littered the council room, but their wicks were cold and dry. Rarely did the sun set in the summer. The coming of autumn, however, made itself known with the first dusting of snow.

The clear, crystal windows of the east-facing wall bounced colourful flecks of rainbow along the shimmering walls of rough, white quartz. While the glass protected the room from the harsh winds of the tundra, they did little for trapping warmth. Those of Karthi blood never minded—after all, were they not created for such a cold environment?

Jannon wore naught but a light jerkin over a pair of thin breeches. His taupe hair was slicked back from his furrowed brow as he pored over the ledgers of the summer taxes.

Why are the funds so low fer the West? Perhaps I should send fer Senator Moira. She never allows such pitfalls. His eyes travelled down the page. *And the North's numbers are all wrong ... again. Gnomes be merciful, Siobhan, if I must protect ye from the banks again—*

The echo of shoes clacking on stone approached the council room. He sighed. "Senator Kiera, now is not the time. I must rework yer daughter's—"

"Has me sister fergotten her maths again? Pity."

Jannon snapped his head up as the woman across the elongated marble table arched a sharp eyebrow above her sapphire eyes. "Senator Moira. A pleasant surprise."

The woman smiled tightly. "Me laird." Moira removed her fur-lined gloves and placed them on the table. She wore a simple dress of pale blue silk with a matching summer cloak. Fine silver thread weaved into her ash-brown braid and around her head, dangling a single tear-shaped sapphire upon her porcelain forehead.

Jannon frowned at her grim expression. "I was just thinking about ye."

"Were ye?" Moira cocked her head. "Surely it's not about last season's numbers."

She's too much like her father fer her own good. "I was going to send fer ye after finalising. Perhaps I should—"

"Is there a reason the republic's treasury has cut our funding, me laird? Are we not in charge of the tundra's winter agriculture?"

Jannon set his jaw. "Gnomes, Moira. I be the bloody duke. Ye're not to interrupt me when I speak."

"And I am the representative of the West. We are a republic, not a monarchy." Moira's tone pierced like a falling icicle. "As such representative, I come to petition on behalf of my people—yer people—the safety and welfare of whom have fallen so far to the wayside that it must no longer be ignored."

"And what problems have arisen that require such prompt attention, besides the funding of the West?"

To Jannon's annoyance, Moira sat. *I didn't invite ye to sit, Senator. Mind yer form.* "If I knew no better, I would say this hostility comes from a being who wishes to see me hanged."

The senator's eyes narrowed. "Hostility, ye say? Why would I wish to see ye hanged, Father?"

Jannon's eye twitched. *I swear to the Wizards, ye're going to be the death of me.* "Ye still haven't answered my question."

"The Áfgalese." The fire behind Moira's sapphire eyes flared at her enunciation of the word.

Jannon, however, chuckled. "Ye'll hafta be much more specific than that, daughter. The Áfgalese have given us many problems over the past hundreds of years, not excluding their halfbreed bastard 'hero.'"

"I never had the pleasure of meeting Sólan the Grim before Diarmuid's son took his head."

Jannon's stomach sank. *Ye don't know. Gnomes, please tell me she doesn't know who he really was.* His heart raced. The silence, as short as it was, threatened to break his composure.

"But a dead halfbreed is not why I come, me laird."

Oh, thank the Wizards.

Moira looked down at the table and clasped her hands together tightly, enough to blanch her knuckles and fingertips. "We need knights. We need dotaires. A plague is sweeping through the villages, and it's already decimated our barley farmers in Sraevorna."

"What does this have to do with Áfgal?"

"I'm not finished," Moira hissed.

Her father closed his eyes to hide their rolling, but she ignored him.

"The Maseño District of Áfgal has failed to rein in the continued assaults on our caribou drovers," Moira continued. "Two of them—and their families—were slaughtered. Half their herds were stolen. Ye know as well as I how preciously rare Karthi children are, particularly Karthi sons. Two boys lost their lives to that raid, one of them unborn."

"Káil." Jannon could no longer hold back his tears. He clamped a hand over his mouth and trembled. *What have I done? Killed me son. Such a rarity in these lands, yet I rejoiced at his death.*

"I've already spoken with Sir Cadman, lead treasurer and chief commander of Karthénos. Me words fell upon deaf ears, I'm afraid."

Bloody Prasti. The lot of them. "Have ye spoken with his first knight?"

"I have."

"And?"

Moira rolled her eyes. "Would I be here speaking with ye if she could do anything? Her title is just that—a mere title. Dame Saoirse has no—"

"They're both Prasti. I'll have the second treasurer speak with them."

"Saoirse was raised here. She may be Prasti by blood, but she is Karthi in every way. If even *she* can't get through to her uncle, how will a banker?"

"What would ye have me do, Moira?" Jannon's teeth clenched tight enough to cramp his jaw. "Throw gold at ye and tell ye to begone?"

"I'm not me sister."

Jannon gaped. *Gnomes be merciful, ye're just like yer mother, too.*

"But ye could move up the wedding." Moira's head cocked, an eyebrow arching high once again.

"What wedding?" Jannon's smile was strained as he fought against the pounding of his heart.

Moira scoffed. "Please, like Siobhan can keep a bloody secret. Ye know the laws, Daela. She can't marry until I do, and yet she has a suitor before me? The *prince* of Prastömin, no less?"

Jannon's gaze flitted around the council room. "No one was to hear of this. Not even Siobhan."

"Oh? She must take after her mother, then. Kiera's conniving has always found a way to gather information like mountain tops gather snow." Tears formed in the corners of Moira's eyes as she bounced her leg and took a shaky breath. "I shouldn't be upset, but what woman wouldn't wish to marry a prince?"

"Gnomes be merciful, Moira. Don't do this."

"Do what?"

New tears threatened Jannon's eyes. "It pains me enough fer ye to discover this from shrouded hearsay. I was going to wait. I was going to tell the both of ye. I may have found one for ye, a *better* one than that bullheaded Prasti."

A sad laugh escaped Moira's chest. "I didn't mean to bother ye about this. I never thought I'd be wanting a husband."

Jannon stood and walked around the table to embrace her, giving his daughter a kiss on her forehead. "'Tis never a bother to see ye, daughter." He cradled her face in his hands and wiped a tear from her cheek. Pinching her chin, he smiled. "Ye don't deserve a mere prince, Moira. Ye deserve so much more. I have no doubt ye'd find yer own suitor should ye put yer mind to it. However, Diarmuid tells me he's found ye a better fit."

Moira rolled her eyes in disgust. "I'd rather marry that asshole, Sir Cadman, than anyone of Diarmuid's choosing."

JANNON PACED THE MAIN HALL WITH DEEP WRINKLES CUT ACROSS HIS brow. The afternoon sun made the polished, white quartz sparkle like fresh ice crystals after a winter storm. Ivory and grey tables of marble and gleaming chairs of silver lined the walls, interrupted only by the massive hearth of bright marble. The duke's breath fogged as he quickened his pacing.

"Two boys lost their lives to that raid, one of them unborn." Gnomes, *they grow bolder every summer. If Cadman could only see beyond his inexplicable feud with Moira, perhaps—*

"I know that look."

Jannon jumped, spinning to lock his panicked eyes with a well-known topaz gaze. He slumped his shoulders and sighed. "Gnomes, Kiera. Ye startled me."

Kiera smiled and rubbed his shoulder. "I didn't intend fer that."

Jannon allowed a smile to touch his lips. "I know, and ye never will." He wrapped an arm about her hips and pulled her close. After a soft kiss and a tight embrace, he released her. "Ye look ravishing today, lover."

His partner giggled. "I wish I could say the same. Ye look sour. Was it another poorly timed letter from treasury?"

Jannon shook his head slightly. "Not entirely, though there is one thing I wish to speak of regarding the movement of coin."

"Hmph. Has our daughter forgotten her maths again?"

"That is exactly what Moira asked when—"

"Moira? She's *here*? Why?" Kiera's expression suddenly twisted.

"The same reasons any of our other senators would be—to bring attention to the needs of our people." The duke narrowed his eyes. "And I did charge her with the safety and welfare of the West."

Kiera rolled her eyes. "As though the West is the only corner of Karthénos? She toys with ye, Jannon, and it makes ye look sour. Aged. Like a mortal, almost. Much like her mother did to ye."

"This *conversation* is what's making me feel sour." Jannon turned away and crossed his arms. "She's still me child. Just as much as is Siobhan."

"So was Sólan the Grim, yet I don't hear ye—"

"Ye *dare* utter that name here?" Jannon hissed. He spun and clasped his hand around Kiera's throat, snarling. "That monster was a scourge upon these lands. A taint on me bloodline that was necessary to remove."

Kiera's eyes widened. She tugged at the duke's hand to no avail. Her face flushed, her lips turning purple. "Please," she choked. "Stop."

"Káil." Jannon released his grip and trembled. The woman crumpled to the ground, wheezing. "Gnomes, I'm ... I'm so sorry, me love."

"Don't be." Kiera rubbed the front of her neck and gulped cold air. "I went too far, me laird. I should have known better."

Jannon grimaced. Stooping, he helped his lover to her feet. "No, Kiera. 'Twas I who went too far. I should never have touched ye." Moira's words again echoed in his ears. *"Ye know how preciously rare Karthi children are, particularly sons."* Gnomes, only too well. "What have I done?" he whispered, his icy gaze threatening to melt into tears. "Ye're right, Kiera. He was my child."

"That mongrel was nothing more than a halfbreed bastard, Jannon—a dangerous one, at that." Kiera's voice dripped with malice. "He was nothing more than the product of an Áfgalese seductress who dared to accuse ye of the unthinkable. He should never have lived as long as he did."

The duke swallowed the lump in his throat, but it merely grew larger. His voice now shook as much as his hands. "He was me firstborne—me only son." *A son I should have held close, title and power be damned.* He dropped to his knees and hugged himself as the sobs overtook him. "I have been blessed with more children than any elf can dream of in a thousand years. Yet, I've murdered one of them for the sake of power. For the sake of secrecy. For pride."

Kiera placed a gentle hand upon his shoulder. "Ye did what was necessary, me laird. The Dark held him long before anyone else could."

"What are yer intentions, senator?" said Jannon, suddenly venomous. "First, ye defend him. Now, ye imply that he was worse than the sprites we fought more than a thousand years ago. Do ye forget so easily what those demons were?"

"I merely intended to clarify yer own words, Jannon." Kiera crossed her arms, towering over him with a scowl. "Did ye love him, or no? Did ye thrust our people into the Crusade of Light because of him or in spite of him? Karthi blood has been spilled in the name of this war! And now, ye regret achieving yer goal?" Her shrill voice echoed off the stone walls and tables. "I will not have the father of *both* of my children—"

"Both?" Jannon snapped his gaze upward. "Ye're with child?"

A smile crept across the senator's face. "The dotaires say I've been with child fer a season, confident that I carry a son."

Another son? Ina, Gnomess of Fertility, ye're too kind to me. "Kiera, this is wonderful news!" Jannon leapt to his feet and embraced his lover, twirling her until they were both dizzy. He kissed her hard. Burying his face into her neck, he whispered, "Marry me. If this be a son, I want him as my heir."

Kiera giggled and tangled her fingers in his feathery hair. "'Twould bring me no better joy, me laird."

The duke slid himself back onto his knees and kissed her belly. "Ye deserve no less, me lady."

20

ISLE OF DEATH

"Móta! You are dead, hármenato!" Twelve-year-old Montrél giggled, poking his sibling in his chest. Silky black ringlets of hair bounced around his olive-toned face as he dissolved into hearty laughter. A playful grin dimpled his cheeks.

Montrél's little brother, however, merely whined. "You promised I would win this time!" The boy threw his stick to the ground and crossed his arms, his bottom lip pushed out.

"I know, I know. Sorry," said Montrél through another giggle. "I forgot again." He stooped to pick up his brother's stick and broke it against his knee.

"*Montrél*! That's mine!"

"I know, Sólan! Just wait!"

A warm breeze kicked small plumes of red dust around the boys, coating their hair and faces with its fine particles. Sólan simply kicked at the pebbles on the ground, huffing while Montrél tied a piece of bark to the broken end of the stick.

"You broke my sword, Montrél. When Mother—"

"You will say nothing to Athóta, Sólan. Here." Montrél handed the new toy to his younger brother. "Now you have an haché, just like Ignacio the Grim."

Sólan's eyes lit up. The bright specks in his eyes danced in the Áfgalese summer sun as his smile widened enough for his baby fangs to show. "I *love* Ignacio the Grim!"

Montrél chuckled and tousled Sólan's wavy brown hair. "I know you do. I would tell you none of his stories if you hated them, silly."

"Yes, you would. You tell me those stupid girl stories too." Sólan snatched his toy from his brother's grasp. He clumsily waved it above his head and around his body, leaping, somersaulting, and twirling in a fit of glee. "You think I will be grim like Ignacio, Montrél?"

"You can be whatever you want, little brother. You could be a blacksmith, like Hidalgo, or a baker, like Átha!"

Sólan's smile disappeared. "But … he's not *my* átha."

"What!" Montrél grasped Sólan's shoulders. His deep hazel eyes bore holes into the sad gaze of his brother. "Of course he is your átha! Who else could there be?"

"Then why are my ears and teeth so pointy?" Sólan bared his fangs in show. "Am I cursed?"

Montrél's nose twitched. "No, you are not cursed. None of the Gods would curse a six-year-old boy like you."

Sólan's lip trembled again. "But … he calls me a mastázo," he whispered. "He says that I am not his son."

"He's a liar, Sólan. If you were not his son, why would he stay with athóta when that elf—" Montrél shut his mouth and winced.

"You mean … 'tis true? We do not share a father?"

Montrél fidgeted with his fingers and shifted his weight as he considered what to say. "I want you to remember something, Sólan. Never forget your family. Your *real* family. Mother … me." Tears pooled in the older boy's eyes, matching Sólan's own watery gaze. "When you are old enough, I will tell you about your real átha, okay?"

Sólan looked forlornly to the ground and nodded with a sniffle. "Okay."

"Hey," said Montrél. He lifted Sólan's chin with a finger. "Would Ignacio the Grim let these things keep him from doing what is right?"

Sólan's mouth broke into another impish smile. "No. He would fight."

"Exactly." Montrél straightened his posture and rolled his shoulders. "Sólan the Grim"—he pointed the end of his own stick at his brother's chest—"I challenge you to a duel."

The young boy beamed with delight. "I accept your challenge, Montrél the Mean!"

SÓLAN'S EYES FLUTTERED OPEN, AND THE IMAGES OF HIS BROTHER FADED to the deep recesses of his mind. It had been a happy time, despite the knowing—before the baker took his innocence, and before Hidalgo shared in such abuse. Sólan rubbed his face and inhaled deeply. His breath caught as a sob threatened to emerge. *I have not forgotten you, Brother.* Sitting upright, he lowered his forehead onto the heels of his hands. *Nor have I forgotten you, Mother.* He released a ragged breath, shaking his head vigorously as though he could erase his memories.

Even his pleasant dreams broke him—sometimes, more so than his nightmares.

A faint knock in the darkness interrupted his grief. Welcoming the distraction, he wiped the moisture from his eyes and grunted, "Come in."

The hinges of the door creaked as Dakil slipped into the room. *I have to oil those damned things.* "What time is it?"

"Midnight," whispered Dakil. "We need to talk."

Sólan yawned. "What happened?"

"We found land." Dakil's voice quivered with fear.

"Is it not the intention of sailing from one place to another to find land?" Sólan stretched, his body popping with the movement. He scooted himself to the edge of the plush feather mattress and readied himself to stand but didn't.

"It is Isli O Kamotiyen, Captain." Dakil wrung his hands, his breath shallow. "The Isle of Death. We *cannot* land here."

Sólan groaned and rubbed his face. "Of course we can land here. Mere legends scare me not."

"It is no legend. I've seen—"

"The dreaded aswang that haunts its beach?" Sólan's voice dripped with mockery. "And here I thought you to be a man of courage."

"You insult me." Dakil bared his teeth. "I'm not fearful like the others. I have seen the dead on the isle's shores and watched countless souls enter its jungles in search of food, never to return." The swordsman took a defiant step forward. "We cannot land here. Even Kadek avoided this place."

Sólan bared his own fangs. "How long until we reach the Island of the Chainbreakers?"

Dakil's nose flared. "Fourteen days, if the wind stays strong."

Gods, that is far too long to be trapped on this ship with you without— "And if they don't?"

"Twenty—or more." Dakil shrugged. "It all depends on the currents."

Sólan looked at the ceiling. *Fantastic.* "How much water do we have?"

"Enough. We gather it with every mist."

"And food?"

Dakil fidgeted and looked to his feet. "Three days."

"Three days?" The air left Sólan's lungs. "Gods, that is not sufficient. What the hell happened? Was Kadek not prepared?"

"*You* weren't prepared! We had more food coming in Bansungei, but you insisted we leave that drowned valley!" Dakil snarled. "And now you want to risk your crew's lives on this—"

"You never mentioned how little we had in provisions! I had no choice in Bangsungei. I am being hunted, Dakil. *And* we were under attack!"

"We all are being hunted. The cavalry hates me too." Dakil crossed his arms, lifting an eyebrow as if challenging Sólan to argue further.

The captain didn't take the bait. For a tense moment, both men stubbornly glared at each other. When Sólan's eyes pulsed in pain, Dakil blinked. "Wait. You have magic. Can you—"

"I cannot create something from nothing, sañero. I am not a god."

"Really? You act, curse, and give orders like one."

Sólan glowered. "I am not so self-indulgent. I do not ask for sacrifice, for worship, for anything." He grabbed two fistfuls of his own hair in frustration. "I wield The Dark. Nothing more. Such powers are limited, Dakil. Perhaps you should think before you speak."

The swordsman rolled his eyes. "I am no child for you to scold."

"Then what are you?" Sólan jumped to his feet and puffed out his chest. "Because you stammer and argue like my late wife."

Dakil snorted. "You mean the child you didn't rape but still married? The child you killed?" His words pierced Sólan's chest, but he wasn't done. "I will take my leave, unless you're finished insulting me."

The Áfgaliard swallowed. "Quite."

They stared at each other once more in stubborn silence, Dakil, again, breaking the trance. "I know who betrayed us."

Sólan blinked. *Us?* "And who would that be?"

"Do you remember the man who brought you and Bayani aboard?"

Kalasin. I knew he was worthless. "Is there a reason you came to me at midnight? You could have told me all this after dawn."

Dakil's angry façade was betrayed by the hint of a smile. "I sleep as well as you do—not at all."

"I was asleep when you knocked," grumbled Sólan.

"Hard to believe." Dakil reached up and brushed the back of his knuckles against Sólan's bare shoulder; he froze at his own audacity.

Sólan's heart pounded in his chest. He prepared to take a small step forward when—

"I should leave. I've overstayed my welcome." Blushing, Dakil turned toward the door.

"Wait." His gentle hand around Dakil's elbow stayed the swordsman's departure. "I did not say you had to leave, sañero. You may stay."

"Don't say that."

"Why not?"

Dakil faced Sólan again. "Because I *will* stay." His voice asked for Sólan to let him leave, but his smoky russet eyes begged for his touch.

Sólan tightened his jaw. His gaze flitted between Dakil's longing gaze and his eager lips. Tugging on the swordsman's arm, he pulled him closer. "Then stay. Please?"

"One dangerous love has already hurt me," whispered Dakil. He stared at Sólan's mouth as they intertwined their fingers. "I can't have another."

"Who said anything about love?"

Dakil's breath hitched. The room reeked of lust as each man stared at the other. Their faces inched closer together, and Sólan inhaled in the swordsman's scent of salt and fine brandy. Goosebumps exploded on Sólan's skin as Dakil's hot breath teased his mouth with wanting.

Finally, Dakil's lips brushed against Sólan's. The sensation sent fiery bolts down his jaw and into his groin. He released Dakil's hand only to wrap his arm about the man's waist, drawing him closer.

Sólan shivered as Dakil's tongue opened his mouth and touched the sharpness of his fangs. All of the captain's senses flared, throbbing through his hands, his chest, his manhood. He felt Dakil's hand travelling up his muscular flank while his other wrapped around him, beneath the hem of his low waistband.

Gods, you taste incredible. A stiffness pressed into the front of his pelvis, and he shivered again. His heart pounding with anticipation, 'twas as though his hips moved of their own accord. He ground himself against Dakil, each movement sending tremors through the body of the man in his arms.

Sólan caressed Dakil's jaw and neck, sliding his hand to the back of his head to grasp a fistful of his luscious, unbraided hair. Dakil, broke their kiss, leaned his head back with a groan. Sólan nibbled and sucked his earlobe, moving his mouth down the swordsman's neck and stopping just above his collarbone. His free hand gently tugged at Dakil's shirt.

"Wait." Dakil released his embrace and pushed himself away.

No! Sólan's heart thumped, his throat dry with desire. His erection throbbed beneath his trousers, but he stepped back. "What's wrong?"

Dakil grimaced, looking to his feet with a flushing face. "I'm no smuggler's whore." He looked into Sólan's pained gaze with a trembling lip. Taking a sharp breath, he added, "Get some sleep. I'll get some men ready to land."

"Okay." Sólan stared longingly at the door as Dakil left. *Medría. Why him?* He winced as a twinge of victory pierced his mind. They were to land at this supposedly haunted island, despite the swordsman's initial protests and the palpable fear in his mesmerising eyes. *Halaña, why must you torture me so?*

THE MORNING MIST BURNED AWAY WITH THE RISING OF THE WESTERN sun. Sólan peered over the railing toward the island before him—a beach of fine white sand that enveloped a dense jungle of green. The salty air was heavy with moisture, exacerbating the growing heat. Beads of sweat dripped down Sólan's face and neck, saturating the collar of the thin cotton shirt he had stolen from Kadek's vast armoire. It was bright red and plenty wide at the shoulders, but the sleeves and torso were shorter than his physique required. He didn't mind the awkward fit. 'Twas of higher quality than anything he'd worn in the last ten years, save for the Áfgalese cloak he had collected—and subsequently lost— from the dead slaver seven days ago. He would hardly miss it come winter, though. His Karthi blood made him far more resilient to the cold of the North than the heat of the tropics. Besides, Kadek's Prasti wool cloak fit him just fine.

Sólan squinted and shielded his eyes with his hand as the emerging sun reflected off the clear turquoise water. His face burned and chapped, despite the wet air. Had it been drier, the heat might have been tolerable. In this part of the world, however, the muggy atmosphere dominated.

An unease churned in his stomach as he watched Bayani lead a group of several mates to shore. All of them were young, inexperienced boys. *If this place is as deadly as you claim, Dakil, then why send our youth?*

The smell of salted brandy wafted through his nostrils, and his heart jumped. *Dammit.* He looked askance at the swordsman who'd suddenly appeared at his side. Sweat was also beaded upon his unusually pale brow, though 'twas obvious it wasn't from the heat.

"You look like you have seen your god in the flesh," said Sólan.

Dakil gulped, the threads of silk in his voice unravelling with a tremor as he said, "How long should we wait for them to return?"

Sólan frowned, facing the swordsman. "What is it that haunts this island?"

"The Pontianak," Dakil whispered. "A demon of Misó who hunts any who enter her jungle."

The scent of fear was nearly strong enough to strangle Sólan, and a slow shiver crept up his spine. *Likely just a fellow mastázo, Sólan—one who has made a life outside of Taelonael, away from her captors.* "If they do not return by nightfall, we can assume them dead."

"Nipantot ki," Dakil cursed. "I'm no coward like the rest of this crew."

Sólan crossed his arms with a glare. "Aeh. Fuck you too, pundijo. I never accused you of cowardice. There is nothing more deadly than a woman scorned, particularly one of mortal elf blood."

"Ha! You think the Pontianak is a mere kapiret-liho?"

Sólan's heart flipped at Dakil's chuckles and melted at his smile. *Gods, keep laughing. 'Tis music to my ears.*

"No, Captain. You will pray to all thirteen of your gods when you meet her."

Not a mortal elf. A Sprite. The Áfgaliard shuddered again. *A woman who has lost control of The Dark. A woman who has given her heart to the One who gave her power.* "I stand by my words, Papuan. If the sun sets before they return, we leave."

"And what of food?"

Sólan grimaced. "How is the fishing between here and Chainless's home?"

Dakil glared. "You didn't ask before we landed," he hissed. "You could've prevented this entire problem if—"

"Fuck, Dakil! This is information you could have given me last night!" The Dark flared in Sólan's eyes; he grasped the swordsman's collar and pulled him close enough to whisper, "I think that would have been far more important than that gods-damned kiss." A blunt pain in his chest knocked his breath away, and he released his grip, leaning onto the rail to keep from falling to his knees. *Thank the Gods t'was your fist and not your sword.*

"That 'gods-damned kiss' was important to *me*." Dakil lowered his fist and stomped away.

Sólan blinked, jaw agape. He watched the swordsman climb the centre mast and work with the sail. *What the hell is wrong with you, Sólan? Perhaps 'tis you who toys with him.*

21

THE PONTIANAK

The sky began its colourful transition as the sun descended over the eastern horizon. All had been quiet during the day, and Sólan's unease swelled with each moment. A faint noise at the top of the beach reached his keen ears. Something approached, and he didn't know whether to rejoice or to scream.

All eyes aboard the *Silent Dancer* were on the shoreline as the shrubs rustled. Sólan held his breath, knuckles blanching as he gripped his hatchet. *Show yourself, Sprite.*

Suddenly, a figure burst out of the jungle and limped along the sand toward the lifeboat. *Medría!*

"Pantot!" Dakil's voice called from behind. "It's Bayani!"

Sólan blinked as Dakil's words took a moment to sink in. "Medría!" The captain scrambled onto the railing and dived into the clear, warm water. He glided just under its surface for several metres before emerging to take a breath. Though battling the receding tide, he reached the shore in short time.

He stumbled and cursed as his wet boots sank into the fine white sand all the way to his ankles. Sólan reached Bayani and caught him just as the smuggler collapsed, blood frothing from his nose and mouth.

"Fuck, Bayani. Stay with me." Blood also streamed from Bayani's eyes—well, one of his eyes. The other was a mere fleshy hole where there once had been an earthy-brown iris. "*Gods, what did that thing do to you?*"

"Sólan? How did you—"

"No time. We need to get the hell out of here." Sólan slipped his shoulder under Bayani's arm and dragged him to the lifeboat. "And what the fuck happened to you?" He asked, noting the gnawed stump where his left hand used to be.

"My belly. It ... it hurts," Bayani gargled, ignoring his extremity.

Sólan helped him rest against the side of the boat and lifted his bloody shirt to inspect. *Shit.* Blood oozed from wounds deep enough to cut through muscle and—*is that a piece of entrails poking out?* The captain gulped. His eyes burned with The Dark's flames, and he placed a hand on Bayani's abdomen. "This will sting."

"What you are—*ouch*!" Slowly, the flesh closed to rough, purple scars.

"*Pantot*, sañero. She almost disemboweled you." Sólan flashed a mischievous grin.

"I *know* t'at!" Bayani grimaced, baring bloody and cracked teeth. "We need to go. T'e sun almost set."

"Yes, yes. I know." Sólan quickly went to work healing the man's arm, face and mouth before loading him into the boat. He pushed, but the vessel wouldn't budge. *Fucking piece of—* a loud cry of what sounded like an infant suddenly echoed over the beach, and Sólan froze. "Wait here."

"Where you going?"

"I need to find that child." Panic settled in Sólan's chest as he snapped his gaze to the edge of the jungle.

"T'at no child, Sólan." Bayani trembled. A sweet scent of floral perfume wafted through the air. So sweet, in fact, it forced them both to gag. "She's here."

Not a Sprite, thank the Gods. "The Pontianak, yes?" Sólan's eye twitched at Bayani's nod of confirmation. "And she killed the others?"

"Ta. We need to—"

"I *know*." The Dark flared, and Sólan resumed pushing. Finally, the boat launched. A thick purple fog engulfed them, and the sweet perfume gave way to a stench that could only be described as death. The infant's cries quieted to a distant whimper. Once Sólan was waist-deep into the sea, he scrambled aboard the boat.

"I t'ought you no able to swim," said Bayani.

Sólan grunted. *Where are the damned oars?* "Now is not the time to question my honesty. Help me find the oars."

"Why you save me?"

"*Gods*, Bayani! We are not safe yet!" At his words, the fog thickened. The men lifted the boat's floorboards and fumbled under the seats, searching for oars. Searching for … anything.

Sólan's hand landed on a cold and clammy piece of flesh. A foot. "Bayani, why did you remove your boots?"

"I didn't."

What the hell? The captain froze. The surrounding fog cleared just enough for him to see an ashen and half-rotted foot attached backward to its ankle. He moved his gaze up the leg to the ragged hem of a creature's dirty, white gown. Stringy black hair tangled its way down its shoulders to its womanly hips. The creature turned, revealing a grey but surprisingly beautiful face. Rounded, upturned eyes were of the purest black onyx, and nothing else.

The Pontianak.

Definitely not a Sprite—Sólan removed his hand from her ankle and gulped—far more terrifying. The creature snarled, baring jagged shark-like teeth that were stained with blood, bits of flesh stuck between them. She lifted her hands, bringing them close to his face. Her fingers were nearly as long as her forearms, and her nails were the size and shape of an eagle's talons.

She lunged. *Fuck!* Sólan dodged just enough to save his eyes. His cheek burned as her thumb sliced deep into his flesh. He healed to a fresh scar before she pounced again. He ducked. She screamed. Her high-pitched wail pierced his ears, and he grimaced.

His eyes pulsed with a searing heat again. He growled, jumping to his feet. The boat rocked, but he kept his footing. "Vita i le medría, le putathóta!" He launched himself into her abdomen, wrapping his muscular arms around her. She grasped his ribs, embedding her talons into his lungs as he flung himself over the side of the boat.

SÓLAN AND PONTIANAK DISAPPEARED BELOW THE WATER, LEAVING NO trace for Bayani to see except the growing swirl of crimson at its surface.

Where he go? The purple fog thickened once more, watering the air enough to block any echo of Bayani's screaming. He tried anyway. "Sólan!"

Dread set in, and his breath caught in his chest as tears welled up in his remaining eye. Bayani resumed his search and found the oars beneath a pile of rope and burlap, cursing he hadn't found them sooner. Fumbling with his half-healed stump, he slipped each oar into its lock.

He trembled. His ears rang in the silence, and his shredded clothing was soaked by the fog's chill. Clumsily, he rowed towards the ship. The Pontianak's stench faded from his nostrils, but he didn't slow to notice, didn't stop to see the gloom fading from purple to grey. He couldn't slow down—not, at least, until the burble of disturbed water froze him.

His heart pounded in his ears as he held his breath. "Sólan?" Bayani whispered, only to be met with more silence. The cold bit him again, and he shuddered; water lapped against the side of the boat. *Oh, Yusa, protect me.* Slowly, he peeked over the edge. He fixed his eyes on the moving water when—

Splash!

A head of tangled black hair burst from the water just millimetres from his face. Bayani shrieked, falling backward and hitting his head on the boat's opposite edge. He shook his head to focus his blurred vision. Long arms reached themselves into the boat, and broad shoulders slowly followed.

"Medría," said a familiar, husky voice.

"Sólan! You alive!" Bayani clambered to his knees and opened his arms with joy.

"Touch me and you will end up like this fucking undead *bitch*!" Sólan slammed the creature's head onto the floor between them. Stepping on her hair, he yanked his hatchet out from her skull. "Did you find the oars?"

Bayani nodded. *How did you do that? With just a hatchet?* "I just need that rope to tie my arm to—"

"Stop it. I row, you rest. That thing nearly took your life."

You stubborn kapiret-liho. "And almost yours."

Sólan shrugged, grasping at the handles and pulling them through the water with great force. "I always cheat death. Javiento taught me how when I was a boy."

"Javiento?"

"Tí Dioses lío, indionta." Sólan grumbled but never answered.

I no speak Áfgal-ish, asshole. "I … um … I want to t'ank you for saving—"

"Will you please stop talking for *one* fucking moment?" Sólan hissed. "There is nothing to thank. I already owe you for several of my lives, so I am merely repaying that debt. Medría, Bayani. When we met, I fucking hated you, and you know it. Your mouth, your temper … *Gods*, you tried to kill me based on a damned children's story."

Bayani fidgeted with his hands and looked to his lap. "I know." He tried to swallow the forming lump in his throat, but it remained. "I try to keep calm, but sometimes I can't stop it. It like my own version of The Dark."

Sólan clenched his jaw with a nod. "I used to be as reactive as you." He frowned as though in thought. "Actually, I still am."

At least I know you honest there.

"Look, I had convinced myself that you were a coward. But you have proven yourself otherwise."

The young smuggler gulped at Sólan's confession. "You should've let me die. I useless now. Wit' one hand and missing eye, I no can do anything. I better off dead."

"You are worth more alive than dead, regardless of the number of limbs you have," the captain snapped, though his expression softened. "I can, at the very least, give you that."

"Why? If you hate me so, why you save me? Why you do this?"

"Because I *want* to trust you, Bayani, and ... well. I no longer hate you. You and Tirsen were the first Nethuanians I met, and despite your lies and your temper"—Sólan shook his head and cursed—"fuck, never mind. 'Tis too complicated even for me."

Bayani flared his nostrils. "I only enjoy women."

"You think I was trying to *seduce* you? Gods, Bayani, you are hopeless." Sólan's laughter forced him to stop rowing and wipe the tears from his eyes. "If I wanted to bed you, you would already be naked and hanging over the side of this boat, screaming my name in pleasure."

"T'at is disgusting," said Bayani, shuddering. "I never touch another man like that. And it—"

"Forbidden by Yusa. Yes, I am aware, cabróde." He raised an eyebrow and gave a mischievous grin. "Besides, Tala was probably a much better lover than you would ever be."

Bayani gasped. "Aha! You did fuck her! You lucky son of Misó!"

Sólan laughed. "I thought you knew all along, for I am 'terrible at lying.'"

"Just like I knew you lie about no being able to swim."

"It does appear you have learned how to read me." Sólan leaned forward with a smirk. "But I feel you are still lying about never touching another man. How else could you manage lonesomeness on the sea?"

Bayani glared, waving his stump in Sólan's face. "I can't anymore, thanks to t'at Pontianak."

Another moment of silence, save for the rhythmic sound of rowing oars on the glassy water, and Sólan added, "I am glad you survived, Bayani."

Liar.

"You remind me of myself at your age."

I nothing like you, tulalo. "How so?"

Sólan shrugged. "Too many ways to list." The boat thunked against the side of the Silent Dancer's hull, thus ending their conversation. The Áfgaliard winked as he flashed a grin. "I think, someday, you and I can be friends, Bayani Lin."

As the fog's edge slithered toward the *Silent Dancer*, Dakil paced and cursed. *Why did you jump? What will your death accomplish if it kills us all? Nipantot ki, Sólan! I told you about this place, and you laughed at me.*

"Help! Bring us up!"

Dakil's attention snapped to the starboard rail. He peered over the side to see two silhouettes waving from a lifeboat. *The* lifeboat. "Shit!" He turned and called over his shoulder, "Ng ma nakologtas!" *Survivors!*

At once, three other men appeared to help Dakil hoist the boat to the deck with ropes and pulleys. Bayani was the first to fall clumsily aboard, Sólan close behind.

Thanks to Yusa you're alive, you reckless man. Dakil shook the thoughts from his head to maintain his indifferent façade, one he knew Sólan would see through with ease. "What happened? Where are the others?"

"Dead," said the captain. "As is that demon you warned me about."

The ice in his tone tore into Dakil's chest. He bit back his bubbling temper before speaking again. "I see you made the island safe again. We should rename it Isli O Pagnakato Kamotiyen—Isle of *Defeated* Death."

Sólan smirked tiredly before melting into his usual sad scowl. Dakil's breath hitched at the sight of his dilated pupils. *Stop it, Dakil. You're nothing more than a whore to him, remember?* "Shall we weigh anchor?"

Sólan frowned. "Not yet. With this *thing* no longer a threat"—he held up the Pontianak's mangled head—"we still need provisions. Limes, mangoes, anything we can get that will prevent scurvy."

"Scurvy?" Dakil blinked, his mouth agape. "After everything, you're afraid of *scurvy*?"

"I have suffered from it, and I wish to prevent that from happening again." Sólan raised an eyebrow. "I will go ashore myself to collect food should any others need my protection."

Dakil grumbled, "Your command, Captain." *Fucking tulalo.* The swordsman turned to give orders, but a hand on his shoulder stopped him.

"We need to talk. Alone."

Yusa save me, what now? Why do you insist we be alone? You tempt me, kapiret-liho, you seducer of Misó. "About?" Dakil peered over his shoulder at the beautiful man behind him. His heart skipped at the silver specks dancing in Sólan's deep amber gaze, a gaze that answered his question without a single word uttered. Goosebumps tingled his skin, and his tension melted away like a candle beneath a flaming wick.

As though reading him like a freshly carved wax tablet, the Áfgaliard stepped close and whispered, "Us, of course."

Us. Dakil shivered again. *There is nothing between us. There can never be anything between us. You stole my vengeance.* "Not now. We have repairs to make, food to gather."

A strained exhale escaped the captain's lips. Relief? Annoyance? *Yusa's grace, he's impossible to read.* Sólan's hand rubbed along Dakil's back and shoulders as he brushed past him to his quarters. His hatchet was hung on his belt, and he still held the Pontianak's head with his other hand. Dakil bit his tongue as he followed, against his better judgement.

The captain stopped in the doorway and turned. His gaze was unfixed, as though he were in deep thought. "Perhaps we should weigh anchor." He locked his intense eyes on Dakil's. "Only a fortnight until we reach the Chainbreakers?"

"Ta." The swordsman opened his mouth to ask more, but Sólan answered before he could ask his question.

"The wind will stay strong enough, I can promise you that. We have work to do, and I still want to wait until dawn to leave, if possible."

Dakil's nostrils flared. "Your command, Captain."

Sólan pursed his lips, an unfamiliar emotion sliding across his face, before slipping into the room. Stopping just inside the doorframe, he whispered, "Would you like to come in and talk?"

"Hundi. We still have repairs to make—I'll go ashore at dawn to collect timber and food if you still want me to do that." The door shut between them, and Dakil closed his eyes with a sigh at the interruption. *He just wanted to talk, tulalo. Why couldn't you just talk?*

22

LAIRD OF THE FOREST

"Of all the bloody women in the Eastern Lands, ya hafta fall f'r the one ya can't have." Naoise clutched his full mug of ale and stared muddy daggers at Alsantör.

The tavern was fuller than usual, the cheers of drunks as they clanged together their pints drowning their conversation enough that they felt safe from any spies. Not that anyone in those parts gave a damn about what conversations were had in a room of drunkard knights and their whores, even if a prince was amongst them.

Two women worked the ale bar, which was odd. Many knew Wizard's Wand for its expensive escorts and cheap drink. Men, women, oddlings ... the variety matched even the most voracious of appetites. 'Twas a central part of Prastömin's heart, located just outside the fortification of the royal keep. The tavern was where the bulk of all trade into the forest occurred, and with the autumn equinox quickly approaching, the border patrols were making their seasonal exchange of knights. It was a mere two-day hike to the westernmost border and half a day's ride eastward to the keep.

Alsantör refused to meet Naoise's gaze. *Gnomes, Neesh. You're not my father. Stop.*

"Just doen't make the same mistake I did, ya ken? I couldn't bear ta watch ya go through that."

"I won't, alright?" The prince rolled his eyes as he added, "You always do this. You lecture me on what's proper and what's not proper, regardless of *your* mistakes."

Naoise frowned. "At least I own 'em." He took a gulp of ale and wiped his mouth with his forearm. "How long've you two been ... ya ken?"

"We're not talking about this." Alsantör flicked his pinkie, sucking the back of his teeth. "I wasn't in my right mind that day, alright?"

"Clearly." The Veer grumbled something else inaudibly—likely, the prince assumed, another lecture on morality or proper form.

We're in a fucking brothel, Neesh. What's proper about that? Taking a cleansing breath, Alsantör finally took a draught of his own pint.

"So, how did that conversation with y'r father go?"

Alsantör finally met Naoise's gaze. "About as well as usual. I said something to trigger him, and he forgot who I was, and where he was. It was like he was at the battlefield all over again, I guess."

"Fookin' hell. He's gon' kill ya during one of his spells if y're not careful, Tör."

"Eil. He could have this time—he had a knife instead of a quill."

"Wizards, that's close."

The prince shrugged. "It's nothing, really. He didn't even strike." He took another sip and licked his lips. "But we spoke on more than just the Taelas."

Naoise lifted his cup to his mouth, his gaze burning in morbid curiosity. "Do tell."

"I ... I've been promised."

"Y've what now?" Naoise blew drink from his nose and coughed.

"Eil. 'A marriage fit for an emperor,' he called it."

"Ha! He must've found the missing Princess of Garmath!"

Alsantör gave a tired chuckle. "Not quite. But I told him I'd only consider if I got a new First Knight." He squinted and fidgeted with his pint. "So, I need your help to find a suitable candidate, since—oh, come on, Neesh, don't look at me like that."

Naoise stared at the prince with wide eyes and a furrowed brow. After a moment of obvious confusion, his expression twisted to a scowl. He slammed his pint onto the table with a growl, the drink sloshing onto the table from the force. "After ev'rything we've been through!" His shouting was loud enough to still the tavern's noise, but he took no notice. "Ev'rything I've sacrificed for—"

"Calm down, Neesh. I'm not taking any titles from you." *You and your fucking temper. And now I don't have Giaven to calm you.* A lump formed in the prince's throat at the memory of Naoise's brother. The carefree nature of his heart, and his impeccable ability to keep his older brother level-headed. Alsantör flitted his gaze around, relieved to see the Wand's patrons returning to their boisterous conversations.

Naoise bit his lip hard enough to draw blood, the silver droplet threatening to trickle down his chin and onto the table. A look of grief flashed across his face before disappearing as he said mockingly, "'Calm down, Neesh. I'm only betrayin' ya to my madman of a father.'"

"Stop calling him that," snapped Alsantör. "He's still my father, dammit. And will you fucking *listen* to me? You're getting promoted."

Naoise stiffened, his pupils suddenly dilated in fear. "What d'ya mean 'promoted?' I doen't want your job, Tör. It's bad enough that—"

"I'm still chief commander. No need to get your knickers in a twist. But I'm going to need your help with this."

"Well, I can tell ya now—I already know who'd be a good fit to replace me. He is young, but if it weren't f'r him and his quick thinkin', you'd be dead." Naoise downed the last of his ale and belched. "But what else would ya need me for?"

"I've drafted a treaty. But it has to be presented to all in the Eastern Lands. Not just to the Taelas and the Karthi. We need Nethuania, Orovín, Áfgal ... maybe even the dwarves up on the mountains."

"And ya need my help to negotiate the terms and sanctions, is that it?" Naoise grimaced at Alsantör's slow nod. "Shite. Y're makin' me the new bloody duke of Prastömin, aren't ya?"

"Eil. I am." The prince smirked and finished his pint. "I told my father that you're the best man for the job. He's never once argued against your merit."

"I doen't wanna be a royal."

"You don't have much choice." Alsantör reached into his pocket and slid a scroll of parchment sealed with green wax and the royal emblem. "He signed it at noon." As Naoise reached across the table to snatch it, the prince continued in a softer tone, "I know it's a lot to take in right now, but—"

"I need another pint." Naoise's voice cracked as he read through the scroll. "Ya want another pint? Perhaps some mead? Wine? Absinthe, heavy on the wormwood?"

Alsantör snorted. "Mead's fine. Though, you'll likely want two for yourself."

"Fookin' 'ell, now what?" Naoise rolled his head back and groaned.

The prince squirmed as he said, "You remember how I told you I'm promised?"

"Y're marryin' me off too, aren't ya?"

Scrunching his nose, Alsantör nodded.

Naoise rubbed his face in both his hands. "Who's the not-so-lucky lass?"

"You're going to need that refill before I tell you." *And you're still going to kill me.*

"Just get on with it, Tör. Unless ya got me marryin' a bloody Sprite or one of Jannon's daughters, I'm sure I can handle it."

The prince's pained expression suggested otherwise, but he still spoke. "So … eh … you're promised to Moira O'Jannon—"

"*What!*" The knight jumped to his feet, knocking the table's bench onto its side. The tavern went silent again, and again Naoise didn't seem to care. "I'm promised to *that* power-hungry beast?"

Alsantör reached across the table, beckoning his friend to sit. "Wizards, Neesh. Calm down. Diarmuid hasn't even announced this yet."

THE GRIM

Naoise trembled as he righted the bench and lowered himself back onto it. "Y're the bloody prince. *You* should marry her."

"O eil. And if I marry her, she'll be right by my side if I ever ascend my father's throne." Naoise opened his mouth to argue, but the prince wasn't done. "I can't marry Siobhan until Moira marries first. It's Karthi law … and I wasn't even offered Moira's hand. Besides, you don't want her anywhere near that crown."

"I doen't want her anywhere near ma cock, either. But here we are."

Alsantör chuckled at the favourite saying. "Here we are, indeed."

"Shite." Naoise ran his fingers through his copper curls and grumbled. "How's y'r mother feel 'bout all this?"

The prince blushed, looking to his clasped hands. "She doesn't know yet."

"Of course she doen't."

Neither does Rhona, for that matter, thought Alsantör, gulping nervously. "I'll tell her on the morrow."

Naoise waved a lazy hand. "Doen't bother. I'll tell 'er. I doen't wanna know what she'd do to me if I didn't—" He clamped his mouth shut, freezing.

Wizards be good. "What do you mean by that? What does my mother have on you?"

"Nothin'," the knight squeaked. "She doen't have nothin' on me."

"Neesh. Tell me everything."

NAOISE APPROACHED THE QUEEN'S CHAMBER WITH A SOUR STOMACH AND a chafed groin. *Gnomes be merciful, I shoulda stopped at the mead.*

After their conversation, he and Tör had drunk enough wine to poison nearly half of Áfgal. He'd then called on his favourite whore, Bessie. Wizards bless Bessie and her strawberry-blonde hair, overly freckled skin, and bright green eyes that reminded him of—

A wave of nausea hit the new duke as he knocked on the queen's gaudy door. He let out a quiet burp, taking care to prevent the contents of his stomach from also escaping. The door opened enough to reveal half of a sleepy face with pale green eyes and tangled ebony hair. "Good morrow, Maid Rhona," he said. "Is the queen available?"

"She's not yet appropriate."

Of course not. Naoise nodded and closed his eyes for a moment as a second wave of nausea rolled through his stomach.

"Are you alright, Neesh?" Rhona whispered.

"No." Sweat dripped down his forehead, and he hiccoughed. "Too much wine last night."

Rhona snorted. "Can't help ye much there. That's yer own doing."

"Ah ken." Naoise tried to moisten his palate, but his tongue was just as cottony as the rest of his mouth.

The handmaiden giggled as she shut the door again.

This is gon' be a long morning. The Veer leaned face-first against the wall. His heart raced and head pounded. *Damn you, Tör. Ya know I doen't drink wine.* Naoise remained still for so long he lost track of time. He only knew that he wanted to sit. To sleep. To get the nightmare of a morning over with.

"You look like shite."

Naoise bolted upright, swallowing the heave that crawled up his throat. "Good morrow, y'r grace," he whispered.

Ethna closed her eyes and rubbed her forehead. "You reek of wine and piss," she said. She loosely tied the top half of her golden hair back in a braid, letting the rest cascade down her back to her waist. Her gown marked the first day of autumn—rust-coloured silk inlaid with crimson filigree and golden leaves. Behind the queen, her handmaiden was dressed in similar colour and design.

"You should see y'r son. He's likely still at that gnomes-damned brothel."

The queen sucked on the back of her teeth, just as her son did when he was irritable. The curses that floated behind her eyes, Naoise could only imagine. He dared not ask.

"What brings you here in this ... condition?" The venom in Ethna's voice was enough to poison a boar. "Have you come to confess that you failed your quest?"

Naoise frowned. *My quest? What was my—oh. Right.* "Actually, nai. While y've likely heard the reasoning behind Jannon's arrival last moon, I doubt y've heard the details."

Ethna scoffed. "You think my husband tells me anything? You're gravely mistaken if you do."

"So, ya doen't know about Alsantör's betrothal?"

Queen and handmaiden both froze. Poor Rhona pressed her lips together and squeezed her eyes shut, looking as though she was about to shatter like a dropped chalice of fine wine.

Gnomes, I'm as subtle as a wild stallion in a pottery.

"Rhona, I think you need to go pray to the Wizards," said Ethna. "I need to speak to Sir Naoise alone."

Ah shite. "It's 'Laird' Naoise, actually." The Veer's mouth moved before he could stop it.

Ethna's expression twisted with rage. "Since when?"

"I'll let y'r husband tell ya. But that's not why I'm here, is it? Ya wanted to hear why Jannon came, and I'm here to tell ya why."

Flicking her pinkie, Ethna's eyes flitted in nigh every direction. 'Twas Rhona who finally broke the thickening silence. "I'll let the two of ye alone. Ye're right, yer grace. I have several prayers to lift to the Wizards." Her voice shook, yet she appeared emotionless. Without another word, she left.

Naoise expected her to weep at the loss of her princely love as soon as she was out of sight. *Knowledge be such a gnomes-damned curse, Rhona. 'Nd I doen't wanna be anywhere near ya when ya talk to Tör. But ya swore an oath. Y'r bound by the law. Perhaps this be better f'r the both o' ya.* "Are we to converse here, y'r grace? Or should we meet in y'r solar? Only the Wizards know what rumours would come from—"

"Rumours of which I have control over, Sir Naoise."

The Veer narrowed his eyes. "It's—"

"I don't care. Until proclaimed from the king's lips, you're still a mere knight."

Wizards give me strength with this royal bitch. I hope Moira isn't as— He suppressed a scoff before finishing the thought. Of course, Moira would be just as conniving, just as cold and venomous.

Ethna cocked her head. "You need to sit. Come."

Her tone was far from welcoming, but Naoise didn't care. His head spun and sweat poured down his face, down his back, down his ... everything. He simply nodded and brushed past the queen, focusing on naught but the plush velvet chair by the balcony. Naoise collapsed into the seat and rubbed the dark bags under his eyes. *Damn you, Tör.*

The queen strutted to the balcony and drew the curtains. The sudden light sent sharp pains through Naoise's head, and he yelped while covering his face with his hands.

Ethna merely chuckled in delight at his pain. "So Jannon means to unite the tundra with the forest," she said, lowering herself onto an equally luxurious seat. A small cedar table separated her from Naoise. "I find it odd, considering how much he detests my husband's archaic views of women. Jannon's respect for them in power is his only redeeming quality."

"Except for the fact that he fathered a demonic bastard through rape," said Naoise with a hiss. "I doen't see much respect f'r women there."

"Am I speaking with Sir Naoise of Prastömin or Earl Manstair of Vaoirsen?" The queen tapped her chin with a smirk. "That bastard was mortal, and the woman wasn't his. What did he call her, again? A 'red-blooded seductress, intent on trapping the heart of the tundra,' or some rubbish like that."

"I doen't care if she was a fookin' goat. He never shoulda—"

"What's done is done, and the last shred of evidence against him has supposedly lost his head—though we both know he likely still lives. Alsantör does have a soft place in his heart for that son of Jannon."

Naoise rolled his eyes. "I think we'd likely've heard something from the Taelas 'bout that devil."

"Perhaps." Ethna's ruby-stained lips curled into a mischievous smile. "So, my son is promised to a Karthi, and you have an impending promotion to Duke of Prastömin. Are you also promised?"

I can't tell 'er. I woen't tell 'er. He shrugged. "Ah dinnae ken," he said. "I only heard of Tör's engagement to one of Jannon's senators."

Ethna sucked her teeth. "Likely one of his daughters." She arched an eyebrow and looked Naoise over with a disgusted emerald gaze. "I'm done with you. It seems you've avoided the revelation of your crime against my previous handmaiden. How you have, I cannot fathom."

Naoise rolled his eyes. "Would I have swung that bloody sword if I were the father of that child?" His heart throbbed at his words. Of course, it had been he who swung that sword, he who had murdered the mother of his own daughter just to save his own head. *Gnomes, Ina. Will y'r ghost ever forgive me?*

"Why are you still here, Sir Naoise? Is there something else you'd like to say regarding Jannon's travels? A secondary motive, perhaps?"

No. But I'll lie again. It's easy to get y'r mind jumbled. "Likely to do with the Taelas. They're plannin' something big, 'nd they doesn't have the Grim to hinder them any longer."

Ethna narrowed her eyes. "What did you hear about the Taelas?"

Naoise stood, turning toward the door. "Talk to y'r son. I've done my part in y'r little treasonous game."

23

CHAINLESS

*D*akil paced the deck under the full moon. Shortly after dusk, they'd reached the Island of the Chainbreakers, and Sólan, of course, had opted to rest before rowing ashore. Dakil had protested to no avail. A warm bed in a private room would have to wait until morning.

Just north of the Silent Dancer was the deceptively large island. The opening to a beach of coarse sand lay just beyond a dark, jutted crag, leading to what appeared to be a shallow cave etched into the face of a daunting cliff. Only those granted passage to the island knew that the cliff was an illusion. The orc twins who ran the island were the last beings in the eastern lands known to wield The Light and thus able to create such a trick. Atop the wall of rock stood an ornate building of white ash and alabaster stone that towered over the small village beside it.

A soft click followed by a squeak of hinges piqued Dakil's ears. *My God, he never sleeps. Why did we even wait to land?* He turned to confront Sólan, but the Áfgaliard was nowhere to be seen. *Where did he—*

The shuffling of someone climbing answered his question before he could even finish thinking it. There, atop the cabin's roof, stood

Sólan's muscular silhouette facing the open water at the stern. *What is he doing?*

Heart thumping, the swordsman watched curiously as Sólan disappeared behind the flat roofline. The soft whispers of his chanting soon filled the air. Dakil tiptoed to the captain's quarters and looked up with a sigh. *How in Yusa's grace did he get up there?* Removing his belt, the swordsman propped his rapier by the cabin door and searched for a foothold, a ledge, anything to help him climb.

He attempted to pull himself up by a loose plank but—*crack!*—he fell back with a grunt. "Nipantot ki, bibu ng pentan." *Fuck you, stupid door.* A mischievous chuckle from above drew his attention upward. The silver moonlight glancing off Sólan's teeth made his fangs appear far more menacing than usual. Dakil shivered.

"Are you stalking me, sañero?" Sólan's grin widened. "You are doing a terrible job of it."

"You didn't even know I was out here until now," grumbled Dakil. He scrambled to his feet to find himself suddenly nose-to-nose with the Áfgaliard. The swordsman jumped back with a yelp. *You're so fast and silent.* Sólan laughed again—music sweet yet mournful as it tickled Dakil's ears.

"I saw you, and I ignored you. You looked anxious, so I thought it best not to disturb your pacing."

"I'm not anxious." Dakil crossed his arms with a scowl. "I'm frustrated."

"With what?"

"With *you*."

Sólan stiffened. "Oh," he whispered, looking to his feet with a shallow frown. "Apologies, then. I just …" He shook his head and turned away.

My God, Dakil. You're not his lover. "Why didn't you want to land?"

"I need to rest. At least—"

"You don't sleep. How can you be *resting*?"

Sólan's eyes flared green once more. "*Gods*, Dakil. I need not explain myself to you. I am your captain."

Despite his need for restraint, Dakil couldn't rein in his questions. "What were you chanting up there? Were you casting a spell over us? Was it *you* who called the cavalry? Did you know Kalasin would betray us? Was *he* the one who—"

"'Tis not sleep I need, but rest. My sleep. Is never. Restful. Need I explain any further?" Sólan clenched his trembling hands into tight fists.

Dakil's breath hitched. He knew that pain in Sólan's eyes, the one that burned with nightmares and panic. The pain he'd experienced so many times with his abusive relationship with Kadek. "I'm sorry, Sólan. You don't need to explain anymore." He reached out to place a hand on the Áfgaliard's arm but withdrew it before he could make contact.

Sólan, however, grasped the hand and rubbed it with his thumb. "Apologies for my harshness. I meant not to …" He shuddered. "I am afraid, Dakil. Afraid of the Chainbreakers."

The swordsman gaped. *Why are you telling me this?* "I don't think you need to be. The twins are welcoming to those who save slaves and who pay for their shelter."

"They are orcs, Dakil. They will smell the elf in my blood and—"

"No one can smell blood inside another's body. Besides, you're nothing like those silver-blooded demons of Misó." Dakil clamped his mouth shut and blushed. "I'm sorry. I'll go."

"Stay." Sólan's hold tightened. "Please? This may come as a surprise to you, but I actually enjoy your company."

Dakil failed to stifle a smile. "I wouldn't have guessed."

Sólan chewed on his bottom lip for a moment, just long enough for Dakil to see him losing the fight of lust that raged behind those captivating amber eyes. Just long enough to feel the fluttering of his own heart before Sólan's mouth was on his. Dakil wrapped an arm about the Áfgaliard's waist to keep from buckling under his own weight. Bolts of fire ran down his legs, his arms, his groin, and an urgent longing to remove clothing and fully experience the man in his arms nearly overtook him. But the kiss was over as quickly as it had begun, ending with Sólan's gentle scraping of his teeth on Dakil's bottom lip.

Dakil pulled himself away and freed his hand. "Get some rest, Captain," he whispered. Snatching his rapier from its resting place, he turned and walked away. *Don't look back at him, Dakil. Don't look back, or you'll end up in his bed, just like you did with Kadek.*

THE CREW CLIMBED THE HIDDEN STAIRCASE UP TO THE ISLAND'S SURFACE. They meandered through the village, each with a full purse of silver and their own plans for the day. Dakil, however, stood at the front of the crew, staring at the monstrous alabaster inn. It was time to face the twins—the innkeepers and enforcers of the land.

An intricately designed copper door creaked as it opened into the inn's ground-level tavern, which was complete with a polished ebony bar, matching tables, and serving wenches. The women appeared to be escaped slaves of Taelonael, judging by the branding scars behind their necks. The building then extended upward for three additional levels, all of which contained dozens of private rooms each equipped with a double bed, chamber pot, and window. The dim chandeliers illuminated a silver light engulfed by fine crystal.

Bayani stomped past his crewmates and shoved Dakil to the side. A dirty, linen bandage was wrapped about his head where his eye used to be. "Rum," he growled at the barkeep.

The being scowled. "We don't have rum," he said in his harsh accent. Looking Bayani over, he bared his teeth—four fangs instead of two—and snarled. "And we don't serve pirates." Fine golden scars were etched across the right side of his face and arm, contrasting with his deep umber skin. The silver-clouded pupil of his right eye extended into his blue-green iris, making it look like an abnormally shaped star. Coarse black hair coiled its way down to the middle of his back in tight, locked ropes. He was of a menacing height and breadth, easily taller than the most robust of Prasti elves. However, unlike the warmongering mentality of those light-skinned wielders of The Dark, he and his gold-blooded kin always sued for peace.

Bayani, you tulalo. What are you doing? Dakil grasped the collar of Bayani's shirt and shoved him away. "You know who we are."

The orc's mouth twitched. "And *you* know the words, Papuan. I don't serve any of you until—"

"Siso no dens-i kami," hissed Dakil. "Call us pirates again, and you will lose your head like—"

"Nino kone-andela, Rasheed?" asked a velvety voice from somewhere behind the hulking figure.

The barkeep peered over his shoulder with a glare. "No dens-i kami."

An equally dark woman approached the polished counter. She raised a heavily scarred eyebrow over her seafoam eyes and flicked the coiled ropes of brown and black hair behind her shoulder. "Where have you been, Dakil?" The corner of her mouth twitched into a slight snarl before settling again. "Oleg hates to wait like this. He said if you don't arrive by sundown tomorrow, his funding for the orphanage dies."

"We aren't that late, Chainless."

"Five days, Dakil. Five *fucking* days. You'll be lucky if you keep your damned head when you see him tomorrow."

Five days! How did that happen? Dakil gulped. "I don't understand. We were only on Isli O Kamotiyen for one day. And the wind was strong. We even left Bansungei a day early!" His eyes flitted around the countertop, his thoughts racing. *This doesn't make any sense.*

Chainless slapped the bar. "Dakil! What happened? Why did you kill Kadek? You couldn't wait until you arrived? You had a plan, Papuan, but you let the *Silent Dancer's* helm control you. And"—she sniffed the air with a look of disgust—"you stink of elf. Don't tell me you've started spying for that fucking 'crusade.'"

Dakil stiffened. *Pantot. Sólan was right about her nose.* He cleared his throat. "First, how *dare* you think I started working for those silver-blooded monsters." His nose twitched as his thoughts jumped to protecting Sólan. *I'm still the captain's guard, not his whore.* "Second, I lost that fight. I'm still the ship's sword."

"Khopin," cursed Chainless. "How are you still alive then?"

The swordsman snorted and stared at the ceiling. "Call it luck, the power of Yusa, or of whatever god you worship." He locked eyes with the orc and squinted. "He's not from Bansungei and is far more … *Grim* than Kadek could ever be."

Chainless cocked her head. "Grim? *The* Grim? The Áfgalese myth?" She scoffed. "I wonder how many young Áfgalese boys were named 'Sun-Child' and felt destined to become 'the Grim.'" Peering over her shoulder she called to her brother. "You hear that, Rasheed? The Grim is the new captain of the *Silent Dancer*!"

"Ha!" Rasheed's booming voice echoed from behind the pantry's door.

The orc woman wiped the smile from her face. "I swear, Dakil, you need more than just fruit to help your head, as mere scurvy doesn't seem to be your problem."

Dakil flushed and flared his nostrils. "Pantot, Chainless! The man beheaded the Pontianak of Isli O Kamotiyen with nothing but his bare hands and a small hatchet!" He banged his fist on the counter. "Ask any of the men. Did you not see Bayani? He lost an eye and a hand to that demon, and if Sólan hadn't killed her, he would be dead."

Chainless rolled her eyes. Before she could respond, however, a tall, cloaked figure approached the bar. He wore what appeared to be a dark green cloak of Prasti wool. No brooch to identify him, but Chainless sneered anyway. "Get out. I have no business with elves." She reached her hand beneath the counter.

Shit. Her iron tiger's claws.

Rasheed quickly emerged from the pantry, wielding a closed katar in one hand and several chakrams in his other. Both orcs' eyes flared bright red.

The figure merely set a heavy burlap sack onto the counter. Tangles of matted black hair splayed from the top, and a rotten stench filled the room. "You will have business with *me*, sañerota." A pulsing green stare glowed from within the deep shadow of his hood. "I am of crimson blood."

Chainless's red glow faded at the newcomer's thick Áfgalese accent. Rasheed, however, tightened his grip on the katar, splitting it into three with its spring-loaded handle. "Prove it," he said through a growl.

Dammit. Dakil prepared his own weapon, despite knowing he was far outmatched against the twins.

"Open the bag," said the Áfgaliard.

The orc woman twitched her mouth but slowly obliged. Inside was a half-decayed head with gaping black eyes and shark-like teeth. Chainless snorted. "I see at least half of your story is true, Dakil." She returned her glare to the hooded figure. "If you are no elf, why do you stink like one? Why do you carry The Dark like one?"

The man removed his hood, revealing a familiar, sharp, olive-tanned face covered in dark brown scruff, and a head of matching wavy hair that stopped at his earlobes. As the green glow faded, his twinkling amber eyes bit into the woman before him like iron hooks. "I never said I was no elf. Only that I am of crimson blood."

Dakil fought the urge to slap his forehead, though a groan still escaped his throat. *You and your mouth, Sólan. I swear to Yusa that will kill you faster than your reputation.*

Chainless suddenly laughed—a genuine laugh that made the chandeliers brighten and change to a warm golden glow. It was a laugh that Dakil had never before heard, one that made her brother join, and one that even tempted Dakil to smile. He looked over to Sólan and flinched, seeing the forced smile that even now never reached his eyes. The slow flexion of his jaw as he clenched his teeth. *They aren't laughing at you, Sólan. I swear.*

THE ORCS' LAUGHTER PIERCED SÓLAN'S EARDRUMS LIKE SCALDING needles. He clenched his fists at his sides, trembling. He willed his face not to turn as red as their eyes had been. *So much for wanting your help. I fucking knew this would happen. These orcs are no longer who you think they are.*

Chainless stopped laughing enough to wipe her nose with her hand and lock eyes with the Áfgaliard. Her tone immediately changed, and the chandeliers darkened and cooled once more. "If you knew how wrong I have been these last three hundred years, you wouldn't be so ashamed by our laughter."

¿Mondé? How did you know—

"You are a myth, Grim," said Chainless. "A legend to the whole of the Chainbreakers, to the orphaned children who swear to have seen you. The 'glowing-eyed angel of Áfgal,' they call you."

Sólan's chest fluttered. "And I thought I was merely the 'orange-eyed devil' of the Eastern Lands. The most hated man in the desert of Taelonael. The man who should not be alive." He forced a smile again, refusing to trust her words. If there was any truth to the stories about orcs, 'twas that they were expert liars. The Light gave them the power of illusion—beautiful, yet deceptive and dangerous. cCeatures of golden blood. He shook his head, as though ripping the woman out of his mind.

"Those children were wrong," she said. A coy smirk curled her lips.

"Tíal? And how is that?"

"Your eyes aren't orange."

Sólan shook his head. *What am I to you, sañerota? A friend, a foe, or a joke?* "What does the colour of my eyes have to do with my reputation?"

"Nothing." Chainless's pupils dilated. "I just find them fascinating."

"I see." Sólan leaned onto the counter and inhaled. The change in her scent was subtle, nearly masked by the stench of the Pontianak head. "And what is it about my eyes that fascinate you, Kil-Alira-non?"

Chainless and Rasheed both stiffened.

Thank the Gods—perhaps they are who I thought they were. "Do you not still answer to that name?" Sólan continued. "Or do you simply go by 'Alira'?"

"My *only* name is Chainless," the orc hissed. "Alira is dead along with the rest of the Kil family."

"Princess Alira and Prince *Rasheed* were the only members of that royal family who were never found after the massacre." Sólan straightened his posture, one eyebrow arched. "The Áfgalese are descendants of Garmath, 'Chainless.' I know my history."

Rasheed grumbled, slipping his hand out of his katar. "Fucking halfbreed." He returned to his duties in the pantry, whatever they were.

Chainless rolled her eyes. "Ignore him. He's never liked anyone." She flicked her gaze to Dakil and then back to Sólan. "You've made a mess on my bar. The cleanup will cost extra."

"Of course," said Sólan as he flashed a mischievous smile. He tossed a leather purse of coin onto the counter. "An expense for which I have prepared." A second purse clinked onto the ebony wood. "Please give me regards to Oleg. I know the impatience of oddlings quite well."

"Hmph." Chainless snatched the purses and assessed their weight. "You're to meet him today. Are you prepared for *that*?"

"Is he prepared to meet me?"

Chainless smiled, but it never reached her eyes. "I'm unsure if anyone is ever prepared to meet you. Were you, Dakil?"

Dakil swallowed. "No … and neither was Kadek."

"There were many things for which that man was unprepared," Sólan grumbled. "How many rooms do you have available?"

"Forty." Chainless's eyes lit up with thinly veiled greed. "I always kept forty rooms set aside for Kadek. He said it 'kept the men pure' from whores, since—"

"I have eighty men to house, not including myself, nor my *piñatorio*. I was told you have rooms that are designed to be private?"

Dakil cocked his head with a frown. "What's a piñatorio?"

Sólan and Chainless ignored him. "It's ten coppers per room, per night," the orc said. "I don't have eighty-two rooms available to give to one single client." Looking to Dakil, she mouthed, "Second-in-command."

"Medría, that is a steep price," said Sólan, unaware of the wide-eyed stare of the swordsman behind him.

Chainless crossed her arms and scowled. "I have a business to run. My guests usually look for ways to kill each other. And these lights?" She motioned to the dim chandelier directly above them. "Candles are cheaper, but these last ages longer."

"Long lost secrets of Garmathian technology?" Sólan stared at the lights with a slacked jaw.

"Something like that."

"Hmph." *I suppose 'tis the end of this bargaining.* "Fine. Two nights, forty-two rooms."

Chainless flashed a bright white grin, revealing her two pairs of upper fangs. She watched in earnest as Sólan counted eighty silver coins, clinking them onto the bar.

He hesitated with the final four silvers. *Dammit, Sólan. Dakil does not want you like that. He needs a private room—away from you.* He gulped, swallowing the knot in his throat. *I have been rejected thousands of times before. Why does this one hurt so much?* He slapped the last four coins onto the counter and spun, hurrying to the exit with fists clenched. He needed to escape, needed some air. No—he needed *Dakil*.

24

SMUGGLERS AND SCOUNDRELS

*D*akil stood beside Sólan, the latter's hood up and arms crossed. They watched the bustling village on either side of the main road, cursing the sun as well as the man beside him.

Sólan finally broke the silence with a grunt. "Oleg Kinev of Orovín, aeh? What does he look like?"

Dakil chuckled. "A pig, tulalo. A pig on two legs." *Just like every goddamned oddling here.*

"I know that, but I have seen several oddlings during our travels to this meeting place. Will he be alone? What colour are his eyes? His skin?"

Yusa save me, thought Dakil. "You ask so many questions."

"And you give so few answers."

The swordsman grumbled, "Nipantot ki. You'll know him when you see him."

"Aeh. Fuck you, too, pundijo."

Finally, a familiar oddling approached. He looked different from the rest, with pieces of one floppy ear missing and the other pierced with five golden hoops. Standing no taller than a metre, he waddled toward them with a heavy limp. One hoglike leg seemed shorter than the other and heavily scarred. The skin that peeked out from under his short breeches and thin cotton shirt was mostly pink. Splotches of black dotted his legs, and his pig hooves were multi-coloured. As he drew closer, the violet in his beady eyes glowed in the afternoon sun.

Oleg Kinev, the largest seller of Taela drugs in the southern half of the Eastern Lands, held a scowl that could strike fear in many. "Five days, Papuan," he said.

I still don't see how that's possible.

"Five days, and you couldn't even tell me you offed Kadek early and took a holiday on the fucking Isle of Death?"

Dakil tapped his finger on the hilt of his rapier, teeth bared. "I wonder, Oleg, if you squeal as much in slaughter as the pig you look like." His nose twitched. "Though, I doubt you'd make a good adobo."

Sólan's let out a quiet sigh, as though he craved the Nethuanian staple.

The oddling ignored him, snorting at Dakil through his flat nose. "I dare you to try a bite, mate."

"Someday, maybe I will." The swordsman shifted his weight. "But I'm not the one who killed Kadek, nor am I captain of the *Silent Dancer*."

"Well, tell this new 'captain' that he's wasting my time. Who the fuck is he anyway?"

Sólan cleared his throat, his eyes glowing green from beneath his hood. "If you are going to shit from your mouth, at least wait until I cannot hear you, putathóta."

"Oh, I see," said Oleg. He flashed a toothy grin before scowling once more. "Take off that fucking hood, halfbreed. I'd prefer to look at you while I think about how I'm gonna kill you."

"Ha! The only ways you could are far beyond your arms' reach." Sólan removed his hood, mirroring the Orovite's scowl. "Take it in, pundijo. Soak in the sight of my face."

My God, Sólan. You're going to get us killed.

"So *you're* the new Kadek, just prettier," said Oleg, scratching his decorated ear with a stubby four-fingered hand. "How much do *you* charge for a night?"

Dakil gripped the handle of his weapon, but Sólan waved his hand low to stop him. The Áfgaliard bared his fangs and growled. "You talk big for someone who can suck my cock while standing."

"How witty"—Oleg snorted and rolled his eyes—"a short-man joke from a halfbreed oaf." He unsheathed a curved dagger from his belt and waved it around as though 'twas naught but a child's toy. "Keep it up, and I might have to cut out your tongue in order to keep business with you."

"You will have to reach it first." Sólan reached behind his back to loosen his hatchet from its holster. "I wish you luck."

I'm tempted to do Oleg the favour. Dakil didn't dare speak his thoughts, however. If he ever wanted to kiss that mouth again, he'd have to tolerate the verbal vomit.

Each armed, the three of them stood, waiting for another to strike. Oleg was outnumbered but far from outmatched. Oddlings were deceptively cunning and swift.

Without warning, Sólan and Oleg burst into hearty laughter and slapped hands. "*Jidir,* Oleg. How the fuck did you get out of those gods-damned gallows?"

Dakil flitted his gaze between the two, lips pursed and nose wrinkled. *What the fuck just happened?* The Áfgaliard and Orovite paid him no mind.

"I thought you'd died of boredom in that damned dungeon, mate!" Oleg shook his head, chuckling. "Ilarion was so indecisive with what he wanted to do with you."

"Ha! Remind me not, sañero. I still have not repaid you for the shit you pulled that day."

Oleg waived a hand. "You killed Kadek, my weakest smuggler. I say your debt's been paid, hey?"

"A favour for betrayal? An odd payment." Sólan wiped the smile from his face. "Niníl, Kinev. I am still in your debt."

"I don't understand," said Dakil. "How do you know each other?"

"A long story, mate, and not one we have time for." Oleg's toothy grin stiffened. "I need a fucking drink. Who'da thought the fucking Grim would slither his way into my gang?"

Ta. He's famous for that.

The Orovite clapped Sólan's forearm and shook it. "Come! Let's talk business over ale, mates. I'm parched and ready for Chainless's hospitality."

"Lead the way, sañero," said Sólan, smiling through gritted teeth. "Putathóta," he whispered just loud enough for the swordsman to hear.

Dakil stifled a snort. On this, at least, they both agreed: Oleg was a bitch to work with.

"So, what the hell happened, hey?" Oleg grunted between sloppy gulps of ale. Cold liquid dripped down both sides of his chin and neck as he continued, "The Hillgard's been shittin' bricks of Prasti granite since you escaped."

Gods, you are a disgusting creature. "Nethuania, obviously." Sólan's mouth flicked into a smile before he took a slow draught of his own pint. "I can imagine, however, that your kinsmen might find it difficult to find a 'halfbreed oaf,' as you would say, by the name of 'Humbírto de Sólanat.'"

Oleg snorted, dribbling more ale from his mouth. "Where the fuck's 'Sólanat'? Is that a new district?"

"Tí Dioses lío, Oleg. *Sólan-at*. I made a fake district to keep them guessing."

"Ha! And they couldn't figure it out? Gods, the oddlings are dense."

As are you, indionta. The Áfgaliard gritted his teeth and haphazardly chuckled. "No need to insult yourself, amógo. I think you have done quite well for such a dense Orovite."

"I'd like to think I'm an exception." Oleg finished his ale with a loud belch.

Sólan was close behind with his drink, but far more graceful. He held up two fingers to Rasheed and muttered, "An exceptional pain in my ass." The barkeep approached with his usual scowl and two full pints.

"I heard that," said Oleg. He crossed his arms, glaring. "And you're not much of a gentleman to be around."

Sólan's glower matched the oddling's. "Glad to hear we agree. I am not called 'the Grim' because of my cheerful nature. Yet, it has never before hindered our relationship."

"Look, Sólan. You work for me now. I can't have you going rogue and challenging my authority. If you do, what's to stop my other smugglers?"

"With," corrected Sólan. "I work only for myself and the gods." He leaned forward and bared his fangs. "And you are quite brave for accusing me of 'going rogue.' I have never challenged you or your abilities, Oleg. Not even when you fucked up that last slave raid."

"What!" Ale sputtered out of Oleg's nose. "That was going completely according to plan until *you* lost your damned—"

"That Taela boy did not have to die. He was more than willing to unlock those fucking chains. He was trying to when you shot him. I had them, cabróde. That Maseño girl would be home with her family, and I would still be 'alive.' You made me murder a *child*, Oleg. You know how I feel about that. Saving *them* is why I became a gods-damned slave scout to begin with."

"I know, I know. Fuck, mate, what do you want me to do? Apologise? 'Cause I won't. I ain't sorry for doing what I did to make sure Khalid got his, and to make sure I still had you to help me with those fucking deserters."

Oh, Oleg. You will be sorry someday. "Fine. But I will not thank you for 'saving me' from that boy."

Oleg shook his head. "You should—I won't be so kind next time."

"There will not be a next time," Sólan hissed.

"Maybe not, though I don't care how close we are as friends."

We are not friends, sañero.

"Besides, mate," Oleg continued, "regardless of what you think, you still work for me. I tell you where to drop, you drop there. I command you to drown, and you ask, 'in the river or the sea?' I don't care if you weep over me for a hundred fucking years once you outlive me—"

"I will not shed a tear for you. I can promise you that."

"*Dammit*, Sólan, I'm not kidding! I'm gonna cut out your fucking tongue if you keep this shit up. You're not scouting anymore. You're not on private contract anymore. You work for me."

"You tell me where to drop, and I will find a better place to drop it," said Sólan. "You command me to drown, and I will tell you to go fuck yourself with a spiked mace or Dakil's rapier." He lowered his voice menacingly. "Must I remind you of what I am capable? Of what I am willing to do to those who cross me?"

Oleg shuddered. "Fine, fine," he whispered. "You work with me." He held his palms out in surrender.

Sólan nodded once with a chilling smirk. "Now that we agree, we must discuss other problems with the *Silent Dancer*."

"Such as?"

"The Nethuanian Temple Cavalry. A man named Kalasin, to be precise. Do you know him?"

Oleg scratched his flat, chinless jaw. "He's one of my land mules. The young one, right?"

"Niníl. Bayani is here and still as loyal as ever." *Even if he is a damned thorn in my foot.* "No, no. Kalasin is much older. And half blind."

"Hmm." Oleg wiggled his pig-like nose and grunted. "I don't know him."

A mole, then. A very convincing mole, at that. "It sounds as though you have a problem. The estuary at the mouth of the Runedein is no longer safe. He alerted the cavalry guard."

Oleg narrowed his beady eyes. "Fuck. He wouldn't have gone all the way through that temple unless …"

Sólan raised an eyebrow. "Unless what? Do you have competitors?"

"Yeah, one from Morinalo and the other from Tianag. Why? You think he worked for one of them?" Oleg licked his lips. "'Cause the last thing I need is a fucking territory war after losing two consecutive shipments from that fat asshole."

"*Two*? Gods, that is a lot of lost gold." Sólan's jaw hung open. "I see his newfound faith made him several enemies."

"He was scheduled to die, Sólan. Dakil wanted him dead—some kind of lovers' spat, I guess."

Far worse than that, I imagine. Dakil seems quite damaged from his relations with that coward.

"I needed to cut my losses, and find a new Bansungei man to reestablish my hold on the slums there. I had four barrels of the new shit in each lost shipment."

"What 'new shit'?"

A toothy grin spread across Oleg's face. "I have something to show you—but first, I need to know that you won't betray me like—"

"Like Kadek? Kalasin? I thought you knew me better than that." The Dark pulsed through Sólan's gaze as he leaned forward with a snarl. "I have my own plans with Kalasin, sañero. Ones that you will enjoy. You *have* forgotten of what I am capable. You have forgotten that I was not just an independent slave scout for the Áfgalese crown —I was your contract assassin. Kalasin is going to *beg* me to burn him alive before I am done with him, I can promise you that." Leaning back, he took a long draught of his ale.

Oleg snickered. "You vengeful fucker. This is why I kept you around, despite your mouth."

Sólan flashed a mischievous smile. "I like my mouth, thank you very much. As do most of the men and women I fuck."

"Gods, you're as lustful as an elf."

I am half elf, indionta. You must have forgotten that as well.

"Now that I know I can trust you"—Oleg pulled a small, wooden box out of his pocket—"this is the new shit." He untied the twine and slid open the top to reveal a fine, white powder.

Sugar? Flour? "What is it?"

"Kabotay. Purified, dried, and milled to *look* like flour."

Sólan rubbed the scruff under his chin with a raised eyebrow. "How is it consumed?"

Oleg shrugged. "However the hell you'd want to use it. Some scoop it into their tea. It's odourless, tasteless, and dissolves undetected. I've seen the Taelas melt it down and drip it through a hollow sewing needle straight into their blood."

"Willingly?" Sólan shuddered at the oddling's nod. *Gods, what have you created?* "Fuck, Oleg. How much will a gram of this cost?"

A wicked smile stretched across Oleg's face. "Ten gold."

And Kadek lost eight barrels of this? Sólan let out a low whistle. "How do you expect the common folk of Nethuania's slums to afford this?"

"I don't." Oleg closed the box, replaced its twine, and slipped it back into his pocket. "I still send in the oil to the slums for the poves. But the wealthiest of my buyers prefer the pure shit. I've even got Prasti crusade hunters drooling over this."

"Medría, amógo. What were you going to pay Kadek had he been compliant? How much per barrel of powder? Of oil? Per brick of apyin bud?"

"Two hundred fifty gold for the flower. Half a thousand for the oil. I was hoping seven and a half hundred per barrel of the powder, but … you see how that ended."

Sólan pursed his lips with a nod. "I want more. If I am also to 'contract' as your Bansungei enforcer, I will need more." He rolled his shoulders back with a pop. "Fifteen hundred for the powder. One thousand each for bricks of apyin and barrel of oil."

"Ha!" Oleg slapped the table and snorted. "I'm not paying you a fucking silver above what I pay my other smugglers. You work—"

"*With* you." Sólan's eyes burned again. "I am not your smuggler. And if we cannot agree on payment, then the *Silent Dancer* will no longer be in your service."

Oleg glared. "You're hardly in a position to negotiate, my friend. I'm the biggest sponsor to this fucking island. That orphanage across the way? My gold built that. My gold keeps it running."

"You are hardly in a position to fuck with me, Oleg. I was paid handsomely as a slave scout. 'Twill take little effort on my part to overtake your hold on the Chainbreakers."

"Dammit, Sólan I can't—"

"What? Cannot what? I lost *ten thousand gold* on that slave raid, pundijo. And now, the Maseño District is on the verge of war with the rest of Áfgal and the tundra's elves. They have aligned with the Taelas, Oleg. 'Tis but a strand of thread keeping this peace together, and I am the one who is cutting the rope." Sólan leaned forward with a snarl. "I will kill you if I have to. So, either you pay me, or your head will be buried on the opposite side of the Eastern Lands from your carcass."

Sólan's eyes burned as the colour drained from Oleg's face. "I can't give you that much, mate. The best I can do is five hundred per brick of apyin, seven and a half hundred for the oil, and a thousand for the powder." He held his trembling hands up in surrender. "Please take it."

"Done," growled Sólan, his chair scraping across the floor as he stood.

"Don't you want to know where to pick up your first—"

"I have Dakil for that."

25

THE ROAD TO BAFOREIS

"*No*, Faerin. I doen't need a bloody escort." *I need to get the hell away from ev'ryone.* Naoise shifted and fidgeted in his formfitting doublet, the linen tunic beneath doing naught but bunch and pinch. He sucked and bit the inside of his lip as he pulled his breeches up to his waist—again.

The quilted silk itself was pleasing to the eye—heavy green inlaid with a golden filigree twisting and swirling like the creeping vines on the outer walls of the keep. Black breeches and matching black boots with golden buckles completed Naoise's royal ensemble. He'd fought to keep his heavy wool cloak from his knighthood. There were few material things he held dear to his heart, and that damned cloak was one of them. He'd won that battle.

Naoise tied and secured his four-horned and stirrup free saddle, his full bags, and his favourite weapons onto his steed. His horse, Denni, merely grazed beneath the weight. After all, he'd trained and fought wearing leather and iron armour himself for the past fifteen years. Denni was Naoise's most prized possession; a descendant of Alsantör's first mare—a pure black draft from Vaoirsen who'd been bred with the finest sprinters of Prastömin.

Denni's line breathed naught but power and calm. Fearlessness.

A loyalty to Naoise unmatched by even his closest friends. He brushed through the stallion's brilliantly white mane and tail, even combing the feathers around Denni's hooves before finally mounting. He nearly fell off the other side of his saddle with the lack of the weight he was used to wearing.

"Fookin' hell. These damned silks're far too light f'r me," he grumbled.

Faerin snickered. "You need an escort, m'laird. Ya can't even ride proper anymore."

"Káil ti pashti, Faerin." *Fuck you, Faerin.* "Doen't make me revoke y'r title."

The young knight clamped his mouth shut and flushed. "Apologies. I—"

"Fook. Doen't apologise neither. I'm just not accustomed to bein' gnomes-damned royalty. Just as y're not accustomed to bein' the first knight." Naoise grimaced and bit his lip again. Locking his mossy brown gaze on Faerin's wide-eyed one, he nodded. "Y're a good lad, Sir Faerin. Y'll serve the kingdom well."

Faerin's jade eyes lit up in spite of the smile he tried to stifle. "Thank you, m'laird. I hope to be half the first knight you were."

Naoise chuckled. "Eil, y'll be more than that." *A hell of a lot more than I was. Welcome to the inner circle. May the king find ya harmless.* He wiped the smile from his face. "Keep Prince Alsantör out of trouble while I'm gone. It's harder than ya think."

THE FIRST THREE DAYS TO THE NORTHEASTERN EDGE OF THE FOREST WERE uneventful, and Naoise welcomed the isolation. The past several fortnights had been rife with politics, threats, and too much anger.

The new duke shuddered at the inner workings of the royal court. *Gnomes, I shoulda stayed a bloody knight. Damn you, Tör.* A chill breeze cut through his lightweight clothing, signaling the impending arrival of winter. Denni grunted at the cold.

"Hush now, lad. We're not in the tundra yet." Despite the heavy load and long days, Naoise was two suns ahead of schedule. That damned escort woulda slowed me down by half a fookin' fortnight. Not once had he anticipated needing half a dozen knights surrounding him. He still didn't. Being Veers, he and his brother were the best damned warriors in the forest. 'Twas the sheer numbers of Diarmuid's army that wiped out his father's people—*his* people. Naoise shook his head and cursed. *I'm a Prasti, through and through. Not a fookin' Veer; not a traitor like my father.*

Tears stung his eyes as images of his brother flashed in front of him. *Not now, Giaven. Gnomes be merciful, doen't haunt me now.* But all he could see was that mischievous grin, those honey eyes that had nearly glowed gold in the setting sun's light, perfectly matching the bronze in his curly hair. His brother had taken more after their mother: more elegant and beautiful—almost like a Wizard in the flesh. He knew it too, the reckless prick. *What I wouldn't give ta knock ya senseless. Ta spar 'til we both sweat blood, drank ourselves silly, and fought over the same damned whore 'til she wanted neither of us.*

Another breeze bit through his clothes, and he looked up at the sky through the thick trees. *Shite.* Streaks of red and purple filtered through the top of the forest, signalling the departure of the sun into the east.

Naoise dismounted and loosely tied Denni's rope to a sturdy branch before reaching into his pack for his rations. The horse grazed and sighed as the duke loosened his heavy leather saddle. "Eil, Denni. That's a good lad." He ran his fingers through the horse's mane, picking out bits of twigs, flowers, and mud. "Shite. I need to stop ridin' ya so hard. I promise we'll take it easy on the morrow, yeh?"

Denni lifted his head and grunted, and Naoise snickered. "Here." He snagged an apple from his pack and tossed it to the horse. "It's y'r only one tonight, ya hear? They doen't grow these up north. The roots get too cold." He shivered. "Everything's too damned cold up there."

Naoise went to work grooming Denni. He hummed an old lullaby that Ina had taught him when she first discovered she carried his child. *O Gnomes, Ina.* The grief came suddenly. A crushing weight that knocked him to his knees. His lungs deflated, and he stared at his shaking hands, remembering so vividly that fateful day—the day he was commanded to swing that damned gladius and execute the woman he loved. Naoise's eyes remained dry, and everything else went numb. Weak.

A faint rustling behind him drew his attention. Hushed whispers and strange bird whistles filled his keen ears. Áfgalese bandits. Denni fidgeted and tugged on his rope—he must've heard them too.

"Hush now, Denni. It's just odd birds," said Naoise. He knelt, brushing the stallion's feathered ankles and slipping a dagger from his own boot. He whistled a nameless melody, hummed his favourite pub songs, and muttered nonsense in his native tongue. To any who might've observed, he was oblivious. The rustling continued to surround him. Three men, Naoise guessed, and likely a fourth in the trees, poised with a bow.

As predicted, one pounced from his left. Naoise jumped to his feet, armed and ready. "Ték!" he shouted. Denni bucked. The force of his kick cracked the man's skull, and he fell to the ground with a thud. *Dead. One down, three to go.*

The remaining two bandits attacked in tandem, hatchets at the ready. Naoise spun, disarming one with his foot and stabbing his dagger into the other's chest. *Fook! Missed the gnomes-damned heart.*

Without warning, Naoise fell to the ground with a grunt. At the twang of a bow, he rolled just as an arrow whistled past and dug into the dirt by his head. *Predictable cunts.* He kicked himself up only to be met by a thin rope that coiled around his neck. *Shite!*

His windpipe shut, and panic threatened to overtake him. The injured bandit limped toward him, his eyes wild and his mouth frothing crimson. He gripped a hatchet in one hand and in the other ... Naoise's dagger?

When did I lose that thing? "Fuck you," the elf tried to say, but his vision tunnelled as the rope tightened even more around his throat. His lungs burned, and his heart raced. 'Twas only moments until he would lose the battle. He kicked—the hard impact and the following thump on the ground told him he had landed his foot on the man's chest. Naoise swung his leg back, hooking his captor's ankle. The bandit yelped and released his grip on the rope.

Naoise fell forward onto his knees and gasped. *No time f'r this, Neesh. Get oup.* Another arrow whistled by his ear, or rather, nicked his ear. The sharp pain threw him off balance, and he rolled onto his back. Upside-down, he searched for his packs, his weapons, anything. *My bow!* He scrambled to his feet, dodging yet another arrow. One bandit writhed and gasped at his feet, while the other stalked him from behind. The Veer snatched his bow and a single arrow. He spun, embedding the pointed tip into his attacker's throat. The man collapsed with gargles, his crimson blood spraying Naoise's face, torso ... everything. He didn't care—*couldn't* care. There was still that archer to confront.

Another arrow sliced past him. Snarling, he rubbed his thumb up his thigh to position his archer's ring. A second later, with another arrow nocked and bowstring pulled taut, he twisted backward and fired.

A yelp and subsequent crash from a nearby tree tickled his ears like music. The arrow had hit home. *Oh, thank the Wizards.*

Three dead and one maimed. *Almost finished with these fookers.* Naoise turned toward the battered and bloody Áfgaliard at Denni's feet. The stallion merely snorted and grazed beside him. *I swear Denni. Y're dense as a fookin' red-blood sometimes.* Naoise crouched in front of the bandit, who'd dropped both his weapons. "Ya speak Garmathian, arsehole?"

He was met with a blank scowl and a wet wheeze. That would be a no.

"Fine." Naoise wiped the blood from his face. "Tese a lí maldónta cutillla, cabróde," he said in nigh flawless Áfgalese. *That's my fucking knife, bastard.* He grasped the handle and wiped the sticky blood onto the man's trousers.

"Qor fivár, sañero," said the bandit through gurgles. "Mersicorda, qor fivár." *Please, sañero. Mercy, please.*

Naoise grimaced. *Ya tried to kill me, ya radge. I should let ya suffer.* The pleading in the man's eyes was palpable, and the elf sighed in defeat. *Alright, fine.* "Javiénto mo llevilú te Terría Vareno cil pizo." *May Javiento lead you to Terría Vareno with peace.*

The Áfgaliard closed his eyes, tears dripping down his cheeks.

Before he could thank the elf, Naoise thrust his dagger into the bandit's heart. Twisting and removing the blade in quick succession, the man was dead before he could finish his breath.

Too damned young—naught older than thirty years. Naoise shuddered. *Stop it. He tried to kill ya, Neesh. Y're already too kind f'r showin' such mercy. No Prasti woulda given him that. Not even Tör. Curse this "honourable" Veerish blood of mine.*

Four days came and went without further hindrance. Despite the stench of rotting flesh, Naoise displayed four mangled heads on his saddle bags. 'Twas brutal—barbaric, even—but it stayed any more attacks from bandits; man, elf, or otherwise.

To his relief, the approach of winter signalled few active predators, particularly the venomous tiger bears of the southern Blue Eye Mountain bases. The forest soon thinned to lone trees and then to shrubs. Naoise'd passed the tree line and entered the southern part of the tundra—Karthénos. There, the soil never thawed, the sun hid in the winter, and the freezing temperatures hardly warmed.

Once he reached the outer quartz walls of the border's city, Baforeis, he tossed the Áfgalese heads aside. Baforeis meant "Border Town" when translated to Garmathian, though it was more than just a mere town. It was the main hub of trade between Karthénos and Prastömin, where Prasti carpenters and loggers exchanged raw lumber for precious gems, metals, and caribou meat and furs from Karthi miners and herders.

Naoise entered through the silver-plated gate with a blank face. A frigid breeze bit through his doublet, and he pulled his cloak tight around his body. *I knew I shoulda worn my winter tunic. Damn this ice.* The gate boomed as it shut behind him.

"Būedich o vothmache!" *Wizards be good!* A familiar stony voice made both Naoise and Denni startle.

The stallion twitched under Naoise, and it took more effort than he would have liked to calm his steed. "Dammit! Who the fook—

Cadman!" The newcomer quickly dismounted and embraced the Karthi knight, clad in silver armour, who approached.

Dirty blond hair frizzed around Prasti eyes and a freckled face which beamed a dimpled grin. "Of all the bloody elves in Prastömin, they got *you* into that damned court? If anyone'd told me that Naoise McManstair of Vaoirsen would show up here in Prasti silks, I'd have walloped him upside the head. Are you mad?"

Naoise snorted and rubbed his neck with icy fingers. "Yeh, didn't expect that m'self, either. But Tör said he needed the help."

"Ha! I told you that friendship would get you in a heap' o' trouble," said Cadman. "I'm surprised he didn't get your brother for the job. He's always wanted to play at those politics."

"He prob'ly woulda had Giaven …" Naoise's throat clamped shut at his brother's name. A single tear emerged and fell down his cheek before he could stop it.

Cadman's smile disappeared. "Ah, shite. I didn't know. Fuck. What happened, Neesh?"

"Bad crusade hunt," was all that Naoise managed to squeak.

"Shite. And now you're promised to that bitch of a senator, Moira O'Jannon."

"Eh. It's a mere hundred years. I can prob'ly handle 'er. At least she woen't get the Prasti throne."

"Hadn't thought about that," said Cadman. Another freezing gust whistled by, and both elves shivered. "Damn it all. Two hundred and fifty gnomes-damned years, and I still freeze in this place."

"Ha! That's on *you*, Cad. Ya didn't hafta run away with y'r sister like that."

"Ah, but I did, Neesh. Couldn't take the tyranny any longer. I don't wanna be anywhere near that forest when the rebellion starts and the trees go up in flames." Cadman raised an eyebrow and smirked. "Besides, there was nothing there for Saoirse. She's too much like her father—quite the warrior, he was."

Naoise frowned. "Y'r niece, right? Who was her father? Did I know him?"

"Oh, you knew him." The twinkle of mischief flashed through Cadman's eyes. "Likely better than most."

Dammit, Giaven! You knew better than to fook with Cadman's sister! Naoise rolled his eyes. "That bloody prick."

The Prasti merely winked before he motioned toward the nearest stable. "Come on, Neesh. Let's get you settled and out of those blood-soaked clothes."

CADMAN ESCORTED DUKE NAOISE TO HIS OWN BAFOREIS HOME AND showed him his quarters. "I don't have a servant boy for you, but you can call on mine anytime," he said.

Naoise grumbled. "I doen't need a servant boy, Cad. I'da brought my Prasti one, if I did." *The poor lad. I should bring 'im back something nice f'r his family.* "But I *do* need a bath."

"Agreed." Cadman clapped Naoise on his shoulder with a grin. "I'd forgotten how much you stink after a long patrol."

Fook ya. I nearly died on my way here. I prob'ly shoulda taken that damned escort.

"There's a hot bath and some towels in your privy chamber. Just leave the dirty shite on the floor. The maid will launder it later."

O, thank the Wizards. "I'll be a while," said Naoise. "Who else is escorting me to Meaforlath?"

Cadman grinned. "Saoirse. She'll come for you in a while. I'll take you to my favourite meadery tonight. It's got a hearth the size of your bloody room, and the roast caribou is exquisite. Second to none, I say."

Gnomes, you sound like a posh nobleman. "Lookin' forward to it—and to meetin' Lady Saoirse."

"*Dame* Saoirse," snapped Cadman. "She's a knight. And a damned good one at that. She's Prasti, remember?"

Naoise stiffened. "Sorry, Cad. Didn't mean ta—"

"Get bathed. Get dressed. I'll see you before evening." Cadman spun on his heel and slammed the door shut.

Shite. What's shoved up y'r arse?

Naoise shook his head and grumbled. He locked his door and undressed, savouring the warmth of the chamber's hearth. He quickly found the privy room and a wooden tub lined with metal that steamed with hot water. The duke groaned as he lowered himself into the bath, his freckled skin turning bright red at the heat, but he didn't care. He was warm. At the least, the water wasn't as boiling hot as the sacred pool in Prastömin. Unlike his forest—or tundra—kin, he was susceptible to both heat and cold. Yet another curse of his bloodline to add to the list.

He scrubbed, lathered, and scrubbed some more, his copper curls glistening brighter than they'd been in days. In fact, his whole body was brighter. Stepping out of the tub, he left behind the blackened bathwater and spent soap.

He'd hardly finished buttoning his long-sleeved surcoat in the Prasti royal colours when a sharp knock gathered his attention. Rustling a towel through his hair one last time, he unlatched and opened the door, the warmth draining from his face at the sight of the woman behind it. She stood half a head shorter than him, her straight coppery hair feathering down to her hips, and her pale face littered with small freckles below a pair of rounded, deep-set eyes.

She smiled and bowed her head. "I'm honoured to make yer acquaintance, Laird Naoise McManstair," she said in an unexpectedly thick Karthi accent. Her mossy brown eyes glistened in the flickering lamplight. "Me name's Saoirse."

Gnomes, ya look just like ... Naoise couldn't finish his thought. Cadman's niece wasn't his niece, after all. Nor was she *Giaven's* daughter. Naoise's breath caught, and he trembled while locking eyes with the young woman. *Saoirse. Fook, Cad, ya had to name her "Freedom."* "The honour is mine," he whispered through the lump in his throat.

Saoirse frowned and placed a freckled hand on his shoulder. "Are ye alright, me laird?"

Naoise grabbed her hand and squeezed. The warmth in her fingers thawed through his own better than had the bath, all the way to his heart. "All these years, I thought you were dead."

"I think ye might have me confused with someone else," said

Saoirse as she freed her hand and stepped back. "I don't know who she was, but she must've been very special to ye."

"Saoirse." Cadman's voice was hard, and Naoise could all but glare at the man. "We need to talk."

Naoise clenched his fists, seething. "Why didn't you tell me, Cad? Why didn't you tell me she was alive?"

Cadman took a deep breath. "Reese," he said to the woman, "Laird Naoise doesn't have you confused with anyone. He knows *exactly* who you are."

26

DAUGHTER OF VAOIRSEN

Reese. Doen't call 'er that, Cad. Her name is Saoirse. Freedom. The freedom her mother never had—that I never had. "Saoirse," whispered Naoise. The name felt sweet, like honey on his tongue after a bitter ale. "Gnomes, ya look just like y'r mother."

Saoirse shook her head, her gaze shifting between her uncle and Naoise. "I don't understand."

The walls around Naoise's heart shattered once again. Growling, he threw a punch, his fist hitting Cadman's nose with a satisfying crunch.

The Prasti's head snapped back, and he fell on his arse. Saoirse gasped and elbowed Naoise's ribs, hard, sending the man to the ground. "I don't know who ye are, or what ye have against me uncle. 'Nd I wouldn't care if ye were the bloody emperor of the Eastern lands. Ye'll not strike him in front of me, understood, *me laird*?"

"Perfectly," said Naoise through a grunt. *Eil. Y're just like me.*

Cadman chuckled, scrambling back to his feet. "I swear, Neesh. Your fists've gotten soft since I last saw you."

Naoise scoffed. "Káil ti pashti, Cad. Y'r reflexes have slowed. I wasn't even tryin'."

"Ha!" Cadman helped the duke to his feet and brushed the wrinkles out of his surcoat. "You need a pint." He looked over to Saoirse, whose face was as sour as an unripe peach. "As do you, Reese."

"What I need," she said, "is fer ye to talk, Uncle. Why does this man know who I am, yet I don't know who he is? He says I look just like me mother, yet I don't look a thing like maela."

"Reese, it's not that simple."

It's clear, Cad, that y've lied to the both of us f'r the past two 'nd a half hundred years! Naoise chewed on his bottom lip. "This be a load o' shite, Cad. I need more than just a pint. I need answers … and to drown in a bloody barrel o' whisky."

Despite Cadman's denial of any pain, his nose had swelled and bruised by the time the trio reached the local tavern. *Serves ya right, arsehole.* As Saoirse opened the heavy door, a gust of heat blew through Naoise's hair, and he sighed in delight.

Cadman was, at least, honest in one thing: that hearth was bigger than Naoise's room. A roaring flame filled the stone hole in the wall, fuelled by logs nigh the size of a grown man. The warmth heightened the delicious aroma of roasting caribou slathered in garlic, rosemary, and butter. Naoise's inhaled deeply, already drooling. *Gnomes be merciful, am I on assignment or holiday?*

"I'll get the pints," said Saoirse.

All the anger, grief, and frustration came crashing back to Naoise as he watched her weave her way through the crowd toward the bar. 'Twas only then that he noticed her leather scaled armour and the silver-sheathed gladius at her waist. On her opposite hip she bore an Áfgalese hatchet, complete with a bearded blade and a rounded hammer on the reverse. While the steel wasn't anywhere near as special as the water steel out of the District of Casaca, it was a tough, high-carbon metal that gleamed in the fire's light.

Naoise's chest swelled with an unfamiliar emotion, one he'd never thought possible for himself. *That's my daughter. A warrior of my blood, a daughter of Vaoirsen — Prastömin. A daughter of Prastömin.*

He didn't realise he was smiling until Cadman nudged him with a chuckle. "I swear, Neesh. You look just like your brother with that stupid grin."

The duke's expression flattened. "Ya bastar,'" he whispered. He knocked his shoulder into the knight and trudged to the table closest to the fire. The two sat, awaiting their drink and companion. Fresh tears threatened to spill from Naoise's eyes, and his voice shook as he said, "Why didn't ya tell me, Cad? Two hundred fifty years. The missed name days, the growin', the chasin' boys away from 'er … Gnomes be merciful, everything! Fook, ah dinnae ken if she even *likes* boys."

Cadman rubbed his face with both hands. "I know. Shite, Naoise, I wanted to tell you, but … it's complicated."

"Complicated?" Naoise bared his fangs and snarled. "She's my daughter, Cadman. D'ya forget how hard it is f'r an elf to conceive? How rare a child is to anyone? How many women did you marry, yet still never fathered?"

"I didn't steal Saoirse from you, if that's what you're trying to say," said Cadman. He crossed his arms and scowled. "If I'd told you what I did, you would've broken your oath to Ina."

"My oath!" Naoise slammed his fist on the table and jumped to his feet. "You thought my gnomes-damned *oath* was more important than—"

"You promised Ina!" Cadman also rose to his feet. "You swore to her the night before you swung that *fucking* sword you wouldn't forfeit your life for her. That you'd continue to live like the free man you are."

Naoise grasped his own hair with both hands. "I thought our daughter was dead. *You told me she was dead, Cadman!*" Hot tears flowed down his cheeks, onto his neck and his chest.

A woman cleared her throat, gathering the men's attentions. "The two o'ye gonna make up and fuck yet, or do ye need more private quarters?"

"Fuck, Reese. I told you not to interrupt like that. Remember what happened last time you disobeyed? Leave the men to discuss—"

Naoise's fist on the table cut Cadman's words short. "Y're not Diarmuid, and this isn't the bloody palace." He looked over to Saoirse, who chewed on her lower lip.

"Should I leave, then?" she asked.

"Absolutely not," said Naoise. He sat, motioning to the empty seat beside him. "As we're *both* victims of Cadman's lies, I think now's a good time to talk." He shot a venomous glare toward his host. "And I'll need someone to hold me back from killing him."

Cadman snorted as he sat. "There's the Naoise McManstair I remember. Couldn't go more than one day without you threatening me. Gnomes, she's just like you, temper and all."

I wouldn't fookin' know, ya son of a—

"I'm right here, Uncle Cadman. Ye can stop speaking about me as though I'm not." Saoirse clunked three wooden mugs onto the table, all foaming with mead. She plopped into the empty chair and eyed her uncle, arching her brow before moving her gaze to Naoise. "Who's Ina?"

Naoise also bit the inside of his lip. *Only the fiercest woman to've ever graced the Eastern Lands. A woman whose beauty woulda shamed the Gnomess of Love after whom she was named. The queen's handmaiden*—the *only untouchable woman in the bloody forest.* "Y'r mother." Another tear trickled down his cheek. "And ya look just like 'er."

"Is this true, Cadman?" Saoirse shot daggers at her fellow knight. Tears pooled in her mossy brown eyes, as though waiting for his answer to fall.

Cadman gulped again, fidgeting with his pint. "Eil, Reese. Ina was your mother."

"'Was?' So, she's dead." Saoirse's voice trembled yet escalated in volume. "Me real maela's dead, and ye didn't think to tell me that might be why yer sister raised me so coldly? Is me father even alive? Who was he? What was he like? I was told he had Veerish blood, but now—"

"He did," said Cadman, motioning toward Naoise. "Does, rather."

Saoirse merely gaped, looking Naoise over with what seemed to be judgement. "One of the last Veers in the Eastern Lands," she whispered.

The Vaoirsen Massacre. Isn't that what they call it here? A rebellion built on lies, treason, and abandonment. "Last," said Naoise. "Giaven McManstair is dead." *Wizards, if he'd be here now. I wonder if he knew about—*

"Did he know about me?"

Wizards be good, we even think alike.

"No." Cadman lowered his gaze and squirmed. "Not even Prince Alsantör. 'Twas just me and Cara. I swear, Reese, I did it to protect you and your father."

"That's not me name, 'nd I don't need protecting," Saoirse said through a hiss. "I need integrity. Is that not what ye taught me?" She looked over at Naoise and gritted her teeth. "And if he's a pureblood Veer, I doubt he needs protecting, either."

Ya seem quite smitten with the idea of bein' half Veer. There's so much ya dinnae ken about them ... about me. Naoise cleared his throat. "When do we leave f'r Meaforlath? I'm not sure if ya heard, but I'm not here on holiday."

"It must be urgent if you're already moving on from *this* revelation," said Cadman. "All the senators are gathering for this 'emergency council.'"

Naoise nodded. "Eil. 'Nd the follow-up will likely take place in the coming season. Cad, this is the largest negotiation since the end of the Great War, if history taught us anything. Mortals, oddlings, elves. Hell, we even sent a bloody pigeon to the dwarfs in the Blue Eye Mountains, though they'll likely not respond."

Saoirse let out a low whistle. "Damn."

Cadman bit through his fingernails. "We leave on the morrow. With a proper escort, it'd take us a fortnight to get there, but we should reach Jannon's palace by the full moon if it's just the three of us."

"Good. 'Cause haste is more important than anything else right now." Naoise's walls threatened to crack once again as that unfamiliar emotion returned. *Second to Saoirse, of course. There's nothin' in these gnomes-forsaken lands more important than my child.*

27

A CURSE OF SILVER BLOOD

Sólan leaned against the limestone wall that surrounded Chainless's orphanage, arms crossed and head cocked. Young children of both mortal and oddling blood played and laughed amongst each other. Some Taela boys built dolls and played with most of the girls, while others kicked a pig bladder and leather balls. A satisfied grin slowly grew across Sólan's face as he watched a group of nearly a dozen Áfgalese children swing curved sticks at a polished, wooden ball in a game of "balo de pola"—"stickball" in Garmathian.

The game itself was simple: goals made of rope nets and wood frames were placed two dozen metres apart. Each team would strike, pass, and shoot the lemon-sized ball into the opposite team's goal, using only their sticks. The older the children, the more violent the game could be. As a child, 'twas one of Sólan's favourite pastimes to watch his brother play. Montrél'd always said he was "too young" to join.

In his periphery, a young Nethuanian girl was attempting to weave a shallow basket. She scrunched her nose and stuck her tongue out of the corner of her mouth in a look of intense focus. The smile disintegrated from Sólan's face as images of Elena in her bright orange wedding dress flashed before his eyes. That sad brown gaze taunted him, and remembering her lifeless body in Tirsen's arms sent shivers throughout his body. He shook the memory from his head and stifled a sob. *I am so sorry, Elena. You deserved so much better. So much more than the crimes of a monster—than such a violent farewell into an early grave.*

The familiar silk of Dakil's voice piqued his ears, and he snapped his attention to the western side of the fields. There, the swordsman sparred with an Áfgalese boy who appeared little older than twelve. Sólan's feet moved before he could stop them, and he watched the master teach his apprentice the art of Nethuanian swordplay. *He is being kind to that boy—and patient. Gods, he is stunning with that blade.*

"Very good, Montrél. Now, thrust!" said Dakil.

Sólan stiffened at the boy's name. *Montrél. Jidir, harméno, do I miss you so.* His breath caught on a sudden lump in his throat, and he didn't realise he'd made a sound until Dakil turned toward him. A huge grin stretched across the swordsman's face as he approached, young Montrél in tow. *He knows not the weight of that boy's name, Sólan. Not yet; nor will he ever deserve such knowledge.*

"I wasn't expecting to see you here," said Dakil. "The Áfgalese children will be excited to meet you."

A shy smile curled on Sólan's blushing face, and the flutter in his chest made him cough. "I doubt many of them will know who—"

"Injál de Áfgal," the boy whispered. His eyes grew wide, the colour draining from his face. "You *are* alive."

Sólan clamped shut his mouth. *"Angel of Áfgal." Gods, Chainless was right.* "Tíal, I am alive. What is your name?"

"Montrél de Casaca. You saved me and my baby sister after the bandits took us. I will never forget those orange eyes that glow green like spring."

Tears threatened Sólan once again. *This, Sólan, is why you are a scout. Why you sought the Chainbreakers.* "'Tis a pleasure to meet you, Montrél de Casaca." He swallowed the ache inching its way up his chest. "I had a brother named Montrél. Montrél de Maseño. He, my mother, and his father moved to Ciudelago shortly before I was born." Reaching out, he squeezed the boy's arm and grinned. "He also trained in swords, like you. But he was lazy at time, and never developed such muscle, as his master was far less skilled than yours." He winked at Dakil.

"You didn't tell me you had a brother," said Dakil, frowning. "What happened to him?"

Sólan shrugged, though his jaw was tight. "I outlived him."

The dull clang of a bell rang through the fields, and the boy averted his gaze to the orphanage's adobe brick building. "I have to go," he said. "Will I ever see you again?"

"I hope so."

"Probably," said Dakil, smiling once again. "Go inside. It's time for your studies."

Montrél nodded and sprinted toward the building. As the remainder of the children followed suit, Sólan wrapped his arm around Dakil's waist from behind and nuzzled his jaw. "We need to talk," he whispered.

Dakil broke the embrace to face him. "About what?"

"Us."

The swordsman blinked as his breath hitched. "There's nothing between us to talk about."

Sólan frowned. "I think there is much between us to address. I want to clarify something you said the night before we landed on that Isle of Death."

"I thought I was quite clear with my words."

"Tíal, your words were clear. But your actions? Call it a 'language barrier,' if you prefer." Sólan's mouth dried as the scent of salt and spice teased his nostrils. He leaned in, hovering his lips over Dakil's. "Perhaps we can speak over a pint of ale."

"I prefer brandy," said Dakil, brushing his lips against Sólan's before pulling away.

Goosebumps prickled the Áfgaliard's skin. *This is what confuses me.* "As do I."

K H NELSON

This needs to end. Just tell him, Dakil. Tell him you won't be his whore, that you won't give in to his seduction like you did Kadek's. He just wants to use you.

Dakil opened his mouth to speak, but Sólan spoke first. "You are a confusing man, sañero. Confusing, fascinating ... frustrating."

Rasheed approached their table with two crystal glasses half-filled with a brown liquor that smelled of cherries. He and Dakil exchanged nervous glances, with Rasheed motioning to the pantry entrance. The swordsman broke his gaze as the barkeep stole away from them. *Thank God. I'll need someone to fuck after this conversation.* "Conflicting? Frustrating? What makes you say that, *Captain*? I just exist, and we've kissed. Nothing more then and even less now."

Sólan winced. "That is not what I had in mind with this conversation."

"And what *did* you have in mind? I told you, I'm no smuggler's whore. I made that mistake with the last captain, and I won't make it again."

"¿Mondé?"

Pantot, Sólan. Are you stupid, or do you simply refuse to listen?

"Dakil, do you believe I wish only to *fuck* you?" The Áfgaliard sipped on his brandy. "If that were true, then there are plenty of other men aboard the *Silent Dancer* who would be willing to indulge me."

Dakil stiffened. "Like who?"

"Ha! If you wanted me not, why should you care?"

Well played, Grim. "I don't know. I mean, I don't care." Dakil fidgeted with his glass before drinking half of it in one gulp.

Sólan arched an eyebrow and snorted. "As I said—confusing." He finished his brandy and shuddered. "Gods, Dakil, why do you do this to me?"

"Do what?"

"Toy with my heart." Sólan ran a shaky hand through his hair. "You come onto me, embrace me, *kiss* me—then turn me away like a piece of rotting meat. Why?"

Yusa's Grace, he really is so hurt. "I'm sorry, I just"—Dakil swallowed the sudden lump in his throat—"I'm just trying to be cautious with my own heart."

Sólan's eye twitched. "I thought 'caution is for the child that steals copper coins from the Temple of Yusa.'"

You remembered that? "I'm not ready, Sólan. I need more time." Dakil threw back the last of his brandy. *You still can't trust him, Dakil. He's half elf. He's the Grim. He's the man who killed Kadek with his seduction.*

Sólan looked to his lap, blushing. "I can give you that," he whispered. He took a shaky breath and turned his empty glass upside down. "Enjoy the rest of your night, sañero Papuan." His chair scraped the floor as he stood and trudged over to Rasheed.

The orc handed him his room key and growled, "Two eight four."

Sólan merely nodded and made his way to the closest of three staircases. He looked over his shoulder at Dakil. "If you change your mind—"

"I won't," said Dakil.

Sólan snatched a bottle of liquor from the bar's counter on his way to the stairs. *Gods, I hope this is strong.* He flipped a gold coin to Rasheed. "For your trouble."

"This is too much. That bottle is only—"

"I care not, Rasheed. Just fucking take it." *Take it as payment to also burn my body when I die of drink tonight.* He clenched his jaw against the intrusive thoughts. *Medría, what has he done to me?* Hurrying up the stairs, the captain entered his room and plopped himself on the lumpy mattress. There, he guzzled the cherry brandy—the same bottle from which his first glass came—as though it were water.

His stomach churned, his heart pounded, and his skin grew slick with sweat as the drink leaked its poison into his veins. Vision spinning, he tried to sleep. The Dark, however, burned through the liquor faster than desired. *Fuck. Why does this curse never let me die of my own accord?* His thoughts, of course, meandered to Dakil, to his words of rejection and the look of doubt and mistrust in his eyes. He thought of the salty taste of the swordsman's lips and the music of his laughter. Sólan's manhood swelled, stiff enough to stab into the mattress. *Gods-damned elf blood in these maldónta veins of mine.* He squirmed and cursed, attempting to rid his mind of Dakil. 'Twas for naught.

Sighing, he finally acquiesced to the pain and loosened his trousers, muttering a prayer to Halaña asking forgiveness. He prepared to relieve himself when …

Knock, knock, knock.

Sólan jumped to his feet, hatchet in hand. He tightened his trousers again and tiptoed to the door. *Please, Dakil. Let it be you.* He shook his head and cursed. *'Tis a fool's hope, Sólan.*

His muscles tensed as the scent of orc slithered through the barrier between him and his coming fight. Unlatching the door, he held it just open enough to see a petite figure, hooded and holding her hands in front of her. Chainless.

"What do you want, sañerota?" Solan's hand tightened around his hatchet.

"It's not 'want', Grim," said Chainless. The coy mischief in her voice was palpable. "You have something I need."

Sólan's mouth dried. *Gods, I love the scent of lust.* He opened the door and stepped aside. "Your timing is virtuous, as I am also in need."

Chainless stepped into the room and removed her cloak. "I know. I could smell it from across the tavern."

A smile danced across Sólan's lips. "I have had to be content with my hand, as of late."

"Ha!" Chainless rolled her eyes and kicked the door shut. "And yet, you have a willing being in front of you. But if you'd prefer your calloused hand above the warm caress of a woman, then I suppose I am wasting my time. I took you for a devout man of your gods. Does Halaña no longer forbid the act of self ecstasy?" She arched her scarred eyebrow over her seafoam gaze. "Perhaps Rasheed may be of some comfort? He, like you, prefers the company of men. And since Dakil has clearly rejected you …"

You wound me, sañerota. "And you think 'tis merely men who satisfy me?" Sólan stepped forward and wrapped an arm about Chainless's waist. He dropped his hatchet with a thud and kicked it hard enough to slide it across the room. "I am a man of eclectic taste, though orc is not one yet familiar to me. For a being who detests the scent of elves, you seem to be quite … enamoured." The smells of smoke and lily blossoms reached his nostrils, sending his heart into a flutter. He entwined his fingers with a lock of her hair and played with it as though entranced. "Why have you made an exception with me, my dear Chainless?"

"Alira," said Chainless. She leaned into his embrace and whispered, "Tonight, I am Kil-Alira-Non, and you … Sólan de Ciudelago."

A bolt of lust shuddered through the Áfgaliard at the utterance of his name. *Halaña, you bless me with this gift of lust.* Without another word, he planted his mouth on hers. The two fumbled with each other's clothing, catching the fabric on his ears and her earrings.

Sólan buried his face into her bosom, and she moaned beneath his hot breath. He stooped to lift her to his level, and she locked her legs about his hips. There, her entrance teased his erection, and he shuddered at the warmth and the tantalising wetness. Plopping her on his bed, he slid beside her and teased her nub with a finger. They kissed again, teeth clacking against each other and tongues intertwining.

Chainless—no, *Alira*—broke their kiss to whimper. "Oh, Sólan. Take me now, you torturous fox."

As you demand, my sweet-smelling vixen. Sólan nibbled her jaw and groaned, unable to speak his thoughts. Slowly, he made his way down her body with feather-like kisses, flicking his tongue against her erect nipples. She loosened beneath him as he slipped his torso between her legs. His mouth reached her belly, her pelvis, her groin.

Alira gasped as his mouth met her entrance. He kissed, licked, and sucked. His hands travelled up and down her abdomen and chest. "Fuck," she whispered. "Don't stop." She stiffened as her pressure built beneath him.

Despite her plea, he halted, his chin slick with her as he crawled onto the bed. "You are a thirsty woman, Alira. Would you like a taste?"

She grasped a fistful of his hair and pulled his face toward her own. "Shut up and fuck me, Angel of Áfgal."

Sólan kissed her again, allowing the taste of her womanhood to seep onto her tongue. He grasped his erection and rubbed its tip against her; teased her until his own desires overtook him. He thrust into her, filling her completely. His body moved of its own accord, and he stood at the bed's edge. He helped her wrap her ankles about his neck before hugging her knees, writhing. *Oh Gods, I need this.*

Alira arched onto her own shoulders. Upside-down, she nigh ripped through the sheets with her fists and let out a guttural cry as she climaxed.

"Medría, Dakil!" Sólan cried. He removed himself from Alira and fell to his knees, spilling his seed onto the ground. He shivered with ecstasy. His heart raced, and his breathing deepened.

Alira giggled. "I may have your cock tonight, but I see your heart was stolen by another."

Sólan gasped. *Oh Gods. I called the wrong name. Fuck, Dakil, what have you done to me?*

28

DANGEROUS LOVE

*D*akil sat at the bar, sipping sage water and cursing its bitter taste. His head pounded with spent drunkenness, and his groin burned with skin chafed by an impassioned night with Rasheed. *Yusa bless you, Rasheed.* Always the willing lover and never attached at the heart. His cock and ass were the reasons Dakil had remained sane during his relationship with the manipulative Kadek.

Chainless slapped the bar, laughing at Dakil's painful yelp. "I hear you and Rasheed rekindled last night."

There was nothing to rekindle. I didn't want to fuck my hand anymore. "You already know that what happens between me and Rasheed is nothing more than our bodies."

"What a relief. I can't have you falling in love with my brother. He's not one to commit."

Dakil grumbled, shifting his attention to his water.

The orc lifted an eyebrow and leaned forward. "I know that look. I saw it every time Kadek broke you."

"Dammit, Chainless. Leave me alone," said Dakil. He bared his teeth and twitched his nose. "I don't have the patience to deal with you."

"Oh? Perhaps you have the patience for the man who holds your heart. This one is much darker than your last *inamorato*."

"And whose lover is he, exactly?" *Dammit, Dakil. You fell into her fucking trap again.* "I saw you last night with Sólan."

Chainless giggled. "And I know that tone. You gave it to me every time Kadek turned you away after ... well, after he decided to throw you to the side." She pulled out a pitcher from under the counter and topped off the swordsman's water. "But we're not talking about your dead partner, are we?"

Dakil grumbled and took a sip from his glass. "Kadek was hardly a *partner*—just a man who thought his cock was more deadly than Misó."

"Ha!" Chainless poured her own pint of sage water and gulped it down. "No need to feel threatened by me, Papuan. What happened between me and the Grim was nothing more than what happens between you and Rasheed."

"Were his words true? You and Rasheed are the lost heirs to Garmath?" *I need to get my head away from that man.*

"Be careful, Dakil. You know better than to cross me." Chainless's eyes pulsed red with the sudden shift in her tone. Her crystalline lamps darkened with the change.

"Fine. I'll ask him." Dakil peeked over his shoulder to see Rasheed wiping down tables while humming a happy tune. *After all, he tells me everything when he receives.*

Chainless slapped the counter again. "I mean it, Papuan. Keep this shit up, and you're no longer welcome on this fucking island."

"Maybe that will get me thrown off the *Silent Dancer*. I can always go back to Morinalo."

The orc scoffed. "What, and leave the man whose heart you stole? I thought you were better than that. He called out your name last night."

He what? Dakil feigned indifference. "Unluckily for him, I called out Rasheed's."

"No, you didn't," said Rasheed, snickering. He slapped Dakil on the back before walking around the counter. "How's your head?"

"Nipantot ki, tulalo," said Dakil. Rasheed roared in laughter and disappeared into the pantry. "I hate you both."

Chainless snorted. "You and Grim just need to claim each other and fuck already. This tension between you two is suffocating everyone."

Dakil turned red. "There is no tension between us. And what do you mean, 'claim each other'? You know men can't marry men. It's forbidden to even—"

"Have you forgotten that it's *not* forbidden in Áfgal?" Chainless's stare bore holes into Dakil's chest, though her was wide enough to show both pairs of her fangs. "The Áfgalese don't marry except to place heirs on their throne. And that marriage is never loving ... nor does it last long. To claim a lover over there is to commit to them for life—they don't do so lightly."

Sólan shouldn't want to claim me, Chainless. He needs someone less broken ... someone like you. "How do you know so much about Áfgal?"

Chainless slid a full pint of frothy ale to Dakil and winked. "Because that's what the Garmathians did. The Áfgalese are our descendants, remember."

How long ago? Yusa's prophets forbid it in all their teachings, yet the Book of the Sun never says—"Tell me more."

"First, a toast. This pint's on me." Chainless lifted her own mug with a smirk, and Dakil forced a smile as he clacked his against hers. Ale spilled from both pints. "To life, to love, and to the liberty to fuck."

To the liberty to claim Sólan the Grim as mine.

SÓLAN DRUMMED HIS FINGERS ON THE CAPTAIN'S TABLE AS HE PORED over the map of Bansungei. *Gods-dammit. I understand none of this.* He squinted as he tried to make out the lettering of each landmark's title, but to him, 'twas nothing but scribbles. Numbers, he knew, for they never changed regardless of the language. Words, however? He was never given the luxury of learning, even after three hundred years of trying to teach himself.

A faint knock made him flinch. *You are safe, Sólan. 'Tis merely the door. You are safe.* He took several calming breaths and shook his head. "Come in."

The smell of salt and brandy tickled his nostrils. Dakil. *Halaña, will you not take this desire from me? Am I to suffer until his death to be free of his spell?*

"The land runners are done loading, and we've filled our galley with enough provisions to last us an entire moon," said Dakil.

"Good," said Sólan through clenched teeth. "The winds are a bit calm for a successful launch." *Do not turn around. Do not look at him, Sólan.* The captain peeked over his shoulder and twitched as that cursed flutter returned to his chest. *Dammit.*

"By the look of the clouds and the open sea's currents, we should be safe to do so by dusk." The floor creaked as Dakil shifted his weight, fidgeting with his sword.

Sólan turned and leaned against the table's edge with arms crossed. "Thank you, Dakil. Is there anything else?"

The swordsman scowled. "No." He spun on his heel and reached for the door.

"Wait. I need your help with something."

Dakil let out a deep sigh. "What do you need, Captain?"

You. All of you. Nothing else on this gods-damned ship, except you. "I am unfamiliar with the southern coast."

"Just read the map. You don't need *my* help with—"

"I cannot read." Sólan's ears burned, and he looked to his feet, rubbing the toe of his boot into a divot on the table's leg. "I never learned, except with numbers. And, I am still unfamiliar with your tongue." *Both spoken and tasted.* He winced at the intrusive thought.

Dakil's face softened into a sad smile. "I'm sorry. I didn't mean to be rude. Too much port last night."

Sólan snorted. "For me, too much brandy."

"And Chainless."

Fuck! How did you know? "¿Mondé? I had just enough of Alira last night."

"For Yusa's grace, Sólan! You even use her real name? You promised you would wait."

"I said I could give you time! Not *once* did I promise you anything!" Sólan's eyes pulsed in pain as he clenched his shaking fists at his side. "And who the fuck are you to get jealous? You reek of Rasheed. I doubt you cared when you were with him. I doubt you cared about *anything* beyond what got your cock wet."

Dakil's face flushed. "I care because I just ..." He rubbed his face and panted shallowly. "Pantot."

"Close the door, Dakil. We need to talk. Now." *No more wasting time. No more toying. Just you and me.* "Tell me, what am I to you?"

Dakil stiffened. He opened his mouth as though to answer, but snapped it back shut.

Your silence says everything. Turning his face away, Sólan grimaced as a jolt of pain stabbed his stomach. *Be this my punishment, Halaña? To be used as nothing more than a wet dream for your games? Was the baker not enough? The blacksmith? The women of your Holy Place in Ciudelago?* "Get out," he said through a heave. "Bayani can help me with this fucking map."

"Oh, now you want to fuck Bayani?"

Ansalá, give me patience with this man. "Dammit, Dakil, why do you care?" Sólan took a step toward the swordsman and snarled. "Just make your decision and tell me." Grabbing two fistfuls of his own hair, he took a shaky breath in a failed attempt to calm his racing heart. "I cannot claim someone if they are unwilling, Dakil. You should, at the least, know this about me. I know not if you reject me or want me. *Medría!*"

"I don't want to be used again, Sólan! I want to trust you, but I don't know if I can." Dakil trembled, though his eyes stayed stubbornly dry. "If you knew what it's like to be taken unwillingly. To be coerced and have your family threatened by the one man who claimed to love you."

But I do know, Dakil. I know more than you can possibly understand.

"Kadek broke me—my heart, my spirit, my everything—all so he could use me for his own twisted games." Dakil bared his teeth at the memory. "But you? If you could understand what it's like—"

"Is that not what you are doing to me?" Sólan gasped, covering his mouth with his hand. *Fuck.* He shook his head and pounded the table with his fist. "You were right, Dakil. I know I refused to believe it before, but ... you were right." His jaw trembled, tears dripping down his cheeks. "I am a broken man."

Dakil's breath hitched. "I know." He looked to the ground and rubbed his toe against his opposite shin. "We both are ... maybe even beyond repair."

Sólan shook his head. *Stop it, Sólan. He is merely toying with you again.*

"What was his name?"

Memories flashed behind Sólan's eyes. He could smell the stale wheat flour and apyin smoke, feel the pressure that tore into his rectum, and hear the devilish groans and chuckles from the men and women who swore to protect and love him. "Please, Dakil," he whispered. "I wish not to remember them. Especially now."

"*Them*?" Dakil's face grew pale. His knees shook, and hands trembled as he shuffled his way to the map table. There, he leaned onto his fists as though weighed down with a blacksmith's anvil. "Pantot, Sólan. I—" he hiccoughed "—I'm sorry. I got so lost in my own weakness, that I forgot you're nothing like Kadek."

The Áfgaliard cleared his throat, but the stubborn lump remained. "Nimíl, Dakil. I am nothing like that devil of a man." Sólan's breath shook as he looked to the ceiling, tears flowing freely down his face. "I need you trust my intentions, Dakil. But, if you do not, just tell me. Tell me to fuck off and pretend we never felt for each other. Either way, I trust you."

Dakil froze. He gazed at the table with wide eyes and a partially open mouth. *Say something. Gods, please say something.*

After a long and painfully silent moment, the swordsman stirred. He placed a hand on Sólan's shoulder and righted himself. Without making eye contact, all he managed to whisper was, "Why?"

Sólan wiped his eyes with the back of his wrist. "Because I know, Dakil. I know how Kadek used you—'twas evident the moment I saw you in the damned 'kitchen,' or whatever you call it." He took a breath and grasped Dakil's hand, holding it tightly to his chest. "I tell you this not for your sympathy. That I neither need nor want. Just understand, sañero. *Please.* My heart is a brittle thing that has never been stolen by anyone." *Until you.*

Dakil slowly exhaled, finally raising his gaze to lock eyes with the man before him. He reached up and swept a loose curl of deep brown hair from Sólan's face, caressing his cheek to rub away another tear. "I trust you, Sólan." He brushed his lips against the captain's, branding his words into flesh. "And I claim you."

Sólan gasped, staring into Dakil's gaze as though searching for deceit. With bated breath, he intertwined his fingers with his companion's. "Do you even understand what you are saying? The weight of the words you have just uttered?" His speaking accelerated alongside his heart, and his voice cracked with the pain of hope. "Dakil, please tell me this is real. That you are not merely pretending, like you claim to do with Rasheed. You realise, Dakil, that I will outlive you by at least ten of your lives. Are you prepared for that? For watching me stay youthful like this while your bones grow thin and dry?"

Dakil bit his lip and winced. The scent of fear slithered up Sólan's nostrils, and new tears filled his eyes. His heart pounded in his head, mouth dry from longing.

"I only need one life—only have one life. Let it be this one," whispered Dakil. "I claim you, Sólan de Ciudelago."

"Oh, thank the Gods," whispered Sólan. He planted his mouth onto Dakil's and pulled him into a tight embrace. "And I claim *you*, Dakil Papuan."

29

THE SENATE'S GAME

*D*uke Naoise wrapped his heavy cloak about himself as he entered the glassy council room. He shivered, his breath misting from between his chattering teeth. *Gnomes, what I wouldn't give to be back in Prastömin right now.* He peered at the massive windows with awe. Despite the cold and prominent desolation, the colours of the eastern horizon as the sun descended behind the mountains would make any man weak. 'Twas a beauty rarely seen in the forest, and Naoise was no exception to its trance.

The soft fragrance of perfume wafted through his nostrils, and when he turned his ear toward the western entrance, he heard the soft arrival of a woman's gait. He peered over his shoulder to see a tall figure of porcelain skin, wavy taupe hair, and brilliant blue eyes that matched the sapphire resting on her forehead. Her expression exuded a strength that made Naoise's breath catch. *Gnomes, y're beautiful, Siobhan. I wonder if y'r sister—* The intrusive thought startled him. He wasn't much attracted to brunettes, unlike the prince. *Tör, ya lucky bastar'.*

"I see punctuality is one of yer strengths," she said through clenched teeth. "A rarity amongst the Prasti."

Naoise arched an eyebrow and opened his mouth to respond, but a sudden chill stayed his voice. He shivered again.

"I keep telling me father to build a hearth fer foreign ambassadors, but he seems quite intent on torturing those who have the ability to disagree with him." A smirk pulled at the corners of the woman's mouth, and she eyed the massive marble table, flitting her gaze to and from its foot. "Ye're doing well with the cold, considering. Shall we sit?"

The Prasti duke merely nodded. Turning his back from the windows, he lowered himself into what he assumed was his seat. The woman followed suit with her own. *The western seat? I thought she was senator of the northern corner. Isn't Moira*—he gasped. He watched her fidget with her forearms beneath the thin sleeves of her pale blue dress. A wet stain developed on the bottom of her wrist. Perhaps 'twas sweat? Melted ice? A faint metallic scent reached his nostrils. *Not sweat. It's blood*. Naoise gulped, though not in fear. 'Twas in admiration. "How many knives do ya carry?"

"Pardon?" The senator stiffened, her face somehow growing even more pale. What was she afraid of? Being caught armed? Seen as weak?

"Ya need new sheaths. Those ones are either worn down, or they doen't fit y'r forearms." Naoise gave a warm smile, praying to the Wizards it wouldn't come off as threatening. "Apologies, I haven't introduced m'self proper. I'm Laird Naoise McManstair, Duke of Prastömin. You must be Moira O'Jannon?"

The woman's musical laugh sent butterflies through the duke's chest and stomach. "Gnomes, me laird, I'm usually mistaken fer *Siobhan* to newcomers."

Wizards be good, this is my future bride? What have I done to deserve this?

"And I see that Diarmuid's made the last of Vaoirsen his duke. He's either denying his hatred toward yer father, or he's keeping ye closer than a lover to control ye better. 'Tis what he *tried* with the earl of Vaoirsen." Moira's smile disintegrated into an emotionless slate of porcelain. "Manstair was no traitor, Laird Naoise. He was merely a threat to Diarmuid's tyranny."

Naoise stiffened and bit his cheek. Locking the gates to his heart and wiping all emotion from his face, he said, "Any threat to His Grace's rule is treason, senator. My late father included. 'Nd I think it'd be wise to avoid such talk today. I'm not here to rejoice—nor lament—the past. I'm here to secure peace f'r the bloody future."

Moira's eye twitched, though she showed not whether 'twas in humour or anger. "Ye may survive us, after all, me laird."

Wizards be good, y're nothin' like I expected. Naoise rose to his feet and leaned onto his fists, knuckles blanching with the force. "This is no game, Senator. We're speaking on—"

"Tell that to the others, Naoise McManstair. I, at least, understand the gravity of yer visit, and the 'promise' of peace it brings. However, I also know this hollow act is less than helpful to the Karthi. *Particularly* the West."

Naoise and Moira stared at each other in stubborn silence. The duke opened his mouth to argue but was interrupted by the bubbly exclamation of a newcomer.

"Laird Naoise! Welcome to Karthénos!" The woman was of similar height and stature as Moira, yet her glacial eyes and snowy hair made her appear as white as the snowy summits of the eastern mountains. She skipped and giggled to the duke, embracing him. "Just think of the fun we'll have when we're brother and sister by law!"

Gnomes be merciful, that sounds terrible. At least I'm not promised to this giggling dunce. Naoise stifled a snicker at Moira's rolling of her eyes.

"Calm yerself, Siobhan," hissed another woman, who appeared behind her. Senator Kiera.

"Oh, but Mother! He's such a huggable Veer!"

Moira groaned, Naoise swallowed a scoff, and Siobhan merely pouted like a young child. Kiera rubbed her forehead with a wince. "Apologies, me laird. She frequently forgets her *place*."

Naoise forced a smile. "No apologies necessary, Senator." *Get me the fook out of here. Damn you, Tör.* He took his seat at the foot of the table. All eyes were on him as he fidgeted and shivered once more in the cold.

More elves entered, including Cadman and Saoirse. *Where's Jannon?* Naoise had little time to say anything as the tension in the room spiked. The hairs on his neck stood on end when he noticed Cadman scowling at Moira. Though, 'twas more than a mere scowl—he looked like he wanted to murder her. The duke then glanced at his betrothed, who matched the knight's face with her own hot glare. *What the hell happened 'atween you two?*

"Apologies, senators, knights … Laird Naoise." Jannon's voice pierced the air like an icy dagger. Moira and Cadman hardly took notice, except that they finally broke their malicious stare down. The duke of the tundra took the seat at the head of the table and smiled. "Welcome to Karthénos. It's been quite some time since a Prasti has crossed our shared border for such an important council."

Ears burning, Naoise took a calming breath to stay his racing heart. *Giaven, I hope to the Wizards y'r ghost helps me now.* "It's an honour, Laird Jannon, that I be privileged with such a task. The hospitality of y'r republic rivals—nai, exceeds—that of Prastömin."

Saoirse rolled her eyes in his periphery. *Doen't say anything, Neesh. No one can know y're her father.* "Shall we discuss the matter that brings me here?"

"That depends, me laird," said Kiera, cocking her head. "As none of us know the importance of this meeting, I'm unsure if we should even be involved. The last time we met at the whims of a Prasti, yer king started a war."

"A massacre," said the man sitting between Moira and Cadman. The southern senator. *What's his name again?*

"And, even before that, the infamous Massacre of Vaoirsen," said Kiera. "Ye, of all beings, should understand our wariness."

"And now, he wishes to take Karthénos through marriage," said Cadman.

Oh, shut the hell up, Cad.

"I suppose we should let the man speak?" asked Saoirse. She arched an eyebrow and pressed her lips together, as though stifling a smile. "He is our guest, after all."

Cadman groaned, but Naoise shot him a glare of warning before saying, "Thank ya, Dame Saoirse." He opened his cloak and pulled out a large vellum scroll. He then broke the green wax seal and passed it to his right, to Moira. Their fingertips touched, and he stifled a gasp at the warmth of her hand. *Not now, Neesh. We have more important things to discuss.* "This only be a draft. The final is to be negotiated before signatures from every corner of the eastern lands are sealed with ink."

The senator clenched her jaw as she read the document, passing it along to the rest of the council. Varying expressions of doubt, mockery, and anger littered the room as the scroll passed from one pair of eyes to the next. Siobhan frowned, as though confused, and Jannon's eye merely twitched once he finished reading.

"Why are the Taelas deciding when I can marry Prince Alsantör?" A strange emotion flashed across Siobhan's face. At least, it seemed strange to Naoise, given her giggling mere moments before.

Naoise could feel Moira's stare boring holes into him, and he refused to look her way. "The Taelas are breeding their mortal elves with giants. Imagine, beings who were once docile and kind controlled by The Dark."

"Káil."

"Wizards be good."

Whispered curses and gasps bounced through the room. Moira's gaze, however, didn't change. "Then why should we wait to unify? If the Taelas are trying to start a war, should we not already be aligned with Prastömin?"

"We unify now, and we've all but declared war on that desert kingdom," said Naoise. He looked at her and was surprised by her gaze. While he expected a glare, he saw naught but intrigue. Fascination. Was that a twinkle of lust in her fiery eyes?

"We're already aligned with Prastömin," said Cadman, crossing his arms with a scowl. "I, for one, would like to prevent this union. I refuse to be back under Diarmuid's thumb."

"Being 'under his thumb,' as you call it, is the purpose of these betrothals," said Jannon. All eyes snapped to him. "I refuse to sign this."

"Yet, this is no permanent agreement, Jannon," said Kiera. "I will sign it, should it mean peace, even fer a short while."

"But I want to marry the prince," whined Siobhan.

Wizards, that screech, lamented Naoise. "Senator Kiera's right. This is temporary. And y'll get ta marry Prince Alsantör, but we need ta sue f'r peace, first." He looked to Siobhan with a deceptively warm smile.

"Would this peace include the Áfgalese?" The crack in Moira's voice was subtle, but still there. "Because the West needs—"

Cadman groaned in interruption. "Oh, for Gnomes' sakes, will you shut up about the bloody West for once! Every fucking time, Moira. You're not the only fucking senator here."

Moira's chair slid back as she jumped to her feet. "The West oversees our grain stores fer winter, Sir Cadman! It seems that mass starvation may be a bit lower on yer priorities than it should be!"

The knight balled his fists as he stood to match her glare, his chair tipping over with a crash. "Like you give a fuck on my priorities, Moira. I'll be damned if the bitch-daughter of Jannon tells me how to do my job!"

"*Enough!*" Naoise pounded his fist against the table, causing it to quiver. "Doen't tell me that the gnomes-damned foreigner has better sense than the lot o'ya!" He scowled at Cadman and bared his fangs, despite his need for restraint. "I swear to the Wizards, Cad. Call my future bride a 'bitch' one more time, y're gon' regret ever knowin' me."

Saoirse remained silent but smirked at Naoise's outburst. Cadman righted his chair and sat. The Prasti duke exchanged a knowing glance with his daughter before saying, "Yes, Senator Moira. This treaty means peace with *ev'ryone.*" His stomach flipped as he and the senator locked eyes once again. *Gnomes, to know what y're thinking this very moment.* She silently lowered herself back into her seat before finally breaking her gaze with him.

Jannon cleared his throat. "This republic has been humiliated by the minions of the crown fer long enough, Laird Naoise. I will not allow it any longer."

Naoise bit his cheek and grimaced, slowly shifting his gaze between Cadman and Jannon, careful to hide his disgust for them both.. "Do ya f'rget, m'laird, how expensive war can be? Diarmuid'll raise the taxes on all the common folk, Karthénos included. We, in the forest, can get by growin' our own grains, and raisin' our own stock. But you? Winter'll be here in two moons: the weather's already turnin'. Y'll need our grains to survive as y'r agriculture's been cut in funding this past season. But ya woen't be able to afford them. Y'r people'll starve, Laird Jannon. And when they do, y're gon' have a rebellion on y'r hands. Is that what ya want?"

A quiet murmur swelled amongst the senators, knights, and dukes. Moira, however, remained silent. Naoise leaned over to her and whispered, "And you? What is it that ya want from this treaty?"

"Peace," she said. Her eyes flared with a brilliant sapphire flame as she arched an eyebrow. "And freedom."

30

BRITTLE HEARTS AND BITTER DREAMS

Sólan's teeth chattered as he paced the cabin, wringing his hands and licking his lips in anticipation. He kept glancing at the open jar of hardened coconut oil and the clean bowl of water set on his mahogany table. *You have bedded so many men before, Sólan. This is nothing new. No need to be so—*

A faint knock snapped his attention to his door. He trembled as he opened it, grimacing at the sharp sound of the creaking hinges. He locked his gaze on the smoky russet eyes of his lover. Dakil was the most beautiful man he'd ever laid eyes upon. Sólan's heart lurched into his throat as the scent of salt and brandy consumed him, intertwining with the erotic incense of lust. Dakil smiled—a coy yet inviting smile that sent a shiver ricocheting up and down the Áfgaliard's spine.

"I have been expecting you," said Sólan.

Dakil merely bit the corner of his lower lip before grasping Sólan and pulling him in for a passionate kiss. Teeth clacked together as hands pulled on each other's hair, shirts, and necks. It took Sólan every gram of strength he had to keep himself from stripping and sucking off the swordsman right there on the deck in direct view of the stars.

Dakil shoved Sólan inside, kicked the door shut, and continued his passion. Unlike the Áfgaliard in his arms, and unlike anything he'd done to this moment, he held nothing back. The two crashed into the mahogany table, knocking the oil to the ground, before a shirt was finally removed. The other quickly followed.

Sólan took a sharp breath at the sight of Dakil's decorated torso. A sun made from ten black triangles like shark teeth encircled his left breast. Inside the circle were dozens of spearhead shapes that were layered in a perfect circle. Simple lines depicted fish, birds, and—Sólan assumed—waves that extended from his chest to his shoulder and down to his bicep. He didn't realise he was staring until his lover chuckled.

"You look confused," said Dakil. He cocked his head with a mischievous smile. "They each have a story."

"I look forward to hearing them," Sólan cooed. He wrapped his hand with Dakil's braid and pulled to expose his neck. Latching his mouth onto the side of his throat, he slid his free hand down the swordsman's trousers, into their waistband. Slowly, he loosened them as he inched his kisses down to his collarbone, his sternum, his breast.

By the time Dakil's erection was free from its covering, Sólan was kneeling, kissing down his abdomen and hip.

"Wait," said the swordsman.

Sólan grimaced but looked up with pleading. *Gods, not again. Please, Halaña stop torturing me with this man. Make him stop.*

Dakil tugged Sólan to his feet. "Me first." Without another word, Sólan's trousers dropped around his ankles, and Dakil was on his knees.

"Oh Gods," said Sólan, gasping. His legs threatened to buckle beneath him as his lover slid his mouth over the tip of his manhood. A sharp pain jolted through his inner thigh, and he didn't know whether to yelp or moan. The repeat on the other side gave him his answer. A guttural groan escaped his throat and left him begging for more. *You are a biter. Gods! You feel so—*

His thought never finished as Dakil swallowed him all the way to his hips. Finally, his knees gave way, but his lover was ready to catch him. To hold him. To *fuck* him.

Dakil eased him to the ground and climbed on top to straddle him. *Wait, am I ready for this? To receive him?* Sólan's breath caught, and his lust gave way to fear.

The swordsman reached across the floor and slid the jar of hard oil toward them. Leaning over, he kissed Sólan's cheek, then jaw, then earlobe. "Your eyes—they're afraid. Why? Did you forget I receive *you* tonight?"

"For a moment, tíal." Sólan caressed Dakil's jaw and coaxed his mouth down to his own. "I wish not to stop. I have waited so long for you, my heart could not bear your rejection again."

Dakil dipped his fingers into the jar and melted a dollop on his lover's manhood. "I've claimed you, Sólan. There is no more rejecting you—especially tonight." The swordsman shifted his weight and gripped Sólan's erection with a tight fist. Slowly, he eased himself down, panting as he inserted.

Medría, Dakil! Sólan rolled his hips upward. The warmth. The pressure. *Gods*, he threatened to burst far too quick, but Dakil stopped. *You torturous man.'Tis no wonder Rasheed is addicted to you.*

More movement, and Sólan went deeper. Got harder. Breathed louder. Moaning, his hips soon moved of their own accord, and Dakil pinned his torso to the ground with a straight arm to the chest.

"Oh, Sólan," he whispered to the ceiling. His eyes rolled up, and a visceral growl echoed from his throat, as though the silk of his voice was ripped by a dull knife.

Sólan arched his back, crying out through clenched teeth. What felt like bits of fresh honey sprinkled onto his chest and neck in rhythmic pulses. As quickly as his lover had finished, so did his own pressure burst.

There, they panted, both shaking in ecstasy. "Gods, Dakil," said Sólan, hardly able to catch his breath.

Dakil inched himself to his feet, using the table as leverage. The Áfgaliard dropped his head against the floor with a thunk after a failed attempt to sit up. Soon, the swordsman was back at his side, wiping his chest with a damp cloth and chuckling. "You're a mess, mintaki. But I won't say sorry."

"Ha!" Sólan sat upright and snatched the cloth from his lover's hand. Wiping his deflated manhood, he snickered. "Apologise not." He cradled Dakil's jaw with one hand and brought him in close for a soft kiss and frowned. *What the hell is "mintaki?"*

"Um … it … nothing. Just a nickname for—" Dakil looked to his lap and blushed. "Never mind."

Shit. I meant not to speak that. Sólan grinned through his wince, kissing Dakil again. "I like it. Have you washed?"

"Not yet."

Sólan planted another kiss on his cheek. "Do not let me stop you, lover."

Dakil beamed. "Just give me a moment, and I'll join you in bed."

For you, I would give anything.

Dakil was jolted awake by the sound of Sólan gasping. His lover was sitting up, hunched over his knees, the silver light of the moon gleaming off the cold sweat on his trembling back. "Sólan?" Dakil reached out and brushed his fingertips across his clammy elbow.

Without warning, the Áfgaliard's arm swung back and collided with the swordsman's nose. Dakil yelped at the flash of pain and the dotted lights crossing his vision. Sólan quickly mounted him. Both his hands wrapped tight around Dakil's throat, squeezing his airway shut. He writhed and fought, flailing his arms in attempt to breathe —to survive. The edges of his vision began to collapse. He was going to die at the hands of the devil of Áfgal—the Grim.

Suddenly, the pulsing green glow in his lover's eyes faded. Sólan released his grip and slid backward, slamming his back against the wall at the bed's foot. Trembling, he curled into a naked ball. "Medría, I—"

"Nipantot *ki*, Sólan!" Dakil wheezed and coughed, rubbing his throat with a grimace. He lifted his fist, but the terror that blanketed his lover's face held his strike. "Oh, Yusa's grace," he said, lowering his arm. "That wasn't you."

Sólan trembled. His face dripped with sweat, his pupils naught but black pinholes in his piercing amber gaze. "I almost killed you." Teeth chattering, he buried his face in his hands and rocked himself back and forth, hiccoughing.

"What happened, mintaki?" The swordsman reached out to place a gentle hand on his lover's shoulder, but Sólan shied away. "It's just me. It's Dakil."

Another shaky breath, and Sólan flitted his gaze around the ship's cabin. "Where am I?"

"The *Silent Dancer*, Sólan. Where else would we be?"

"No. No, no, no—'tis impossible. Where is the blood? The shattered glass? The burning walls?"

"Sólan! What did you see?"

Sólan scrunched his eyes shut and shook his head. When he opened them again, his pupils doubled in size, his breathing slowed, and the tremors ceased.

Calomot i Yusa, you're back.

"Gods, you are still alive," said Sólan, whimpering. Fresh tears flowed from his eyes, and he let out a heavy sigh. He reached out with a tremulous hand and placed it on the swordsman's forearm. "If … if you want to leave—"

"Hundi." Dakil grasped Sólan's elbow and pulled him in close. "I'm not leaving you like this. You're not safe to be alone."

Sólan buried his face into Dakil's bare chest and sobbed—no—wailed incoherently, begging some unseen entity for peace. For strength. For rest. *"My heart is a brittle thing."* Memory of his words pierced Dakil like a knife through the centre of the sun tattooed on his chest.

"Hush, mintaki. You're safe with me." *You'll always be safe with me.*

There, they lay embraced, Sólan's sobs slowly dying into quiet whimpers as he fell into an uneasy sleep while wrapped in Dakil's arms.

BAYANI SHIFTED HIS WEIGHT AND FIDGETED WITH HIS STUMP AS HE STOOD outside the captain's quarters at the western rising of the sun. *What's taking him so long?* He raised his arm to knock a second time when the door finally creaked open. Sólan's tired face and bed-matted hair appeared, squinting in the merciless sun. "Is it dawn, already?" the captain croaked.

"Ta. It's morning," said Bayani curtly. "You said you want me here, so—"

"I know, I know." The Áfgaliard rubbed the sleep from his eyes and yawned. "Please, come in."

Bayani rubbed his head and sighed. *This going to be long morning.* He trudged into the cabin, and the sudden movement in the bed made him yelp. Dakil was lounging, arms behind his head, with naught but the corner of a linen sheet covering his groin. His smug grin taunted the confused smuggler. "Yusa's grace, Dakil! What you are *doing*?"

Dakil burst into laughter. "I swear, tulalo, you're denser than a Prasti."

Bayani flushed and tightened his fists at his side.

Before he could shout anything obscene, Sólan gave a sharp whistle. "Bayani, look at me."

The smuggler turned his glare onto the other half-naked man. "You seducer of Misó. I knew I should let you—" A sharp poke on his back made him stiffen. Dakil's rapier.

"Careful, Bayani. I don't take kindly to men who threaten my lovers." Dakil's voice was smoother than silk, but his threat was clear. "You don't want to end up like Kadek, do you?"

Sólan's face stretched into a wicked grin. "Sit down, pundijo. We need to talk."

Pantot. They perfect for each other. "Fine," Bayani grumbled. He plopped himself into one of the lush chairs and crossed his arms with a scowl.

Sólan slipped into a shirt and crossed to the other chair. He leaned on his elbows and rested his mouth against his clasped hands. "Tell me about Kalasin."

Wait. What? "What ... um. What you need to know?" *Oh Yusa, help me.*

A fully-clothed and armed Dakil slipped behind Sólan and stood, twirling a finger in the base of his lover's hair. He lazily propped his other hand on the hilt of his rapier. "Everything," the swordsman said. "Let's start with where he's from."

Bayani pursed his lips. "I think Tianag. He wore amulet of horse 'round his neck."

Dakil hissed. "Shit. Those grassland zealots." He removed his hand from Sólan's scalp to tug his own hair with a grimace. "Do you think he works for the temple?"

"Hundi. He can't! He too savage for t'at."

Sólan pawed at his scruff and stared blankly at the table. "Jidir," he whispered. "'Tis *precisely* what Oleg was hoping to avoid." He locked eyes with Bayani. "A territory dispute." The captain stood and crossed the room to snatch a large papyrus scroll from a shelf. He untied it and plopped it carelessly onto the mahogany table. "We cannot land at the river mouth, as you both are well aware."

Bayani leaned forward and flattened the scroll's rolled edges. A map of Bansungei. *I told that to Kadek two years ago.* "We need to land here." He pointed to the opposite side of the drawn rocks—the bay.

"That's the port market," said Dakil, crossing his arms in defiance. "We'll get caught."

Bayani shook his head as he pointed to the easternmost point of the coast. "Not if we land during busy times. I know Bansungei better than you know Morinalo." He locked eyes with Dakil before continuing, "I smuggled product under t'at city belly for nine years, Dakil. I watch what come in and what go out."

"That place is *crawling* with cavalry guards, Bayani, even more so at night. Do you really—"

"He has a point, Dakil," said Sólan. An eyebrow arched as he clenched his teeth in thought. "What does Morinalo import to Bansungei?"

"Rum," said Bayani. "Rum and sugar. The only things that no get tax. They no even check barrels. Just show t'em scroll from Morinalo, and they stamp it with yellow wax of the sun."

"'Tis settled, then." Sólan clapped once as he spoke. He jumped to his feet and planted a kiss on Dakil's mouth. "See? I told you he was still of use to us."

"Nipantot ki, Sólan!" Bayani banged his fist on the table. "Why I bother to help you if you insult me?"

"Because helping him helps me," said Dakil. "We have a plan now, thanks to you."

Wait. Does that mean Sólan finally trust me?

As though he heard his silent thoughts, Sólan nodded. "Yes, Bayani. We still need you, as you have become an irreplaceable member of this crew. Kadek was a fool to ignore your insights."

Bayani's heart swelled. *That the kindest thing you ever say to me.* "What else you want to know?"

Sólan smirked once again. "Tell me everything you know about this Kalasin."

31

DAELA

*N*aoise watched the sparring Karthi knights with his arms crossed and his brow furrowed. *Gnomes, they swing those swords so fookin' wide. They wouldn't last half a moment in a real battle.* Flurries of snow dusted the arena and soaked through the quilted linen armour of each knight, but they showed no sign of cold. Naoise, however, shivered as an icy breeze bit his face and neck. Though padded, his leather armour did little to keep him warm—nor did his heavy cloak. His ears piqued at the sound of boots crunching over the frosted ground.

"I'm surprised to see ye outside yer silks, me laird."

A warm smile stretched across his face at the familiar voice. He turned to face Saoirse and startled at her scowl. *Just last evening, you were proud to know me. What happened?*

The woman snatched a gladius waster and covered hatchet from behind her father with a huff. "Tell me, *Father*. Is it true? About me mother? What ye did to her?"

Naoise's breath hitched. *Fook ya, Cadman. That was* my *story to tell.* He chewed on his bottom lip and nodded shallowly. "Eil," he whispered. "It's true."

Saoirse inhaled deeply. Her face contorted and twitched, her freckled mask cracking and chipping under the weight of this revelation. "Then I was a fool. A fool to think that, perhaps, me father could possibly love me." A single tear betrayed her, sliding down her cheek and stopping at the corner of her jaw.

"Saoirse, I do—"

"*Fuck* off! Ye dare slither yourself into me life and think ye can take me from the one man who's ever loved me? The man who raised me?" Saoirse's voice trembled as its volume grew. "I see why Cadman lied to me all these years. He merely protected me, didn't he? Protected me from *you*."

Naoise winced. "That's not fair, Saoirse. 'E lied to me too. Do ya think—"

"I don't want yer excuses. My life would be in danger if he'd told ye! Gnomes, it'd be in danger now if ye were armed!"

Dammit, Naoise! Ya shoulda told her in Baforeis! "As though I had a fookin' *choice*, Saoirse!" Tears threatened his eyes, but he wouldn't let them fall. He couldn't. He'd shown enough weakness around her, and now she loathed him. His heart shattered once again, but she wouldn't see. Not that she cared if she did, anyway, he gathered.

"The choice was to let her live, which ye *did* have."

"Ya think she woulda lived? That you and I woulda lived? It's a fool's hope, Saoirse, to think that Ethna'd let either of us walk away with our heads!"

"Perhaps better to die with yer dignity intact than to live with the guilt of what ye've done to yer family." Even the sharpest sword was dull compared to the spite that thrust from Saoirse's lips.

Naoise turned his head away and squeezed his eyes shut. *Stop it, Neesh. Doen't let her see.* "If ya think so poorly of me, then ask f'r reassignment. There's no point in protecting a man ya despise."

Silence.

Her sharp inhale cut through his ears into his chest, and Naoise peeked over his shoulder to see her blank face, wet with tears. "Well?"

Her face twitched again. Tossing her gladius waster at his feet, she grabbed another one before trudging out to the arena.

Naoise stooped to pick up the weighted stick. His gaze flitted between the armoury and the arena, between battle and peace—dignity and cowardice. All for what? To prove a point? He sighed and unclasped his brooch, his cloak collapsing on the icy ground.

Already defeated by the woman's challenge, he trudged toward Saoirse, stretching his neck and arms in the cold. Fingers still numb, they slammed their swords together, each with a scowl. "Let's get on with it, shall we?"

Saoirse bared her fangs and lifted her weapon in front of her face. "We shall."

They assumed their fighting stances. Naoise rested very little weight on his front foot, merely his toes, in fact. Saoirse shuffled to his left. A quick step, and he'd followed while still square with her shoulders. The duke struck, easily parried by Saoirse's flick of her wrist. He dodged her counterattack.

The two twisted and parried with increasing speed and agility. Every thrust, every shuffle was matched. It was nigh a draw until, "Shite!" Naoise's hand oozed with silver blood as a splinter cut him, and he dropped his waster in pain. He rolled to avoid his daughter's final blow, kicking behind her knees. Losing grip on her waster, she slapped the dirt with her arm to soften her fall. Grasping both weapons, he kicked himself up and stood in front of her with a grin.

Saoirse merely snarled. She dodged his attack with ease, rolling and scrambling to her feet. Her face was flushed in anger or fatigue, Naoise couldn't tell which—until she screamed and swung her hatchet wildly. A hatchet he'd completely forgotten she wielded until its uncovered blade came barreling toward his neck.

The force of her blow split one waster in half, and he jumped backward to dodge the next. "A *live* blade? The hell ya thinkin' lass?" It was his turn to snarl as he attacked.

Naoise snatched her wrist and twisted. Her axe clattered to the ground, and he punched. Hard. Silver blood spattered her face, and she fell to the ground with a yelp. Her father tapped the tip of his blade on her throat. "Dead. 'Nd *I* still live, despite y'r reckless efforts."

Saoirse wiped her face, smearing the blood across her cheeks.

The duke offered his hand, but she only glared at him. His jaw trembled at the growing lump in his throat. *Take it. Please, Saoirse, take my hand.* Despite his silent plea, she turned her gaze away.

Dropping his arm with a sigh, he spun on his heel and trudged off the sparring grounds. His waster clattered to the ground, but he didn't care. He needed to kill something. Shoot something. He eyed a rack of bows and growled. *Not as good as mine, but they'll do.* Quickly sizing them, he grabbed one to his liking and slung a quiver over his shoulder.

NAOISE STOMPED TO THE ARCHERY TARGETS. HE WAS FAR ENOUGH AWAY from the arena to cool himself with the icy atmosphere, but close enough that he wouldn't freeze to death without his cloak. In front of him stood a woman of slight build wearing the same padded armour as the other knights. Braided taupe hair clung to her head in an intricate twist that made Naoise stop and gape. Senator Moira.

He cocked his head and watched. The cracking leather bracers on her forearms still held four small blades each that chafed and stabbed into her skin, though she seemed to take no notice of the pain. She took a deep breath, and her body moved like an avalanche —fluid and beautiful, yet deadly.

She twisted, turned, and flicked, launching each of her eight blades into the centre of the straw target. The final knife burst through the back and stuck into the wood frame with a thunk.

The duke gulped, releasing his breath in a slow blow of awe. "On y'r right," he said, voice cracking. The senator's fiery sapphire eyes sliced into him as she glanced his way.

"Done with sparring already?" Her mouth twitched with the hint of a smirk.

Naoise glowered and strung his bow with a grunt. He reached behind his back, grabbing a fistful of arrows. *Shoulder quivers. What pointless pieces of shite.* Flipping his brass thumb ring around, he shot three arrows in rapid succession. They formed a small triangle in the middle of the bullseye, but he bit his bottom lip with dissatisfaction and plopped the quiver to the ground.

The duke stroked the fletching of the fourth arrow. He nocked, drew, aimed, and ... *twang!* The arrow failed to hit the centre of the triangle he'd created. It failed, even, to hit the blue of the bullseye. He wiggled his shooting thumb and frowned when he discovered it was bare. *Shite. I knew I shoulda sized that one better.*

Moira moved in his periphery, and reached out her hand, bouncing the archery ring in her palm. "It's not the size of yer ring, if that's what ye think. Yer fingers are just cold."

"Hmph." Naoise plucked his ring from her hand. He fidgeted before slipping it back onto his thumb. "It's still new ... a gift from a friend, actually. Was loose even in the warmth."

He shivered at a sudden gust that sent a flurry of massive snowflakes around them. Drifting his gaze to the senator's target, he said, "That's quite the precision ya got there."

"Well. Accuracy's necessary when yer home's ransacked every autumn and winter," said Moira, rubbing her neck. "Not that it matters much when the rest of yer senate's more focused on their own power than the welfare of their people."

"I know this hollow act is less than helpful to the West," she'd said. What's so hollow about peace? Naoise nodded, her previous words echoing in his ears. "What'd ya mean by 'hollow act' when speaking of the treaty?"

"In short? I'd hoped for Prasti aid to hold off the Áfgalese raiders." Moira crossed her arms. "Our funding grows thinner each season, no thanks to our chief commander and treasurer."

"Cadman controls the treasury, too? What the hell does 'e have against ya, anyhow?" *How the fook did that bastar' weasel his way into the banks?*

"I don't know, honestly. I'd like to think jealousy, but ... he did steal yer daughter from ye. He must have something against ye, too."

The blood drained from Naoise's face. "'E doen't have any children, Senator. Hardly a theft."

"His 'niece'?"

How the fook would ya ken? Doen't say anything Neesh. Not a word; if she finds out ...

"Yer silence is telling." She raised an eyebrow and cocked her head. "I told her to take care with Cadman's words. To ask—"

"I doen't have any children either," Naoise said hotly. "Not that I'd ever want any." *Isn't that what ya want, Saoirse? F'r me to denounce ya as my child?*

"Please. I know yer blood runs in Saoirse's veins. She looks just like ye."

"Are we done here? I'd like to finish my day without playing some political game with anyone."

"She's me closest friend, Laird Naoise. If ye're to break her heart, consider our betrothal annulled. I'm not playing games with ye, merely protecting those I love."

Naoise ran a shaking hand through his curls. "Fookin' 'ell. Ya think it's *her* heart that's breakin'? That I'm the one who's rejecting her?" He snarled. "Ya doen't understand what's happened 'atween us, so doen't pretend to. And eil, I have some choice words f'r Cadman, as well. That fooker's lied to all of us f'r far too long. Now, if y'll excuse me, *Senator*." Naoise crossed the range to collect his arrows. Sudden tears flooded his eyes, and he shook his head in a failed attempt to stop them. Another gust of frigid air, and his sinuses dripped with the cold and his sorrow.

"Ye want me to talk to her?"

"What now?" The duke stiffened at the closeness of Moira's voice. "Nai, nai. I ... shite. I should let her make her own choices about me 'nd how she wants to know me."

"She had, until Cadman interfered."

Naoise turned to face her, chewing on his bottom lip in thought.

"Gnomes, ye both do that, too." Stepping closer, she grasped his freezing hand and squeezed once. "Ye deserve each other. She needs her father—her daela, 'nd Cadman is far from one. And ye? I know the look of unresolved grief quite well." Moira lifted herself to her toes, kissing Naoise on his cheek.

His heart leapt at the warmth of her lips feathering against his ice-chapped skin. *I'm sorry, Moira. I'm sorry I let the words of that prick determine my thoughts against ya. I'm sorry y're betrothed to this ... this bastar'.* A small turn of his head, and his mouth met hers. *The fook're you doing, Neesh? She doen't wanna kiss ya yet. She hardly knows ya. Merely bein' kind to ya's all. She*—

Moira wrapped an arm about his waist and stepped in closer, kissing him deeper. She ended with a gentle tug on his lower lip with her teeth. "Ye've surprised me, Naoise. Ye're nothing like yer warmongering king." Her gaze flitted from his eyes, to his lips, back to his eyes. "I hope to see ye again—before our wedding night, should it ever come."

JANNON STARED AT THE GRID ON THE STONE BOARD WITH A FURROWED brow and clenched jaw. His finger still pressed against the small black stone sandwiched between two white ones of similar sizes. Waning light glittered through the crystalline walls of the main hall, and the oil lamps flickered awake as the sky transitioned to black. Finally, the duke removed his finger from the stone. *Damn. I see three moves for her now.*

Dame Saoirse chewed on her bottom lip as she studied the board. Twirling a white pebble between her fingertips, she placed it diagonally from Jannon's black one.

"Ye're getting too good at this game," said Jannon, quickly placing a black piece to block one side of her white row of four. *Far better than you are at sparring, I see.* He studied her swollen and bruised nose with thinly veiled amusement.

The knight grinned, ignoring him as she placed a final pebble on the board. Five in a row—game over. "Don't be silly. Ye've merely been distracted, me laird. Between planning two weddings and hosting the Prasti duke, ye're stretched nearly as thin as Sir Cadman. He's far behind schedule on his treasury duties."

"Three weddings." Jannon cleared the board of stones and piled them together in front of him. "Kiera and I are to be wed before the solstice." He stared at Saoirse, waiting for her façade to slip. It didn't.

"Congratulations," she said. A warm smile spread wide across her face. Collecting her own pebbles, she stared curiously at the duke. "Another round?"

A true politician. Perhaps I should nominate ye as a senator. But who could possibly replace ye in the military? "Ye must care deeply for yer uncle to be so concerned with his duties."

"I'm more concerned with the safety of Laird Naoise. Since Cadman is so distracted with this treaty, the treasury, and assisting with the new recruits, I am afraid the Duke of Prastömin may be too low on his priorities."

Jannon silently placed a black pebble in the middle of the game board. "Are ye suggesting he be removed from this assignment?"

"Eil, I am. I believe Sir Heugan would be of better assistance. He's just returned from holiday." Saoirse made her move. "I'm sure ye're aware, me laird, this fragile peace hinges on the safety of Diarmuid's ambassador."

How kind of ye to consider the Prasti king's cunt of an ambassador. "When does Laird Naoise leave?"

"The morrow after next."

The duke of the tundra's eye twitched. Scratching his chin, he took a deep breath and placed another black pebble on the grid. "I will have yer answer on the matter before then. First, I must speak to yer superior." Saoirse merely nodded before making her next move. If she felt any frustration, fear, or victory, she certainly didn't show it. *Nearly as flat as her mother, Cara. She's learned this court well.*

Naoise entered a rundown alehouse with a deep scowl, wrapping his heavy cloak around himself with a shiver. His chapped skin was bright red, and he sniffed loudly as the rush of warm air thawed his face and sinuses, the burning tingle of returning sensation making his eyes water. *Damn this cold. I need to get home.* Once his vision cleared, he took in his surroundings. The place was crowded with merchants, farmers, herders—not the most ideal place for a laird, but better than being anywhere near that bastard Cadman. At least it was warm.

A throat cleared behind Naoise. "Ye've wandered into the wrong place, Prasti," said a cold, gravelly voice. "We don't take kindly to warmongers."

Dammit. Can't I just drink in peace? He turned to face the *diddy* behind him with a snarl.

But before he could speak, a familiar voice cut in: "Lucky fer him, he's not Prasti. Now get on, ye pox. Wouldn't want our laird to hear ye've been threatening the last of the Veers, would ye?"

A swirling current of emotions tore through Naoise's chest at the sound of his daughter's voice, pride included. The man slinked away without another word, but Naoise didn't turn around, the cracks of grief widening as the memory of their spar flashed behind his eyes. *"I see why Cadman lied to me all these years. To protect me ... from you."* Naoise swallowed back his tears before facing Saoirse. "I can handle arseholes like that. I doen't need y'r protection." He brushed past her and found an empty table in the far corner. Pinching the bridge of his nose, he finally released a sniffle.

He flinched at the thud of a full pint half-slammed in front of him. "Ye need a pint," said Saoirse. "At least, I hope ye do. 'Cause I need several."

Naoise rolled his eyes but grabbed the mug. "What're ya doin' here? I thought ya requested a new assignment." He guzzled half his ale in one swig and belched into his fist before continuing, "Come to insult me some more?"

Saoirse winced and gently rubbed the bridge of her nose before taking a long draught of her own drink. "I didn't get reassigned, as ye can see. And I came here to apologise fer the spar ... fer the axe. I don't know what came over me, but it wasn't becoming of a knight."

"Ya what, now? Y're the one with the broken nose, and y're apologisin' to me? Ha! What kind of—"

"Do ye accept it or not, me laird?"

Naoise clamped his mouth shut. "I accept it, though there's no reason f'r it." He finished his ale and set the empty mug at the table's edge, buying some much-needed time to gather his next words. "I'm sorry Cadman's torturing ya with refusing to reassign ya."

"No need. I didn't ask fer it, and Cadman's not here anymore to torture either of us while we talk. Laird Jannon made sure of that."

What! How the hell did that happen?

"And as for me"—Saoirse tossed a bundle of scorched parchments onto the table—"I found these in Cara's hearth. The wood must've been too damp fer the fire to blot the ink."

Naoise frowned, sliding the burned papers toward himself. Carefully, he opened one and read. "These were addressed to Giaven. And this one, to Alsantör. How did she wind up with them?" *Nai. This isn't possible.*

"She never sent them." Saoirse's teeth chattered, fresh tears streaming down her cheeks. "She was going to until she heard of Giaven's death. She told me that she'd written them nearly two hundred years ago—said, 'I won't be responsible fer the final eradication of Vaoirsen.' Wizards be good, why don't any Prasti like ye?"

"Apparently, I'm too much like my father," Naoise sighed. "You were right, by the way. I *did* have a choice. Y'r mother 'nd I coulda run away together with you, but I was a fool. I killed her anyway. Bloody hell, Saoirse, she was the queen's bloody *handmaiden*. Ah didn't think o'the consequences when I sired ya." The weight of his own words crushed him like an avalanche. His mouth twitched as another sob bubbled up his chest. "I deserve this, ya ken—losing you, losing y'r maela. You were right: Cadman was merely protectin' ya from me."

"Nai, I was wrong, alright? Wrong about Cadman, about ye, about me." Saoirse suddenly buried her face into her hands and sobbed, body shaking with heaves and muffled cries. "I'm sorry, daela. I'm so sorry."

Naoise sprang from his chair to kneel beside his daughter and embrace her. "Gnomes, what're ya sorry for?" he whispered. "Doen't cry, Saoirse. Please doen't cry. Y've done naught wrong, ya ken. Naught."

"It's my fault she's dead. My fault ye had to execute her like that."

Naoise stiffened, planting both hands around Saoire's cheeks and staring deeply into her eyes. "Stop it. Ya did naught wrong. Bein' born's no crime, regardless of the king's law. 'Nd if I ever hear anyone tell ya otherwise, their tongues'll be cut out and fed to their dogs, ya hear me? I loved y'r mother more than anything else in these gnomes-forsaken lands. And I will love *you* even more. Y're my child, Saoirse McNaoise. Wizards curse any man, elf, 'r otherwise who tries to take ya from me again."

The woman coughed, choking on another sob. "McNaoise," she whispered, falling into his arms and squeezing him tight. "Don't let me go, daela."

"Never again. I promise ya."

32

SONS OF WARMONGERS

*A*lsantör fidgeted atop his painted palfrey stallion. There, unarmed in the middle of Áfgal, he was vulnerable—or stupid. He wasn't sure. *Gnomes be merciful, I shoulda sent Naoise here instead of to Karthénos.* Though he'd made his intentions clear at the ominous steel gate, the prince still faced peril. His escort of half a dozen knights were blocked at the border of the central district, leaving him alone—and unprotected—in the heart of Áfgal.

Statues of winged beasts topped the expansive wall of King Arsiño's palace—thirteen of them, to be precise. Some bore wings of feathers while others had wings of skin, like a bat. Each statue represented one of the Áfgalese gods: a bull for Varín, a cat for Javiento, and a rabbit for Halaña. He didn't remember the rest. Alsantör sucked the back of his teeth as sudden memories of Sólan and his tattoo flashed before him. *To think, I actually miss you, friend.* He shook his head and cursed. *Please be alive, Sólan. Your life's the only way I get out of here with my head still attached.*

The gate's massive hinges creaked as one side opened just wide enough for a heavily decorated rider to trot through and meet him. "Alsantör, Prince of Prastömin, yes?" The man's tone stung, though his face showed naught.

"Eil. I come to meet with King Arsiño. My father sends a message of great—"

"The Riátha is not here. Perhaps a pigeon would have sufficed?"

Alsantör's pinkie flicked against his thumb. *Definitely should've sent Naoise.* "Is there, perhaps, an ambassador with whom I may speak? We've sent several pigeons with no reply."

The rider bared his teeth. "Perhaps His Majesty wishes not to align himself with the whims of Prastömin any longer."

I knew this gnomes-damned crusade would lead to a fucking war between us and these allies. Alsantör cleared his throat, opening his mouth to respond, but before he could—

"Yet, perhaps, Prince Irragrin may be willing to … accommodate such urgency?" A wicked grin stretched across the rider's face. He loosened his horseman's axe from its holster before releasing his grip again.

You need to leave, Tör. Get the hell out of here while you still have your head. "I'd like to meet with him," said the prince, even as he barely stifled a wince. *Idiot.*

To his relief, the rider sighed. "Follow me, sañero." He spun on his horse and shouted orders in his native tongue to several men atop the wall.

Alsantör flinched as the gates boomed shut behind him. A chill breeze kicked up tiny swirls of red dust from between the textured cobblestones. This was Ciudelago. The place that raised Sólan, betrayed Sólan, broke Sólan, and created "the Grim."

"You are to stay with me, sañero," the rider said, ripping the Prasti prince from his thoughts. "I am Cabillero Fernandez de Ciudelago, the baron of this district. I will show you to your accommodations, but first, you must meet with Prénsope Irragrin de Áfgal."

The Prasti held his breath in surprise. "Am I not to bathe first? Perhaps make myself more presentable to His Gr—"

"When was the last time you stepped foot inside our borders?" Fernandez's eye twitched as he glowered. "If you wish to speak with our prince as an equal, you shall present yourself as his equal."

His equal, or his prisoner? Alsantör shook his head again. "I see."

Fernandez led Alsantör through the labyrinthine palace. Its architecture was filled with elaborate carvings in stone and windows of stained crystal portraying scenes of the gods in their triumphs. He stopped and gaped at one large window at the end of a hall, flanked by statues of a winged cat and a horned crane.

But it wasn't the grandiosity of the statues that made Alsantör stop, but the man depicted in the glass. It was a man of fiery amber eyes and wavy brown hair. Green flames surrounded his head like a crown, and he crossed his arms while holding a scroll in one hand and a hatchet in the other. Bright white wings extended from his shoulders. Beneath the bust read the words "Injál de Áfgal."

Wizards be good, he's like a bloody god here. The elf shuddered as realisation overtook him. *I'm walking into a bloody trap.*

Fernandez cleared his throat. "I said, follow me."

Alsantör clenched his teeth in irritation. "Of course," he said and followed the rider down two more winding halls. They stopped at a heavily veiled doorway. The sound of rippling water reached the elf's ears, and he stiffened. *They're going to drown me. Káil, anything but drowning.*

The Áfgaliard nudged Alsantör with a grunt, then entered. The sweet scent of rose and lavender wafted through the air as a burst of steam hit the prince's face. He shook his head. *Calm down, Tör. It's just a bath.*

Hushed whisperings echoed from inside the room. After what sounded like a tense moment of wondering, panic, and frustration, an unfamiliar voice said, "Medría. Send him in, I suppose."

Alsantör gulped as Fernandez beckoned him forward. *Here we go.* He cleared his throat and said, "Your grace, Prince Irragrin." He silently cursed the tremor in his voice and the loud echo of his heavy boots. In the midst of the room's intricate tiles and stones, the floor gave way to a massive pool of milky water with floating flower petals and wisps of steam rolling their way up from its surface.

The muscular arms and shoulders of an olive-brown man with ashy blond hair were spread across the pool's edge. The Áfgalese prince was lounging with his back facing the elf, and he turned his head just enough to show that his attention was piqued.

"I pray I haven't caught you at a bad time," said Alsantör, grimacing.

A low growl rumbled from the man's head. "You have."

The Prasti glared at the doorway, but Fernandez had disappeared. *Shite. You conniving bastard.* "Apologies, your grace, but—"

"No need to be so fucking formal, sañero. As you can see, I am certainly not dressed for such niceties." Irragrin turned his torso to stare hazel daggers at his guest.

Alsantör sucked the back of his teeth again. *I knew I should've waited. What the hell were you thinking, Tör?*

A mischievous smirk flashed across the Áfgaliard's face as he chuckled. "Please, come join me. You look as though you have ridden through Enfríno itself." Before Alsantör could argue, he held up a hand. "This is a rare offer from me or any of this royal family. 'Twould be unwise to decline. Besides, Fernandez also tells me of your desire to bathe." A mischievous twinkle in his gaze caught the Prasti off guard. "Given the condition in which you present yourself to me, I understand why you wished to wait—despite your 'urgency'."

"If you wish to speak with our prince as an equal, you shall present yourself as his equal." Fernandez's words echoed behind the Prasti's ears, and he exhaled with a sigh. *Equals, indeed.* "Thank you, your grace. You are most generous."

Irragrin snorted. "Just get in. We have many things to discuss." He cocked his head and raised an eyebrow as Alsantör stripped at the edge of the pool. "I see the stories of the silver-bloods are true. I am impressed."

The elf cupped his manhood and bit his lip. *Fucking Áfgaliards. The lot of you.* He stepped into the hot water and sank to his waist, groaning as the heat began to thaw his tight muscles. "Káil," he whispered.

"The mineral waters of Ciudelago are a rare luxury for us as well. They are dependent entirely on our summer rains to the north." Irragrin dipped his head below the surface and emerged opposite from

Alsantör. Shaking the excess water from his amber curls, he rubbed his face and said, "What brings you here to Ciudelago? I see you come not in the golden armour of your hunters, but rather … in your silks?"

"Eil, your grace. I come for matters beyond a hunt, which is why I seek an audience with your father."

"My father is in Maseño, assisting Cabillero Julio on the growing revolt … and his grief."

Alsantör stiffened with a frown. "What happened in Maseño?"

"You are a very brave man, sañero—or, you are a fool," said Irragrin, suddenly hostile. "You come to the heart of Áfgal hardly announced and alone, after what you have done?"

The elf's heart lurched as panic bubbled in his chest at the possibility of being drowned. His voice trembled as he said, "I don't follow."

"Sólan the Grim was a man of Áfgal. A man of *Ciudelago*, no less." The Áfgalese prince bared his teeth and clenched his fists. "No doubt you saw his portrait above the statues of Javiento, God of Death, and Martím, God of Justice. Was he not the most valiant of their servants?"

"He was a criminal outside of these lands, Irragrin." The elf held his breath as though 'twould stop his racing heart. It didn't. "Responsible for the deaths of hundreds of noblemen and women of Taelonael."

"Noble? Ha! Men and women of Taelonael who abducted, sold, and mutilated Áfgalese women and children for the sake of gold. Tell me, dear prénsope de Prastömin, does nobility preclude you from the laws of your gods?" Despite the steam rising between them, the malice that slithered from Irragrin's voice was chilling. "Sólan was under the protection of my father's crown, and his father's before him, and so on. Yet, you have brought your father's kingdom to the brink of war with the last of your mortal allies with a single strike of your sword."

"He failed to swear the Oath of Light," Alsantör whispered.

Irragrin's glare deepened. "Oath or no oath, Alsantör, Sólan de

Ciudelago was a fucking hero. A legend. The man eternally blessed by Javiento to never leave this life until the whole of the world—"

"Are you going to kill me as payment, *your grace*?" The room felt suddenly cold and dark, as though a winter storm had swept into the bath house and was threatening to freeze the naked men. "You seem quite pleased with the idea of going to war with my father's people."

The Áfgalese prince blinked, lifting an eyebrow. "And you do not." His expression softened to a mischievous smirk, and he leaned himself back against the bath's ledge. "What business do you have with my father?"

He knows something. "I come to prevent this war of which you seem too fond."

"Truly? What of the rumours I hear coming from the tundra … ?"

"Have you not read any of the notes we've sent to you?" Alsantör didn't try to hide his irritation.

"I thought you desired an audience with my father, dear prince." Irragrin's nose twitched, as though stifling a snarl.

The icy grip of panic let go of Alsantör's throat only to stab into his chest with vengeance. "You're being impossible," he muttered, then squeezed his eyes shut at the words he meant to be thought, not spoken.

Irragrin snorted. "You come to me as I am *bathing*, wishing to speak on the business of war and politics."

That's on Fernandez, not me, arsehole. "Had I known what you were doing—"

"Please, spare me your niceties," said Irragrin, rolling his eyes. He leaned forward and studied his guest with an intensity that made Alsantör squirm. "We are alike, you and I." He chuckled at Alsantör's look of confusion. Closing his eyes, he ran his fingers through the surface of the milky water. "Tíal, very alike. The sons of warmongering kings and the leaders of their armies. Consider yourself fortunate, sañero, that you met with *me*, rather than my father. He has been begging for your head for nearly two seasons."

Alsantör sighed. "I don't blame him." The hint of a smile threatened to curl his mouth. "But being the *sons* of warmongers doesn't make us like them. Neither do all rumours hold truth."

"¿Mondé?" Irragrin straightened as he frowned. "I follow not."

Gnomes be merciful, don't let these words leave this room. "Sólan the Grim is alive, Irragrin. I made sure of that before I left Nethuania's port of Bansungei."

Irragrin's chest deflated as the Prasti's words appeared to hit his chest. A warm smile stretched across his face, and he laughed; not the kind of laugh that made Alsantör fear for his life. Nay, 'twas the laugh of an ally. A friend. *Thank the Wizards, he believes me.*

"Does your father know? More importantly, does his father know?"

"Do you think I'd still have my head if either of them did?"

Irragrin chuckled again. "A fair point." He leaned his head against the pool's ledge and sighed. "I may be of assistance in your pursuit of peace. But we Áfgalese have terms that must be met."

33

AMBASSADOR OF PRASTÖMIN

Faerin meandered through the hedge labyrinth in half a daze. He didn't know why he wanted to be out here, only that he did. The chill autumn air tousled his feathery hair and sent a shiver through his shoulders. *Why first knight? Why me?* He'd asked the same question daily since his promotion—a promotion he was convinced was unearned. *Shite, I'm younger than most Áfgalese infantry, and the son of a dotaire.* He shook his head in attempt to focus. *How'd I get into this mess?*

Hushed voices in the labyrinth's midst snapped his attention southward. Two intruders? No, three! Two men and a woman spoke in hushed tones, plotting an insurrection, no doubt. Faerin grimaced, cursing himself for leaving his weapons behind in his new quarters. *I'll hafta make do. Treason doesn't sleep, and neither should justice.* Perhaps the element of surprise would keep him alive. Perhaps he should get more knights. He could go back and wake up the royal family ... A dry leaf crunched beneath Faerin's foot. The whispers stopped.

"Who's that?" a smooth, baritone voice barked. The woman gasped.

Faerin gritted his teeth and stooped to pick up a jagged piece of rock before—

"Ya sneaky bastar.'" A rough hand grasped his shirt and pulled him to his feet. The crescent moon's silver light gleamed off Naoise's warm smile. "Almost got y'rself killed, lad. Come on, have a drink with us."

A drink? Not conniving, not planning anything. Just ... drinking? Faerin tentatively followed the duke into the clearing, where the two others sat comfortably next to each other on a stone bench—too comfortably. He stiffened as he recognised them: Prince Alsantör and Handmaiden Rhona. *Shite. I need to arrest her. Fookin' hell, this job gets worse every day.* "So, ehm ... what's all this, now?" said Faerin, fidgeting. "I don't wanna ... if-if-if her grace finds out about Rhona—"

"She won't." Alsantör shot a glare of warning over his shoulder.

Naoise rolled his eyes and groaned. "I told ya you'd get caught, Tör. Now, gimme that gnomes-damned bottle." The prince obliged, and the duke took a deep swig before passing it over to the young knight. "Relax, Faerin. We're not doin' anything connivin'. Just a few friends livin' freely, f'r once. Y're welcome to join our sad adventure."

"B-but"— Faerin chewed on his tongue and tapped his toes on the grass—"the handmaiden." His eyes darted from Naoise to Alsantör, then to Rhona, Naoise, and back to Alsantör. "If-if Her Grace finds out, my hands're tied."

"Oh, fer fuck's sake, Faerin!" Rhona jumped to her feet and snatched the bottle from his hand. "If ye're not gonna drink that brandy, give it to us who will." She took a swig and handed it back to Alsantör. "Now then, are ye one of us, or not?"

What the hell's that supposed to mean?

"Wizards be good," said Alsantör. "Faerin, take a seat and try to enjoy the night. I know your promotion's getting to you, so please let yourself relax. It's not treason to take a fucking break."

"Y'r grace." Faerin sat on the bench across from them, stiff as a Taela shield. "I don't think I should be here."

"Ha! I should be with the queen, keeping her bed warm and cunt wet, but here we are."

"Here we are, indeed," said Naoise and Alsantör in unison.

"I think he needs a good fookin' down at The Wand. What do *you* think, Tör?"

A mischievous grin stretched across the prince's face. "I'm sure Ellie's free tonight, considering …" He wrapped an arm about Rhona's waist and pulled her close, nuzzling the back of her ear.

Faerin scrunched his nose. "No, thanks. I'd rather not fook anyone tonight—or, ever."

Naoise and Alsantör stared at Faerin with gaping mouths, bewilderment, confusion, and perhaps a flicker of disgust passing over their faces. Rhona, however, kicked the duke's shin and elbowed the prince. "Stop it, both of ye." She smiled warmly at the knight. "So, what brings ye to our break in duties?"

Faerin watched as Alsantör raised the brandy to his lips, and swifter than Naoise's deadly arrows, he snatched the bottle from the prince, mid-swig. Three gulps later, the fruity spirit was gone. *Hmm, black and blueberries. A Karthi staple.* "Can't sleep." It took little time for the drink to cloud his head. He hiccoughed and handed the empty bottle to Naoise. "Sorry m'laird. Didn't mean to finish it."

Naoise snorted. "Ya needed it."

"Where'd ya get it, anyhow?" The knight winced at the slur in his words, though his stutter seemed to disappear. "I don't remember you havin' it on ya when we picked you up in Baforeis."

"That's 'cause I hid it in ma saddlebags. Didn't want Sir Cadman to see it was missing."

"Ha! You stole from that bastard? How the hell is he? Haven't seen him since … well … since." Alsantör clacked his mouth shut and sucked his teeth. "Shite. Never mind."

"It's the only thing I could do short of killin' 'im, Tör. He stole from me, so I stole from him." Naoise plopped himself on the ground and sat cross-legged, chewing on his bottom lip.

Faerin shivered. *What in Sprite's Hell did he steal from you to get such rage?* He opened his mouth to ask, but Rhona was first.

"What's he stealing, Neesh?"

Naoise's lip trembled, but he shook his head. "Never mind," he whispered. "He's just a pretentious bastar', is all."

The prince merely snorted. "Tell me something new. Like, his niece is really another bastard of Jannon, or something outlandish like that."

Naoise bit his lip and grimaced, looking away as both Alsantör and Rhona snickered in oblivious amusement.

Faerin, however, took notice. Before he could speak, however, Rhona was moving on.

"So, which one o'ye is going to the Oasis City fer the final negotiations?"

Alsantör sighed. "Káil. I was hoping to avoid this gnomes-damned conversation."

"There are many conversations ye try to avoid, Tör. This shouldn't be one of them. One of ye leaves in half a fortnight."

Faerin frowned. "You've been to Taelonael before, y'r grace. Why can't ya go again?"

Naoise grumbled. "'Cause I'm the bloody ambassador now. Tör needs ta stay here an' keep his father in line. Besides." He looked over at the prince, who merely rubbed his toe in the grass. "He just got home from Áfgal."

"What's wrong, Tör?" asked Rhona, rubbing the prince's shoulder.

Alsantör looked up to her curious gaze. "Oh, nothing. I just miss who my father used to be, that's all. When he actually wanted to be 'Daela,' you know?"

"Y're not guiltin' me into stayin' here, Tör," said Naoise, arms crossed. "Despite the Taelas' hatred of Vaoirsen, I'm a lower risk. The Prince o' Prastömin would bring too much temptation f'r a ransom."

"The Taelas wouldn't dare ransom the man who executed their most hated enemy," argued the prince.

Faerin gritted his teeth and interrupted with a grunt. "I'll go." Six eyes stared at the young knight, their weight crushing him to the size of an oddling child. "They don't know me. M-ma father's a dotaire—not many beings in these lands hate a healer—and I have no secrets to-to hide." *Shut up, Faerin.* "Besides, it's not like there aren't any b-better qualified knights here to replace me, should something happen." *Damned stutter.*

Rhona grimaced. "Oh, Faerin. Ye're not expendable."

"He's right, though," said Naoise. The duke rose to his feet and clapped a hand on the knight's shoulder. "Y're the best chance we have at keepin' the peace."

What the hell am I doing? "I-I don't, ehm, don't, ehm, know the, eh, first thing ab-about politics."

Naoise grinned, a mischievous glint sparkling in his eyes as he said, "Neither do I."

34

MIDNIGHT

*R*hona closed the queen's door behind her and held her breath. Her ears twitched as she searched for signs of spies, watchers, or whomever else might report her whereabouts to her mistress. But there was nothing, save for the snores echoing from Alsantör's room. *Thank the Wizards.* She clutched her cloak, along with a satchel, close to her chest, tiptoeing down the dark, stone corridor with naught but the filtered moonlight to guide her. Her bare feet made no sound as she sneaked down the winding servants' stairs and stole her way into the kitchen. The handmaiden flitted her gaze through the room.

Still nothing.

She poked through the pantry, finding leftover uncooked carrots, day-old oat honeyed bread, and apples. She filled her satchel to the brim and crossed to the cooking corner. Embers long extinguished sat in the brick oven, though the bricks themselves were still warm to the touch. Rhona felt her way around the back corner, searching. At last, a loose stone gave way, and she pulled a hidden lever. A slab of granite slid down, revealing a gaping doorway—her secret.

Though it was not much of a secret, for 'twas a hidden passage built to lead any members of royalty or nobility to the outside should enemies siege. Rhona rolled her eyes at the thought. *How could anyone siege this place and expect to win?*

She passed through and rounded a sharp corner. Within the trunk of a fallen cedar tree lay two bundles. One held her Garmathian dagger and matching long sword, gifted to her by her father before they'd parted. The other contained a pale blue cloak, breeches, and thigh-high leather boots for riding. The last remnants of her past life.

Changing into her old garb, Rhona darted across the courtyard toward the royal stables, leaving her weapons behind. She grimaced at the quiet creak of the barn door's rusted hinges. *Oil. These things need oil!*

She slid through the stables, stopping before the queen's blue roan mare, Misty. "Are ye ready for a night ride, girl? I brought ye some apples this time."

Misty perched her ears forward and chewed an invisible bite, sighing.

"Hush, Misty," said Rhona. "Ye don't want us to get caught, do ye? Here." She reached into her satchel and removed an apple. Taking a large bite, she handed the remainder to the mare, munching. "Happy now?"

Misty merely snorted and rested her head on the handmaiden's shoulder.

"Good."

Rhona went to work grooming, humming, and giving treats and kisses as she brushed through Misty's tangles and dirt. She placed a quilted saddle pad on the mare's bare back.

"Where are we going?"

Rhona froze. *Shit! Who saw me?* She pressed her lips together to keep her teeth from chattering. "I just came to be sure the queen's mare is ready for her ride on the morrow."

The familiar smooth, baritone voice chuckled. "You really don't have to lie to me, Handmaiden."

A smile danced across the handmaiden's face as she spun to face her accuser, and she failed to stifle her giggles. "Me?" Lie to the prince of Prastömin? However shall I defend meself for such a crime?"

Alsantör stepped into her view and snickered. "How'd you know it was me and not some other knight?"

"I know yer voice too well." She leapt into the prince's arms and pressed her face into his neck. "What are ye doing here? I never see ye this time of night."

Alsantör's arms tightened around her. "Couldn't sleep."

"Ye were asleep when I left yer mother alone." Rhona inhaled with a snore and giggled. "*Deep* asleep."

Misty snorted and pawed the ground, nudging her dark nose against Rhona's shoulder. Alsantör chuckled, motioning to the satchel. "So that's why she's getting fat." He snatched a carrot from beneath the leather flap and bit off its end.

Rhona rolled her eyes. "Perhaps she's just getting into season."

"It's almost winter, and she didn't season last moon." The prince crossed his arms with a frown. "Slow down on the apples, will you? Her line's more sensitive to colic than the others." He reached around the handmaiden's shoulder and tousled Misty's mane between her ears. "You're a good girl, Misty. Don't let that Rhona tell you otherwise."

He coughed as a sharp elbow jabbed him in the ribs. "Fuck you, Tör," said Rhona.

Misty nodded her head and pawed the ground again. *I know, Misty. Just hold on.* "Are ye gonna stop me, or—"

"Of course not. I'm riding with you tonight." Alsantör wrapped his arm around Rhona's waist and nuzzled the nape of her neck. "Where are we going?"

Rhona trembled at the warmth of his breath in her ear. "The falls," she whispered. Running her fingers through his mahogany hair, Naoise's words came crashing down on her like a thunderclap. *"So ya didn't hear? About Tör's betrothal?"* She stiffened.

"What's wrong?"

Everything. Our lives, yer father's laws, this fucking crusade and the even larger war that's brewing from it … Rhona smiled. "Nothing. Let's go."

THE HALF-MOON ILLUMINATED THE FOREST, ACCENTING THE SHADOW OF every tree and rock. Fireflies—the last of the season—danced around Rhona's and Alsantör's heads as they walked their steeds alongside the bubbling midnight brook. A distant rumble of water falling on granite echoed through the narrowing ravine. The trail then opened to a bright pool surrounded by a myriad of glowing plants: bright green mushrooms, orange and yellow fire primroses, and pink flowers that were otherwise pale when the sun was out.

Alsantör took a sharp breath as they entered the clearing. The falls' water shimmered in the moonlight and glowed in an unnatural blue wherever it landed on the rocks and pools below. "*Gnomes*, I forget the beauty of this place after sundown."

A sour taste entered Rhona's mouth, but she smiled. *There's naught ye can do, Rhona. Stop it. Ye're breaking yer own heart by continuing this.* "I do too." She quickly dismounted and tied Misty to a low-hanging branch to let her graze.

The prince quickly followed suit, loosening his stallion's saddle. "There you go, Murtaugh." He scratched Murtaugh's splotchy black ear before turning to Rhona with crossed arms. "You're upset. Talk to me."

"I don't know what ye mean." Rhona raised an eyebrow and pressed her lips together, forming a fine line across her mouth. *Damn ye, Tör. Ye know me too well.* "I am perfectly content with—"

"Bullshite, Rhona. You've hardly said a word since we left the stables, you refuse to look at me, and you're doing that *thing* with your mouth again."

Rhona hadn't noticed the chirping crickets until they stopped their song. She gulped, failing to rid her throat of the growing lump. "Who is she? The woman ye're promised to?"

Alsantör closed his eyes and slumped his shoulders, grimacing. "Fuck," he whispered, nigh too quiet for Rhona to hear. "Where'd you hear?"

Who do ye think? The last honest man in this gnomes-damned forest. I can't believe I fell for this. "Naoise told me." A tear trickled down her cheek, and she nigh drowned in her watery sinuses. "Rather, he told yer mother. I just ... I just happened to hear."

"That blubbering ..." Alsantör's flicked his pinkie against his thumb. "I'm trying to break it. That treaty Naoise's negotiating in Karthénos removes my betrothal to Siobh—" He clamped his mouth shut and winced.

"Siobhan? Siobhan O'Jannon?" Suddenly, Rhona burst into a laughter that forced her to her knees. "Oh Gnomes be merciful, ye poor fool! This kingdom's all but *ruined* with that conniving wench."

Alsantör stiffened. "Conniving?"

Rhona wiped the smile from her face and frowned. "Eil, conniving. She's become quite the favourite of Jannon's daughters, and she's far from the giggling dunce she portrays. Ye'd best hope that treaty gets signed, Tör. That yer betrothal be nullified before she's had a chance to sink her claws into yer father's mind." Her eyes narrowed at the sight of the prince's sceptic face. "Ye think it's jealousy, don't ye?"

"Well ..." Alsantör sucked his teeth. "Not really, I suppose. You've never ... eh."

"I'm not a jealous lover, Tör. I share ye with Ellie, remember?" *I need to see her. I hope she's got a new batch of that—* "If I were to carry yer child, ye'd have the same grief as Naoise."

The prince sighed. "You're ruining the mood, Rhona." He wrapped an arm around her waist and pulled her close to him. "You're not sharing me with anyone tonight. Not Ellie, not Siobhan, not anyone. I'll be the unwed prince forever—unless I can have you."

"But, ye're betrothed—"

"Against my will." Alsantör brushed a strand of hair from Rhona's face. "I made no promises, and I don't intend to keep the ones my father made for me." Leaning in, he kissed her cheek before resting his forehead on hers.

Rhona's sad smile trembled. "And if Jannon refuses to sign?"

"He won't. He loves his people too much." The prince brushed his lips against hers. "We're not in the keep. We're not surrounded by any spies. Please, Rhona, let us have this moment together, without politics and fear mongering. Without—"

She interrupted him with a kiss, a simple one which quickly

turned into passionate hands and the stripping of clothing. There, amongst the glowing flora, they made love. They writhed in unison, savouring every touch, sight, and smell of each other as though 'twas their last time. Perhaps it was. It didn't matter anymore. For that moment, under the waning moon, Rhona was free.

The front tavern of the Wizard's Wand was, per the norm, full. Lustful beings and half-naked workers bustled around each other, the sale of food, ale, and escorts dominating the atmosphere. The back, however, offered a sharp contrast. There, the workers' common area and private apartments extended from the southern walls of the building. It took at least two to afford such luxury, as opposed to a mere room—except one. Queen Ethna's handmaiden sought out its tenant.

Rhona entered the Wand through this back entrance. She wore her plainest evergreen cloak, its deep hood covering most of her face. Still, the wool was of higher quality than anything these workers could afford, and her hopes for anonymity were quickly dashed as she approached.

"A royal! How delightful!" a deep voice shrieked.

Rhona gasped, locking her panicked gaze with a broad-shouldered woman who was drinking what smelled like berry wine from a glass bottle. "Nobody knows I'm here, Laurie," Rhona whispered sharply. The sound of coins clinked through the air as she pulled a small leather pouch from inside her cloak. "And ye didn't see me."

Laurie giggled. "Save the coin f'r someone else. Her Grace don't fuck elves like me."

"Her Grace won't fuck *anyone* right now, as she's on this year's flow. Take it. The herbalist behind Craigen's forge just got a shipment of sinsaflower root from the dwarfs. It's the biggest one in ten years."

"Oh, thank the Wizards for ya! I've been without f'r nigh a moon, 'nd my beard's been comin' back far too thick!"

"Gnomes be merciful, Laurie. Whispers." Rhona gritted her teeth at the woman's squeals. "I'm not here, remember?"

"Right, right. Apologies ... eh ... m'lady. In ya go." Laurie stooped to snatch the purse at her feet. "Who you looking for, then?"

A dull tingle threatened to stab through Rhona's chest and down her arm. "No one in particular," she said through clenched teeth. *Just someone I can trust to get me some of that damned piarab—*

"Ah, I see." Laurie rubbed at her scruff. "I think Ellie's workin' the ale."

Thank the Wizards. She's precisely the woman I seek.

"She's havin' a slow night. Most of her usual clients aren't around. I can have Frieda fetch her."

"Ye're too kind." *But not kind enough to trust with me life, should it come to that.*

Laurie escorted her into the workers' common room and slid out a rickety chair. "Not sure if you've eaten yet, but there's some roast boar 'nd sour bread if ya haven't."

"Thank ye." Rhona clasped her hands together to keep them from shaking. She couldn't understand why. Ellie was always willing to sell her some piaraberry tea for the queen. Every autumn, Ethna would be bedridden from the mere pain of her flow. The tea was all that could relieve it well enough for her to sit upright without vomiting. Rhona grimaced at the thought. She was a mere season away from her own, if she was careful. Gnomes knew she hadn't been, of late.

A familiar coin purse thumped onto the table beside her. Rhona flinched at the sudden noise, her heart lurching into her throat. A mousy giggle filled her ears, and she found herself glaring at the petite woman standing in the doorway. Her wavy hair was pulled up into a messy knot with curly wisps and baby hairs perfectly framing her heart-shaped face. Ellie. The prince's favourite whore.

"Ya don't hafta bribe anyone to come see meh through the back," she said. She spoke just as high-pitched and nasally as she laughed.

Gnomes, I should've waited until I'd rested. I can't handle her squeaks right now.

Ellie sat at the table next to Rhona and tore a piece of bread from the still-steaming loaf. "Thanks, by the way. I hate workin' the damned ale." Her pitch lost some of its sharpness as she spoke through full bites of bread. Reaching over, she flicked Rhona's hood off her head. "You're quiet tonight—'nd broody. Her Grace turn ya down f'r a good fucking?"

"She's on her flow."

"Oof. That's never fun. I just got a fresh batch of her tea two nights ago, if y're lookin' for some."

Rhona couldn't stifle the relieved smile that twitched across her lips. "Ye should know that be the reason I come. The equinox was a mere moon ago, was it not?"

"Eil, it was. Alright, then." Ellie stuffed the last chunk of bread into her mouth and swallowed, hard. She stood and stretched, breasts slipping out of her neckline as though she was seducing a client. "Ya look like you could use a good fucking too, eh? I know I could, 'nd I'm not much in the mood f'r cock."

"I don't have enough gold for that, Ellie. Just for the tea—and double the dose this time."

"Oh?" Ellie's doe-like eyes sparkled with mischief. "I was wrong. You've already *had* a good fucking. Now we really need to talk, Maid Rhona. 'Nd my apartment's just out back, detached from the rest of this place."

"I don't fuck 'nd flab. I'm not telling ye. I don't want to hate ye if her grace finds out."

"Fine then, keep meh bored. Likely better for y'r health, anyways." Ellie motioned to a narrow corridor with her eyes. Silently, she mouthed, "Before anyone comes by."

Nodding, Rhona covered her face once again, finding herself pulled rather than led to the far back. They glided across a thin walkway before reaching the raised porch of a wood and stone home. Ellie removed a flap of floorboard, reaching inside up to her wrist. A series of hidden latches clicked and whirred, and the front door suddenly popped ajar.

"What kind of door—"

"*Shh!* Get inside."

Rhona silently obliged, waiting to speak again until Ellie had followed her and slid the advanced latch back into place. "Garmathian?"

Ellie smirked. "Eil. Garmathian. If not f'r the king's ridiculous hatred toward the orcs, we'd be far advanced from that fallen empire. But here we are."

"Here we are, indeed." Rhona took in her surroundings with a sigh. Ellie's quarters were quite large. Nearly as large, in fact, as the queen's own chambers, yet much simpler. A long cedar table with two chairs sat opposite the bed, with a wardrobe and full bookshelf flanking the ends. A vanity and an expensive Orovite looking glass were wedged in the corner between the doorframe and closest wall, while the back one was naught but a massive hearth. While the apartment was a far cry from the keep, 'twas luxurious for a commoner.

"So." Ellie plopped herself onto her bed and winked at Rhona. "How long've you been secretly fucking the prince?"

What! Rhona's heart thumped and her hands trembled with a sudden sense of dread. "I don't follow," she whispered.

Ellie sprang to her feet with a giggle. "Ya reek of 'im. Of all the women in the damned forest, ya think you'd be able to hide y'r affair with him from meh? Don't worry, I won't tell Her Grace. Gnomes know I wasn't the one who told 'er about Ina, either." She crossed to her wardrobe to rummage through its drawers. Tossing a leather pouch onto the table, she followed with a half-empty bottle of vibrantly purple liquor.

"Is that Ethna's tea?" said Rhona, motioning to the pouch.

"Eil." The smell of berries filled the room as Ellie removed the stopper from her bottle. "Brandy? It's Maseño berry from Áfgal."

"Dammit, Ellie. Now I'm gonna go back to the queen reeking of her son *and* brandy!" Rhona sniffed. "How large are yer glasses?"

"Ha!" Ellie filled two wooden goblets and handed one to Rhona with a wink. "Finish this off and y'll only reek of the liquor." The women knocked their drinks together, and each took a long draught. "I knew he's been pining away after some garl, just didn't realise it was you. How long's it been, really?"

Rhona shrugged. "We've only ... eh ... ye know ... twice? Once when I healed him from that arrow wound—though I hardly count that. The other was just last night, at the falls."

"*Oh!* The falls! I miss those damned things! Does the water still glow at their base?"

Rhona nodded with excitement.

"We must toast, Maid Rhona. Now that we share a lover, we must be closer than sisters, ya hear? Ya need an ally in the forest, especially now. On the brink of war with yer mother's kingdom and now a forbidden affair with yer employer's own son? This kingdom won't last long should Her Grace—"

"I know, Ellie. I know." Rhona swirled the bottom half of her goblet and gulped some more brandy. "I have Tör. And Naoise. But yes—I need ye too. Thank ye."

"To the Royal Cock!" said Ellie, lifting her empty goblet to the sky.

The brandy burned Rhona's sinuses on its way out of her nose. Tears filling her eyes, she coughed and sniffed through the pain. *To the Royal Cock, indeed!*

35

THE COUNCIL OF NATIONS

Faerin gulped at the size of the Taela's massive wall. Behind it was the Oasis City, capital of the desert kingdom. His golden armour flashed bright in the merciless sun, and the heavy green cloak pinned about his shoulders did naught but make him sweat. The hard brick wall extended at least a hundred metres high, if not higher. Even Faerin's keen eyes saw nothing but black specks representing the men guarding the parapets. The wall's intricate stone gates were closed flush with the fortification. *How the hell do they even open this thing?* He fidgeted atop his steed, ignoring the approaching Áfgalese escort—at least, he tried to, until their emissary spoke.

"I expected your prince to be here. Or, perhaps, your Veerish duke. Who are you, sañero?"

Faerin bit the tip of his tongue to stay his racing heart. "Sir Faerin, First Knight of Prastömin." He met the man's hazel eyes with a stiff smile. "And you are?"

"Irragrin de Ciudelago, Crowned Prince of Áfgal." The Áfgaliard raised an eyebrow and cocked his head. "You look like you could use a good fucking. Men or women?"

"N-neither." *Why does everyone think I need to fuck to relax? What I need is a bloody drink.*

"I see." Irragrin flashed a mischievous smile and winked. "Not yet."

The knight rolled his eyes. A second set of escorts arrived, this time hailing from Karthénos. *Thank the Wizards, a true ally.* Before Faerin could say a word, a sharp, wailing horn sounded before a clap of thunder shook the ground.

The heavy gates popped and grated against each other as they opened just wide enough to allow a single rider to emerge from within. The being wore an iron helmet and veil of chain. The only part of his face that was visible were his eyes—heavily lined with black makeup hardly darker than his natural skin and creased in the corners as though he were smiling.

"His Sovereign Excellency, M'flū Jabali Nir, welcomes the foreign ambassadors of Áfgal, Prastömin, and Karthénos with an open heart," the rider said. "Please accept these gifts of gratitude for your travels and the promise of peace they bring."

Faerin trembled as three Áfgalese boys and three Nethuanian girls approached. Iron collars were wrapped about their necks, and heavy chains extended to their pelvis—branching off to shackles around their wrists and ankles. Each pair carried a heavy golden chest, which they placed on the ground in front of each ambassador. The boys then opened the chests, revealing them to be filled to the brim with gold coins and precious gems. Faerin's tongue bled as he bit it to keep his thoughts silent. *They're children. Why the hell are they slaves as children?* Though he'd heard the thousands of rumours floating from the southern desert, he never believed them, until now.

Irragrin flashed a stiff smile, his posture tense and erect in his saddle. "I thank you, sañero, for your impeccable generosity. Do send our regards to His Excellency, King Jabali. However, I cannot help but ask—how did such *strapping* young boys of Áfgalese descent toe into your market? I recall not such transactions out of our prisons. Have the orphanages been added to your ... selections?"

The rider glared. "Perhaps it is a question for the slave masters here, as I am but a humble servant of the M'flū himself."

"Ah, yes," said Irragrin. "Apologies. We have all travelled very far to meet as a council for this unprecedented time."

Somethin' tells me you're not sorry in the slightest.

A sharp whistle made Faerin flinch. The children snapped the chests closed and carried them back into the city.

"I pray you find our city to your liking, ambassadors of the North. We have prepared accommodations of the highest quality set aside for the bringers of peace."

Faerin merely smiled with a nod. *What the hell am I doing here?* He nudged his horse forward as the others around him followed their guide. *Gnomes be merciful. I'm just a knight.*

Faerin sat at the window of his guest chambers, taking in the sights of the sprawling city. Below him, spiraling towers of carved stone flanked the tiered brick structure of the main palace. To the south, he watched the Umfila River meander its way to the Dragon Sea. Along its bank stood hundreds of date palms, followed by thousands of apyin bud plants, their skunk-like smell wafting upstream and into the back of the knight's nostrils. He scrunched his nose at the pungent scent.

A soft knock on the chamber door stole his attention from the mesmerising view. "Who is it?" he asked.

"Irragrin."

Káil. Fuckin' red-blood. He shook his head at the intrusive thought. Of all the mortals he'd encountered these last moons, the Áfgalese prince was the least intolerable. He crossed to the entryway and unlatched the door.

Irragrin slipped in and replaced the lock. "Thank the gods you are still awake."

"*Still* awake?" Faerin squinted. "It's hardly after midday."

Irragrin seemed to take no notice. "I am unsure if I can handle another moment with these desert putathótas." He plopped himself on the knight's feather bed and sighed. "Áfgalese children. Can you believe the gods-damned gall to use child slaves from *Áfgal* to welcome us? Medría, they are conniving—"

"Are y-you really here to-to just blather shite on the T-t-taelas *in* Taelonael?"

"And if I am?" The Áfgaliard sat up with a glare. "You must be much younger than your peers, sañero. Or, perhaps, just dense. Which is it?"

"I b-beg your pardon?"

"Where is your wine?"

Faerin blinked. *My wine? What the hell?* He watched the prince closely as he crossed the chamber and snatched the corked bottle. "Y're confusing me, y'r grace. Why—"

"Shh!" Irragrin held up his hand and stilled his breath, tilting an ear to the outside.

Faerin's heart screamed, *Danger!* His pulse pounded in his head, but he stifled his questions. Uncertainty lingered in the air, thickening the already humid atmosphere to near suffocation. He whispered, "What are you listening for?"

Irragrin shushed him again. Finally, after a moment that felt like moons, the Áfgalese prince whispered, "Tell me you have drunk none of this."

"W-what did they put in-in it? Did any o' your men drink it?" Faerin winced at the squeak to his voice.

"Have you had any of this wine?"

"Nai, I haven't. Have you? What did they t-t-taint it with?"

"Oh, thank the gods." Irragrin dropped the bottle out the window. A faint crash soon echoed from the ground far below. "They speak words of honey and yet try to poison us. The conniving *pundijos* think they can outsmart us, aeh? This was an act of war, Sir Faerin de Prastömin. You should be thanking your gods that Alsantör is absent in this—"

"Irragrin! I'm n-not gonna ask again! What were you lis-listening for, and what the *fuck* did they put in-in that wine?"

"It matters not, sañero. They tried to fucking poison us. Two of my men are waiting—"

"It *does* m-m-m-matter, 'cause I know the antidote to-to-to some of the most ancient Taela poisons." Faerin grasped the prince's tunic with a tight fist. "What's going on? What did they use?"

The prince opened and closed his mouth as though he gasped for air. "Any moment, I expect an ambush on us. After all, they did poison the wine, no? The Karthi girl called it 'Dragon's Blood.'"

Káil. That one's the worst. Chewing on his tongue, Faerin frowned. "Did any of y'r men drink it? Any of the Karthi? How did she find out?"

Irragrin shook his head. "We drank it not, but one of my men spilled while pouring his first glass. It completely ate through the stone table and nearly through the floor."

Faerin cursed. "We'll hafta mention it at-at-at tomorrow's gathering. We c-can't let him get away with this."

"You wish for war?" The prince smirked. "Accusing a king of attempted murder in his own home is one of the quickest ways to start one."

The Prasti hung his head with a groan. "I swear, I shouldnnn't've come here. I'm a knight, not an ambassador."

Irragrin clapped Faerin on the shoulder. "Just follow my lead, sañero. Our kingdoms are still allies, remember."

FAERIN FIDGETED WITH THE VELLUM SCROLL'S TWINE. IN HIS HANDS WAS the solidifier of peace: the Treaty of Taelonael, as it would soon be called. He shifted his gaze around the room, taking in the luxurious setting. Dozens of sharp arches transformed the circular shape into that of a star. High above, the ceiling was domed with a perfect symmetry of bright tiles swirling into vibrant blue and green mosaics. Not once did he find a missing piece in the design—the builders were as meticulous as they were creative.

The rounded table and intricate chairs of acacia wood and tiles matched in both quality and design, yet the gold, brown, and black contrasted enough with the surrounding decor that their importance was doubly highlighted.

A graceful being approached through the western entrance,

tearing Faerin's attention away from the fascinating architecture. He glanced over his shoulder to see an elf woman of confident stature. The top half of her loose curls was pulled back into a braid interwoven with silver threads, extending across her hairline. A teardrop sapphire dangled in the centre of her porcelain forehead, matching perfectly with her deep blue dress and silk gloves. Clenching her jaw, she inched herself to a stiff seat on Faerin's right and eyed him curiously. Per the ledger of ambassadors' names, this was Jannon's eldest daughter, and senator to the western corner.

"Has yer king already grown tired of his new duke?" asked Moira.

The knight cocked his head and frowned. "No. He—ehm—L-laird Naoise needed t-to-t-to stay behind." Smiling stiffly, he asked, "Why d-didn't Jannon come down? Couldn't-ehm-trouble himself with suing fo-for peace?"

Moira frowned. "Be careful, Sir Faerin. We're in hostile lands, and we're supposed to be allies."

Shite. That was supposed to be funny.

"He did what!" A husky shout echoed through the geometric room from the eastern entrance. Quickly, an escalating argument in Taela ensued. Something about dragons? Or drinks?

Drinks! Of course, not dragons.

Prince Irragrin stole his way into the room and snatched his seat on Faerin's left. "I believe the king of the desert has discovered the alchemy in our beverages." Running a hand through his wavy hair, he chuckled nervously. "Thank the Gods he appears to take the attempts on our lives harshly, aeh? Perhaps 'twasn't him at all."

Faerin gulped. *Just what we need. An angered Taela king on the cusp of negotiating a treaty.*

The clacking of hooves echoed from the southern entrance. Faerin glanced over his shoulder to see a short, portly being with bright red hair and yellow eyes approach. His legs, ears, and nose resembled those of a boar, while the rest of him attempted to resemble a mortal man. He clambered up to the seat next to Moira.

"Yer Grace, King Ilarion," Moira greeted the Orovite newcomer. "A pleasure to make yer acquaintance."

"The pleasure is mine, Senator Siobhan."

Did he not read the bloody ledger?

Irragrin coughed. "Moira."

The oddling king stiffened. "Senator Moira. Apologies. I thought—"

The clang of metal-on-metal rang through the air as two Nethuanian men also entered from the southern entrance. "I pray we're not late to t'is council." The deep, sandy voice of the taller one pierced the council's ears. He stood a head above his companion and was covered in an armour of bronze and leather scales. His black-and-grey hair was slicked back, resting in a low braid that ended at his tailbone. The second guard wore the same garb, but in leather and blackened iron.

"Of course not, Roman Ho'su." The Áfgalese prince grinned at his fellow mortal's words. "I have two available seats next to me, for you and …"

"Lubiyo Maniki," the second guard answered.

"You're too kind, Prince Ir'greem." Roman nodded once as he and Lubiyo sat at two of the four remaining chairs across from the Áfgaliard.

In surprising silence, Irragrin scrunched his nose and glared.

Faerin chewed on the tip of his tongue, stifling the urge to correct the man's pronunciation. *Wizards be good, who's denser? The oddling or the red-blood?*

Moira leaned to her left and whispered, "Thi senn cüer mis i daoise cìrth e thi'sa." *We are doomed if these fools are peacemakers.*

A smile curled up Faerin's mouth. *Eil, we're gonna be friends.*

Movement and the clearing of throats brought everyone's attention again to the southern entrance. There, a golden-brown man in the silver, slim-fit coat and matching turban of Taelonael's royalty, stood. A thin layer of black paste covered his lower eyelids, accenting the gold streaks in his bright brown eyes. "Welcome, leaders of the Eastern Lands," he greeted with a warm smile. "I would have my vizier with me, but we had an incident of great importance."

"No ap-ap-apologies necessary, Y'r Grace Ja-jabali," said Faerin.

"We are m-m-most grateful for for for y'r hospitality and willing-g-gness to meet with us."

"This *is* an unprecedented day, I agree," said Irragrin. "Perhaps later we can toast to a resolution of these newly established hostilities."

Jabali wiped the smile from his face as he locked eyes with the Áfgalese prince. "Hostilities, you say? Do tell."

The Áfgaliard opened his mouth to respond, but—

"Gnomes be merciful, Irragrin. I thought ye were a peacemaker, not a warmonger."

Irragrin clacked his mouth shut at Moira's taunt.

"Ah yes. I heard about the incident with the wine," said Jabali. "My son, Kabir, forgets that our *alchemy* is no plaything." He glared daggers at the southern doorway, where a young boy of perhaps ten spied around its corner. "I apologise for such a lapse in his judgement … and for my oversight."

"On b-behalf of of of all y'r guests, King Ja-ja-jabali, I accept y-your apology," said Faerin. "As you can see, there was n-n-no true harm done." He shot a menacing glare at the scowling Irragrin. Without breaking his sharp gaze, the Prasti continued, "Now then, would any of of of ya like to discuss the the end of this w-war?"

36

KALASIN

Sólan buried his face into the nape of Dakil's neck as he thrust, his body pressing against Dakil's and sandwiching him against the wall.

Sighing, Dakil arched his back to lean his head on Sólan's shoulder. "Faster, mintaki," he whispered.

With a passionate growl, Sólan obliged. He grasped a fistful of silky black hair with one hand and reached around his lover with the other. Faster. Sólan stroked Dakil's oiled erection with a tightening grip. Pressure building, his hips moved of their own accord.

Dakil's legs buckled, and he fell to his knees with a thud. He sighed, panting as Sólan spilled himself onto his ass cheeks. "Yusa's grace, Sólan," said Dakil.

Sólan shivered before helping his lover to his feet and planting a kiss on his mouth. Inhaling deeply, he said, "*Gods*, you smell good."

"What?" Dakil chuckled as he broke the embrace to wash. "What can I possibly smell like?" He tossed a rag to a beaming Sólan.

Only of fine salt and the most luxurious of brandy. Sólan shrugged. "Nothing in particular. You are just ... intoxicating." After wiping his deflating manhood, he crossed to Dakil, nuzzling his earlobe.

Dakil shied away, blushing as he hoisted his trousers to his hips.

"You're a strange man. But I like it. Tell me something. How do you know Oleg? Slave scouts rarely mix with the Taela drug trade."

Still naked, Sólan plopped himself on his feather bed and groaned. "I often kill those I scout against. Funnily enough, many of them are also scheduled to die at the hands of Oleg and his minions." He smirked. "Oleg sought me out. At first, he wanted to kill me for my 'interference' with his own career, until he discovered I was of more help than his own assassins. 'Twas an easy thing for me to accept his gold, as I was soon richer than any scout could ever dream. Tell me about Morinalo." With a coy pout, he beckoned Dakil to bed.

Dakil obliged with a grin, sinking himself into his lover's muscular arms. "It's like Linget in this life. You can see the most vibrant of colours in the sun as it sets behind the sea. The aroma of fresh sugarcane and coconuts ..." He closed his eyes and gave a sad sigh. "I loved my home. But I'll never be able to go back."

"Why not? I would follow you there, and 'tis not as though you have been banished."

"But I have." Dakil's voice quivered. "When you said I was likely noble, you were right. My father was a member of Morinalo's Cavalry Guard. When he died, his replacement knew me as a boy—he would recognise me anywhere."

Sólan gulped as Bayani's words from Bansungei's kitchen echoed in his ears, *"It unnatural. Disgusting. A vile abomination." Gods, this idol called Yusa is a tyrant.*

"We land at Bansungei tomorrow," said Dakil. "We know what we pretend to deliver, but ... they will suspect an Áfgalese captain."

"Which is precisely why I have asked you about Morinalo." Sólan intertwined his fingers in Dakil's hair. "Do all Morinalans grow their hair this long?"

"What does that have to do with—"

"Nothing, of course," said Sólan, still playing with his lover's lock. "I just enjoy your hair. So, do they?"

Dakil gave a sheepish chuckle. "Only the men, actually. The longer their hair, the higher their status. The women keep it short to keep it out of the way of their household duties." He frowned, looking up to Sólan with a curious gaze. "So if you won't be on the *Silent Dancer*, where will you be?"

Sólan flashed a wicked grin at Dakil. "Bayani and I will be inside the city, of course. We have a traitor to find."

Dakil crawled on top of his lover, straddling his waist and planting a wet kiss on his mouth. "Not just find, mintaki. We have a traitor to *kill*."

The western port of Bansungei bustled with merchants and customers of every age, social class, and nationality. Even elves from as far north as Karthénos shopped amongst the various colourful tents that littered the walkways between the ships and city walls. The mid-morning crowds exacerbated the still, muggy air of a late fall heat wave, creating a redolence of rotting stench from the port and body sweat of both men and elves alike. 'Twas enough to make Sólan gag.

The gang of smugglers anchored at the end of the massive limestone dock. Dakil conversed with the local patrols, paying them for their use of the slip as he pretended to be captain of the *Musina Pinoy* —the *Summer Lands*. A falsified receipt and a confident handshake later, the men offloaded the bricks and barrels without so much as an eyebrow lifted in their direction.

Sólan slipped off the disguised *Silent Dancer* into the warm, murky water. Bayani followed close behind, clutching the slimy dock walls with his remaining hand. As they inched further away from the ship, Bayani clutched Sólan's shoulder to keep from drowning.

Just beyond the sight of the closest patrol, the Áfgaliard clambered up the rocks and hugged himself against the smooth, limestone wall. He balanced with caution as he helped his one-handed companion out of the water. "There," he whispered, pointing to his immediate left. "Our entrance into the city's belly."

"Nipantot ki," whispered Bayani. "I thought you hate t'e sewers."

"Of course I hate the sewers, indionta. But I hate traitors even more." The two climbed over the slippery rocks to a metre-wide grate that covered a drainage exit. Sólan's eyes glowed, and the rusted metal disintegrated to fine sand. Flashing a grin toward Bayani, he said, "After you."

Bayani slithered through the opening, and Sólan stifled another gag as the smell of the slums' waste assaulted his senses. Eyes watering, he held his breath and plunged into the dark stink of Bansungei's sewers—a place he'd foolishly hoped he'd never see again.

An echoing choir of boos and angry cheers from above vibrated through the tunnels. Sólan tensed. *Likely the murder of a raped child. The fucking monsters.* Beside him, Bayani muttered curses in his own tongue.

The tunnel widened, accommodating a narrow walkway beside the slimy deluge through which they crawled. Once out of the muck, Sólan retched. "Gods, I will never get used to this." He vomited again.

Bayani belched beside him. "You will, I promise." He placed a grimy hand on Sólan's shoulder. "Use your mouth to breathe. The smell no bad when you—"

"Dammit, Bayani, I have the nose of a fucking *Karthi*." Sólan spat a sour glob of saliva to the ground. Shuddering, he shuffled along the walkway and into the subterranean heart of the city.

The duo rounded a corner and found a narrow staircase leading away from the sewer. Sólan angled his ear toward the top of the steps. "Up there. I can hear him coming from the northeast."

Bayani gasped, his breath sharp against Sólan's eardrums. A swift backhand to his ear silenced him.

Dull footsteps approached. The smell of fear engulfed the tunnel, overbearing the wretched scent of the putrid waste beside them. Sólan and Bayani pressed themselves against the tunnel's wall, hiding behind the corner they'd just passed.

The flicker of an approaching oil lamp illuminated the hall, followed closely by the broad silhouette of a weathered smuggler. "I know you here," said a familiar voice. Kalasin. "I saw Dakil on t'e *Silent Dancer*. You can come out, Bayani. Is no what you think."

Ninil, sañero. 'Tis precisely what we think.

"No need to hide, Bayani. It no me you want. Maybe Dakil the one to look at? Did he no want the *Silent Dancer*, instead?"

Bayani balled his fist to stay his trembling. Placing a gentle hand on his shoulder, Sólan beckoned him to reveal himself.

"T'ere are you, binyego! I wonder why you no come from drowned valley," said Kalasin. "What happen to you!"

Sólan could nigh hear Bayani roll his eye. "I no have time for t'is, Kalasin. Where our buyers now since the cavalry took our last hiding place?" He shouldered past the traitor and grumbled.

"They what?"

You are a terrible liar, putathóta.

"You know what I say, tulalo. You no need to lie. I tired of it."

Kalasin growled, raising his hand to strike when Sólan approached and cleared his throat. The smuggler stiffened. "Who you are!" Spinning, he gasped at Sólan's devilish grin. He stumbled backward, colliding with Bayani. A burlap sack plopped over his head, and before he could scream, Sólan punched the side of his skull.

The two eased Kalasin's limp body to the ground and dragged him up the northeast corridor, Sólan whistling a merry tune.

Bayani tapped his foot, arms crossed, as he watched Sólan hang a naked Kalasin by his bound wrists on a hook. "What if he no talk?"

"He will talk. My only concern is whether or not we will be heard," said Sólan. Binding the traitor's ankles with rope, he then chained his feet to the ground. "You are certain we will not?"

"As certain as I have cock."

A mischievous grin stretched across Sólan's face. "That, sañero, makes me even less confident."

"Nipant—"

"Yes yes. *Nipantot ki*. Fuck me. You need to learn some new curses, or else I may begin to take that as an invitation. Dakil is a jealous lover, you know."

Bayani groaned. *Yusa's grace, you are a disgusting man.* "This is old slaughterhouse for pigs, Sólan. This built so children no can hear t'e squeals of death. We no can be heard."

Kalasin stirred, and both snapped their attention to the bound traitor. "Where I am?" said Kalasin through a croak, his voice muffled by burlap. "And why it smell like death?"

"You at the entry to you grave, tiksal. That why you smell death. You death."

"Tiksal? You call me 'traitor,' Bayani?" Kalasin struggled against his bonds to no avail. "Perhaps is *you* who traitor!"

"Believe me, if this pundijo were a traitor, you would never see him again," said Sólan. He lifted the sack from Kalasin's face and smiled. "Hello again, *minion.*"

Kalasin snarled. "You. I thought you die at hand of Kadek."

"Ha! Like that fat indionta could lift his own weight, let alone a sword. No, sañero. 'Tis I who commands the *Silent Dancer* now."

"Who you really are!"

"Some call me a demon of Misó, while to others, I am the Angel of Áfgal. As for you, dear Kalasin, I am a servant of your god of death—a servant of The Dark whose vengeance is unmatched. I am the man they call 'the Grim.' Yet, you believed me not when I first told you."

The air grew suddenly cold, sending a shiver down Bayani's spine. *Yusa's grace.* The familiar green glow pulsed around Sólan's bright amber irises, and Bayani stiffened at the sight. *Ta, tual. You truly t'e Grim.*

Sólan appeared to take no notice of his comrade. "You have betrayed your crew. You have betrayed your master, Kadek the Vile. And now, you have betrayed me. Who sent you?"

Kalasin glared and spat in Sólan's face. "I never tell, kapiretliho."

Sólan wiped the saliva off his cheek and snarled. Grabbing Kalasin by the hair, he thrust the spike of his hatchet into each of his eyes. The traitor screamed as Sólan, in a whisper, asked again, "Who sent you?"

Bayani squirmed at the sight of the oozing eye sockets.

"Myself! No one send me!" Kalasin's voice squealed like a pig in slaughter.

"Ha! Listen to him, Bayani! He thinks he has outsmarted the man who should not be alive!"

Gulping, Bayani merely nodded. *My God, this no is t'e Sólan I think I know.*

Sólan, however, continued his maniacal laughter. "You say to me that you will never tell who sent you, and now you tell me that you worked alone. My dear Kalasín, do you truly think I could be so naïve?" He grabbed the man's ear and sliced it off. "Tell me—who do you work for?"

"I work for Kadek," Kalasin said, sneering, "And you kill him!"

"Well, then. It looks as though I will have to kill you, too, sañero." The captain scraped through the layers of skin on the traitor's chest, exposing the bone of his sternum. Kalasin's screams pierced through their ears as Sólan continued, "But not until you tell me who sent you."

The traitor snarled, cursing at the Áfgaliard in both the common tongue and Nethuanian. Sólan appeared unfazed, however. "I have been kind to you this far, sañero. Who sent you?"

Kind? I no see kindness here!

"Fuck you, kapiret-liho! I am man of Yusa! Not a demon of Misó like you! May you soul burn in Yirno! I will no—"

"Bayani. Will you remind me what I did on the 'Isle of Death'?"

"You behead t'e Pontianak bare-handed, tual." Bayani's voice trembled. Whether in fear or excitement, he couldn't tell.

"Yes. How could I have forgotten? I beheaded that demon with my hands." Sólan chuckled and averted his attention back to Kalasin. "So, you can imagine what I am capable of doing to you, dear traitor, to have my way."

"You torture me and kill me, halfbreed. I still tell you not'ing."

Give up, tual. You lose, and I no can watch this torture anymore.

"I am not going to kill you *now*, sañero. No, no, no, no. You forget that a halfbreed such as myself can keep you alive for as long as needed." He rubbed the sticky edge of his hatchet against Kalasin's cheek. "You will not die on me, pundijo," he whispered. "I will not let you." Sólan grasped the flap of skin on his hostage's chest and pulled. It tore and bled as he ripped his way down Kalasin's sternum.

Bayani stifled a heave as fresh crimson blood flowed from the wound, his ears ringing from the traitor's screams.

"Who sent you!" Sólan demanded.

"Stop! Please stop!" Kalasin begged.

"I will stop when you tell me what I want to know!" Sólan then dug the tips of his bare fingers between the muscles of Kalasin's ribs and continued to tear through his flesh.

"Roman!" screamed Kalasin. "Roman Ho'su sent me!"

Sólan stopped. His eyes faded to their natural amber state, and he looked to Bayani with victory blanketed across his face. "The High Guard of Nethuania," he whispered.

"T'e attack at t'e river mouth … it was plan long before you kill Kadek. He was after—"

"I knew you no can be trusted!" Bayani cried. He lunged forward and snatched Sólan's hatchet from his grasp. Swinging clumsily with his good hand, he chopped through Kalasin's thigh, shoulder, ribs— anything he could reach until Sólan pulled him back by his shirt.

"Perhaps you should know who sent *me*, aeh? There is a phrase in Áfgal: 'Óligo e tuas enomógos cil carño.'" Sólan grasped Kalasin's hair. "'Choose your enemies with care.' And you, pundijo, have chosen carelessly."

Kalasin's bottom lip trembled. "Are you to kill me now?"

Sólan chuckled as he brushed the man's face with the back of his knuckles. "Of course I am, dear Kalasín. But I am unfinished with you yet." He held out a hand to Bayani, silently asking for his hatchet. "Oleg Kinev sends his regards, traitor."

Stomach twisting, Bayani obliged before looking away with a wince. *I no can watch this anymore.* He didn't need to watch. The gurgling screams, the squelching sounds of flesh, and the smell of blood knocked Bayani to his knees. He heaved, spewing forth what little food he'd eaten earlier onto the dusty ground of the abandoned slaughterhouse. *Yusa's grace, make him stop. Please, make him stop.*

Despite his desperate pleas to Yusa, Sólan continued the

madness. Blood dripped down the Áfgaliard's forearms as he slowly skinned Kalasin alive, laughing louder with each scream he let out.

Bayani couldn't take any more. "Binyego, stop!" He leapt forward and grabbed Sólan's wrist, yanking the hatchet from the halfbreed's bloody hand and tossing it across the room.

Sólan grasped Bayani by the throat and snarled, his fangs bared and his mouth drooling with malice. "Who are you who *dares* to stop the work of the Grim?" he spat. His voice was not his own—and those eyes. They burned with a bright green flame that was brighter than Bayani had ever seen, even covering amber in his natural eyes. Their pupils thinned and stretched upward like a cat's.

"It me," choked Bayani. "It Bayani Lin."

A wet scream from their prisoner seemed to bring the Áfgaliard back to the present, as he barked, "Fuck!" Sólan threw Bayani to the ground and fell to his knees, grasping his left shoulder in pain. When he met the smuggler's terrified gaze again, his eyes had returned to their natural amber state—and his pupils were large and round once again. He looked to his trembling hands and whispered, "What have I done?"

Bayani ignored him, standing on wobbly legs. He snatched Sólan's hatchet from the ground and sliced through Kalasin's throat. The traitor's cries turned to gurgles before finally silencing altogether.

Sólan, however, never looked up from his hands. "What have I done?" he repeated.

"It no matter now," said Bayani, placing the hatchet at Sólan's feet. "Kalasin dead, and we have information we need. Time to go back. Dakil waiting for us—'specially for you."

37

BROKEN MEN

*B*ayani was the first to climb over the railing of the *Silent Dancer*, clumsily thudding to the deck as Sólan followed. The captain's approach was, of course, far more graceful.

Dakil grinned at their blood-soaked appearance. "I see you found him." Sólan merely winked in response before slipping out of his shirt.

Bayani's face grew pale. "I never see something so grim. Kalasin beg us to kill him."

"That tiksal deserved it," said Dakil. "Now we can send the message to Tianag's—"

"He was a spy for the cavalry guard," said Sólan. Slicking his hair back, he scrunched his nose at his own scent. "Gods, I smell like an Orovite."

Dakil snorted. "I wasn't going to tell you, but ..."

"What we do, Dakil? If Roman finds out what we do to Kalasin, we have all Nethuania on us," said Bayani through teeth suddenly chattering.

"They won't find out, binyego," said Dakil. "It could've been anyone who killed him. Roman made many enemies today." *Pantot. He's still alive? And the high guard now?*

"Ha! As though he had so few to begin with," said Sólan, ripping Dakil back to the present. "How young was the child he executed today? Five? Ten?"

This is still my home, Sólan. Not everything is terrible here. Dakil scrunched his nose. "There were no executions today."

Sólan rolled his eyes. Yawning, he rolled his shoulders back with a pop. "Good. I grow tired of hearing about them. I see there were several gold-clad elves within the crowds this morning. If I am seen, I am merely your halfbreed slave from the Oasis City, my tongue removed so I cannot speak, and I was bound by the Oath of Light at the time of my—"

"There's no need to worry about hunters, mintaki. They all left and won't return."

Confusion contorted Sólan's face, followed closely by a flash of joy, and then ... fear? *What are you possibly afraid of?*

"How can we be certain of this?" Sólan whispered. "Surely they seek to surprise us all."

"The Crusade of Light is over," said Dakil. "That's what the crowd cheered about."

Tears moistened Sólan's mesmerising amber eyes just enough to make their blue and silver specks dance in the sunset's light. Swallowing, Dakil rubbed his lover's arm. "The elves made a treaty with Taelonael. You're safe now, Sólan. Safer than you've ever been."

Sólan clenched his jaw. "I need to get this fucking blood off of me." He shouldered past Dakil, slamming his door before the swordsman could respond.

Not again. Yusa's grace, Sólan. You need to talk to me. Taking a shaky breath, Dakil turned to Bayani and said, "We sail in four days for Oleg. Make sure our buyers pay us in full."

Bayani nodded but didn't move. "Why you love him so? Is he seducer? Did he make you sin wit' him?"

"Kilak ng ki, Bayani," snarled Dakil. *Shit on you, Bayani.* "Are my relations with Sólan any worse than old men who marry young girls? Or more sinful than you trying to steal a married woman like Tala? If you're going to use the Book of the Sun against me, be sure you completely follow it too. Or else, you're no different from those prophets who use it for their own sins."

Blushing, Bayani shut his mouth and shuffled away.

Dakil crossed the deck toward his lover's quarters. *Fuck the book, and fuck Yusa. I can't do this anymore. I need Sólan.* With heavy feet, he approached Sólan's door. Lifting his arm to knock, he stopped and cursed. If he'd learned anything these past weeks, it was that Sólan needed time. He turned his attention to the ship next to the *Silent Dancer*. 'Twas a shallow merchant vessel of Áfgal that had travelled down the length of the Runedein. Curiosity piqued, Dakil meandered his way toward it, in search of something for his lover. *I can give you time. And maybe something to celebrate.*

THE FRESH WATER WAS A LUXURY—AT LEAST, IT WOULD HAVE BEEN HAD Sólan sworn the Oath of Light during the crusade. Even the briny water of the northernmost Karthi Sea could be made fresh in the blink of an eye with The Dark. As greedy as the powers were, they were quite useful most of the time.

He wet his hair, lathered a bar of Taela soap in his hands, and scrubbed. Flakes of dried blood dissolved and stained his fingers, dripping down his face. The smell was nearly as fresh as when first spurting from Kalasin's flesh.

Next, Sólan addressed his body. He stripped out of his crusted trousers and kicked them to the side. A sour belch escaped his chest, making him shudder. *Gods, pure mortal men are disgusting.* Scouring his skin until it felt raw, the captain scrubbed vigorously, yet nothing would lessen the stench. Nothing could numb the sudden pain pulsing through his throat and chest.

Vision blurring, Sólan's sinuses flooded and mucus slid down his chin as his teeth chattered. Soon, his body was trembling hard enough to knock him to his knees. "Grachoas, Elek," he whispered through his sobs. "Li protigest e trovas de luste crusede. Javiento, lo hambode servente lo doba lu eterdando." *Thank you Elek. You have protected me through the crusade. Javiento, your humble servant owes his eternity to you.*

Sólan shook his head. *I still smell like death and sewage.* He scrubbed some more. With a second basin, he rinsed his hair and skin, the water turning maroon with his filth. Though he still felt dirty, he stepped into a clean pair of loose trousers and plopped himself onto his bed.

There, Sólan muddled feelings struck his gut. He buried his face into the mattress and screamed. It was a scream of sorrow against joy, anguish against solace, despair against hope. Despite his father's efforts, he'd survived the war ... he'd survived the massacre. *Dakil is right. I am finally safe.*

A sharp knock on his door jolted him back to the present. Wiping the fresh salt from his eyes, he padded over and cracked it open. A shallow smile crept across his lips at the sight of Dakil. "I thought you knew you never have to knock. These are your quarters, too. Remember?"

"You seemed upset. I didn't want to startle you."

Sólan embraced Dakil with a kiss on the mouth. "What do you have behind your back?"

Dakil's smile widened as he revealed a corked glass bottle. "Some wine."

"Where did you get it?"

"You'll see. Here, open it." Dakil handed the bottle over, making Sólan's frown deepen.

He instantly recognised the bottle's distinct shape. *Áfgalese. Likely their terrible port, but I cannot disappoint.* He flipped the bottle over to read the numbers etched into it—*1-0-1-1*— and his jaw dropped. "Dakil," he whispered as the air escaped his lungs. "This ... Dakil ..." He couldn't speak. Words flooded his throat, but he couldn't slow them enough to form on his lips. *This is twenty-five years old! Arriya Taca—the wine district! This is the best vineyard in Áfgal! How did you know my taste in wine? Why did you get this? Do you realise how much gold this cost in Áfgal? How did you know that I love wine more than brandy?*

"I hope it's a good one. The merchant said it was the best in Áfgal, but you know how merchants can be."

Sólan gulped, gripping the bottle for fear of dropping it from his trembling hands. "How did you know?" he finally squeaked. "What is it ... why?"

Dakil's smile lit his face, making the smoky streaks in his deep, russet gaze smoulder like a blacksmith's forge. "We need to celebrate, mintaki. It's the end of the crusade."

"I ..." The floodgates behind Sólan's eyes burst open, and he sank to his knees in a sob.

"Sólan, what's wrong?"

Dakil's warm hand on his shoulder brought more tears to the surface.

"Nothing. I just ... I am so surprised by the wine, is all."

"Kilakahon. Bullshit. *Look* at me." Dakil grabbed Sólan's chin and stared into him with those perfect brown eyes. "You're a terrible liar. Talk to me. I can't know all of you if you only give me half. I don't want to love a stranger, but I'm in love with you. Talk." He quickly blushed and shut his mouth.

Gods, Dakil. Have I not yet told you the same? I love you more than anything I have ever held—than anyone I have ever met. Yet, you love me as well—this halfbreed monster? This man who caused the longest war in the history of the Eastern Lands? Sólan shook Dakil's hand off his face. "I was the cause of the crusade, Dakil. Not the Taelas. Not the Prasti nor the Karthi. Me."

"How old were you when the crusade even started, mintaki? Ten?"

"Twelve." Sólan's eye twitched at the sting of Dakil's skeptical frown. "My father raped my mother hundreds of years ago, and I was the result. When I met the man who fathered me ... well, the crusade began less than a season after."

Dakil rolled his eyes. "That doesn't make you the reason for it. Perhaps it was just—"

"Why do you think it ended today? I was 'executed' by the fucking Prince of Prastömin! A mere two seasons, and 'tis over?"

"That still doesn't mean it was because of you."

Sólan's lip trembled. "I wish your words were true. Gods, do I wish …" His words trailed off into more whimpering sobs. "Look at me. A blubbering fool who weeps more than smiles, of late. How can you possibly love such a coward?"

"*Coward*?" Mouth agape, Dakil grasped his lover's face in both hands. "After everything, you think I'd believe such lies? After Kalasin? The Pontianak? Kadek?" He awkwardly smashed his mouth onto Sólan's. "Are these your nightmares, mintaki? That you are weak when you really are strong?"

"Nintl. My nightmares are far worse." Taking a shaky breath, Sólan asked, "Do you want to hear? You say you wish not to know a stranger any longer. Though I wish not to speak on them, I trust you. Perhaps"—he shook his head—"never mind. You would discover my cowardice. You would hate me like you hated Kadek in the end."

"Stop it, Sólan. You are no coward, so stop saying it! Talk to me, mintaki. You aren't Kadek, and you never will be!"

I said I trust you, but, Gods, why is this so difficult? Why are my words so fucking hollow? Sólan fidgeted with the wine bottle still clutched in his hands. Gulping, he finally looked deep into Dakil's concerned gaze. "I need some wine first."

A sad chuckle escaped the swordsman's mouth. "I'll pour while you talk."

Letting out a sigh, Sólan finally obliged his lover's demands. "Fine." He inched himself to his feet and crossed to the bed. "When Duke Jannon forced himself onto—"

"Jannon of Karthénos! He's your father?"

Sólan scrunched his nose. "Do you want to hear, or not?"

Dakil pressed his lips together and popped the wine's cork as Sólan continued, "As she carried me, my mother, Lorrita—along with her lover and my brother, Montrél—fled Maseño. I was born in Ciudelago, where she became an herbalist, and her lover, a baker." Sólan shuddered. "The man hated me. After all, I was a mastázo. A halfbreed bastard who should have been sent to Taelonael to become a slave."

Dakil inhaled sharply but kept quiet.

"I was eight years old when it started. He used it as a punishment, but it soon became something more for him. For four years, I was his plaything. I was his little whore he could fuck and sell to others for the night ... 'We need the coin for winter grain,' he would say. And I fucking believed him."

Dakil brought over two pewter chalices of wine and scrambled onto the bed. "Yusa's grace. Eight years old and ..." He shivered.

Sniffling, Sólan grabbed a chalice and sipped. The spicy tartness and dry finish soothed his throat. "I was twelve when Montrél discovered his secret and threatened to expose him. The baker murdered him to keep his crime unknown.

"I was accused, of course. No man would murder his own son, especially when he had the luxury of accusing the mastázo he hated. My mother was thirty-five when she died. She hanged herself when her grief and guilt became too much to bear. I know not what happened to the baker, but I wish I had killed him. I wish I had not been so afraid." He took another sip and savoured it. "*Gods*, this is good wine. They blend it so well with their pepper ..."

Dakil cleared his throat. "I ... I'm not sure I like it. My mouth feels too dry."

"¿Mondé? This is the best vineyard in all of Áfgal!" Sólan gaped at Dakil's offensive words. "If you will drink it not, *I* will. There is a bottle of blueberry brandy in the map cupboard."

"Calomot i Yusa," whispered Dakil. Handing his wine to Sólan, he jumped to his feet and pattered across the cabin.

Sólan drained both cups with ease. "You have strange taste."

Dakil snorted. "And you don't? You drink dry, bitter wine, and you think it's the 'best in Áfgal.'" With a mischievous smile, he guzzled the blueberry brandy.

"Ha!" Sólan's face grew hot as the alcohol finally reached his head. "Come here. And bring that 'dry and bitter' wine with you." He opened his arms with a coy pout. "I suppose you are right. I should be celebrating tonight rather than wallowing in self-made despair."

With a sigh, Dakil grabbed the bottle of wine in one hand, taking care not to spill the brandy in his other. "Sólan. Why do you think you're a coward for what happened to you?"

I thought we were done with this shit. Sólan clenched his jaw against the sudden onslaught of emotion bubbling in his throat. *I thought you were listening.*

"Mintaki. None of this is your fault, ta? That monster took your innocence at eight. It's not your fault. Your father's cowardice for not accepting you as his son? That's not your fault, either."

Stop it, Dakil. Please stop. I grow tired of weeping in front of you.

"It's not your fault, mintaki."

Those words again. "It's not your fault ..." *It is my fault. Had I stayed with Alsantör in Prastömin, or died at the hands of the Cabilleros, or avenged my brother and stayed within Áfgal. Had I—*

"You're not saying anything, but I know you disagree. It's. Not. Your. Fault."

Again, his sinuses flooded. Tears formed. His throat closed. "It's not your fault." *Did you hear nothing of which I spoke?*

"Tsst."

Sólan snapped his attention back to his lover. "What?"

"Are you going to say anything?"

Tell him, Sólan. Tell him you love him. How you will crumble the mountains and flood the valleys to be with him. Sólan opened his mouth, but the words wouldn't form.

"Sólan?"

"Promise me something." Sólan's heart suddenly thumped in his throat, fear engulfing him for what he was about to ask. "That you will help me claim the *Silent Dancer* completely. That we will remove it from Oleg's grip."

Dakil stiffened. "Oleg is the most powerful drug seller in the southern half of these lands. Do you want that target on your back after all these years running from the elves?"

"This is different, Dakil. He fights not rivals from Tianag, Morinalo, or any other territory. He will want war with all of Nethuania." Reaching, Sólan stroked Dakil's jaw with the backs of his knuckles. "I am not a smuggler, Dakil. I am a man who fights the oppression of such markets, not an enabler of another. And with you by my side, we can topple that trade and help the Chainbreakers expand beyond the island."

Dakil looked at the ceiling and pursed his lips. "You're going to cause another war, mintaki. Are you sure—"

"As sure as I know that I love you." Sólan quickly gasped, clamping a hand around his mouth.

"Hah?" With bated breath, the swordsman locked his smoky gaze with Sólan's. "What did you say?"

"I …" Sólan trembled, flitting his gaze around the cabin as though searching for an escape. Without another word, he planted his mouth onto Dakil's with passion.

They fumbled with each other's clothing, tangling joints and fingers with linen and cotton. Dakil's shirt still hung around his neck, and Sólan's trousers were stuck around his ankles. He didn't care. All he wanted was to savour Dakil—to taste him, to love him. "Oh mólamí," whispered Sólan. "I love you."

PART III

THE BREAKING OF PEACE

TEN YEARS LATER

38

SECRETS OF THE FOREST

*N*aoise tentatively entered the Wizards' sacred cave. It had been years since he was last there—before Saoirse had been born. With all his hardship and conflicting emotions in the past ten years, he decided 'twas time to reach out. He needed to rekindle his faith with the Wizards and Gnomes, or, at least, to see if they were even real.

The pungent steam from the pool assaulted his nostrils, and his eyes watered, blurring his vision as he stumbled into the cave. *Gnomes be merciful, to think this is a sacred place to 'em. What kind of putrid horror do they—*

"What brings you to the sacred pool today, Laird of the Forest?"

Naoise jumped at Brayson's silent approach. Despite his decrepit and twisted limbs, he'd made no sound. Naoise shuddered as he met the speaker's gaze. Those eyes—what was left of them, anyway—were terrifying. "Ah dinnae ken, Speaker o' the Wizards. Ah dinnae ken where to begin."

"It has been a long while, Naoise McManstair," said Brayson, placing both hands on the duke's head. "I sense a great fear in you. A fear of betrayal—of doubt. You question the existence of our creators, do you not?"

Based on what, exactly? All y're doin' is holding my hair like a lover. Of course I question their existence, Speaker! Of course I question their motives, their—

"Their motives?" Brayson removed his hands and stepped back. "What blasphemy do you bring into this holy place?"

Naoise gasped. "I—That's not ... what?"

"Then perhaps, son of Vaoirsen, you may enlighten me on your thoughts, rather than hide them behind the same veil as did your father."

Tears flooded the duke's eyes—whether in anger or sorrow, Naoise didn't know. *I'm no traitor, Speaker. I don't blaspheme. Oh, Giaven, I wish you were here. Y'd know what to say, how to explain ...*

"Sorrow, child. Your mind is clouded with it."

"I miss 'im." Naoise's chest tightened with the swelling grief. "I wasn't ready. I doen't think I ever could be. But ... I seek ..." He cleared his throat. "My mind is a mess, Speaker. Too many thoughts muddy me, and I need help." He'd said it. Finally. After hundreds of years of refusing to accept it, of trying to hide it, of being the "strong one," he'd done it. Naoise's breath came easier than it had in over two hundred and fifty years. *Please, Speaker. Will you help me?*

Brayson's knees popped as he lowered himself to Naoise's level. "Of course, child. The Wizards rejoice that you've returned to them." Grasping his hands, he muttered incoherently.

Distant memories flashed behind Naoise's eyelids.

His father's teachings of honour and dignity. Him and his brother as children, bickering over their alpine village's lone archery target.

The sight of Ina, wisps of her strawberry-blonde hair floating in the gentle breeze kicked up by the falling water in front of their secret cave. Her eyes glittering with tears in the sunlight as she begged him for help. Naoise reaching out and placing his hand onto her swollen belly, his long-lost daughter growing inside of her. "I promise, my love," he'd said. "Our child will not die at their hands. You will not die by their hands."

"Ahhh," said the speaker through a sigh. "Y've met her, at long last. Dame Saoirse."

Naoise was violently ripped out of his memories. Cold beads of sweat trickled down his forehead as his chest clamped tight once again. "What did you say?" he whispered.

"A fitting name for a forbidden daughter, son of Vaoirsen. *Saoirse*. The freedom she bestows to you and the gift such freedom brings."

Gift? Naoise's breath shallowed. "Apologies, Speaker, but ... I doen't do well with riddles."

"Freedom through *death*, dear Naoise, the gift from betrayal that shall bring such freedom."

Again, images flashed behind Naoise's eyelids. This time, he saw his hand wielding a golden gladius and striking through Alsantör's back. He jumped to his feet, knocking the elf to the ground. "Fook off!"

The Speaker hissed at his outburst. "You dare insult—"

"*You* dare imply I'd betray his grace? That I'd strike down the man I trust the most? My last and dearest comrade in these gnomes-forsaken lands? I'm no *traitor* like my father was, Speaker!" Naoise grasped the frail elf by his white robe and lifted him to his level. Baring his fangs, his mouth sprayed with saliva as he hissed. Brayson cackled, and Naoise threw him to the ground, spitting on him as he did so. "If this be the way the Wizards treat their most loyal followers, then *fook them*!"

The duke stomped out of the cave, fists clenched. Behind him, Brayson screeched and laughed, "The Dark consume you all! A slave of the shadows, you shall become!"

NAOISE'S KNUCKLES BLANCHED AT THE FORCE OF HIS GRIP AS HIS MARCH turned to an agile sprint through the dense forest. He stopped, punching the nearest cedar tree until his hands bled. Reaching inside his tunic, he retrieved his brother's ring, ripped the necklace off, and threw it as far as he could. The clang of metal on rock echoed through his keen, pointed ears as it bounced to the ground nigh a hundred metres away. Naoise fell to his knees and pounded the earth with his hands, screaming a guttural cry until his voice grew hoarse.

Tears flowed from his eyes, down his face, and into his nose, his body heaving with sobs. "I'm so sorry, Giaven ... I ... Gnomes, I shoulda been there. I coulda saved ya."

"Laird Naoise?"

He startled, jumping to his feet into his fighters' stance. Behind him stood Rhona, cloaked in green silk and jewelled with gold and emeralds. His voice cracked when he said, "You should be preparing her grace for the breaking of her fast."

A sad, crooked smile reached Rhona's eyes. "And ye should be counselling his grace on this treaty ye and Tör made him sign. Yet here we are."

"Here we are, indeed." Running his fingers through his copper curls, he shivered as Brayson's voice echoed through the trees. "Dammit. He's still cackling."

Rhona playfully frowned. "And I thought 'twas Giaven who was the jester among the two o'ye."

A quiet snort escaped Naoise's nostrils. "My first damned visit with the Speaker in two 'nd a half hundred bloody years, and he tries to call me my father. Says I'll betray Tör with a golden gladius to the back." He reached into his tunic to fiddle with his brother's ring, but it wasn't there. *Shite. Why the hell did I—*

"Ye were the closest thing to a father Giaven had, and have been a better mentor to Alsantör than Diarmuid could ever *dream* to be." Rhona stepped forward, holding out a fist. "Never do that again, Neesh. Don't ye dare try to throw away the last of yer family's memory."

Naoise held out his hand beneath hers, and the tarnished silver ring plopped into his palm. Fresh tears filled his vision. "Thank you, Rhona," he croaked.

"I'm afraid the chain's ruined, but—"

"Easily replaceable." Naoise slipped the ring onto his middle finger. "But I think I'll have it where it belongs, f'r now, rather than hidden away. 'Specially now that my daughter"—he froze.

"Yer what!" Rhona grasped his elbow. "Ye have a child? Why haven't ye told us? Who's her mother? When was she born? Where is she now?" She could hardly contain her happy squeals, bouncing eagerly on the balls of her feet.

Naoise, however, fidgeted and gave a tense smile. "Yeh. Ehm ... doen't let her grace find out, will ya? Please?"

Rhona stopped, the joy on her face washing away like dust.

"I only just met her, 'nd. Well ..." The duke swallowed the growing lump in his throat. "Please don't tell Ethna," he whispered. "Or Tör, f'r that matter. I wanna be the one to tell 'im."

"Yer secret's safe with me, Neesh." Rhona cupped her hand under his chin, wiping a tear away with her thumb. "Don't let some blind man's prophecy ruin ye. There's more to this life than tiptoeing around the whims of madmen. And I don't merely speak on Brayson."

"Ah ken." Naoise nodded gravely, clutching the silver ring about his finger. "I shouldn't keep ya from y'r prayers, Handmaiden. Good morrow." Stiffly, he gave a shallow bow, as though there were spies surrounding them. He wasn't wrong—even the still air could whisper his deepest thoughts to the Wizards.

"Good morrow, me laird," said Rhona. The strain in her voice and curtsy told him that she felt it, too. "Take care of that ring. I know how special Giaven was to ye." She lifted her hood and covered her head before gracefully slipping down the road toward the sacred cave.

"We can't keep doing this, Tör," whispered Rhona. Despite her words, she slipped her hands up his shirt and squeezed his muscles until her fingers ached. *Just tell him, Rhona. Tell him why—*

Burying his face into the nape of her neck, Alsantör groaned with pleasure. "I know," he whispered. "But you're so addicting."

The prince lifted her by her buttocks, pressing her against the stable's wall as she wrapped her legs about his waist. He ground his pelvis against hers, trembling as she dug her nails into his back and scratched him down his ribs.

"Gnomes be merciful, how I wish it was you I could marry instead of that fucking Karthi dunce."

Rhona winced. *I'm Karthi, too. Remember?* She shook the intrusive thought from her head—he didn't mean for the insult to affect her. With his breath hot against her neck, her skin prickled with arousal. "Just shut up and fuck me, Tör. I can't wait fer ye any longer."

A mischievous smirk curled the corners of Alsantör's mouth. "With pleasure."

He eased her to the hay-covered ground and slipped his hand up her dress.

Hips wriggling with anticipation, Rhona pulled his face into her breasts. "Wizards, Tör, ye're a terrible tease with that hand."

A soft chuckle escaped through his nose. "If I knew no better, I'd say you're begging me."

"Then, ye don't know better."

It took mere seconds for Rhona and Alsantör to strip themselves from the waist-down. Teeth rubbing and tongues fighting, the prince thrust himself deep inside of his lover. The act itself was over before Rhona could climax, though she panted as though she had anyway.

Slipping back into his breeches, the prince helped Rhona to her feet to straighten herself and pick the hay out of her hair.

She grunted at the sharp pain in her breast as Alsantör caressed it.

"Please tell me that pains because you're close to your flow," he whispered. "Winter, correct?"

Rhona remained silent. *Just tell him already!* her heart screamed. "We can't keep doing this," was all she could squeak out.

"What's wrong, Rhona? Does my father know about us?"

"No, thank the Wizards." *Tell him!*

Alsantör closed his eyes and leaned his head back with dread. "Then my mother does. How did she—"

"Ye don't need to know, Tör. And … y-yes. Winter." She pressed her lips together at her own lies—her own cowardice. "But we need to stop doing this. We made a promise to stop years ago, and I know we've broken that promise, but we—"

"Winter's not your flow," said the prince, face suddenly pallid. "Last year, during the harvest, you were bedridden. You and my mother."

The sudden whinny of a horse at the stable's other end jolted Rhona into a panic. "There are many reasons fer a woman to be bedridden during the harvest. That doesn't mean—"

"Dammit, Rhona! How did my mother discover us? *Please* tell me you are not with child."

He needs to hear the words, Rhona. Tell him. Rhona shook her head, tears suddenly flowing down her face. "I can't," she sobbed. "I can't tell you I'm not. I had to tell her what happened—why me flow never came. I had to tell her whose child I carry." Curling herself into a ball, she rocked herself in a failed attempt to calm her nerves. "She promised she wouldn't say a word, but at a price."

"I can get you a pardon," argued the prince. "Rhona, do you understand how freeing this is? I now have a reason to permanently revoke my betrothal to Siobhan!" Alsantör grabbed her face and stared deep into her sad gaze. "Let me talk to my mother. I can free you from your duties as handmaiden and marry you instead. If this be a son, I can even make him my heir." Fear had apparently given way to joy—according to the ignorant grin across his face, that is.

"I'm not keeping it," Rhona blurted. "I can't. There's far too much at stake."

"Of course you can keep it, silly. This is your chance to—"

"*Tör!*" Rhona ripped her face away from the prince's grip, her tears glistening as they trickled down her cheeks. "Ye're going to start a bloody war if ye do this. I'm half *Taela*, remember?"

Alsantör took a sharp breath at her words, and his smile all but disappeared. His silence, however, was more telling than any words he could have said in that moment.

"If ye're gonna break yer betrothal," Rhona continued, "don't do it with a crimson-blooded heir. I couldn't bear being the cause of the next war."

"This would be a fulfilment of that treaty, Rhona," argued the prince. "Don't you see what a child of Taela blood would do for peace? And if that starts a 'war' with the Karthi, so be it." He tugged her close to wrap her in a desperate embrace and whispered, "I would start a *thousand* wars if it meant I could be with you forever."

Oh, darling. If only ye knew the truth of me duties here.

39

SOLSTICE OF WINTER

*C*hainless's inn was busier than the norm. A frigid storm had announced the coming of winter, and the whole of the town had gathered inside the tavern for a warm hearth and a hot meal. Bayani sat next to the fire, drinking his usual warm rum with coconut milk. Shivering, he couldn't hear the being who approached him from behind, until it spoke.

"Something is bothering you, sañero. What is it?"

Bayani groaned. *Why, Yusa? Why you still torture me with this kapiret-liho and his prying?* Glaring over his shoulder, he said, "Why you care?"

Sólan snorted at his ferocity. "Back to your chipper self, I see." He slipped into a chair across from the smuggler and stared chasms of bright amber into him. "I never know which version of Bayani Lin I will receive when you speak. Which one is it today?"

The one that want to be alone. Bayani looked to the ceiling, grimacing. "Yusa, save me from this tulalo," he whispered.

A soft snort from Sólan's mouth snapped his attention back to his loathsome captain.

"What?"

"That hurts. I am no idiot."

"What? I thought you no speak Bankun?"

"Please. Look at the man I have been fucking for the last ten years—who I have been surrounded by for that time. One does not stay ignorant of such tongue after so long an immersion." The blue and silver specks in Sólan's eyes sparkled with his mischievous grin. "And now, I know how to insult you in four tongues."

Bayani lowered his forehead into his hand. "Pantot. You act like child sometimes." Without warning, two pints of frothy ale thumped onto the table between them.

"What this is? I no pay for these." Bayani looked up at a scowling Rasheed.

"No. But he did." The barkeep motioned to Sólan with a snarl before sulking off. Sólan merely smirked at his back.

"He really no like you," said Bayani. "Why? What up his ass?"

"Ha! Rasheed is a trained and seasoned Shinjai from ancient Garmath. You should never insult him like that."

"Shin—what?"

Sólan chuckled. "Shinjai. The champion of the Garmathian Empire. A prince, of sorts, but also the head of their military. The empire fell during the Great War when the royal family was slaughtered like cattle."

Bayani's eye widened. "Rasheed is prince of Garmath? So, that make Chainless—"

"Yes. Yes, it does." Sólan leaned forward, lifting a finger to his lips. "They are the last of their line and in hiding for a reason. By the looks of their scars, they have already died once."

"Ano? What?" Bayani felt his jaw hanging open like Kalasin's ravaged skull. Despite his best efforts, he couldn't close it.

Sólan chuckled. "We are all given two chances at this life. The one we are born with and the one returned to us by the Gods. Of course, only through those who wield The Light."

"I no can tell if you lying again."

"I suppose it matters not," said Sólan, smirking. "There is no one left in these lands who can command such power. That *thing* that took your eye and hand—"

Pontianak, tulalo.

"—was a mere annoyance compared to the abomination that The Dark would bring back from the dead."

"You are here to tell me fantasy stories? Or something else? Because I no want to hear anything from you right now."

That damned Áfgaliard looked offended, but Bayani knew better. If he truly was offended, he would again be without another body part of some kind.

Suddenly, Sólan plopped something heavy onto the table between them. Bayani jumped, nigh tipping over his chair. He cursed, having fully expected to lose his other hand, an ear, or, perhaps, a toe. His heart rate settled, and he stared at the odd-shaped package in front of him.

"What this is?" he asked, reaching tentatively across the table with his stump. He nudged the package but flinched at the weight.

"'Tis a gift." A warm smile stretched across Sólan's face, which only heightened Bayani's anxiety. "In Áfgal, we celebrate the Solístia de Énvrino as a 'thank you' to the Gods for a successful harvest season—and as a plea for protection through the winter. We give gifts, sing songs, drink hot, spiced wine ..." His gaze drifted to faraway places for a moment, leaving Bayani with far more questions than he'd care to admit.

"I no celebrate pagan 'holy' days, Sólan. Hard to believe, but I still follow Yusa and His Words of the Sun." Bayani crossed his arms with flared nostrils. "We no give gifts, especially during Misó's season of darkness—winter."

Grumbling, Sólan scrunched his nose. "I am merely trying to be kind to you. Take this as a ... eh ... a thank you for saving my life back in Bansungei." He squirmed in his seat, refusing to look Bayani in his eye. "And"—he stopped, cleared his throat, and swallowed.

"And?"

"And ... as an apology for nearly killing you alongside Kalasin those ten years ago."

Bayani's mouth briefly fell open again. "What wrong? Were you poison by Taela?"

"Ha!" Sólan's laughter sang through the tavern like a mother singing lullabies to her child.

The smuggler frowned, for there truly was something wrong with him. He was never so happy—unless he was skinning someone alive. "What really is this, Sólan? Why you give gift to me?"

Wiping the happy tears from his eyes, Sólan's chuckling slowed to a mild wheeze before he spoke. "Look, we began our friendship poorly, but we have been through enough. Between our slave raid, Tirsen's extremism, that Ponti … thing—"

"Pontianak."

"—and Kalasin, I think we have come a long way—and that was merely our first year together. This may surprise you, sañero, but I have learned to enjoy your company." Sólan pushed the gift closer to Bayani. "Here, open it. Please?"

Bayani rolled his eye, grumbling as he pulled the loose strand of twine to untie the burlap that covered it. A sudden lump formed in his throat, hitching his breath. "What this is?" he whispered. He held up what looked like an eyepatch—wait, it *was* an eyepatch! The engraved leather was polished on one side and padded with the softest cotton he'd ever felt on the other. And the straps? Intricately braided leather, one end ending with a buckle and the other riveted to keep from fraying.

Yet it wasn't the quality of the build that made Bayani's tears threaten to flow. Nay, 'twas the perfection of the ten-pointed sun carved onto the patch's front, a beautiful rendition that made the symbol of Yusa in the high temple look simple.

"Sólan, I …" He cleared his throat. "I no know what to say. Thank you."

His smile warmer than the crackling fire, Sólan took the patch from Bayani's hand and wrapped it around his head, buckling it snug against the fleshy socket. "There. You no longer look like a damned beggar. And thank me not. Besides, 'twas Dakil was who ordered it from the tanner down the way."

Bayani's cheeks reddened with his sheepish grin. "Why you do this for me? You also give gift to the rest of crew?"

Sólan lazily flicked his wrist as he returned to his seat. "I gave them larger shares of gold from this last drop. I need not be brothers with every man on this ship."

Brothers? Why? You say youself you hate me. Bayani fidgeted with his stump, waxy with tough scar tissue.

Seeming to read his thoughts, Sólan continued. "Tíal. Brothers. I have no family left, sañero, so I must make one. Just ..." He shuddered. "Not with children. I would make a terrible father."

Bayani snorted. "We finally agree on something."

"Ha!" Sólan's eyes lit up once more, their colourful specks dancing in the hearth's flickering light.

It was a strange thing, this side of the halfbreed. Was Yusa responsible? Perhaps the baptism really did change Sólan. Or, even better, perhaps he'd repented for his disgusting crime of impurity with Dakil. The latter was unlikely, though. After all, the gift was a joint effort.

"There is another piece, Bayani. The one from me." Excitement blanketed Sólan's face as he nudged the half-open package forward. "I had to borrow a forge to make it."

Make? Bayani dug into the burlap. If he thought his breath was difficult to catch with Dakil's gift, his lungs would surely collapse at the sight before him. It was a hook, built to slip over his stump and buckle around his forearm, forged from the finest of metals the eastern lands had ever known: Casacan water-steel. That wasn't all, however. A sliding lever at the top of his arm revealed a double-edged blade nigh a cubit in length.

Yusa's grace, it was too much. Bayani burst into tears, his thoughts racing with questions, gratitude, and curses. *Damn this confusing pagan!* Perhaps his false gods taught love after all. Or, perhaps, the grace of Yusa finally penetrated his soul, thawing his icy heart into a flaming beacon of kindness and faith.

A soft hand on Bayani's shoulder brought him to the present. He stared into Sólan's warm grin, though it wasn't his hand that touched him. Bayani wiped his eye and peeked over his shoulder to see Dakil. *Oh Yusa, how you bless me with these friends.*

"Happy Solístia de Énvrino, binyego. May Yusa bless and protect you in this coming season of Misó," said Dakil. He leaned over and kissed the top of Bayani's head, prompting further tears and heavier sobs.

I never feel love like this with Kadek. Even when he found God, I never feel this. Bayani opened his mouth to thank the men beside him, but his voice caught on the lump in his throat. "O how blessed am I that Yusa gives me these brothers in Him." Oh, how the words of Great Prophet ring true.

Dakil brushed his fingertips across Sólan's neck and whispered something Bayani couldn't hear. Not that he wanted to hear. Who knew what sins they spoke of in that moment?

A seductive smile crept across Sólan's face as his gaze followed his lover to the tavern's exit. Finishing the last of his pint with a dramatic gulp and a tilt of the head, he stood and winked.

"Apologies for my prompt departure, amógo. I have an appointment of special importance."

Bayani rolled his eye. *I guess Yusa need more time for them to repent some immoral ways.*

SÓLAN FOLLOWED DAKIL WITH BATED BREATH. THE "HIDDEN BEACH" was far enough from the village to be secluded from prying eyes and ears, yet close enough for Sólan's keen hearing to listen for trouble. Even in his happiest moments, he could never fully relax. But, Gods, did Dakil's presence smooth the ragged edges of his worry.

The northeastern locale of the beach both sheltered it from the island's winter winds and provided the most spectacular views of the stark white crags along the southern coast of Orovín.

Kicking off his boots once they reached the coarse sand, Sólan inhaled deeply to savour the scent of saltwater and the glowing purple blossoms littering the surrounding cliffs. He picked one of the largest of the star-shaped flowers and brought it even closer to his nose, its bright glow fading to a deep indigo as the life faded from its petals.

"Gods, Dakil. I have not had the pleasure of salt lilies since my last coastal raid seventy years ago. They grow by the thousands on the shores of the Dragon's Horn." *And their scent is nearly as intoxicating as yours, mólamí.*

Dakil scoffed. "Flowers? Really? This Solístia de Énvrino messes with your head, mintaki. Makes you different—like a woman with your interests."

I refuse to take your words as insulting. Sólan tossed the flower to the ground with a playful snarl. "And what the hell is wrong with that? If only you knew their true strength. The way they carry and bring life into this world. Their perseverance in the face of what we men do to them. Perhaps your temple merely oppresses them because they are afraid." *Surely, they would have learned to fear Tala and Elena Bonlak of Bansungei, should they have ...* The sting of guilt flashed through his chest at the thought. *Ten years, and I still ache for that family. Why?*

Nose twitching, Dakil unsheathed his rapier and twirled it as if in challenge. "I never said you were *weak* for it. Just ... different."

Sólan's knees threatened to buckle at the embers smouldering in his lover's russet eyes, and he could feel his manhood beginning to swell. *O Halaña, how you have blessed me with this man.* He loosened his hatchet from its holster with a mischievous grin. "A challenge, aeh? You seduce me, mólamí."

"Of course, I do, mintaki. How else can I fuck you here?"

Sólan licked his lips. *Gods, do I love you.*

Without warning, Dakil lunged the tip of his blade to his lover's face. Sólan, however, dodged and parried with ease. "You always begin these spars with the same move. If it killed me not when we met, 'twill not kill me now."

"Ha! That's the idea, my love. I don't want to kill you. And this is the only way cavalry guards begin their duels."

Sólan let loose a deep growl of lust through his chest. "Nor I, you." He flinched once, twice ... *thrice,* all the while circling Dakil like a predator ready to pounce. Dakil, however, was undeterred. "Ay, mólamí, you are learning."

"More than you, it seems."

¿Mondé? What can you mean by—

A sharp, burning pain to his wrist made his hand go flaccid. He dropped his weapon, stunned. *What?*

"You keep losing your weapon, mintaki. You need to hold it tighter," said Dakil, snickering.

Sólan grunted. "'Tis not what you said last night." He dodged the swordsman's next two moves, somersaulting behind him and grasping his hatchet with his other hand. He jumped to his feet, ready to touch the back of Dakil's neck with his edge when—

"Dead."

Sólan gulped. The tip of Dakil's rapier hovered over his trachea mere millimetres from slicing into its flesh. He groaned, knees growing weak again. He reached up to caress his lover's jaw, flicking his blade away. "You are, no doubt, the most successful at that," he whispered seductively.

Dakil's breath quickened, and he lowered his rapier with a lustful sigh. "At what?"

"Finishing me."

Dakil fell into Sólan's arms and kissed him. The two quickly dropped their weapons, their pants, and their plans for further sparring. Spinning into the sand, they made love, embracing the crisp winter air and sweet aromas of the lilies surrounding them.

40

ROMAN

"Where you have been?" hissed Bayani. "We have problem."

"What kind of problem?" Sólan's ears twitched at the man's tone. He flitted his gaze around the half-empty tavern, searching for anything that may be amiss. There were tradesmen making deals in the southern corner of the room. Nothing new there. The hearth was in near desperate need of more logs—still naught of worry. Along the northern wall, all he saw was the exchange of coin for Taela and Orovite drugs, a blacksmith collecting his dues for his work, a tanner receiving the deed for new skins, a cavalry guardsman at the bar— He froze. *A cavalry guardsman! Here?*

"Medría. Bayani, I was never here." Sólan whispered, turning to leave the way he came but was stopped by a Nethuanian man in armour of black iron and leather. He forced a smile and nodded. "Pardon me, sañero. I—"

"Have questions to answer for me."

Sólan rolled his eyes and turned to face a bronze-armoured man behind him. A smug, toothy grin stretched across the guard's face, wrinkling in the corners of his monolid eyes. The man stood nearly as tall as Sólan, lifting his chin as though superior to all in the building. He held his horned and crested helmet in one hand and rested the other on the hilt of his decorated rapier.

Pretentious bastard. You must be this 'Roman' I have heard so much about.

"I was not speaking to you, pundijo. Now, if you will excuse me." Sólan bared his fangs and pushed his way toward the exit.

"Ah, perhaps Kalasin was wrong, then, when he described the man who killed Kadek. A shame he met such a violent end, that Kalasin. The man who murdered him must be quite brutal."

Sólan stopped in the doorway and grimaced. *You fucking piezo de—*

"I thought, perhaps, his slave could give me some answers."

Slave? Is that what you think of us who are of mixed blood? That all of us are mere slaves? Sólan's knuckles blanched at the force of his clenched fist. Gritting his teeth, he half-whispered over his shoulder, "I am a slave of no one." He turned, his nose scrunched into a snarl. Heat pulsed through his eyes as The Dark bubbled to the surface. By the look on Roman's face, he gathered that his eyes must be glowing green again.

Roman grinned again, and Sólan wished for nothing more than to punch out his teeth.

"I am looking for a man who claims the name 'Dakil Papuan.' He's wanted for the murder of my cavalry guard, Kalasin Yu—my second in command over Tianag."

"Fascinating," said Sólan with a strained smile. "I am afraid, however, I am unfamiliar with the name 'Dakil Papuan.' Perhaps you have me confused with someone else." He turned to leave once again but was stopped by a hard hand on his shoulder.

"Please, tual. Join me for a drink. Perhaps you can still help me in my search."

Sólan swallowed the curses that threatened to escape his lips. He would do anything to defend his lover, even deny his existence to that putrid demon who thought himself a man. With clenched teeth and a furrowed brow, he led Roman to his favourite corner of the inn. It was secluded enough that no one could spy, yet open enough that he could see the comings and goings of all in the room.

Rasheed followed close behind with two brimming pints of ale. They splashed onto the table's polished wood as he set them down.

Roman handed two coppers to the barkeep before averting his attention back to Sólan. "Well, then. I suppose I owe you an apology after our mix-up. What's your name, tual?"

"Montrél de Maseño. And apology accepted—for the moment." Sólan never broke his gaze on Roman as he took a deep draught of his ale. "Tell me, how long ago was this murder of—what was his name again? Kalasin?"

"Ten years."

"Ha!" Ale spilled out of Sólan's nose with his sudden laughter. "Ten years and you still have not found the man you search for? Are you certain he is even *alive*, sañero?"

Chuckling along with him, Roman took a small sip of his own drink before grasping Sólan's wrist with a force that felt it might crack the bone.

A tingling pain shot through Sólan's hands as Roman's tightening fist forced his grip to go slack. "What the f—"

"You are a terrible liar, *Moon-treel*. Or should I say, 'Grim'?" Roman sneered. "I was there, kapiret-liho. Your baptism and wedding in Yusa's Great Temple, when you married that young girl you raped. She would be twenty years old today—likely with several sons—if not for you."

Sólan simmered at the high guard's irritating butchering of his late brother's name. Memories flashing behind his eyes, panic nigh overtook him. *Those sad, rounded eyes that glared with undeniable malice. The bronze-armoured guard with the face of a demonic lizard.*

"Fuck," he whispered. With a sudden ferocity, he spat into Roman's face and growled. "I never touched that child, putathóta. I was forced by your 'god' to—what did her father call it—atone for the sins of the monsters I killed. Must I be punished for my deeds in her honour?" Sólan loosened his hatchet from its holster with his free hand. The conversation with the high guard was getting dangerous, and he could see the strange twinkle of victory in his opponent's eyes.

"Murder for a rape. There is no honour in such crimes, even if your false gods say otherwise. But that is not the purpose of my visit, Grim. I still search for the deserter, Papuan." A smile inched its way across Roman's face. "He and Kalasin were charged with flushing out the smugglers of Oleg Kinev—that Orovite wretch who sells Misó's grass and oil to the sacred people of Yusa—until Kadek the Vile seduced Dakil to the ways of Misó and damned his soul to Yirno. To think he also murdered his brother in arms? Abominable."

"Ho'su," said a silky voice behind Roman.

Roman snarled. "Papuan." Gripping his rapier, he spun to meet the tip of a similar weapon at his throat.

There was something irritatingly familiar about Roman's features, Sólan realised, as Roman stood face-to-face with Dakil. The streaks of ashy grey in his eyes, the long braid that ended at his tailbone ...

"I never understood why you kept your *mother's* family name," said Roman. "You should've been proud to be a Ho'su."

Oh Gods! Sólan's face burned with the same rage he always felt when betrayed. Swallowing his outbursts, he clenched his jaw to keep it from falling open. "Quite the doting *father* you are, searching for your son only to kill him based on lies. Ha! You must have learned such a trick by the duke of Karthénos."

"It's no lie, Montrél," said Roman's companion. "Dakil Ho'su deserted the temple as a boy. He murdered countless cavalry guards under the direction of the Vile, and now has murdered Kalasin Yu."

Sólan flinched. He'd forgotten the man was still there—the man who'd obviously failed to hear the beginning of the unfortunate conversation. "I doubt not that he has killed many men of your god. However, I *know* he is not the one who—"

"I'm done talking to you, kapiret-liho. I have found my man," said Roman, never breaking his gaze with Dakil.

His son. Gods, the one time I finally learn to trust someone—to love someone—and he lies to me for ten fucking years! How could I have been so foolish? Why did I allow myself to be so naïve to fall in love with a man like him? Sólan shook the malicious thoughts from his head. "Tíal, you have found your man, but he is not the man who killed your precious Kalasin."

He could nigh hear the roll in Roman's eyes as he turned to face him once again. "And how would you know who did?"

"*I* killed Kalasin, indionta. I am Sólan the fucking *Grim*, remember? And I enjoyed every moment of his tortured suffering." Sólan gripped his hatchet tighter, baring his fangs as he rose from his chair. "Give me one reason, cabróde. *One* reason why I should not skin you alive as I did that Tianag spy."

"You would start a war with Nethuania," said Roman, shrugging. His companion grunted in agreement. "I think that should be reason enough."

Sólan and Dakil both snickered. Leaning forward, Sólan brought his face close to Roman's and inhaled. "Your face hides it well, Ho'su, but I know the scent of fear better than anyone. Try again."

"You wouldn't dare," said Roman.

"I would. And, as with Kalasin, I would enjoy every moment of your pain."

"Dakil," whispered Roman. "Don't listen to this black-blooded demon of Misó. Come home … *please*. Come home and be Ho'su once more. I will make this right, my son. I swear by the Book of the Sun and God himself, I will make this right."

"You made it clear to me as a boy that I'm *not* your son. Why would I help you now? Because you fear death?" Dakil rested the tip of his blade at the base of Roman's skull. "I am a Papuan, like my mother and her father before her. You are no more my father than Yusa is real. If he is, why are you so afraid of entering Linget?"

Roman gulped, panicked eyes staring into Sólan's at his son's words. "You cannot mean that, Dakil. Please. You will be forgiven of all, as you were seduced by the Vile and acted not of your own will."

"Perhaps I didn't, then." Dakil tightened his grip on his weapon to stay the shaking in his hands. "But I do now. And I don't take kindly to those who threaten my lovers. May Javiento and Martím have mercy on your soul."

The sting of betrayal faded with the sudden swell of pride in Sólan's chest. Heart skipping, he stifled his desire to pull Dakil into his arms and fuck him right there, in front of his father, for the world to see their love. Their commitment. *Gods, how could I have doubted you?*

The sound of an unsheathed dagger snapped through the tavern. Sólan flinched at the sight of Roman's companion holding his thin blade against Dakil's throat. "You do this, and you die, tiksal. The lines of both Ho'su and Papuan will die with you."

Panic shot through Sólan. Roman had gained a surprise upper hand. *Medría.* Sólan's thoughts froze. *Shit, shit, shit.* He scrambled for words, ideas, anything that would save his lover from the maiming injury that would certainly kill him.

"I have a deal," he heard himself say, though the words didn't hit him until after several agonising breaths. All eyes now on him, he cast about his empty mind for a follow-up. "I ... aeh."

The look in Dakil's eyes asked him, "What are you doing?"

Saving your fucking life, mólamí. That is what I am doing! Still fumbling for an idea, Sólan merely started talking. "I noticed that many of your lesser temples in Bansungei have fallen into disrepair. The slums? Riddled with disease, starvation, and death. Much of your infrastructure is crumbling into the Southern Sea, and even your most wealthy citizens struggle to traverse the disintegrating cobblestone streets."

"Your point?" said Roman. Clearly, he was uninterested in useless babble from a foreigner of such dark repute.

Sólan flashed a desperate look of help toward Dakil. "You have a problem with gold ... or lack thereof."

"Five percent," said Dakil, suddenly.

Fiver percent? Five percent of what?

"Five percent of our profit from Oleg's business," Dakil continued, "and we can rebuild Bansungei."

Roman turned to face his son once again. "Do you take me for a fool, *deserter?*"

Ah. No longer his son, I see. 'Tis only when convenient for him. Sólan cleared his throat. "Would you rather we kill you? If so, I would be happy to oblige." He flashed a mischievous grin at the man still holding his blade to Dakil's throat. Turning his attention to Roman, he said, "I took you for a man who serves your 'god.' Is kindness not one of your ten rays of sunshine—or something idiotic like that?"

"Hollow words from a nonbeliever," said Roman.

"This is a generous offer, sañero. I suggest you take it. Five percent—and we allow you to sail back to Bansungei alive," said Sólan.

Dakil nodded firmly in agreement. There was nothing to break their resolves in that moment, and Sólan's heart beat wildly.

Roman, however, scowled. "I want ten percent and for you to leave Bansungei after it has been rebuilt."

"Seven percent, and we stay," said Dakil, arms crossed. "Or else we reveal to the temple *how* you got the gold to improve our people."

"Tsst." Roman's nose scrunched as he flitted his gaze between the lovers.

Do not make me kill you, sañero. Your son would never forgive me. Hands shaking, heart thumping, Sólan's thoughts spiralled as he struggled to maintain his menacing façade.

"Fine," said Roman, grimacing. "Seven percent. But know this, Dakil. My offer of returning to the Ho'su family is revoked."

"It was a shit family, anyway," grumbled Dakil.

Roman's companion dropped the blade from Dakil's throat and slipped it back into its sheath. "This is a mistake, Roman."

After taking a deep breath, Roman held out a stiff hand to Sólan.

"No more a mistake than coming here for the purpose of murdering the man I love," said Sólan. Grasping Roman's wrist to seal the pact, he yanked him close enough to whisper into his ear. "If you betray us, I will hunt you down to the edges of this world *and* the next. Even your god will be unable to save you from my wrath, for there is nothing in this world more dangerous than the Grim when scorned. Nod if you understand."

Trembling, Roman's forehead was slick with cold sweat as he nodded with fervour and released his grip from Sólan's forearm. "Lubiyo, pay the dark-skinned man. We leave tomorrow."

Orc, pundijo. He is an orc—and 'tis Alira you must pay, as she owns this place.

Roman's nose twitched before giving his parting words to Dakil. "If you fail on your payments, consider your life forfeit. I can still *make* a new son." He spun on his heel and marched out of the inn, his companion trailing close behind.

"I'm surprised you haven't yet," spat Dakil.

Sólan sighed, slumping his shoulders as the tension momentarily released from the tavern's corner, until a new wave of distrust and anger swept over him. With the threat to his lover's life gone, the threat to his own sanity returned. Baring his fangs, he glared at Dakil with renewed malice. "Find yourself a new room tonight. I will not share a bed with a traitor."

"Traitor?"

The pain in Dakil's voice rang clearer than a temple's bells, yet Sólan refused to look him in the eye. He didn't want to kill the man he thought he loved. *Gods,* did he wish 'twas a mere nightmare! But the throbbing pain in his chest and head were enough to remind him it was his dreadful reality.

I trusted you, Dakil. I gave you my heart, and you have shattered it beyond repair. Did I not tell you 'twas a brittle thing? Did I fail to say to take care of it? Dakil Ho'su ... son of the gods-damned head of the cavalry guard—the highest nobility in that fucking place. Perhaps I should have killed you those ten years ago after all.

Tears streamed down his face as he hurried up the steps toward his room. *Will I ever love again?*

DAKIL SAT ON THE END OF BAYANI'S RICKETY BED, NUMBLY STARING OUT the western-facing window as he had for most of the afternoon and evening. No amount of rum, brandy, nor ale would curb the aching pain tearing through his chest, cutting him deeper than the lowest trench of the Dragon Sea.

Bayani paced while fidgeting with his hook. "I no understand, Dakil. Why he do that? You no do anything to him to make him so angry."

Swallowing a heavy sob, Dakil broke his gaze with the orange clouds outside. "I lied to him," he said, yet the tears still refused to fall. "I failed to tell him about Roman when—"

"Kilakahon! He no ask who you papa was! Why you share that with him if he no ask?"

"We claimed each other, Bayani! Do you know what that means in Áfgal? We are husbands, and I kept this a secret from him. My husband, Bayani! He doesn't have a family anymore, and that is the most precious thing to him. And I *lied* to him. I told him my father was dead!"

A cold gust of wind whistled through cracks in the window's frame as though taunting Dakil's pain. *Yusa's grace, I should never have let him take me. Is this how the Gods treat love? Is Halaña truly so vile? How could I ever doubt the Book of the Sun? I should have gone home with my father when I could. Now, I have no one.*

"Dakil," said Bayani. "I no want to be harsh, but ... perhaps this Yusa's way to tell you of you sins. Two men you lay with, and both men break you. Maybe—"

A swift punch in the nose shut him up with a yelp.

"Nipantot ki, Bayani! Stop talking to me about sin as though you never tried to steal someone else's wife!" Dakil bared his teeth, paying no mind to the throbbing pain in his hand nor the blood that now oozed from Bayani's nostrils. He'd broken the younger man's nose, no doubt, but he didn't care. The only thing he could think about was Sólan. Sólan and the gaping hole he'd left in his heart. *I need to make this right.* Forcing a calming breath, he stood with a grimace.

"Where you are going?" said Bayani. "You know better than me how he dangerous when angry like this."

"Ta, Bayani. Maybe he'll simply kill me and rid me of this fucking heartache. I have nothing left to lose. Does that make me stupid? Or does that make me dangerous as well?" Dakil's stomach heaved as another sob threatened to escape, but that one he swallowed as well.

Bayani snatched Dakil's shoulder with his hand and turned him around. "Look at me, Dakil. He no will kill you. He will take you sword hand—maybe even you eyes—but it will be something that you love."

A single tear finally escaped Dakil's eyes and meandered down his cheek and onto his jaw, where it sat in waiting for either a wipe or enough time to evaporate from existence. "He already has my heart, Bayani. I have nothing left for him to take." He shrugged off the man's hand and barrelled toward the door. Before he could open it, however, it swung open and slammed against the wall.

Before he realised what was happening, Dakil had been scooped up into Rasheed's arms and bombarded with passionate kisses.

"I can't do this anymore," said Rasheed, tangling his hand in Dakil's hair. "I can't—"

"What are you *doing*!" Dakil squirmed out of Rasheed's embrace and kneed him in his erect manhood. The orc fell to the ground with a wheeze. "You had your chance ten fucking years ago, so kilak ng ki! I'm a claimed man now."

"You sure about that?" said Rasheed. "I heard him call you a traitor."

"You sleep wit' Rasheed too?" Bayani smacked his own forehead. "You have *ever* not sin?"

"Fuck off, Bayani!" Dakil and Rasheed both snarled in unison.

Dakil turned back to the orc, glaring. "My heart is Sólan's and Sólan's alone. Get out of my way, Rasheed. I need to talk to my *husband*." Without another word, he shouldered past his former lover. No, not a lover—just the man he used to fuck when he felt lonely. The man for whom he'd never felt anything besides lust. *I'm not sorry Rasheed. And I never will be.* He wiped the remnants of that single tear from his chin as he stomped to his husband's room. Lifting his hand to knock, he heard the thing he feared most: Chainless's voice.

41

TREASON

$\mathcal{A}$lsantör groaned, shifting his hips this way and that as Ellie breathed into his ear. Nibbling his neck, she stroked him fast, then slowly. He knew she was trying her best to keep him hard, but he just. Couldn't. Focus.

"What's wrong, Tör?" She let go of his erection—if one could even call it that—and stared at him with her doe-eyes burning in concern. "I know y'r fake moans when I hear ehm." Her mousy voice dipped in pitch, as though her seductive façade was wavering.

Dammit, Ellie. Just take my gold and fuck me, will you? Alsantör rolled his eyes. "Nothing's wrong, just ... too much wine, I suppose."

"Rubbish. Ya don't stink enough o' that shite." Ellie stood, her loose curls spiralling their way down to her hips and covering just enough of her freckled skin to tempt any man's imagination. When Alsantör shook his head, she added, "Perhaps ya need more? Or do ya want meh to fetch the new garl? She's a Karthi of white hair 'nd skin, just like y'r intended bride." Padding over to her table of cleansing necessities, she reached for her revealing gown.

"If I wanted a woman of fair hair and freckle-free skin, I would've asked for one." Alsantör reached out and softly and touched Ellie's elbow. "Besides, you know me better than any other worker in this place. I need something familiar right now."

Ellie snickered. "Careful now, y'r grace, 'r the whole of the forest'll believe y've fallen f'r a whore."

"Ha! That'd be rich." *But not entirely untrue. Is that not what the handmaiden is, after all? The private whore of the queen?* The prince shuddered at the thought. *Of all the women in the gnomes-damned kingdom ... Naoise was right.*

"Whores have feelings too, ya know. And I think you might've bruised mine," said Ellie, ripping Alsantör from his thoughts and back into the brothel's room. She puckered her bottom lip with a fake pout before breaking into a giggle. "What's 'er name, then? Surely, it's not *Siobhan O'Jannon*."

"Whose name?"

"The garl you've been pining for f'r the last two hundred fookin' years, Tör! Who else?"

The prince sucked his teeth. "I don't know of whom you speak, Ellie. Have I not been your most ... eh ... *loyal* client?"

Ellie inched her way closer to her table, placing a hand on her gown with a smirk. "Ya dodge the hard questions with ease, y'r grace. But that woen't make meh believe y're not in love with another."

I swear, you could've been a lady of my father's court rather than a whore. You have the wit for it, and you know I'd be lying to myself to say that a political marriage to you would disappoint me. Alsantör knew better than to believe his thoughts, of course. Ellie would never wish to be a member of the court. Besides, she was one of the many elf women who'd rather fuck than bear children. She'd removed her womb at will, and whether she'd done so for her career or in a silent rebellion against the king's ideals, he couldn't guess. It mattered not to him, and he knew she'd never tell.

"Come back to bed, Ellie. I paid for the whole night with you." He winced at his own tone. *I'm not my father. I'm not my father. I'm not—*

"Y'r gold's in my reach, y'r grace," she said through a sudden hiss. "I can return it 'nd get someone who's willing to fook meh with a *real* cock."

Alsantör flinched again at that.

"Oh, did I bruise ya?" Ellie smiled, rubbing the tip of her tongue against a fang. "Tit f'r tat, Tör. Y're within my borders, here."

"A deep cut, actually." The prince found himself hardening at the woman's insults. 'Twas a peculiar thing, his cock. Undoubtedly, that was precisely why he came to the Wand: to escape the kiss-arses of Prastömin. *Eil, that treaty's a success. But at what cost? I need some gnomes-damned conflict.*

Ellie's mouth curled into a coy smile. "There 'e is." The triumph in her voice was unmistakable.

Seeing her eyes twinkling in lust, Alsantör's breath soon shallowed with anticipation. His cock was standing straight up like a proud knight after a conquest. He licked his lips as she clambered, still naked, onto his lap. He buried his face into her bosom, teasing her nipple with his tongue. She shuddered atop him as his erection gracefully slipped into her.

Pressure building, he panted into her chest. Her freckled skin moistened and dripped from the heat of his breath. "Gnomes," he whispered at his peak. "*Wizards, Rhona!*" He burst, spilling himself inside her with a pathetic whimper.

Ellie, of course, giggled. "Ya couldn't keep a secret even if y'r head was at risk of falling off your damned shoulders." She sprang to her feet and removed the sheep's bladder pouch from between her legs, its contents splattering on the floor.

Alsantör cringed at the noise. *I didn't need to see that. You're not very graceful with the cleanup, are you?* Her words only hit him a moment later. "What do you mean by 'my secrets'?"

"Please, Tör. I already knew about you 'nd Rhona. I've known f'r ten bloody years. But you could at least be subtle about it. Callin' her name out while fucking meh 'nd all."

Káil. Did I really? I hadn't meant to be speak her name. The prince opened his mouth to respond but was interrupted by a sharp knock. Both elves stiffened. *Shite.* He slipped into his loose trousers and padded over, opening the cedar slab just a crack.

Heavy dread washed all feeling from Alsantör's face at the sight of the well-armoured knight. "What's wrong, Faerin?"

Naoise chewed on his bottom lip as he read—and reread—the pigeon's message scroll. *Can't even wait ten fookin' years or write the damned thing himself, the bastar'.* A pair of heavy footsteps echoed through the main hall, though the noise did little to distract the duke from his ruminations.

"What happened, Neesh?" Alsantör's voice was small compared to the weight of the scroll's contents. "You *know* Faerin hates coming to the Wand."

Faerin merely grunted in agreement.

Naoise flicked the message down the table as though he were flicking a fly off his meal. "Best ya stop y'r nights with Ellie, y'r grace. Our brides're on their way down." *Though I don't think I'd be opposed to seeing Moira again. What's the risk of a summer holiday up north?* The intrusive thought made him frown. *Bloody hell, look at me. Born a Veer, raised a Prasti, now longing to be a Karthi. The Wizards're cruel sometimes, aren't they?*

"What!" The prince grasped his hair with both his fists and sputtered. "The fuck is that mad bastard thinking? Does he have the fucking memory of a gnomes-damned oddling?"

Faerin snatched the letter and scanned it with a frown. "Th-this is a wo-woman's writing," he said flatly. "Ya sure it's n-not f-f-forged?"

"That seal look forged to you?" Naoise slumped his head onto his palms. "Fookin' 'ell. To think we actually believed him when he'd signed the damned thing." Alsantör sucked his teeth, the noise stabbing Naoise's eardrums like hot needles. *You and y'r mother both.*

"I'll rally an-an-an escort. C-c-can't have the future princess and-ehm-duchess of the f-f-forest travelling alone, can we?"

Wizards bless ya, Faerin. Will ya lend me y'r calm?

"I'll write to Baforeis's baron. Perhaps we can turn them back at the border," said Alsantör, voice shaking. "Faerin, I'll need you to convince him that despite Jannon's push, we can't be the ones breaking the treaty. Prastömin's the one who *wrote* the bloody thing."

Naoise bit his lip again. "And, if they refuse, make sure they get here safely. We'll house them as long as needed to get them back to their homes unwed." He stifled a grimace at the word. *"Unwed." I'd hate to be so brash, but I hope Moira'd understand—better than 'er sister, anyway. Wizards, what has that woman made me?*

"Eil, your-your grace. M-m'laird," said Faerin, nodding to each of his superiors. He frowned, eyes flitting around the room in what looked like deep thought. "Wh-what if this whole thing's a-a-a-a ruse?"

"Let me see that scroll again." Naoise flinched at the sharp whistle of Alsantör still sucking on his teeth. "F'r fook's sake, Tör! Stop doing that stupid *thing* with y'r mouth, will ya?"

A quiet snort escaped Faerin's nose, his face turning bright red as he swallowed his giggles. Alsantör, however, looked far from amused. "I'm surprised you still have a fucking lip, Neesh. And you, Faerin? You're apt to bite your bloody tongue off."

Faerin and Alsantör both howled in sudden laughter. Despite his foul mood, Naoise joined in with a soft chuckle. "Fine, fine. Faerin, I really need to see that scroll." He snatched the paper and looked it over once again. *It's not Saoirse's hand. Who's else? Any o' Jannon's senators, of course, or even a scribe.* He carefully rubbed the back of the parchment, feeling for anything. *Fookin' 'ell. Faerin's right.*

Apparently, Naoise's face showed his surprise, as the prince took in a sharp breath. "Is it forged, Neesh? Is Jannon even aware of this?"

With a trembling hand, the duke dropped the scroll onto the cold cedar table. "Faerin," he whispered. "You cannot allow those women to cross that northern border, understood? 'Nd take a dozen upper knights with ya. They're walkin' into a trap."

4 2

AMBUSH

*B*aforeis in the winter was cold—colder than Faerin had ever encountered. The extra layers of wool and quilted linen beneath his gilded armour didn't seem to be helping much, either. Each breath stung on its way in and fogged on its way out, but that wasn't even the worst of it.

The well-travelled road was wrought with frozen puddles, brown slush trying to be snow, and piles of shit and mud that caked his horse's legs nigh up to her belly. *And I thought the Karthi were quite fond of their cobblestone streets. Why the mud?* Teeth chattering from an icy gust, Faerin dismounted with a squish into the ankle-deep muck. The dozen knights he'd brought with him begrudgingly followed suit, and all thirteen steeds were ushered away to the closest stables after the exchange of coin and parchment receipts.

"And they call this a warm fucking winter? Mah balls are nigh frozen enough to shatter!" said one knight to another.

"I'm sure they got plenty o' brothels here to warm them up. Did ya not see the size of the city inside those massive walls?" said a second.

Faerin willed himself to speak in protest, but his constant shivering wouldn't let him. *Fuck. I'd hate to feel what a* cold *winter's like in these parts.*

The massive portcullis of silver fronting the main city silently rose to allow a single Karthi knight to approach on foot. "Sir Faerin O'Aiden, I presume?" said the bright, feminine voice beneath the silver-crested helmet. Her silver armour glistened in the setting sunlight—at least, what bit of armour was visible beneath the massive grey and blue fur cloak draped about her shoulders and down to her ankles.

Blinking, Faerin cleared his throat to stutter. "Ah-Eil. Yes-ehm ... Y-you have the right m-man. Forgive me-ehm. D-dame? I was-was-was expecting Sir C-Cadman?" *Damn this stutter.*

The newcomer nodded. If she was smiling beneath that lowered visor, he couldn't tell.

"Sir Cadman has fallen ill. Name's Saoirse, First Knight of Karthénos."

"A p-p-pleasure," said Faerin through his chattering teeth.

Saoirse raised her visor to look over each of the thirteen knights before her.

You're no Karthi. Why, you almost look like a Veer!

"Gnomes, why those royal bastards sent ye this far north amid winter's beyond me," said Saoirse, mumbling. "Come on, then. Let's get ye warmed up." Without another word, she nodded toward the gate and trudged through the slush in a hurry.

Faerin would've sighed in relief, but his lungs just couldn't work well enough to do so. *You'll hafta burn me alive in a hearth to get me warm again.* He followed Saoirse closely. So closely, in fact, they were nigh abreast. His fellow Prasti marched behind in single file by order of rank, as was tradition. They slipped on the smooth cobblestone road, their boots slimy with mud.

Saoirse, however, continued to walk with ease. The extra crunch from the metal spikes tied to the soles of her boots forced Faerin's curiosity to pique and lower his eyes—just enough for him to slip and land hard on his hands and knees. "K-káil," he hissed. If it weren't for the cold, the pain might not have stung so much. It was only then, he realised, that his fingers were stark white with a concerning shade of blue at his nail beds.

"We're almost there, Sir Faerin. I'll be sure ye get some furs and gloves before ye return home," said Saoirse. "We of Prasti blood aren't built for the ice and snow."

If he didn't know any better, Faerin could have sworn he saw genuine concern blanketed across her face. Taking her hand to scramble to his feet, he took in his icy surroundings to find that most of the locals wore naught but summer-like clothes. Perhaps heavier on the wool, but nothing that would indicate that they felt the cold.

Gnomes, I'm gonna die up here. Was that Jannon's intent? Faerin shook his head at the thought. Of course not. *He hardly knows who I am.*

A BLAST OF HOT AIR ENGULFED FAERIN'S FACE AS SAOIRSE OPENED THE meadery's heavy door of imported oak. As his fingers thawed, they ached and burned, turning from white and blue to bright red. His nose tingled and dripped with previously frozen snot. Despite the war inside his sinuses, the smell of roasting meat and garlic managed to distract him from his discomfort. His fellow Prasti knights sighed in obvious relief, and all immediately removed their helms. Warm food and mead were on the menu, and Wizards curse *any* who stepped in their way of full bellies.

The barkeep was less than enthused to see more than a dozen Prasti enter his meadery and showed his disdain through snarls, curt tones, and an overall demeanour that was colder than the weather outside. Even Saoirse seemed to take notice. "Prasti aren't well liked in these parts. Particularly after the treaty."

Faerin gulped. *And to think I had a part in those negotiations. What the hell did I get myself into?*

"Worry not, Sir Faerin. Seeing as how the lot of ye are so heavily armed, there likely won't be any violence."

"I ... ehm ... th-thank you," said Faerin, still rubbing his burning fingers together haphazardly. "Is—ehm ... is there a place we could talk privately?"

Saoirse raised a mischievous eyebrow. "So bold already, yeh? I suppose—"

"Nai! Not like that!" Faerin shuddered at the thought of fucking a complete stranger. Or really fucking anyone at that moment. "N-no. It's about th-the-ehm. W-well ... the unity. Y-y-you know? The ... ehm." He grabbed both his wrists as the typical signal of the elfish marriage.

Annoyance flickering across Saoirse's face, she motioned to the back corner of the meadery. "Follow me, but be silent. Can't have spies or rebels hearing this needed conversation." Straightening her posture, she said louder, "Gnomes, Sir Faerin. Ye flatter me. Perhaps we should take this somewhere a bit less public, yeh?"

Faerin smiled through clenched teeth. "I-i-if you insist." Knots tied up his stomach, despite the obvious ruse. *Just a conversation. We're just talking, Rin. Just talking, nothing else. Just talking, no fucking. Just talking about the treaty and this forged letter from "Jannon." Just talking ...*

FAERIN CHEWED ON HIS TONGUE AS HE FLICKED HIS EYES BETWEEN THE two seated Karthi women and Dame Saoirse in the secret room. Only the light from a single candle lit the place, and the cold ... Wizards be damned, it was bloody cold in that room. The few pieces of furniture were a single table, two wooden chairs, and a bench. 'Twas not for hiding in comfort. Faerin noted odd markings on the stone wall. *Gnomes be merciful! This was once a slave scout's hideout!*

"Why the secrecy? Why can't we just go to Prastömin like the prince wants us to?" The whiny voice grated against Faerin's ears like a tanner's scraper.

You must be Siobhan.

The other woman snorted. "Fer fuck's sake, will ye shut up about the damned prince, fer once?"

"Shut it, the both o'ye," said Saoirse through a hiss. "This room isn't completely silent. And fer the last time, Siobhan, the secrecy is 'cause that tavern out there is crawling with rebels who'd rather see ye drawn' n quartered than marry a Prasti—particularly the prince."

"Though it may satiate their appetites if he's anything like his father," muttered Moira.

Faerin finally cleared his throat to speak. "He's n-not." Six eyes stared at him with varying emotions behind them. "Ehm ..." *Damn this stutter.* "And we've reason to believe he wasn't the one who sent f'r ya." If the room was cold then, 'twas nearly impossible to keep from shivering now. Reaching into his breastplate, he fished around for the prince's letter.

The sounds of clanging, shouting, and violence seeped through the thick wooden door. *Wizards be good, the trap's already been sprung!*

Faerin's exact thoughts must've flashed through Saoirse's mind, as her face grew pale with dread. "We need to get out of here."

Moira sprung to her feet, and 'twas in that moment Faerin realised she was wearing thick boots, and a breastplate beneath her dress. "Under the bench. Quick and silent."

What kind of lady are ya? Nothin' like ya were in Tae— He hadn't the chance to finish his thought. The door shattered open with a resounding boom. Faerin and Saoirse both drew their weapons ... as did Moira. Siobhan, however, merely screamed and crumpled into a corner.

Moira stepped in front, shielding her sister while holding a throwing knife in each hand.

"Na'ames tapa!" a voice called from the smokey doorway. *I found them!*

Faerin gasped. *I knew the Taelas were involved!*

Nearly a dozen men rushed into the small room, each wielding a Khopesh or dagger. "Get out!" shouted Saoirse. "I'll cover ye!" Immediately cutting through two Taelas, she fixed her wild muddy eyes onto Faerin. "Get them out and get them north!"

Faerin sliced through two necks, tossing both heads toward the onslaught of warriors. He went for a third but clanged his gladius against a familiar weapon—another Prasti sword!

"You fucking traitors!" he bellowed with another parry, followed by another thrust. But there were too many, and he was soon disarmed by three of his own men.

Faerin lay on the ground, scrambling for his sword even as a heavy boot was clamped on his chest. Before his opponents could finish the job, however, three throwing knives whistled by and embedded themselves into each of the traitors' throats. Silver Prasti blood spattered and mingled with Taela crimson, and the whole damned place stank of fear, death, and treason. Gritting his teeth, Faerin snatched his sword and jumped to his feet.

Siobhan's grating voice continued to shriek. The secret exit was crawling with more rebels. Karthi, Taela—even the occasional oddling.

Wizards be good! It's like the whole of the Eastern Lands're—

A wooden club to the back of his head turned his world black.

NAOISE CLOSED HIS EYES AND COUNTED HIS BREATHS AS DIARMUID'S incessant tapping on the heavy table stabbed at his ears like red-hot needles. Even worse than the king's impatience was its echo in the vast, empty throne room. *Come on, Tör. Where the fook are ya?*

Diarmuid clicked his tongue. "I see that punctuality is no strong suit of his."

Gnomes, if only he knew of his own shortcomings. Naoise coughed. *What's all this about, anyway? He should know about the purpose of Faerin's travels, shouldn't he? Gnomes be merciful, is he quite the negotiator. I hope to the Wizards he can do this.* Naoise dared not voice such concerns. His father had, and it proved to be his demise. *Except that was on greater treason.* At least Diarmuid was justified, back then. Despite his continued thoughts on the matter, his belief in them waned. Particularly after meeting his daughter up north.

The sound of heavy boots jolted both elves' attention to the main entrance. Naoise gulped at the sight of the terror blanketing Alsantör's face.

Diarmuid seemed to take no notice. "*Finally*, Alsantör! We can begin our talks!" He sighed obnoxiously loud, as though relieved to be distracted from the Veer at his left.

"What happened?" asked the duke.

Alsantör sucked his teeth, much to Naoise's dismay. The prince only ever did that in front of his father when in deep thought or if distraught. Naoise hoped it wasn't the latter, but was disappointed.

"There was an incident in Baforeis. Both Dame Saoirse of Karthénos and Sir Faerin are fighting for their lives in the infirmary up there," said the prince, voice quivering. He dropped heavily into an empty chair. "At least two score of rebels and—"

"Well, what did we expect? How should the tundra react with you breaking that bloody treaty you wrote?" said Diarmuid.

"Six of them were Prasti."

Naoise straightened, his breath leaving him as a thousand curses bubbled to the surface. He swallowed them bitterly. At least, he thought he did. "Fookin' Rowan 'nd his treasonous ideals," he whispered.

The king glared his way. "Perhaps, Laird Naoise, he was *protecting* the Treaty of Taelonael. The only treason I see is from the prince."

Alsantör jumped to his feet, knocking his chair over with a resounding thud. "How *dare* you spout such lies! I worked too damned hard on that treaty for it to be broken in a mere ten years! Jannon sent for us!"

Diarmuid was chillingly calm, and the clarity in his eyes made Naoise wish he could shrink away into nothingness. 'Twas all for naught, however. And Alsantör? Well, he looked as though he might lose his head—both by insanity and by the sword. None of it made any sense. *Dammit Tör, he's the wrong man to lose your temper to.*

"Take care of that tone, Prince. You are not yet king, and you tread on thin ice. You are not irreplaceable."

Chewing his bottom lip, Naoise finally spoke. "If y'll allow, y'r grace, I think we are at a misunderstanding regarding this situation. Ya see, *I* received this." He revealed the forged scroll from beneath his jerkin and passed it over to the king. "It was a trap, and we fell into it arse-first."

Alsantör grumbled as he righted his chair and plopped back into it.

The king took no mind and studied the scroll, rubbing his chin with a deepening scowl. A cloud threatened to cover his eyes, and the entire room felt as though they sat in the tundra rather than the Prasti throne room.

"Perhaps I shall let Jannon know that there is a traitor in his midst. Quite a beautiful hand, is it not? Almost as beautiful as the queen's. I pray the senators have survived this vicious attack?" With unveiled malice, Diarmuid's glare pierced through Naoise's chest like a hunter's arrow before drifting to find Alsantör's.

Alsantör gulped loudly. "Eil, fa—your grace. That we know of, at least. They are not among the dead, nor injured. But that's not what—"

"Well, I suppose Ethar the Gnome continues to protect you and your conspiring ways, though I fail to see why. Perhaps Alvara has grown bored with such peace that we've seen. That Wizardess of War loves to connive with the others for her chance at glory, does she not?" Diarmuid chuckled aimlessly at his own words. "Eil. Perhaps Mûntak has decided that losing my son to a terrible scourge as the Great War was my justice for … for …"

Shite. Not again.

The hurt on Alsantör's face made Naoise's chest ache, and before either of those royal tripwires could snap, the duke cleared his throat to bring their attention onto him. "Whoever planned this had more than just this treaty in mind, y'r grace. This was a calculated attempt to overthrow the Republic of Karthénos and bring this kingdom down with it."

Diarmuid again rubbed his chin, the clarity, Gnomes be merciful, returning to his eyes. "I was told, at one time, that there were many Karthi who believed the fall of Vaoirsen was an act of war." He peered carefully at Naoise. "What are your thoughts, my laird?"

Of course, ya think this was somehow the fault of my kin. Naoise rolled his shoulders back and stuffed the surprising thoughts back into his chest. "Eil, they call it the 'Vaoirsen Massacre.' What they doesn't remember, y'r grace, is the deep-rooted treason in that place.

Giaven 'nd I were lucky f'r y'r immense mercy, and I cannot thank you enough f'r your generosity. You've been a better father to me than my own blood."

He'd thought those same words for years, but this time ... this time was different. A sour taste made his stomach queasy, and his mouth watered as he tried to keep himself from vomiting. *Manstair was a traitor, Neesh. He blasphemed the Wizards and Gnomes, disowning his own sons f'r the sake of his beliefs. Incited a coup against Diarmuid, Wizards bless his crown.*

"There were Taelas in Baforeis, as well. Taelas and mortal elf giants. Dame Saoirse wrote that she's afraid the senators were taken to the Oasis City," said Alsantör. A flash of what looked like rage bounced off his eyes. "If that's the case, we're looking at pieces of the caoiröge board that've been placed unseen."

Caoiröge? Naoise struggled to find the similarities between the Karthi pebble game and war, but—

"You will return the senators to Karthénos unharmed and unwed," said Diarmuid. The sting of his tone was hot. "If you fail, Alsantör, don't bother returning unless you wish to lose your head."

Naoise grimaced. While not uncommon for the king to threaten his own heir, he didn't expect it then. Especially with such clear eyes. *That's not his demons. That's the Diarmuid of which we were warned.*

"Do I make myself clear, my son?"

"Clear as the waters of the sacred pool," said Alsantör, voice cracking.

"Then, I suppose this ends our conversation. I will write to Jannon and tell him of this unfortunate information regarding his daughters. The last thing we need in these eastern lands is for his son to be raised amidst a war."

What! What son? That halfbreed bastard o' his should be dead. A battering ram of realisation hit Naoise in the chest. *Kiera! That's why she's the duchess. Fookin' hell, Tör. We're in deeper shite now than we were during the damned crusade.*

Alsantör locked panicked eyes with Naoise, as though hearing his thoughts. When the king departed, the two elves stared at each other with shared unease.

"Neesh. We're dead men."

"Eil, that we are. What the fook're we to do?"

To Naoise's dismay, Alsantör sucked the back of his teeth once again. "I know someone who may be able to help. But it will require stealth, a lot of gold, and … well … an open mind."

Naoise's stomach sank with dread. "Who the hell're you thinking?"

"A man who shouldn't be alive."

43

GAMES OF THE HEART

"Captured," said Sólan. He placed his jade figurine on a small square and moved Chainless's piece five spaces back. Picking up the four painted sticks, he threw them in the air again. One more move, one more throw.

"You aren't allowed to use The Dark in this game," said Chainless.

"My eyes burn not. Senet is a game of luck as much as skill. I would never use The Dark for such foolish schemes." Sólan shifted his weight from one side of his buttocks to the other. Sitting on the floor for the game because of its unstable board had its advantages, but *Gods* was it uncomfortable.

Chainless snorted. "You're a terrible liar, Grim. Perhaps that's why Roman found you out so easily."

A flash of searing heat flickered across Sólan's eyes at the mention of that damned name. *Roman Ho'su. Father of the man whom I thought I loved — whom I thought I could trust.* He tossed the sticks once more. Two white, two black. He moved his piece two squares and motioned to Chainless for her turn.

"I swear, Grim, you need to talk to him."

"Speak to whom?"

"Your lover, idiot! The man you claimed for *life*. Your fucking husband."

Taken aback at her sudden ferocity, Sólan scrambled to his feet and paced the room with a heavy limp. His right foot had apparently lost all function during his sit. It tingled and burned with each step, indicating the return of its blood flow.

"Ten years, Alira. Ten years, and he hid the name of his father to me? Did he think I would kill him if he told me? Mine is the fucking *Duke of Karthénos!* Mine is the reason for the gods-damned crusade that massacred millions of my kin! Yet he still hid the truth from me? I trusted him—*loved* him. Why the—"

"Do you think he doesn't love you? That he doesn't trust you?" Chainless asked in challenge. "Fuck, Grim. You're as dense as a Prasti! How much of that damned apyin flower have you been smoking?"

The door creaked open to reveal an emotionless Dakil. A wave of conflicting feelings immediately swept Sólan away, sending him churning in a deluge of rage, mourning, and joy. A familiar nagging flutter in his chest returned, and his breath caught at the sheer pain etched across his lover's face.

"I'll leave you two alone," said Chainless. 'Twas only then that Sólan caught her mischievous grin. "Don't squander this chance, Dakil. The Dark is an opportunistic foe," she whispered as she slipped around him through the exit.

Sólan assumed he wasn't meant to hear that, but it still stung. He locked eyes with Dakil's smoky, russet ones and lost his fight with his tears. *My heart is a brittle thing. It cracks every moment I see you—and every moment I look away. Why must you torture me so?*

"Your game isn't finished," Dakil said flatly. "Should I get Chain—"

"No, no. 'Tis quite alright. I care not for this game." Sólan fidgeted, squirmed, and tried to shake the life back into his still-burning foot. "I … aeh … will you lock the door on your way in?"

Dakil blinked. Whether in surprise, mocking, or disgust, Sólan couldn't say, though it mattered not. They needed to talk. Silently,

Dakil obliged, tiptoeing to the bed and placing a hand on the mattress. "I need to sit," he whispered.

"So do I," said Sólan. The thought of leaving passed through his mind, but he squashed it as he would a beetle. Shuffling to the bed, he sat close to his husband, hands clasped on his lap.

"I'm sorry, mintaki. I should have told you." Dakil took a shaky breath, and, suddenly, his words came pouring out like a hole in a ship's hull. "At first, it was because I didn't know if I could trust you, and then I thought he was dead, and now I don't know if you can ever trust me again or if you even love me anymore, but I want you to know that I still love you and I understand why you're angry and if you want to unclaim me I don't know what I'll do but I know that—"

Sólan interrupted Dakil's rant with a kiss. 'Twas a soft kiss, at first, one as light as a velvety feather, but it was heavy enough to stop the swordsman's words. "I am the one who is sorry. I am the one who should be unclaimed, for I have—" He hiccoughed, tears dripping down his face. "Of all the men in the Eastern Lands, I should be the one who understands the most." He kissed Dakil again, harder this time, cradling his lover's jaw with one hand and tangling his other in his loose hair.

Dakil quickly broke their kiss and pinned Sólan to the mattress. He straddled him and attacked with a barrage of kisses and nibbles on his face, neck, ears, mouth, chest …

Oh Gods, mólamí. How could I have ever doubted you? The lovers wrestled, groped, and stripped each other bare. Sólan mounted Dakil, both of them naked and hard, panting with lust.

Heart racing, Sólan reached under the pillow and revealed his favourite vial of oil. To Dakil's obvious surprise, however, 'twas not his own cock he prepared.

"I want to try something, Dakil," whispered Sólan. "I need to show you that I trust you still. Gods, do I need you now more than ever. I want you to fuck me."

A warm smile stretched across Dakil's face as the scent of salt, brandy, and lust thickened the air. "Mintaki," he cooed, rubbing his knuckles against Sólan's jaw. "Whatever you want, I will give. I love you."

Sólan lowered himself onto Dakil, the sensation more familiar than he'd thought—far more horrifying than he'd hoped. *He is not one of them, Sólan.* One look into Dakil's eyes, and he relaxed. Deeper did he guide his lover. Stronger did the threats of memories invade.

Dakil flipped his lover onto his back, thrusting deeper still. Faster.

Fuck.

Panic strangled Sólan. Dakil's hot breath made his ear sticky. Cold sweat accumulated on his brow, and the distant echo of a young boy's screams filled the room.

I can do this. This is for Dakil ... for our love.

He snapped his head back and stared at the wall, upside down.

Where the hell was he?

The smell of brandy faded to acetic wine and stale flour. Apyin smoke clouded his vision, and the baker's hot breath stung his ears.

A young boy of eight sobbed, curling himself into a ball on the floor. The blue and silver specks in his desperate amber gaze flitted around like trapped mice. "Make him stop, Átha! Please!" *The child covered his ears and tucked his head between his knees before screaming again.* "Make him stop!"

"Medría!" Sólan quickly headbutted his assailant in the nose. Crimson blood spattered across his face, and an out-of-place, silky voice yelped.

A naked man of beautiful copper skin and luscious black hair fell off the bed and landed on his arse with a thud. "Pantot!" he cursed, pinching his broken nose to stop the bleeding.

Why is he not attacking again? Sólan stared, dumbfounded. *Gods, 'tis as though you are my lover, not—*

He stopped, reality crashing over him like a Casacan avalanche.

"Shit. Dakil." Sliding off the bed, he crawled to Dakil and reached out to his face. "Gods, I—"

"It's alright, mintaki." Dakil gingerly wiped his watering eyes. "It's not the first time you've broken my nose."

Sólan looked to his lap in shame. "I know." Taking a ragged breath through his nose, he tried—and failed—to ease his thumping heart. He reached up to Dakil's face, hesitating for fear of further heartache. *I just want to heal you, mólamí. 'Tis quite alright. I just ...* Tears threatened his eyes once again.

"Sólan," whispered Dakil. "It's alright."

His breath caught, the shame overbearing. Sólan finally brushed his knuckles against his lover's cheek. "Forgive me. Not merely for your injury, but"—he hiccoughed—"but for my distrust." Despite the likely protests, he healed Dakil's nose with a light touch. He watched a single tear escaping from his lover's eyes. *Gods, am I a fool. Halaña, forgive me, for I have nearly squandered the gift you have given me.*

The lovers embraced, and Dakil kissed Sólan as though 'twas their last time. "I'll always forgive you, mintaki. I love you."

Hours passed, though they felt like mere seconds, Dakil took every moment he could to cherish his time with Sólan. He lost count of the number of Senet rounds they played—Dakil won nearly every game. They ended their night with another passionate moment. Thank the Gods it didn't end in another injury.

Sólan slipped into a deep, yet restless, slumber while wrapped in Dakil's arms. Despite everything that'd happened in the last day, they'd forgiven each other.

Dakil didn't know—*couldn't know*—how his lover had forgiven him so quickly. *Halaña, you bless me. How could I ever doubt you and believe in that false god of Yusa?*

With a soft hand, he swept a loose curl of dark brown hair from Sólan's face. He sighed, savouring the feel of his hot skin against his own. That's what the elf blood did, far as he could tell. It made sense, seeing's how the man was half Karthi. Those damned silver-bloods from the tundra never wore winter clothing, even in the coldest weather.

Sólan stirred, gazing sleepily up at Dakil with a loving smile before adjusting his weight and dozing back off.

Dakil's stomach fluttered at his lover's quiet purr. Yes, Halaña had blessed him, indeed. He lay his head onto his pillow to join

Sólan in sleep, but the shuffle of feet and the hush of whispers snapped his attention to the door. He recognised those accents ... that language! Prasti.

"Pantot," he whispered. "Mintaki. Wake up."

"What is it?" groaned Sólan. Dammit, he hardly slept as it was. After he'd finally found some gods-damned rest, Dakil had to tell him his life was in jeopardy.

"Elves."

"*Medría.*" Sólan bolted upright and scrambled out of the covers. "I thought that fucking crusade ended years ago." He searched through the jumbled pile of clothing, grumbling curses in every language he knew ... which amounted to nearly all of those spoken in the eastern lands.

"It did," said Dakil. "I don't know why—"

"Where the fuck is my hatchet?"

Dakil gritted his teeth as he followed suit. Unsheathing his rapier, he tip-toed to the door. "Under the bed. By our feet."

Sólan nodded and crawled under the furniture with naught but his legs—and that beautiful bare ass—sticking out. The door's latch clicked. Whoever it was, they had a damned key! Sólan must've heard it, too, because he stopped his grumbling and slid out from under the bed. Slinking to the darkest corner of the room, he readied himself with raised fists and glowing green eyes.

Dakil shuddered. Even after ten years of loving him, he could never get used to seeing his lover channelling The Dark. The door creaked open, and two monstrous elves shuffled into the room. Jumping out from behind the door, Dakil thrust his rapier at the closest silver-blood quicker than he'd ever thought he could.

But that elf disarmed him with a move Dakil had never seen, at a speed that made even his quickest reflexes feel sluggish. Was it fatigue? Rusty skill? The swordsman didn't even see the elf move before a hard kick in the abdomen pinned him to the ground. Squirming beneath the heavy leather armour, Dakil found he couldn't breathe. The being was of pure silver blood and Prasti build, unlike his half-blooded lover. Gods, were they menacing savages!

The metallic taste of blood filled Dakil's mouth, and his airway continued to collapse at the sheer weight of his opponent. His vision blurred, and panic set in. He couldn't see what was happening to Sólan, but he knew the worst: he'd failed his lover once again.

"You fucking pundijos!" Sólan punched, dodged, and kicked the unarmed Prasti scum until his limbs felt heavier than a blacksmith's anvil. Where had he put that hatchet?

This elf was slower than his companion, who'd pinned Dakil quicker than a mere mortal could blink. 'Twas almost as though *this* one wanted to keep Sólan alive. *You wish to capture the Grim, aeh? A futile attempt at peace with Taelonael? You should have come to take my head to them, instead.*

A swift elbow crashed into his nose, and a kick to his knee caused Sólan to collapse with a yelp. His eyes watered, exacerbating the heat already searing in his eyes as The Dark surged through him.

The elf mounted him, pinning Sólan's wrists to the ground with one hand and placing his free forearm against his throat. "Stand down," he hissed.

Tíal, this elf was of high nobility. Likely trained at the highest level with his king's own personal guards. Perhaps he *was* of that king's personal guards. Sólan bared his fangs and spat into his opponent's face. To his dismay, it did naught to lessen the silver-blooded fucker's grip.

"Look at me," said the elf. "Look close. You know me. You've known me for years."

Sólan stopped struggling. *¿Mondé? Who the fuck are you?* He stared into that freckled face with fear pulsing through him. That mahogany hair, those evergreen eyes. Gods, he almost looked like …

"Thi a e'dos gid bharbhadh mo aoithniche thi, du graise," said the other elf. *He's going to kill you before he knows you, your grace.*

Peace—that was the only thing way to describe the emotion flooding his veins. He relaxed and closed his eyes, allowing his lungs to deflate with a heavy sigh, tears forming quickly behind his eyelids.

He attempted to flash a mischievous grin—or at the very least, a wink—as he said, "Medría, Tör. You could have written first. Especially before tempting me like *this*."

Something must've worked, as Alsantör rolled his eyes and popped up to his feet. "I swear to the Wizards," he grumbled. Turning to his companion, the prince exhaled sharply. "Get off him, Neesh. He's not a threat anymore."

The other Prasti obliged, drawing Sólan's attention. Wait, he wasn't a Prasti. No, that silver-blood was a Veer! Fuck, he'd only ever heard of those mountain warriors—of their speed and agility—in children's stories. The tales claimed they were nearly as large as a damned giant. This one, Sólan realised with a twinge of disappointment, wasn't as monstrous as he'd imagined—broader, perhaps, than the average Prasti, but nothing more. Despite the incredible respect he felt for the specimen of legends, Sólan couldn't stop his mouth. "And who the fuck are you?"

In his periphery, Alsantör twitched, obviously nervous at the present situation.

"I could ask you the same thing, fooker," said the Veer.

"If you know not who I am, perhaps you should have died with all the rest of your kin. And *what did you do to Dakil*?"

"Who?"

The searing heat returned to Sólan's eyes. Trembling, he clenched his fists and prepared to strike, when Alsantör stepped between them. "He's fine. He should wake up any moment."

"Could also make f'r the both o'ya to put some bloody trousers on."

Sólan cocked his head and bared his fangs. "Apologies, putathóta. Your arrival to my *bed chambers* was unexpected."

The Veer snorted. "To be attacked by a halfbreed 'nd his red-blooded lover-f'r-the-night was unexpected."

"Will you both stop!" Alsantör shouldered his way past Sólan and knelt by the still-unconscious Dakil.

Oh, mólamí, what did that savage do to you?

The sound of a fist to flesh, the prince's yelp, and a thud told Sólan his lover had awakened. Relief turned to fear, however, at the telltale ring of a rapier being readied. "Dakil, mahundi! Suya ng na kikompa!" *Dakil, wait! He is an ally!*

Dakil stopped, yet he didn't drop his sword.

"The fook kinda tongue is that?" whispered the Veer.

"It's Bankun. The Nethuanian dialect out of Bansungei," said Alsantör. Turning his attention back to the naked swordsman, he raised his hands, palms out. "Kaliang ko manaksupang na Sólan, manang." *I need to speak with Sólan alone.*

"Whatever you need to say to him, you can say to me," Dakil growled. "And I'm fluent in Garmathian, so no need to butcher my language."

Sólan snickered as he slipped into a pair of loose trousers. He padded over to Dakil and planted a long, open-mouthed kiss on his lips.

The Veer groaned. "Alright Tör. Y've made y'r arrival clear to this … thing. Can ya tell me who the fook is this, 'nd why are we meetin' with him?"

Alsantör sucked the back of his teeth, and Sólan couldn't help but smirk over his shoulder at the Veer's wince at the sound.

The prince took a long, ragged breath and muttered, "Naoise McManstair, I'd like you to meet Sólan de Ciudelago—or in Karthénos, Sólan O'Jannon."

44

BLOOD AND ALE

Sólan the fookin' Grim! I knew that Áfgalese demon was still alive, 'nd now I'm grovelling to him like my head's on the line!

Well, Naoise's head was, in fact, on the line. He clenched his fists to stay the shaking in his arms. *First Rhona, and now this? Gnomes, Tör has a lot of explaining to do.* But, Naoise knew he couldn't give that arsehole an excuse to murder them both. That Nethuanian swordsman didn't look much kinder, either.

"I need a bloody pint," he said curtly. Marching out of the room and down the stairs, Naoise fought the immense need to shoot something with his bow. He stopped, feeling as though he were being watched. Glancing in his periphery, he saw that orc woman glaring in his direction. What was her name again? Chainless, right?

"What's this? A pureblood Prasti who can't murder his target? How unfortunate for you." The orc's voice dripped with hatred.

Save it, orc. Your kind's no better. He dared not goad her, though—nor her menacing brother. The Oath of Light may protect him from wielding The Dark, but the power of The Light was a whole different realm of chaos. He shuddered at the thought.

"Crusade's over, 'nd we're not here f'r murder." He slapped two coppers on the bar. "I'll need two pints to get through this morn."

"*Or*, just one of mead? Same price, triple the strength of our ale."

Naoise chewed on his bottom lip for a moment. "There's a catch. What is it?"

Chainless grinned maliciously, her eyes pulsing in an unnatural red glow. "Trust me, Prasti. You don't want to know." Leaning close, she whispered, "A fool's hope, really. But if you can deliver your king's head next time you're here … nothing else. Just his head."

"Pardon?" Naoise backed away, horrified at the request. He shouldn't be surprised. Were the orcs not on the losing side of the Great War? Were they not allies of the sprites? Gulping, the duke reached back to the counter to remove his copper coins. Before he could, however, a frothy pint of sweet-smelling mead was slid before him.

"Don't worry," said the hulking man behind the counter. "She forgets about what happened to *your* kin, Veer."

What the hell is so bloody great about the Veers? They were traitors!

Three pairs of heavy footsteps descended the stairs, and Naoise didn't know whether to feel relief or dread. *Fook me. Here we go.* Slapping another copper on the table, he said, "The *real* Prasti's gon' need an ale."

Alsantör and Dakil followed Sólan down the stairs. The swordsman's hot glare made the elf prince want to shrivel away into nothingness. It hadn't taken him long to realise just how close the two men were—far closer than Naoise had seemed to think.

Speaking of that hot-headed duke, there he was at the bar, chatting away effortlessly with the barkeep. Rasheed seemed far more relaxed with Naoise than he'd been with Alsantör, but that didn't surprise the prince one bit. The orcs had always hated the Prasti, especially after Diarmuid had taken the throne.

The crystalline lights seemed much dimmer than when he'd arrived. Colder, too. 'Twas almost as though they were completely controlled by Chainless's mood. They probably were—she was a pure Garmathian, after all.

Sólan picked a table in the far corner, plopping in the chair closest to the wall. Alsantör looked around to see that the location was ideal for monitoring the whole damned building. *Not surprising. You've always been one on edge.*

Dakil scooted a chair close to his lover, hand resting uncomfortably close to the hilt of that decorated rapier. At closer view in the better light, the prince realised the blade was of Casacan water-steel! Wizards be good, Sólan was a master at smithing, wasn't he?

"I never think I will be relieved to see you until I actually see you," said Sólan. "This was, by far, the longest silence I had heard from you. But, at the least, I was not on my knees this time, aeh?"

Oh, that stings. The prince's mouth spoke sooner than he'd liked. "Nai, friend. You were pinned naked on your back this time. I'd always thought you'd enjoy that."

"Ha!" Sólan slapped the table as he burst into a hearty laughter. "*Gods*, 'tis good to see you, Tör. How the hell did you find me?"

Dakil was less than amused. "And how did you get past the cliffs?"

"No need to worry about that ... ehm ... Dakil? I have my connections," said Alsantör. "Nor do you need to worry about my friendship with Sólan. He's never been my type."

"Nor you, mine," said Sólan. He wrapped his arm about Dakil's waist and nuzzled his ear with his nose. He whispered something in Bankun, and the swordsman relaxed his posture with the hint of a smile.

"So, what kind of fuckery has you in need of my services, amógo? The only times would I ever see you were when you were on a hunt or when you were saving my head from the Taelas. With our fathers' crusade now ended, and with me safer than ever ... why now?"

"Am I not allowed to see you just to visit?"

Sólan snorted. "You have a terrible way of announcing yourself, my friend."

"We're not y'r friends," said Naoise, placing a full pint of ale in front of the prince. He sat directly across from Dakil, glaring muddy daggers at him and Sólan.

Alsantör winced at the duke's brash words. He'd nearly forgotten he was there too. *Dammit, Neesh. You and your gnomes-damned temper.* Realisation and dread suddenly fell upon the prince's shoulders. *Sólan's temper too. What the hell was I thinking bringing these two—*

"Apologies, pundijo. Was I speaking to you?"

"I liked ya better when you were whimpering in y'r sleep," grumbled Naoise.

"And I liked you better when you were absent!" Sólan and Naoise jumped to their feet in unison, fists at the ready.

Dakil followed close behind, the tip of his rapier on Naoise's throat. "Sit down, elf, or your silver blood will flow into your fucking drink."

"Oi!" Alsantör slammed his fist onto the table. "We need to talk. *Now.*"

Sólan's nose twitched into a snarl, his gaze never breaking from Naoise's. "Then let us talk...*now.*" He inched back down to his seat but made no motion to prompt his lover to do the same.

Naoise finally swatted Dakil's sword away and clamped his hand over the oozing wound under his chin. "This is a bloody mistake, Tör."

"I will be the judge of that. Sit down," said Alsantör through gritted teeth.

Grumbling, Naoise obliged. And Dakil? He hesitated, but finally re-sheathed his weapon and sat even closer to his lover.

"We need your help, Sólan. This ... task is ... well ..." *Why the hell was it so hard to talk? Sólan's been your friend for over three hundred years, Tör! You can ask for help. You* need *to ask for his help.*

"Come to collect the debt I owe you, aeh? You have saved my life so many damned times, I suppose I should stop taking you for granted." Sólan's warm smile, while reassuring, didn't help the dread still filling the prince's chest.

"Well, I suppose we could start from the beginning." Taking a deep breath, Alsantör explained, "I'm promised to be married, you see. But that would require—"

"Congratulations, amógo!" Sólan clapped with joy, his speckled amber eyes gleaming with mischief. "So, what you do is quite simple, really. You let her get naked, you wait until you are nice and hard, then—"

"I know how to fuck a woman, Sólan! That's not why I need your help!"

Naoise snorted. "He obviously doen't fuck women, Tör. He wouldn't be much help, anyway."

"He does, actually, but that's not the point," grumbled Alsantör. "The woman in question—she and her sister were kidnapped by Taelas in Baforeis."

Sólan stiffened. "*Taelas*? What were they doing all the way in Karthénos?"

"That's the problem, Grim. We dinnae ken what happened, nor why," said Naoise. "They weren't supposed to be there. The treaty says the Karthi 'nd Prasti aren't to unify 'til after a hundred years of peace 'atween the red-bloods and silver-bloods. Someone's tryin' to start a war and blame us."

"Medría," whispered Sólan. "And I thought my father was a warmonger."

Alsantör let loose a sad chuckle. "Mine too."

"What does this have to do with us?" said Dakil. "We're not Taela, nor Prasti. Why should we care?"

Sólan rubbed his face with both hands, sighing. "He wishes to hire us to scout. Gods, the last two times I scouted, a woman and two children died. I know not if I can do it again."

"How many thousands of women and children have you saved since you started scouting?" Alsantör tried not to sound desperate, but he couldn't help it. He was.

"I am a smuggler, now, Tör. Not a slave scout. Fuck, if I go back down that path, that damned crusade will start again, and what little healing I have accomplished will be all for naught."

"They used a mortal elf slave that was bred with giants for this. The Taelas're up to something," said Naoise. He balled his shaking fists until the knuckles turned white. "And if we fail, we both lose our heads."

"I hardly care about *yours*." Sólan glared at the duke. Shifting his gaze back to the prince, however, he sighed. "I still fail to see how this has anything to do with me. There are plenty of Áfgalese scouts who would be willing to keep your secret. Who are these women they took?"

Alsantör gulped. This was exactly what he feared most: telling Sólan about the Karthi duke's other children. "Ehm ... Senators Moira 'nd Siobhan ... O'Jannon."

Just as expected, the colour drained from Sólan's face, and his pupils constricted to fine black pinholes. Dakil gasped, gripping his lover's forearm with a vicelike grip.

Say something, friend. Please, say something.

"There must be a mistake," said Sólan, his voice hardly deeper than a quiet squeak. "Karthi children are too rare. He cannot—no. No, no, no, no ..." He ran a shaky hand through his wavy hair. "Gods, no."

"I know. It's hard to imagine that blue-eyed goblin having more children, but he does. Two daughters and two sons." Alsantör grimaced as soon as the word "sons" left his mouth. *Shite. This won't end well. Don't tell him his brother's the heir. Don't tell him—*

"He what!" Sólan jumped to his feet, paced to the far wall, and punched it hard enough to send a tremor through the whole tavern. "That silver-blooded fucking demon! Gods! He should have been castrated the moment I was fucking conceived! An heir, Tör? He named his *second-borne son his heir*!"

Dammit, Tör! That wasn't supposed to be spoken!

"Not to defend what he did to y'r maela, but ... he does think y're dead," said Naoise.

How the hell that Veer thought those words would help, Alsantör couldn't fathom. "Neesh, don't—"

Too late. Sólan slammed his hatchet's spike into the table, splinters flying everywhere. "And whose fault do you think that was, aeh?" The bright green glow in his eyes never flickered as he bared his fangs at both elves in front of him. "Fuck him. Let the whole damned Tundra burn with Taela fire for all I care. And you?" He turned his ire to the prince. "Exile in the West might suit you better than wasting your time with that fucking forest."

Dammit! Me and my fucking mouth. Naoise was right, I'm gonna start another gnomes-damned war. Gulping, Alsantör lifted his hands, palms out. "Please, Sólan. I'm begging you. Those women didn't ask to be borne of their father, just like you hadn't. Please. They're your sisters ... your kin."

Sólan grabbed two fistfuls of his own hair and choked down sobs, tears and snot running down his face. "So was the baker's boy, but I could not save him, either, could I?"

Alsantör grimaced. He should've known; should've remembered.

Peeling the hatchet out of the table's wood, Sólan wiped his face with the back of his wrist. "Fuck, Tör, I want not to do this gods-damned job, but ..." He took a shaky breath and leaned against Dakil like a crutch. "I have nowhere to stow you on the *Silent Dancer*, but ... find a way to meet me at the Dragon's Horn in one fortnight."

45

OF SCOUTING AND RUNNING

*D*akil paced Sólan's cabin—*their* cabin—aboard the *Silent Dancer*, wringing his hands. "I don't like this, mintaki. I don't like any of this." Shaking, he uncorked a bottle of apple brandy and took a long pull.

Sólan, however, sat hunched at the edge of the bed, hands clasped and knuckles blanched. "Neither do I, but I have no choice," he said, voice hoarse from the tantrum he'd just thrown moments prior.

Yes, you do, Sólan. You chose to be here, to help those silver-blooded monsters. Dakil shook the angry thoughts from his head. "You don't have to do this, Sólan. *Please* don't do it. Those elves do nothing except kill and force their ways onto others. Look at Garmath!"

"Dammit, Dakil! They are my sisters! I have no choice." Sólan suddenly glared, eyes pulsing with The Dark. "And, are the elves really all that different from the Temple Cavalry of Nethuania? Did you forget I was forced to marry a child? *Your* father was the one who gave her away, not hers."

His words stabbed Dakil deep in his chest. Sólan was right, after all. Why else would Dakil have left the Temple of the Sun? Why else would he deny the existence of Yusa? He took a breath to calm his trembling hands and another gulp of brandy.

"Besides," continued Sólan, "I hate silver-bloods just as much as you do—if not more. But Prince Alsantör? He ... well ... he differs. Nothing like the rest of his kin."

Dakil growled. "Keep talking like that, and I might grow jealous."

Sólan sprung to his feet and snatched the drink from the swordsman's hands. Guzzling what remained, he frowned at the empty bottle before tossing it over his shoulder. "There is no need for that, mólamí. I have no desire to *bed* him. I simply trust him."

"Pantot, Sólan! How can you trust anyone of such pointy ears savagery? I don't!"

Sólan stiffened, absently rubbing his own ear with a blank face.

Shit. I didn't mean that, mintaki. I—fuck.

"Well, at least you trust me, tíal? My ears ... aeh ... they are not quite ..."

Dakil pulled Sólan into his arms and embraced him tightly. "I love you and your pointed ears, mintaki." He caressed Sólan's jaw and kissed him softly. "But, please, don't do this."

Sólan's shoulders slumped into Dakil's chest. "*Gods*, I want nothing more than to abandon this entire thing. But a promise is a promise—and I am a man of my word." He broke their embrace to wipe a tear from his own cheek. "Besides, 'tis the will of the Gods."

"Hah?" Dakil pushed Sólan away, incredulous. "The Gods? How can you know what they—"

"I failed to save my brother more than three hundred years ago, and they have been punishing me ever since. This is my redemption."

"Kilakahon. What about all those women and girls you saved? Was that not enough for them? How many times have you sacrificed your reputation, your *life* for them? Even that wasn't enough?" Dakil's jaw fell slack as terror gripped him. *Javiento, don't be so greedy. Don't you dare take Halaña's gift from me!*

"Mólamí," whispered Sólan. "No need to be afraid. This is the will of Javiento and Elek. Perhaps my cowardice all these years will finally be dissolved."

There's that fucking word again. Cowardice! You, of all beings in the eastern lands? Dakil's lip trembled as his heart raced and breath shallowed. "I can't lose you. Not again."

Sólan winced but held his ground. "You won't."

They kissed again. *Please let it not be our last.* "I can't do this anymore," whispered Dakil.

"Do what?"

"*This*. Smuggling. Dealing with fucking Oleg and his godsdamned business."

A mischievous smirk curled one side of Sólan's mouth. "Perhaps we should run away. To Áfgal? We could settle in Arriya Taca or Pueblanrío—there are hundreds of vineyards and villages in need of blacksmiths and farmers."

"Farming? You think I'd be a farmer, Sólan? What's wrong with you? Don't go soft on me like—"

"Niníl. Say it not, Dakil. I never said we would stay that way. Perhaps the slave scouts will still need help."

"And what about the ship?"

Sólan shrugged. "Let them figure it out. Perhaps Bayani would take the helm—I doubt anyone would duel him for it, after all."

Dakil clicked his tongue. *And what of Chainless? Rasheed? The orphanage?* All the questions made his head hurt.

"Mólamí," whispered Sólan, pulling Dakil into a loving embrace. "I am not leaving forever—a mere moon, at the longest. Have you any idea how long I have dreamed of infiltrating this damned city? Of tearing it down, brick by brick, from the inside? This is about more than just my sisters. This is about freedom. Of liberation. The downfall of oppression against all of my kind."

Nipantot ki, Sólan. The crusade is over—what oppression? Dakil dared not question him in this impassioned state. "Fine," he sighed. "But come back to me, mintaki."

Sólan leaned in and gently kissed his lover. "I will. I promise."

"I no understand," said Bayani. "Why you look like that?"

Sólan finished buckling and tying the myriad of chains and ropes around his waist, leaving just enough slack for further bondage, if needed. A laughably small strip of armour criss-crossing across his chest was held in place by large ring of polished steel. Intricately engraved, leather scales covered his shoulders and not much else. His bracers, however, consisted of protruding metal spikes spiralling down his arms from elbows to wrists. Finally, fingerless leather gloves with matching knuckle busters were slipped tightly over his hands.

Looking over to Bayani, he smirked. "I intend to enter the Oasis City, and this is my way into her walls."

"Yusa's grace, you really trusting these elves," Bayani grumbled. "What if it a trap?"

"I already asked him that," said Dakil, pouting in his chair like a child. "He thinks that Prasti prince will save him."

"And he has, many times over. 'Tis now my turn to save *him*."

"Maybe t'at what he want you to think, binyego. Only to fool you, and—"

"Gods, Bayani, listen to yourself. He has had opportunities to behead me hundreds of times. You are simply paranoid."

"I surprised you no paranoid too. After t'e crusade? The elfs' war? You still trust t'is savage? He head of Prasti army! Dakil. Make him stay."

"I tried, Bayani. He won't be stopped—'it's the will of the Gods,' he says." Dakil rolled his eyes before looking to his lover with annoyance blanketed across his face.

"Pantot," whispered Bayani.

"Fuck off, the both of you!" Sólan finalised his garb with his fine leather holster. Slipping his hatchet into its resting place against his hip, he raised his arms in triumph. "There. Do I look like a convincing n'poginat?"

Bayani scrunched his nose. "A what?"

"Pit fighter," said Dakil, rising to his feet. He walked over to Sólan and looked him over with thinly veiled lust. "And yes, mintaki. You fit the look well. I'd be lying if I said I didn't like this armour." Licking his lips, he wrapped an arm about his lover's waist and pressed his hip into his groin.

Sólan's heart flipped, pressure building in the front of his trousers. "Then say it not," he cooed. He caressed Dakil's jaw and brought his face close. Their lips hardly touched before Bayani cleared his throat.

"Now? Really? You no can wait until—"

"Fuck of, Bayani!" said Sólan and Dakil in unison.

Bayani crossed his arms and huffed. "So, what we say to the crew when you gone on t'is … quest?"

Shit.

"You no think about that?"

Dakil snorted. "Of course he didn't. But thank the Gods I did."

"You mean thanks to Yusa,'" grumbled Bayani.

Sólan rolled his eyes. "Kirpa, Goddess of Mercy, save me from this indionta."

"Tsst." Dakil kicked Sólan's toe as he hissed. "We called you in, Bayani, for a reason. You're to help me keep the men under control."

"How, binyego? Why?"

"Because you're the only man on this ship we trust," said Dakil. "You know how much gold Oleg owes us—"

"Too much," chimed Sólan.

"—and he claims it's his seller who owes him."

"Probably lie. So, he go to Oasis City to find seller." Bayani rubbed the sweaty skin beneath his eyepatch.

"Exactly."

"¿Mondé? I am?" Sólan flitted his gaze between Dakil and Bayani with a frown. "I mean … yes. Yes, I am."

"Yusa's grace," whispered Bayani, face in his hand. "We doomed."

"Not entirely. There is something else I need you to do, amógo."

'Twas now Bayani's turn to frown. "What else?"

"When I return, Dakil and I are leaving."

"What!" The colour drained from Bayani's face. "What about *Silent Dancer*? Oleg? What—"

"That's for you to figure out," said Dakil. "The ship is yours."

"And if Sólan no come back? What then?" Bayani's voice shook, beads of cold sweat forming on his forehead.

"Then the *Silent Dancer* is mine ... unless you kill me for it," said Dakil.

Sólan closed his eyes to hide the panic forming in his chest. Ten years ago, he would've believed his lover's words. Now? He wasn't sure what to believe with this man. At the very least, he knew Bayani wouldn't challenge him.

Just stay alive, Sólan. 'Tis all you have to do. Javiento, God of Death, do not take me yet.

The sun descended in the eastern horizon, illuminating the wispy clouds in a myriad of glowing pinks and oranges. The beach where Naoise and Alsantör were resting jutted out half a kilometre from the main shore, curving toward the west in a shallow, horn-like shape—the "Dragon's Horn." While the finger-like beach was like several other shores lining the southern coast of Taelonael, the Dragon's Horn was unique. It was the largest and most protected shore—the locale where most of Oleg's pickups happened. As the sky made its slow transition, the shimmer of the surrounding star-shaped salt-lilies brightened. Their scent was sweet, like honey, and their eerie purple glow lit the entire beach.

"Sólan the fookin' Grim," said Naoise, pacing in the ankle-deep sand. "The one being in the bloody eastern lands responsible f'r the crusade, this cold war with the Taelas, and—"

"The only beings responsible for that massacre were the men who connived to start it in the first place," said Alsantör. "And the Taelas? They've always hated us! It didn't take Jannon's half-mortal bastard for that. Ten years, they've thought him dead, and look at the state of our treaty. Sólan had nothing to do with them."

That's not the bloody point of this all, is it? It doen't matter if the Taelas hate us, y'r father, or the whole gnomes-damned eastern lands. Ya lied to everyone! Naoise didn't stop his pacing despite the increasing load of sand in his boots. "I fookin' knew it. The moment I heard you were the one who took his bloody head, I knew he still lived."

Alsantör rolled his eyes in Naoise's periphery, but the duke ignored him.

"I doen't understand ya, Tör. Y're bloody head is on the line, and ya act like y're the only one who's right. What the fook's wrong with ya?"

"Dammit Naoise, I'm trying to show you my side! Sólan's the gnomes-damned victim here!" Alsantör jumped to his feet, bowing his chest with clenched fists and bared fangs. "Do you think I knew his father would try to kill him the moment they met? Káil, if you knew a mere half of his true history, you'd defend him just the same."

"Then tell me," said Naoise through gritted teeth. "Tell me somethin' about 'im that doen't make him a bloody monster, 'cause all I see in him is a rabid beast that needs to be put down."

That did it. Alsantör's face contorted into the same rage filled sneer his father would make right before his demons took over. "That's all you ever fucking see!"

The prince's booming voice echoed down the beach, bouncing off Naoise's eardrums like a blacksmith's hammer. The duke stepped back, all warmth draining from his face as he stared into the devilish glare that flashed like lightning behind the prince's gaze. Something wasn't right about those damned evergreen eyes—was it the setting sun? The lilies' glow?—but whatever it was, it disappeared before Naoise could make it out. He backed away slowly, praying to the Wizards *and* the Gnomes he wasn't about to be attacked.

As though he could read his thoughts, Alsantör exhaled with a grimace. "Fuck. I'm sorry Neesh. I didn't ... Wizards, I didn't mean to—"

Naoise shrugged, though the nagging sense of panic still simmered beneath his chest. "It's alright. Both y'r parents swore, yeh?"

"Wait—what? Of *course* they swore. Why? What happened?"

Whether Alsantör was offended or concerned, Naoise couldn't tell. He rubbed his neck with a nervous chuckle. "Nothing. My eyes're playing tricks on me, is all. Been quite the season, yeh? Treason, war ... what else happened?"

"Káil," whispered Alsantör. "What the hell *hasn't* happened?" The prince plopped back onto his arse, and a quiet sob escaped his throat as he aimlessly drew circles and swirls in the fine, white sand with his fingertips.

Chewing on his lip, Naoise followed suit. "Y're not you, Tör. What happened? Really?"

The prince sucked his teeth, a tear escaping the corner of his eye. "I made a mistake—a big one. And it has nothing to do with this damned treaty."

Ah shite. Doen't say it. Naoise's heart thumped as he prepared for the worst—something worse than even Sólan the Grim.

"It's Rhona."

Káil, ya said it.

Alsantör took a slow breath, but it didn't stop the mass of water now flowing from his eyes and nose. "The hell is wrong with me, Neesh? Why can't I do anything without harming everyone I know? Gnomes, Sólan was right. Perhaps exile would suit me better than—"

"Ah, fook that halfbreed bastar'. He doen't have nearly the responsibility you do." Naoise rested an arm about Alsantör's shoulders and sighed, staring out at the water with his racing thoughts. "How long does she have?"

"She ... ehm ... she took piaraberry tea after finding out. Lost it right before we left. So long as my mother doesn't tell the king, she should be safe."

Káil. What kind of woman kills her own unborn child? Naoise gulped his insults, though his stomach still churned. "I doen't wanna say it, but ... I warned ya."

"I know," croaked Alsantör. "Perhaps 'tis a lesson I had to learn through heartache rather than lecture." Heaving through a sudden barrage of sobs, he trembled. "I suppose I should thank the bloody Wizards I won't have to execute her. *Fuck*, I couldn't do what you did and live with myself."

Can hardly live with myself, as it is. Saoirse's my only fookin' light of late, 'nd now she's in more danger than she was the day she was bloody born.

"Saoirse? *Dame* Saoirse?"

Naoise stiffened. Had he spoken his thoughts? Was the prince's gift of speaking to the Wizards maturing? "What about 'er? Ah dinnae ken what—"

"You just said that Saoirse's your only light of late. Why?"

"Tell me about Sólan. What's y'r deal with him? Why'd ya protect him f'r so bloody long? Since we're likely to spend nearly a moon with the brute, I need to know a bit o' this 'history' ya speak of." Naoise chewed on his lip once again, hoping the prince would take the bait. To his relief, he did.

"Fine. But I'm not done prying about Cadman's niece."

Fookin Cad. Forgot about that bloody son of a sprite.

"Do you remember that half-elf child, about three and a half hundred years ago? The one being hunted by his own people, driven out of Áfgal? I was only thirteen. I think Vaoirsen was still around then."

Naoise furrowed his brow. "Damn, Tör. I hardly remember what year mah balls dropped, let alone what mortal elf was where and when."

The prince snorted. "And yet, you swore you'd never forget that shot to their archer's wrist. Half of us in that damned patrol wanted to throttle you."

Naoise couldn't stop the silly grin that quickly stretched across his face. "Yeh, I remember that one, now. Heh. I wasn't the most humble then, was I?"

Alsantör jabbed his friend with a playful elbow and snorted. "You're not the most humble now. You just learned to hide it better. That child was Sólan. So, you tell me, Neesh. Did he look like a rabid beast then?"

"What! I'd've remembered *those* orange eyes!"

"They're brown," said Alsantör sharply. "More of an amber or hazel, actually. But it's the silver specks that make them look orange if you don't pay attention."

"So, we both had a hand in savin' his arse back then. Didn't seem to stop him from becoming what he did." A cool breeze sent a shiver down Naoise's spine at the thought of all the blood on that mongrel's hands. "Besides, I don't see the reason behind that tantrum o' his in the orcs' tavern. He doen't seem to enjoy bein' Jannon's bastar', even if he is the firstborne."

Alsantör shrugged. "He doesn't have to enjoy it to be angry. If given the chance, he'd likely give his birthright to his brother … but he never did. Why else do you think he agreed to do this? When you don't have a family, you grasp any kind you can get, regardless of the dysfunction."

Naoise winced. Gnomes, did he know too well what the prince meant. He fidgeted with his own brother's ring beneath his leather glove and fought the oncoming tears seeping through the cracks in his heart. *Dammit, Tör. Y're bloody right.*

"I see it," he finally confessed. "Y're perspective." He sighed, dropping his head in defeat. "Káil, what a fooked life … but that doen't mean I like him."

"You don't need to like him. I just need you to stop trying to kill him every time he says something you don't like. He thrives on that kind of conflict."

"I noticed," said Naoise, grumbling.

"I'm serious, Neesh. Once you get past the brash, angry exterior, you'd be surprised at the amount of kindness of which he's capable. Give him time. His heart's in the right place—it's just damaged."

Bloody hell, Tör. Why doen't ya just suck 'im off 'nd be done with it? Naoise rolled his eyes at the lecture. He was used to giving advice, but taking it? Especially from the prince? Wizards be damned if he listened. But Naoise knew he was right in one thing: Sólan thrived on conflict, and he was prone to all manner of violent outbursts.

"Fine," he said. "Just answer me this: who was the baker's boy?"

Alsantör opened his mouth to answer, but—

"My brother," a husky voice answered from behind.

The elves jumped to their feet and unsheathed their swords, ready to fight the bastard who'd sneaked up on them, but it was just Sólan. He stood facing them, head cocked and smiling curiously.

"Wizards be good, how long've you been standing there?" said

Naoise. Adrenaline shook his hands, even as he slumped his shoulders with a sigh.

"Long enough," Sólan said.

"How much did you hear?" said Alsantör. Obviously, he wasn't ready for Sólan to know *all* of his life, either.

Naoise raised an eyebrow. *Some friend you are, Tör—keepin' secrets from the man ya claim to—*

"Enough."

"Hmph," said Naoise. "Glad t'see y're punctual, if nothin' else."

Sólan flashed a mischievous grin before dropping his expression to a sad scowl. "I hope you are well-rested, as we have seven days of travel until we reach the Oasis City's southern walls." Removing his hatchet from its holster, he rubbed and polished until it reflected the purple lilies and the red sunset in a wondrously water-like glow. He handed it to Alsantör, who frowned in obvious confusion.

"What's this for?"

"I cannot be your 'slave' while armed, amógo."

Naoise took in a sharp breath. "Is that the reason f'r ... this?" He waved his hand around, motioning to the odd armour and chains wrapped about Sólan's torso. "I've never seen anything like it—f'r a slave."

"I have a plan, sañero ... aeh ... Veer."

"It's Naoise." *Prick.*

"Whatever." Turning to Alsantör, Sólan nodded once. "Chain me up. We leave once the first stars are out."

"Why?" said Naoise, crossing his arms. "What's this plan of yours? We've travelled far enough, and we need to know what the hell's going on in that mind o' yours."

"The further inland we go, the higher the heat of the day," said Alsantör.

"And the higher the concentration of Taela patrols. We must get within half a league from the walls, unseen, before we can strike," added Sólan.

"This is Sólan's domain, Naoise. We have to trust him."

The Veer grimaced at the smug grin spreading across Sólan's

miserable face. "I'll trust 'im the moment I leave that damned city alive. Until then …"

"You will have to do as I say, or else you will *not* leave that city at all," said Sólan. He marched up to Naoise and stood in front of him, toe to toe, noses nigh touching. "Now tie me up, you miserable putathóta."

Naoise's nose twitched into a snarl. "With pleasure, *cabróde*."

46

THE OASIS CITY

*A*t the peak of the gibbous moon, Alsantör thanked the Wizards that Naoise and Sólan seemed to tolerate each other for the sixth straight night. At least, that was until Sólan asked, "So, which of my sisters are you to marry, amógo?"

"Siobhan," Alsantör said curtly. "And, you're supposed to be my prisoner, remember?"

Sólan snorted. "Tíal, but you failed to gag me, indionta. 'Tis a shame my previous 'captor' allowed me to keep my tongue, aeh?"

"F'r fook's sake. *I'm* gon' cut out y'r tongue if ya keep talking," grumbled Naoise.

Alsantör sucked his teeth. *This was a mistake. Wizards be good, this was a bloody mistake. I wish Faerin were here.*

"What of ... aeh ... Moira? Is she cursed to remain a maiden for eternity?"

"She's promised to me, arsehole."

Sólan suddenly dug his feet into the sand. "She what!"

Alsantör yelped as he collided into Sólan's clunky armour. "What the *fuck*, Sólan?"

Sólan seemed to pay no mind to the prince. "Tör, I changed my mind. I refuse to—"

"You've *got* to be fookin' me," grumbled Naoise. "I told you this was a mistake. Ya can't trust these bloody halfbreed mongrels."

"Sólan, Naoise, I swear to the Wizards …" Alsantör never got the chance to finish his sentence. The sounds of rattling chainmail averted everyone's attention to the north. "Shite."

The prince flopped to the ground behind a cluster of tumbleweeds, praying to every deity he knew that they wouldn't be seen. In the moon's light, he could barely make out the shadows of Sólan's clenching jaw and the green glow of his pulsing eyes. Behind him, Naoise's nervous breath quivered in his ears, and, and he realised it had been nearly one hundred years since the duke had left the forest for a campaign.

Should've hunted with me during the crusade, Neesh. Maybe you would've learned to bite your bloody tongue like Faerin, rather than your lip.

Sólan wiggled two fingers behind his back, signalling the number of patrols.

The prince silently relayed the message to Naoise.

A countdown began. Alsantör's heart pounded in his fingertips, anticipation fuelling his veins. He was ready.

Three. Two. One. The trio sprang to their feet in unison, weapons at the ready. At least, Naoise and Alsantör had theirs. Sólan shrugged the chains off his torso and whipped them around. Flicking his wrist, he knocked a helmet off one of the patrols, giving Alsantör just enough of a window to drive his gladius between the man's eyes.

The prince spun, facing what he thought was another attacker, but the man collapsed at his feet before he could register where he was. Alsantör kicked the man over to see the shaft of an arrow sticking out of the tiny slit in his visor.

Wizards bless you, Naoise.

"Your marksmanship is unmatched," said Sólan, re-wrapping himself in his chains. "Perhaps I should speak more carefully."

"Eil, that ya should. Oligo e lúas enomógos cil carño, ya radge," said Naoise. *Choose your enemies with care.*

Sólan grinned. "I usually do. Thank the Gods we are not yet enemies, aeh?"

"Nai, not enemies. But, in ninety years, the two of you will be brothers by law, so stop it," grumbled Alsantör. He loosely tied a rope around Sólan's wrists before stripping one of the corpses. "How well do you speak Taela, Neesh?"

"Well enough, I suppose," said Naoise. "Though my accent could use a bit of work."

Sólan snorted. "Perhaps we should have tied you up, then."

"Like you can speak a word o'that tongue."

"Fluently. Slave scouts are useless without communication, though I doubt you would understand, pundijo."

Gnomes, Sólan! Your mouth is going to get the lot of us killed.

Naoise opened his mouth to retort, but—

"Dammit, Naoise, just put this on!" Alsantör tossed the heavy chain mail to his comrade. "If we want to infiltrate this city, we need to look like them."

"Tíal," Sólan agreed. "And we are getting close—we must rest here and move on at first light. This dune should keep us unseen, for now."

Alsantör sighed, but he wasn't relieved in the slightest. *If I don't die in the Oasis City, I will by my father's hand.*

'Twas the end of Naoise's watch. The prince still slept soundly, though Sólan didn't seem to have gotten a single moment of rest.

"The sun will ascend shortly," he said, adjusting his false bonds.

"Eil. That it will," said Naoise. "Did ya get any sleep?"

Sólan shrugged. "I rested. 'Tis the best I can say."

As Naoise watched him stare absently toward the west, he thought he could see the glisten of a tear running down the man's cheek. Chewing on his lip, Naoise pondered whether to converse with the damned brute. Shite didn't matter, anyway. They were all going to die in that gnomes-forsaken desert. "That man in y'r bed back there. Who was 'e?"

The hint of a sad smile tugged at Sólan's mouth. "Only the most important man in my life."

Hmph. Ya sure talk a lot but say nothin'. How the hell does Tör know ya so well?

"Look, we ... ehm ... we started all wrong, eil? I mean, if we're gon' be brothers by law, perhaps—"

"'Tis of no concern whether or not we like each other, Naoise de Vaoirsen. You will never see me again after this."

Naoise flinched. *I'm tryin', Tör. I really am, but this bloody halfbreed ...*

"Tör," said Sólan, breaking his solemnity. "Time to move on."

Shite, perhaps it isn't a façade. Perhaps that's how he really is? Lonely, sad, distrusting. There's more to ya than just Jannon's bloodlust 'nd dark reputation. Naoise drew in a sharp breath as he thought, *Bloody hell! Y're just like Giaven!* His sharp tongue, the mischievous prodding, the angry mask he always wore to hide that distant pain. Yes, just like Giaven, indeed. *Dammit, Neesh. Perhaps* you're *the prick here.*

THE SUN HADN'T EVEN REACHED HALF ITS APEX, BUT THE HEAT WAS already turning Sólan's skin red. It didn't seem to faze either of his companions, though. *Of course not. Fucking Karthi blood of mine. A blessing in winter, but a gods-damned curse in the sun.*

Alsantör held Sólan's chains with a tight grip. "I count six guards at the gate. Any I'm not seeing?" he whispered.

"Niníl. Naoise?"

"Nai. I count six, too."

Perfect.

The three companions made their way over the dune only to be immediately stopped by the closest patrol.

"Chal! Wel-no no nakè?" *Stop! From where you came?*

To Sólan's relief, 'twas Alsantör who spoke. "Pimta ey jaka. Cha nisu-muzalin ak nop-ka." *Dragon's Horn. We bring a halfbreed fighter.*

The patrol grabbed Sólan's jaw in a vice-like grip, turning his head this way and that. He grunted, motioning to the other five to stand down with a quick wave of his hand.

Sólan could hear Naoise's chainmail rattle as he careened his neck upward to check the parapets. "Wall's empty," he whispered, just low enough for the patrols' mortal ears to miss.

The half-dozen patrolmen surrounded the companions, urging them towards the gates.

Thank the Gods, this worked. Sólan tried to hide his relief. Behind him, Alsantör's breath accelerated, while Naoise's chainmail continued to clink. Sólan's own heart thumped wildly as they approached the gate. *Almost there.* The sun was relentless as it beat down on his neck and torso, and the worsening burn made his skin feel tight and hot. *Almost there.* Sand filled his ill-fitting boots with each step. Stumbling, he could feel his bonds nearly unravel, but Alsantör was quick with his hands and ruse.

"Samimi, n'goweh!" said Alsantör, growling. *Stand up, you pig!*

You must be enjoying this, Tör. Perhaps I am your type after all. Sólan's thoughts nearly broke him into laughter. *Stop it, Sólan. Almost there.* He awakened The Dark from its slumber, and the sear behind his eyes began to burn. *Almost there.*

Sólan, the elves, and their escort soon stepped into the wall's shadow, and a moment later, they finally reached the gate. The leading patrol reached up to the massive, gaudy ring that hung as a knocker. Before he could wrap his fingers around the embossed metal, Sólan broke from his bonds. His heavy chains clamoured to the ground, and he snatched his weapon from Alsantör. "Now!"

Chaos ensued. Sólan slammed the spike of his hatchet into the front patrol's eye, ripping flesh and bone from his face as he tossed the man backward from the gate. A stomp on his throat, a kick to his helmet, and the man was dead before he could even make a sound.

Alsantör, too, had cut through the two guards beside him before they'd even realised they were being ambushed.

Naoise's bow remained untouched as he fought off two more with only a dagger. They both collapsed, crimson blood spurting from wounds Sólan hadn't even seen the Veer inflict.

"S'mami-ko weh!" the last patrol cried, too far away for any of them to reach. He fumbled with his belt, snagging a horn. Before he could press it to his lips, however, an arrow pierced his chainmail and into his throat. He fell to the ground and grasped at the shaft in desperation.

With a flick of his wrist, Sólan pulled the man toward him with The Dark. "Kó suna inik afi," he snarled.

The terror in the patrol's eyes was unmistakable, yet Sólan felt no sympathy. All he felt was hatred, rage ... *bloodlust*. He watched with glee as the man's flesh became leathery and ashen before whittling away to dust. A malicious giggle escaped his throat, increasing in volume until—

What the fuck is wrong with me! A sudden pain stabbed through his chest and radiated through his arm and jaw. The Dark whispered in his ears, but he refused to listen.

He tore his eyes away from the carnage and pressed the heel of his hand against his chest. For a moment, the burn in his eyes persisted, and his chest tightened even further. Panic setting in, he feared he'd finally lost control. The Dark was a greedy thing, indeed.

"You alright?"

A soft hand touched Sólan's shoulder, and he spun around with a snarl, a strong grip around the throat of whomever had come to kill him from behind. "Shit," he said, releasing his chokehold with a grimace.

"It's alright," said Alsantör, rubbing his throat. "Shite, I forgot not to grab you like that."

"Hmph. And ya wonder why I doen't trust 'im," said Naoise, grumbling. He walked over to the remnants of the final patrolman and removed his arrow from the body. "Fookin' red-blooded halfbreed."

At any other time, Sólan would have reacted with anger. He would have glared and thrown insults. But all he felt was shame— and fatigue. He desired nothing more than to sink into the sand and disappear until the end of the world. That was what it meant to be a mortal elf. That was who The Dark made him. *That* was why he was the Grim.

Alsantör, however, bared his fangs at the Veer. "Dammit, Naoise! I *told* you not to antagonise him!"

"We're gon' die here anyway, Tör! What does it matter whether it's by his hand or the Taelas?"

Sólan finally gathered his wits and stepped between the two elves. "Do you want your brides back, or not? Because this is how we kill them. I, for one, will not fail my family a second time."

Naoise clenched his fists until the knuckles turned white. "At least y've *got* a bloody family to save," he muttered before stalking off toward the gate.

Alsantör glared at the back of Naoise's head in a stubborn silence —save for the high-pitched squeak of his tongue sucking against his teeth.

Sólan moved toward him with a furrowed brow, all concentration on his evergreen eyes. There was something familiar there. Familiar yet—

"What are you doing?" said Alsantör.

"Looking … I dislike what I see behind your eyes." Sólan leaned in closer, nearly touching his comrade's nose with his own. "Do not let it take hold of you, amógo. 'Twill never let go."

47

FEAST OF NEW SPRING

Sólan's stomach churned as they entered the tunnel beneath the city's massive wall. Naoise and Alsantör had wrapped him again in his chains before straightening their own armour. The six patrols' corpses had been buried beneath the sand, and there seemed to be no sign they'd been there at all.

Echoes of the past sent chills down Sólan's spine as memories flashed behind his eyes. The pit-fighting he'd endured—the scars he still carried on his flesh. The mutilated bodies of mixed-blood men and women who'd chosen death over an eternity of slavery. The slave mothers smothering their children in their sleep in an act of desperate mercy. He'd been told they were being treated better, just like he'd been *told* that his freedom would be granted in the arena. But Sólan knew, as he had then, that words spoken and acts taken were never the same.

The inner gate opened, and two guards frowned at them from outside. At least, Sólan *thought* they were frowning. The piercing, white light from the still-rising sun assaulted his eyes worse than The Dark ever could.

"Wel-no no nakè?" the first guard asked.

A frustrated sigh escaped Alsantör's lips. 'Twas the same

damned question. "Pimta ey jaka. Cha nisu-muzalin ak nop-ka," he repeated. *Dragon's Horn. We bring a halfbreed fighter.*

Without another word, the guards collapsed—dead before they hit the ground.

"The fook just happened?" said Naoise.

Sólan shrugged off his chains for the last time before dragging the corpses into the tunnel. "I grow tired of this disguise, and I refuse to be sent back to those gods-damned arenas."

Naoise startled. "Back? When did—"

"So, what's the plan, then?" said Alsantör. "You were *supposed* to go to the arenas for mere spying—no fights."

"I know that," said Sólan, gritting his teeth. "The plans have changed." *I will not be poisoned by their Viper's Breath again.*

"You've got to be kidding me," whispered Alsantör. "We've made it this far without breaking from our plans, and now that we're inside the bloody gates—"

"I am *not* going back to those pits, Tör!" *I have to make it back to Dakil. We are all dead if I step foot in that arena.*

"Dammit Giaven! Can't ya think with y'r head instead of y'r feelings f'r once?" blurted Naoise.

Sólan froze, looking to the Veer with unveiled confusion. "Who is Giaven?"

The Veer opened his mouth to answer, but quickly clamped his mouth shut. Face flushing, he chewed on his lower lip and turned away.

It seems we have more in common than not, thought Sólan, as the familiar scents of sorrow and shame reached his nostrils.

Alsantör stepped between them. "Why have the plans changed, Sólan? You don't do that lightly."

"What'd ya expect, Tör?" grumbled Naoise. "Look who he is."

"Perhaps you would do better in the arenas," said Sólan. "The pit masters would shit bricks of gold for the chance to see a Veer in a fight."

"I'm *not* addin' to my chances of gettin' killed down here, unlike you."

"If we continue with our original plan, indionta, we *will* be killed, and all your Senet figures will be captured without another toss of the sticks."

"Sólan! What are we *doing*? I need answers, not riddles," said Alsantör. He brought both fists to his face and shook them like a young child throwing a tantrum.

"Do you not see the coloured ribbons tied across the inside of these walls? The silk tents that line the gods-damned road?"

Alsantör stared blankly at Sólan, but Naoise peered toward the tunnel's exit. "Some kind of festival, yeh?"

"'Tis the Feast of New Spring. A celebration of the end of winter —their last fruits sacrificed to their gods as thanks for protecting them into to the new year," said Sólan, stripping naked. "Only the most well-known pit fighters will be in the arenas during this celebration. Only *their* names will be called during the tournament, and mine is dead, remember? We need to blend in." He undressed one of the dead guards, the taller one, and changed into his armour. Despite his best efforts, sand infiltrated every crevice from his chest down to his toes, and his burned skin chafed with each tiny movement.

Alsantör merely rolled his eyes and walked into the light, grumbling curses.

Sólan smiled beneath the chainmail that now covered his face. He dropped it immediately as he met Naoise's anxious gaze. "Neither of you answered my question: who is Giaven?"

Biting his lip hard enough to draw silver blood, Naoise answered without actually answering, "Y're not the only man in these lands who's lost a brother. Despite Jannon and Diarmuid's best efforts, y'r kind wasn't wiped out like mine." He leaned in close, staring mossy brown daggers into the Áfgaliard. "I want to trust ya, Sólan of Ciudelago. I really do," he said. "Doen't fuck it up."

THE COMPANIONS MADE THEIR PLANS AND SPLIT UP. WHERE THE TAELAS had hidden Jannon's daughters was beyond any of them, and since Sólan's escape nearly three hundred years ago, the city had grown at least tenfold. Back then, the architecture had been little more than simple buildings of square brick and wooden beams. Just in the last hundred years, however, imports of marble from Prastömin, quartz from Karthénos, and domestic acacia grew to dominate even the poorest of villages. Every wall and temple displayed perfectly symmetrical mosaics composed of thousands of colours.

'Twas disorienting, to say the least.

Still chafing in his sand-caked armour, Sólan trudged through the easternmost marketplace where farmers, tailors, and tinkerers sold their wares to the most affluent of Taela citizens. Thousands of silk tents lined the sandy streets with bright colours of blues, greens, and yellows. Vendors shouted over each other for the undivided attentions of the hundreds of people that shopped and traded. Bright-coloured spices were piled high out of their barrels, gold and jewels reflected the sun's blinding light on their displays, and the smells of baked bread and fried meats filled the air with heavy goodness.

Sólan's mouth watered as he slinked past carts that sold fresh rotisserie shawarma, pita with hummus, kushari … The buttery scent of cinnamon, cloves, and nuts from fresh baklava made his stomach growl louder than it had in Bansungei when he ate their adobo.

He dodged a drunken street fight as it spilled onto the street, jumping on the opportunity to lift a heavy purse from the man now in shackles.

From there, Sólan purchased a deep blue achkan, ivory silk pants —dhotis as they were called—and a matching turban. Silver filigree and buttons glimmered on the coat in a bright display of wealth. For his feet, he bought a pair of simple leather slippers that sealed the cuffs of his dhotis from the hot sand.

A thin layer of black paste on his lower lids helped with the glare of the high sun but did little to help hide him from the wandering eyes of lustful people. 'Twas likely, to his dismay, that the contrast merely increased the vibrance in his amber irises.

Sólan wandered through the tents, listening to the idle chat regarding the feast—the favourites in the arenas, which of the hundreds of gods had blessed them that day, how they had disciplined their "rebellious" slaves. It all made his skin crawl.

A distant whisper from a poppy farmer at the northern edge piqued his interest. Something about silver blood and appeasing the gods of war with—

Suddenly, Sólan tripped. He fell to the ground with a thud, landing on top of what seemed like a small animal that squealed at the impact. "Shit. Apologies, sir," Sólan muttered. *Fucking Orovite, piezo de medría.* "I didn't mean to—" Sólan stiffened, locking eyes with the unfortunately familiar and buggy violet gaze of Oleg Kinev. Baring his fangs, he hissed. "You."

"You didn't see me, mate." Oleg swung. His fist smashed into Sólan's jaw with a jolting crunch, allowing him to escape.

"Fucking pundijo," whispered Sólan, rubbing his face with a grimace. He flitted his gaze around, The Dark threatening to simmer in his chest. A woman's distant scream snapped his attention westward. *There you are.*

Springing to his feet, Sólan bounded effortlessly through the sandstone streets. "Ruki hopa, m'puzi!" he shouted. *Come back here, thief!* Countless faces looked at him before jumping aside as he rushed past. Say one thing for the Taelas. Say they loved to see the tortured of the world punished by the rich.

Oleg slowed just enough to peek over his shoulder. "Fuck!" he squealed, taking a hard step to the right.

Sólan followed, ready to corner the bastard in the dead-end alley. But it was empty. "Fucking piglet," he muttered, rubbing his sore jaw. His ears twitched at the muffled sound of tip-toeing hooves clicking directly under his feet. A triumphant smirk twitched up the corner of his mouth. *I found you, putathóta.*

SÓLAN SAT IN THE DARKEST CORNER OF AN UNDERGROUND ROOM. IT WAS empty, save for a series of bamboo cots and small chairs. On the walls were dozens of hooks, chains, and ropes—a holding cell for slaves before their days on the open market.

Swallowing a bubble of rising bile, Sólan concentrated on the poorly hidden door opposite him. Tentative footsteps approached, stopping just long enough for the clattering jangle of a clumsy padlock unlatching.

The door creaked open, and the oddling's shadow slipped into the room before it clicked shut. He leaned against the wall and sighed. "Fucking halfbreed cunt," he whispered. "Can't read for shit, but can count like—"

"You should learn to make slippers for your hooves, sañero. Even the dead could hear you approach."

Oleg gasped. "Sólan! What a pleasant surprise, hey? Wasn't expecting you to be wandering the farmers' marketplace of Taelonael's capital!" He paused, as though waiting for a warm welcome in return. "So … uh … what brings you to the Oasis City, friend?"

"A 'pleasant surprise', am I?" said Sólan, lifting an eyebrow. "Because it appears I am only your 'friend' when you are hiding something from me … this 'halfbreed cunt,' as you say."

All evidence of pleasantry was wiped clean from Oleg's face. "What the fuck are you doing here, Sólan?"

Sólan snorted. "I should ask you the same thing. I never thought you were as much of a … aeh … *slaver* as you were a drug seller." Sólan crossed his arms and lounged his feet on the closest cot. "To say I am disappointed would nearly be a lie."

"I'm here all the time, asshole. Call me a slaver again, and I'll have your tongue ripped out through your fucking nose."

"You always threaten my tongue. Why are you so obsessed with it? Are you jealous of Dakil, perhaps?"

Oleg rolled his eyes. "Perhaps I should remove your cock instead, hey? Now, if you'll excuse me, I have an apyin supplier to meet with." Spinning on his hoof, the Orovite retreated toward the door, but—

Sólan's hatchet sliced through the air and embedded itself in the wall, its handle blocking the door's inward swing just outside of Oleg's reach. "Speaking of which, your supplier owes me a great deal of gold."

"Is *that* what you're here for? Fuck, Sólan, you're mad! You jumped headfirst into the fucking dragon's lair for a bit of gold?"

"Four shipments of apyin, two of kabotay oil, and three of

powder. *Shipments,* Oleg. Not mere barrels. 'Tis more than 'a bit of gold.' Besides, you are also behind on your payments to the twins." Sólan stood and stretched lazily. "So, you are either keeping our gold to yourself, or I, too, have a meeting with your supplier."

"Kabir's not a man to cross, and if he finds out you're still alive after all these years—" Oleg clacked his mouth shut, eyes wide.

"Kabir?" Sólan blinked. "*The* Kabir?"

Oleg clamped a hand over his mouth, desperately shaking his head.

Without warning, Sólan doubled over and burst into a heavy peal of laughter. "Gods! You mean to tell me that I have been smuggling for the fucking prince of Taelonael all this time? How old is he? Fifteen?"

"Twenty-one, but—*dammit* Sólan! You were the most hated man in the fucking desert! You've got to get out of here if you wanna survive past the full moon."

Still chuckling, Sólan straightened his posture. "Oh, to see his face when he discovers who his best smuggler and assassin is …"

"He ain't gonna discover nothing, 'cause you're still dead, remember?" Oleg pulled a wooden flask from his belt and chugged its contents—based on the smell, 'twas Orovite vodka.

"Look, Sólan," said Oleg, wiping his mouth with the back of his grubby hand. "You'd be safer as Jannon's personal servant up in the damned tundra. Kabir's ruthless, hey. He's not above murderin' his own father if it meant the crown. King Jabali's youth hasn't helped his health, and there're rumours of a coup. Fuck, folks even think Kabir's poisoning Jabali to make it look natural! They say he was always obsessed with their alchemy, and based on—"

"I have no interest in the intricacies of Taela politics, pundijo," said Sólan, eyes rolling. "I have other business to attend to. If you can ensure that at least half of the gold you owe me makes it to Dakil on the *Silent Dancer* by the full moon, I will let you go with all of your fingers intact."

"Wait, you're not just here for the money, are you? You're here for a hit. I can't have competition for your assassination skills—especially here, dammit." The colour from Oleg's face suddenly drained. "Shit, are you here for me?"

The scent of fear oozing from the oddling's skin nearly made Sólan's cock harden. "That is none of your concern. You should be thanking whatever gods you believe in that I am not here for you, either. I hope to leave this place with no bloodshed." At Oleg's sigh of relief, Sólan added, "However, I am not above spilling yours to protect my end of our business arrangements."

"Of course you can't just let me go without threatening me," grumbled Oleg.

"Nin*í*l. Nor can I let you go without asking more questions." Sólan crossed to the door and loosely wrapped his fingers around his hatchet. "What do you know about this 'sacrifice' at the full moon?"

48

KABIR

*N*aoise stood watch at the entrance of the slave market, nigh half a day's trek from where Sólan searched on the city's eastern side. While his Taela was rough at best, Naoise'd convinced the single guard there to take a break.

The stench of burning flesh and excrement assaulted his nose, and it took all the strength the duke could muster to keep from vomiting. Still, the dull, gargled screams of tortured prisoners and starving slaves threatened to break him. If that was what awaited his future bride, then Wizards curse anyone who got in his way to bring her home.

The piercing scream of a child echoed through the dark tunnels behind him. *Shite. What the hell're they doing to that poor girl?*

"Removing her womb," said a husky voice, as though he'd heard Naoise's pondering.

Naoise gasped and spun, bringing his dagger to the throat of an obviously wealthy man dressed in dark blue and silver. "Fookin' hell."

A scarred eyebrow lifted over a pair of familiar, amber eyes. "'Tis merciful, if you can believe that. Though, I was told they started using kabotay to numb the pain of the process. At the very least, she will never be bred." Sólan flicked away the blade with a scoff.

"Where'd ya get this?" said Naoise, motioning to the odd disguise. "And what're ya doin' here?"

"Change in plans ... again."

"Wizards be good, Sólan," Naoise muttered. "Is there ever a set plan with ya?"

"Not with the art of scouting." Sólan flashed a mischievous grin before looking down the tunnel's entrance. "I saw Tör on my way here. He should be arriving to the rendezvous at any moment."

"Art of scouting?" Gnomes be merciful, Sólan, listen to y'rself.

Another child's scream reverberated behind them, and Sólan grimaced. "Medría, I hate this place."

"Alright, Sólan. Why're we meeting here at midday?" Naoise's voice was strained, as though he'd just finished a fight in the arena. "I thought we were waiting 'til the morrow."

"Unfortunately, we have not the luxury of time." Sólan glared, carefully hiding the sharp points to his canines. "And that is not my name. I am Okeyo! Master of the poppy fields that supply medicine to the whole of the eastern lands!"

Gnomes, was his act flawless! For a man who hated the desert kingdom as much as he claimed, Naoise thought Sólan fit in better there than he would in any Áfgalese village. Gritting his teeth, the duke muttered, "Apologies, Okeyo. I mistook ya f'r someone else."

"See that it never happens again," said Sólan, waving his hand around like a damned theatre act. He suddenly dropped his voice to a whisper. "We are in bigger shit than I thought. We have walked into a gods-damned trap, and *my sisters* are the bait."

"Káil."

Sólan nodded urgently. "We must go to the rendezvous and find Tör." Without warning, he fell forward into Naoise and gave a terrible screech. "Thank the gods I foundeded you, guard!" he slurred in the loudmouthed manner of a drunken fool.

"The fook're ya doin'?" hissed Naoise.

"I need yerrr halp! I've been robbed!"

Wizards, save me. Naoise hoisted Sólan to his feet and said, "Where'd he go?"

"Thisss-a-way!" Sólan pointed to the city's centre and dragged the Veer with him. "Hee went thisss-a-way!"

ALSANTÖR WEDGED HIMSELF BETWEEN THE CORNER OF THE PRISON'S tower wall and a parapet, watching. He'd long since abandoned the clunky Taela armour and slipped into a servant's white kurta dhoti and matching turban, his face covered with a thick white veil. Beneath the flowy pants, his gladius was strapped tightly to his thigh.

The sun was finally setting, but the glare from the eastern horizon made him regret not smearing some kajal under his eyes. A commotion just north of him twitched through his ears. A Taela guard was being dragged by Sólan, who was still in his blue achkan.

Dammit, Sólan! How the fuck are you drunk already? The prince slowly clambered down the wall, gritting his teeth in anticipation of being seen. Thank the Wizards, he wasn't—at least, until Sólan screeched.

"There he iss! Tha'ss the man who robbed meee!"

You were robbed? And why do you have a fucking Taela guard with—

"You sure? Ah doen't see anything on 'im," said Naoise.

Gnomes be merciful, his accent is terrible. "What the hell are you doing, Sólan?" hissed Alsantör.

"Creating a gods-damned distraction. Look behind you."

Sucking his teeth, the prince spun to see a handful of prison guards running out of their hiding places in the tunnel.

"Huwiz o hina! Roni nyamot!" Naoise shouted. *Servant in white! Step back!*

Alsantör was quickly brought to the ground with his hands pinned behind his back. The ruse was complete, though he didn't know what the hell he was supposed to be doing.

Naoise leaned forward and whispered, "He just went inside. Fooker was wearin' that damned arena armour under his coat."

An escaped n'poginat. Of course. Alsantör gritted his teeth. "Now what?"

"Now I arrest ya, 'nd clear us a path f'r escape."

Wizards be good, I hope you find them, Sólan.

SÓLAN TIPTOED BENEATH THE FLICKERING TORCH LIGHT, HIS HAND gripping his hatchet. He tossed the blue achkan into an empty cell, where it fluttered silently to the ground. Unravelling his dhoti, Sólan wrapped the fine cloth about his waist and tied its ends together through the armour's ring on his chest. The slippers, unfortunately, he had to keep—as uncomfortable as they were, they were infinitely quieter than the pit-fighting boots.

The torchlight made the sandstone bricks glow an eerie red the deeper Sólan walked down the corridor. The air was cooler in there, thank the Gods, but 'twas still—very still. And it smelled of ... of ...

Gods, it smells like nothing. What kind of alchemy hides such vile— Fuck. What if Oleg sent me into a trap?

He didn't know why the thought hadn't occurred to him—that oddling always spoke of killing him, cutting out his tongue ... or worse. He shuddered. He had worked with that buggy-eyed pig long enough to know that whatever manner of torture Oleg imagined for him was likely far worse than anything Sólan had ever inflicted on anyone.

Listening at each wooden door he passed, Sólan searched for anything that would indicate where his sisters were.He came to a latched door, but it, too, was silent, the prisoner inside likely dead. From another door across the way, however, came quiet whimpers and the jingling of chain. *Moira! Siobhan!* He peaked into the small, barred opening of the door to see a Taela man wearing what was left of servants' garb. Blood and blistery fluid dripping down the man's back, the smell of burned flesh assaulted Sólan's nose. *Just the first torture of the day, it seems.*

A faint, rhythmic banging grew louder as he sneaked down the hall, cloaking himself in shadow with each patrol that marched by.

Shouts, too, were heard with each passing moment. Medría, how long had he been down there? Hours, at least. Finally, he came to the last door, and he approached to listen.

"Chal!" a voice suddenly shouted. *Stop!*

Sólan froze.

"Uliwen'kaje kat'ka weh? Roni nyamot, n'goweh." *How did you escape? Step back, you pig.*

The Dark rose in Sólan's chest, and the familiar burn behind his eyes returned, bouncing an eerie green glow off the metal window of the door before him. "Ita kuma no biso-una isu nivuk-eh," he said through a malicious smile. *You would be wise not to cross me.*

"Ita kuma no biso-una roni nyamot!" *You would be wise to step back!*

"Oh, sañero, how careless you are with choosing your enemies," said Sólan, dropping the Taela in his voice.

He spun, swinging his hatchet with a blow so forceful that it should've beheaded the guard. The man, however, blocked his strike with his spear. Catching the edge of Sólan's hatchet, he swung upward to expose Sólan's torso. A series of jabs, thrusts, and spins followed as the men danced to their deadly rhythm—Áfgalese mist-fighting and Taela fire-dancing. Neither could overcome the other until—

The spear impaled Sólan's chest. With a wicked grin, he repeated the same words he'd said to Dakil all those years ago: "You missed my heart, putathóta."

Terror flashed through the guard's face as Sólan charged him like a bull, eyes ablaze with a fiery pain that outmatched every other time he'd felt it.

But Sólan didn't care—he had an enemy to kill. Snapping the spear's shaft with a single hand, he ducked and embedded the spike of his hatchet into the guard's groin. The Taela buckled, falling to his knees as crimson blood soaked the ground beneath him.

Sólan pulled the remaining spear from his chest, standing over his victim as a maniacal chuckle escaped his throat. "Kó suna inik afi." *And now you die.*

He finished him with a kick to the head that knocked both his helmet and chain mail off. With a final battle cry, Sólan hammered the blade of his weapon into the man's forehead. Blow after blow, he shattered the man's skull, continuing until his head was naught but a bloody stump atop his neck.

Crimson blood and fragments of bone spattered his chest as he stood, looking to the heavy door before him. He kicked it open in triumph, certain he'd found his sisters.

Empty.

"Medría," Sólan muttered. As he took a step into the room, a cold chain wrapped about his throat and tightened, bringing him to the ground with a hard thud. "Putathóta!" he yelped. He had walked into a gods-damned trap, just as he'd feared.

Swinging his legs upward, Sólan flipped over his assailant and wedged his neck into the crook of his elbow. But a woman's sudden scream stayed his attack. 'Twas not the head of a Taela guard he held, but that of a woman with wavy taupe hair and large pointed ears. *Oh Gods, 'tis you!*

"Káil ti pashti!" the woman snarled, driving her bony elbow into Sólan's ribs.

"Wait! I—"

Crunch. A fist to his nose blinded him just long enough for the woman to knee his groin and jump away.

Fuck. You are a fighter, harmenóta. Shaking the tears from his eyes, he finally regained his sight to see … nothing. His ears twitched at the echo of two pairs of footsteps fleeing down the hall. His sisters had escaped, thank the Gods.

ALSANTÖR FINALLY REACHED THE MAIN TUNNEL AFTER SNEAKING through the labyrinthine prison tower. Naoise was somewhere outside, finding an escape route. Preferably unseen.

From the far end of the tunnel, he saw two beings sprinting toward him, hand in hand. The dull light of the torches finally revealed them to be unarmed women. *Thank the Wizards!* Forgetting he'd changed back into Taela armour, Alsantör rushed toward them with open arms.

The silver-haired one screamed, and the other stepped forward, fists up. "Kill us now, or let us go! We'll not be yer pawns any longer!"

Alsantör stopped, removing his helmet and mail. "It's alright. We're here to save you." *Wait. Where's Sólan?*

"We?" The dark-haired woman lowered her hands just enough to show her face.

You must be Moira. Which means …

"Tíal, 'we,'" said a husky voice from somewhere behind the women.

"And who are ye?" the silver-haired woman asked. "Either of ye?"

Before Sólan or Alsantör could answer, the sound of bells rang throughout the tunnel. Everyone froze. After a brief pause, a second round of bells echoed, and the two men gasped in unison. "Naoise!"

The four grasped each other's hands and sprinted toward the tunnel's entrance, the prince leading the way. Despite the bright light nigh blinding him, Alsantör yelped, sliding to a halt.

Two score of Taela guards suddenly surrounded them, spears raised and ready to strike. In their midst, a young man in brightly coloured armour and a golden turban sat atop a decorated white horse. He held the end of an apyin fibre rope—embedded with shards of glass and metal—which was wrapped around a naked man of freckled skin, copper hair, and pointed ears.

Naoise!

Silver blood seeped from Naoise's nose, mouth, and eyes. Gnomes be merciful, the Veer looked as though he might fall onto his face and die right there.

"I didn't want to believe it when I was told two Prasti had broken into my city and murdered three score of my men," said the head guard. A smug grin stretched across his face as he pulled on the rope.

Naoise grimaced as the sharp barbs dug deeper into his skin.

Moira gasped and rushed forward, only for Sólan to wrap his arms about her waist and pull her back. She screamed, punching and kicking in an effort to free herself, but Sólan's grip was impossible to break.

"'Tis alright, harmenóta. 'Tis alright," he whispered. "He will not die today, I promise."

Alsantör sucked the back of his teeth with a wince. *Don't make promises you can't keep, friend. We've failed ... My father will finally lose the son over whom he so often grieves.*

Moira finally settled, but tears still freely flowed down her face as she whimpered. "Naoise, please. Oh Wizards, save him."

If the guard took any notice of the woman's desperate whispers, he didn't show it. "I must ask, however, why you have freed one of my pit fighters alongside my blood offerings?"

Sólan snorted.

Shite. Don't do it Sólan. Please don't do it!

"You must be the ignorant child who calls himself 'prince.' Kabir, correct?"

You did it. Káil, your mouth is going to get us all killed.

"Ah! A new fighter! One who has yet to lose his tongue," said Kabir. He pulled on the rope again, and Naoise grunted in pain.

Sólan stepped forward, his eyes pulsing in that damned green glow again. "Your masters have taught you poorly, pundijo. I am no slave to you." Slowly, he reached behind his back to retrieve his hatchet. The guards surrounding them pressed in ominously, their spears too close for comfort.

Alsantör gulped. They were going to die except by some miracle of the Wizards.

Siobhan gasped in recognition of that weapon. "The Grim," she squeaked.

Quicker than most mortal men could perceive, a hint of fear flashed across Kabir's eyes at the woman's words. Without warning, he and all his men burst into laughter. "To think I nearly believed you, Karthi girl! The Grim is dead, ten years past. If I remember right, it was your betrothed beside you who took his head."

"Let the Veer go, prince," said Sólan, "and I may allow you to live long enough to see dusk. You have broken your father's oath by taking these women from their homes."

Kabir bared his teeth. "My father is weak for allowing these silver-bloods to control my kingdom. Do you truly believe—"

"Oh, Kabir."

Sólan's chuckle made Alsantör want to crawl out of his already-shivering skin.

"Give my regards to King Jabali. I am sure you are *dying* to tell him of your mistake. 'Chugawa ma'adi wakon'dwa ungalua.'" *Choose your enemies with care.*

All of the guards suddenly collapsed, and Kabir's steed reared at the sudden shift in atmosphere. The Taela prince dropped his rope to regain control.

"Go!" shouted Sólan. "They will not stay down for long!"

Alsantör rushed to Naoise and tried hoisting him to his feet. The Veer merely collapsed. "We need to get the fuck out of here, Neesh. Lean on me." In his periphery, Sólan's posture waver as bright, green embers flickered and sparked around his head, forming a crown. *Wizards be good, he's losing control!*

Tossing a now unconscious Naoise over his shoulder, the prince grabbed the Siobhan's wrist and ran southward toward the wall. Moira, snatching a Taela dagger on her way. *Gnomes be merciful, I wish you were mine*, he thought as he watched her steal a second weapon. An arrow whistled past his ear to bring his attention back to the present. *Though, I suppose it doesn't matter to whom we're betrothed if we're dead.*

49

BROTHER MINE

*A*stinging pain on Naoise's cheek startled him awake. *Where the fook am I?* He was lying on his back, the stars were out, and he was naked. That's all he could gather, other than the spasms shooting throughout his torso that violently told him he was still alive.

A Karthi woman's voice squealed, piercing his eardrums like hot pokers. "Gnomes! We're alive!" she said. "And I have me true love to thank!"

Ah. Heard that damned screech before … He gasped. *Siobhan O'Jannon! Wizards be good, we did it!*

Ignoring the cuts and bruises that littered his body, Naoise shot upright with a grunt, only to collide his forehead with another's.

"Káil!" A woman yelped. "Glad to know ye're still alive, me laird."

Naoise's breath caught in his chest. Never since Ina's death did he think he'd be relieved to hear such a honey-sweet voice. "Oh, Moira. Thank the Wizards, so are you."

Moira smiled. It wasn't the forlorn smile he'd remembered from their last meeting, but one of radiant joy and relief. She wrapped her arms around his torso and planted her mouth on his lips as if it were the last time they'd ever see each other.

Naoise wished he could reciprocate, but the pain was just too damned much. Grunting again, his grimace broke their kiss. "Fook. I'm sorry, Moira. I just—"

"No need to apologise," said Moira, releasing him. "Ye're hurt." She traced her fingers across the cuts on his chest, sticky, silver blood staining her fingertips. With a careful sigh, she leaned forward and brushed her lips against his once again.

Naoise caressed her jaw and parted his mouth to deepen their kiss. "Wizards, I thought I'd lost ya." His own words shocked him. Why was he speaking like this to her? They'd met a single time, ten bloody years ago! Though the letters they exchanged had quickly turned from those of business to those of romance. Diplomacy to love.

Gnomes be merciful, *was* he in love?

"Should probably get ye some clothes. Ye're shivering." Moira's voice dripped with concern, though Naoise hadn't even noticed the cold.

"I'm alright," he said through chattering teeth. "But yeh, I doen't want any more bloody sand up my—"

"We need to get moving, Neesh," said Alsantör. "We only have enough supplies to last us six days, not seven."

Naoise bit his lip, stifling the curses simmering in his throat.

Moira, however, held nothing back. "Can't ye see he's wounded? He'd be lucky to survive the night if ye make him travel now."

"*None* of us'll survive the night if we don't start moving toward the coast. Chainless won't wait for us forever." The prince crossed his arms with a scowl. "I'll bloody carry him if I have to, but we've got to get moving."

The Karthi senator opened her mouth to argue, but a soft hand on the small of her back stayed her voice. "It's alright, Moira. I'll be alright, ya ken?" said Naoise, pinning a loose wave of hair behind her ear.

Alsantör huffed, stomping away with an even deeper scowl.

"Here's at least a bloody cover for your cock," he said, tossing a pair of Taela-made trousers at Naoise's head.

"What's up his arse?" said Moira.

"Gnomes know," grumbled Naoise. "Fookin' bastar's been like this since we left the bloody forest. Though, I should be like that too if I weren't so relieved to be alive. Alive 'nd with you safe." He kissed her cheek before slowly slipping into the clothing. Each breath sent sharp pains down his chest, his abdomen ... his bloody everything. He collapsed onto all fours, starving for air as his heartbeat throbbed inside his head.

"Káil, Naoise!" said Moira. "We cannot move on like this, yer grace. Ye're going to *kill* him."

"I'm alright," Naoise said hoarsely. "I'm alright."

"Maldónta enfríno, amógo," said a familiar Áfgalese voice. *Fucking hell, friend.* "You most certainly are not alright."

Thank the Wizards, it's Sólan the Grim!

Gods, this is all my fault. I should never have exposed them, nor *myself. I should have—*

"Thank the Wizards ye're alive, fighter!"

The voice of Sólan's silver-haired sister was unbearable, and he winced at the ringing that lingered in his ears after her shrill assault. "Tíal, thank the Gods," he muttered, grunting at the squeeze that she probably meant as a hug.

"I half expected to see a flaming crown about your head, friend," said Alsantör, embracing Sólan as well. The prince shivered as though he was about to cry. "It's damned good to see you."

"Heh." Sólan squirmed out of the prince's arms. "Elék be praised, he has protected me thus far." With a clenched jaw, he locked eyes with Siobhan. "Are you hurt, harmenóta?"

"Why do ye keep calling us that?" said Moira.

Sólan turned to meet her fiery, sapphire gaze with a raised eyebrow. "*Surely* you know who I am." Her blank stare indicated she did not. "The Grim? The 'man who should not be alive?' The bastard mortal son of Duke Jannon O'Corin of Karthénos?"

Moira crossed her arms with a furrowed brow. "I'm not convinced. Alsantör took his head ten years ago"—she turned to the prince—"did ye not, yer grace?"

"Well …" Alsantör rubbed the back of his neck, sucking his teeth like he always did when uncomfortable.

Gods, you are going to swallow your whole fucking mouth if you keep doing that. Sighing, Sólan averted his attention to the Veer as Alsantör and the two women began to argue, then cry, then shout …

Naoise had fallen back asleep. He was clammy and pale—well, paler than he had been when they'd met. Shit, was he dead? Sólan moved toward him, and upon closer inspection, a surprising wave of relief trickled through his chest. He was still alive, thank the Gods. But not for long.

"Duke," Sólan whispered, shaking Naoise's shoulder. "Naoise, wake up."

A faint groan escaped the Veer's lips, but that's all he could get out of him.

The sickening sweet smell of fermenting fruit slithered through Sólan's nostrils, bringing vivid memories of madness, blood, sand, and savagery. *Fuck. Not the Viper's Breath! Anything but—*

"Doen't ya dare touch me with that bloody magic o'yours," croaked Naoise. "I'd rather die than—"

"Oh, fuck off, Veer," said Sólan, snarling. "That rope was tainted with Kabir's worst alchemy. He was going to turn you into a pit fighter by cutting out your tongue and wiping your memories until there was naught left but bloodlust and undying obedience to your masters. You will not die, but you *will* kill us all."

A deep growl vibrated through the ground from Naoise's chest, but he finally obliged. "Fine."

With a single nod, Sólan pressed the heel of his hand just over Naoise's heart. "This will sting." The searing heat of The Dark burned behind his eyes, but the pale flesh wouldn't close. *Medría. The oath!*

Sólan's chest tightened in panic—or was it desperation? What was that tincture he'd swallowed so long ago? When he'd been bought out of the arenas by Ignacio the Grim himself?

Harvest to rot
—embers to ice
Yet the salt shall give thee life

Bitter to sweet
—vinegar to wine
So the salt shall make thee mine

He jumped to his feet and sprinted to his other comrades. "Tör! I need saltwater!"

"You what?" Confusion blanketed Alsantör's face. "We don't have salt, and our water is—"

"We have food preserved with salt. I need it. *Now.* Naoise is poisoned."

ALSANTÖR PACED AT THE BASE OF THE MASSIVE DUNE THAT HID THEM from the rising sun. Sólan had taken half the night to mix his damned antidote to the "Snake's Breath," or whatever he'd called it. The prince hadn't studied Taela alchemy as closely as he should have in his youth.

Sólan'd even said the toxin wasn't fatal, so what, exactly, was the problem? Every moment they spent on this gnomes-forsaken dune was one moment closer to being captured by the Taelas.

Wizards be good, what have I become? My father? Alsantör shuddered at the thought. If he kept on *that* trajectory, it would be fewer than a hundred years before he'd start to forget his own family ... *Nai! I won't let it happen!*

The prince trudged halfway up the hill, slipping and stumbling in the loose sand that infiltrated his boots and trousers. *Damn this fucking desert.*

The faint sound of "Shite!" made his heart leap. *He's alive!* His legs suddenly felt light as a rush of adrenaline pulsed through him. Finally reaching the top, Alsantör fell to his knees and nearly wept with joy at the sight of Naoise, sitting upright! The duke was still covered in lacerations and glass, but he was alive. Moira sat behind him, picking splinters and shards from his back while Sólan cleansed and wrapped his wounds.

"The fook're you doin' back there?" said Naoise.

"Cleaning it!" Sólan snapped. "Now, hold still, pundijo."

"Cleanin' with what? Bloody *demon* fire?"

"Wizards, Naoise," said Moira. "Fer the Eastern Lands' greatest warriors, ye Veers know shit when it comes to dressing wounds."

Alsantör cleared his throat to announce his presence. Varying gazes poked at him. Gazes of mischief, pain, irritation, and … whatever was behind Siobhan's absent face.

"Sólan, why aren't you just healing him?" said Alsantör. "I doubt you'd lose control with these superficial wounds, now that he's cleared of the alchemy."

"Tíal, he is cleared," said Sólan, wiping the smirk from his face. "But he is bound by the Oath of Light. He can neither use The Dark, nor can I heal him with it."

What! Alsantör's mouth hung open. "That can't be—"

"Ah ken, Tör," said Naoise. "It doesn't make sense to me, either. But Sólan would likely know his limits better than any of us, eil?"

"Eil," said Moira, turning her attention back to her work. "Pass me that brandy, bhromaeri. This is the last one."

Sólan took a deep draught of the flask—it had been water at one point—before handing it over to his sister. "My job is done here." He rose to his feet and shouldered past Alsantör in a hurry.

Frowning, the prince watched him gracefully descend the dune, despite the deep red burns on his shoulders and torso. *Shite, Sólan. Who are you anymore?*

Thank the Gods, Naoise was quiet during the final days of travel. Perhaps he was grateful for what Sólan had done—or maybe his mind was still wounded from the Viper's Breath.

On the eve of the sixth day, the smell of ocean and salt lilies filled the air, carried by an oncoming breeze from the sea. Spring clouds filled the sky, turning it bright orange, pink, red, and purple. In the distance, the *Silent Dancer* was anchored in waiting for her captain's return.

Sólan leaned against a palm tree and gazed longingly out to sea. Gods, did he miss Dakil. The silk in his voice. The smell of salt and brandy on his skin. *And to think that I nearly left you forever, molamí.*

He broke his gaze with the ship's silhouette to carefully scan the beach. Though Alsantör was on first watch, he was still uneasy. Fuck, he was always uneasy.

Naoise and Moira slept soundly, wrapped tightly about each other like claimed lovers rather than strangers. At first, Sólan had hated the idea of being the Veer's brother by law, but seeing the sheer love he felt for his sister and smelling the joy that wafted from her skin when he was near, he couldn't help but smile. At least *one* of his father's children had found happiness. Besides, that mountain elf wasn't all that bad, after getting to know him.

Alsantör sat cross-legged at the top of the beach. Close enough to be heard should the need arise, but far enough to give the others a head start in escape.

"You should be asleep, friend," said the prince.

'Twas only then that Sólan discovered Siobhan wasn't resting with the others. She was, in fact, sound asleep beside her betrothed.

Sólan shrugged. "You should know how well I sleep, amógo. Not at all."

"Heh. I'd hoped that would've changed by now."

"A fool's hope, perhaps." Sólan plopped on the ground next to Alsantör, staring out to sea as the prince stared inland. "I can see you wish not to marry her," he said, eyes unmoving. "Not like Naoise and Moira, anyway."

"They seem to be the exception to arranged marriages, though I've been told the love can grow ... eventually."

Sólan grumbled. "I would know not. Mine never stood a chance."

"Wait, what!" Alsantör's posture stiffened in the waning light. "You're married? Does Dakil know?"

"Widowed, actually. And yes, he knows everything." Sólan rubbed his sunburned face with a grimace. "Medría. Of all the wounds I can heal with The Dark, a fucking burn from the sun is not one of them."

"Nor trauma." Alsantör raised an eyebrow as he finally broke his gaze from the north. "I'm sorry, by the way."

"For what?"

"For telling you about ... eh ... your father."

Sólan rolled his eyes to hide the burning rage that bubbled in his chest. He failed.

"What? You don't forgive me? It was a mistake, Sólan. I didn't mean to—"

"You meant not for a great many things, Tör. Why should I blame you for *my* father's decisions, as fucked as they are?" Tears rolled down Sólan's cheeks, and he tried to wipe them away with the heel of his hand, but all that did was dirty his face with wet sand. "Gods, I wish not to be his heir. But I would have liked the fucking choice to give that damned birthright away. Throw it back in Jannon's smug face and tell him to go fuck himself with it."

"There's the Sólan I know," said Alsantör, chuckling.

Sólan merely snorted. Looking to the sky, he grimaced at the first signs of twinkling stars.

Alsantör followed his gaze and sighed. "I supposed it's time for Naoise's watch." Scrambling to his feet, a soft hand on his knee stopped him from walking away.

"He needs his rest. Let me take his watch, as I am unlikely to sleep until I get back to Dakil."

The prince sucked his teeth but nodded. "Fine," he grumbled. "Just wake him up at midnight, will you?"

"Just go rest, Tör. You need it, too. Your travels are far longer than mine."

Without another word, the prince trudged back toward the others. Well, almost all the others. Siobhan awakened to lock eyes with Sólan. A deep look flashed across her gaze before she wiped her expression clean—back to the absent look she always carried.

"Where's me true love?" she said through a yawn.

Sólan smiled back at her with clenched teeth. "Down by the water." *Be careful with this one, Tör. She is cunning.* He watched her as she weaved through the palm trees and tropical shrubs toward the main camp. Sighing, he caught one last glimpse of the *Silent Dancer* before finally beginning his watch.

Tomorrow, mólamí. Tomorrow, we leave for Áfgal, and the Grim will be no more.